Sevasadan is not only a gripping novel but also a sensitive and perceptive document on the lives of young urban men and women at the beginning of the twentieth century. At a time when Indian women were being held up as standard-bearers of a nation in chains, Premchand depicts the hypocrisy of the so-called 'pillars of society', who can sacrifice their orthodox principles behind closed doors, yet do not shirk from mouthing moral platitudes in public. He portrays the reality of the Hindu–Muslim divide, but also conceives of an ideal community that gives a new direction to the life of a fallen woman and allows her to lead a meaningful existence.

A hugely popular novel, *Sevasadan* went through several editions after its first publication in 1918. It was made into a film in 1938 with M.S. Subbulakshmi in the lead role.

Snehal Shingavi is pursuing a PhD in English at the University of California, Berkeley, USA.

Vasudha Dalmia is Professor of Hindi and Modern South Asian Studies, University of California, Berkeley, USA.

Sevasadan

PREMCHAND

Translated by SNEHAL SHINGAVI

with an Introduction by Vasudha Dalmia

OXFORD
UNIVERSITY PRESS

YMCA Library Building, Jai Singh Road, New Delhi 110001

Oxford University Press is a department of the University of Oxford. It furthers the
University's objective of excellence in research, scholarship, and education
by publishing worldwide in

Oxford New York
Auckland Cape Town Dar es Salaam Hong Kong Karachi Kuala Lumpur
Madrid Melbourne Mexico City Nairobi New Delhi Shanghai Taipei Toronto

Argentina  :e Guatemala
Hungary Switzerland

(:ss

HJ	13/01/2009	;i
F	£6.99	

First published 2005
Oxford India Paperbacks 2008

All rights reserved. No part of this publication may be reproduced,
stored in a retrieval system, or transmitted, in any form or by any means,
without the prior permission in writing of Oxford University Press,
or as expressly permitted by law, or under terms agreed with the appropriate
reprographics rights organization. Enquiries concerning reproduction
outside the scope of the above should be sent to the Rights Department,
Oxford University Press, at the address above

You must not circulate this book in any other binding or cover
and you must impose this same condition on any acquirer

ISBN-13: 978-0-19-569-658-5
ISBN-10: 0-19-569-658-1

Typeset in AGaramond 10.5/12.5 at Le Studio Graphique, Gurgaon 122 001
Printed in India by Pauls Press, New Delhi 110 020
Published by Oxford University Press
YMCA Library Building, Jai Singh Road, New Delhi 110 001

Contents

*The House of Service or the
Chronicle of an Un/holy City*
Vasudha Dalmia
vii

Sevasadan
1–271

Glossary
272

The House of Service or the Chronicle of an Un/holy City

Vasudha Dalmia

As POSSIBLY THE best known Hindi-Urdu author of our times, Premchand (1880–1936) has found so secure, but in the meantime also so dusty, a niche in the halls of fame as the classic author of rural north India, that it takes some refocusing of our lens to register in any fine detail the fact that when with the publication of *Sevasadan* he first rose to fame, it was as a sensitive and perceptive cartographer of a city. This city was none other than Varanasi[1], the holiest of all cities in India, in the throes of modernizing and refashioning its image, even as it made a bid to drive away its once famed courtesans[2] from the vicinity of the Chauk, or central square, from which ran arteries into its nethermost nooks.

There is much hidden cultural history in the publication history of *Sevasadan*.[3] It was written first in Urdu in 1917 under the titillating title:

---

[1] I refer to the city as 'Kashi' when speaking of it as a pilgrimage site with all the mythical connotations that this conjures up. Otherwise, in order to remain near Premchand's usage—he calls the city 'Banaras' in Hindi—I use the British-Indian term 'Benares', since that was the usage in English till very lately, when the name of the city was officially changed to 'Varanasi', which is yet another older Sanskritic name for the city.

[2] The Urdu term for courtesans is 'tawai'f', the one more current in Hindi now is 'Bai'. For the sake of uniformity, I have used the term 'courtesan' throughout this essay.

[3] The text used for the translation of the novel is from the twenty-volume edition of Premchand's collected works (Delhi: Janavani Prakashan, 1996); *Sevasadan* is contained in the second volume. My own more literal than literary translation for this introduction

Bazar-e-Husn or the 'Bazaar of Beauty', though, given the exigencies of the market and the whimsy of the publisher, it had to wait till 1924 to be published in its Urdu form. However, it shot into almost instant fame, when it was recast in Hindi and published in 1918, under the sober and uninspiring title, *Sevasadan* or the 'House of Service'—the reference was to the educational institution which was erected to house the daughters of former courtesans. *Seva* and *sadan* however also carried other meanings. *Seva*, or service, could also be of the kind which the courtesans of the city supplied to their clientele, and *sadan*, or abode, was also the name of one of the central male protagonists of the novel. An erring and largely unfulfilled young man, Sadan had been in love initially with the one sister, the beautiful and enticing Suman, whom he had first met in the Bazaar of Beauty. Eventually he married the other sister, the more pacific Shanta, to whom he had been betrothed all along and who had suffered the misery of her lot with virtuous resignation. Though the various connotations of the title must also have existed for contemporary readers, it was surely its most apparent meaning, with its obvious allusion to social reform, the puritanical rather than that which suggested the lurid, which accounted for the initial appeal of the novel. It was the era of high nationalism; Hindi was seeking to set up its own respectable literary canon; and if nation, woman, social reform, and the reordering of the city landscape could be brought together thus educatively; the novel could do none other than win public approval. But the novel's enduring popularity may have had more to do with the interplay of the various meanings, and of voices other than the calm, analytical, auctorial, which make possible more than one reading of how *seva* and *sadan* came variously to be conjoined but also queried. This essay is an effort to trace and recover this interplay of meaning in order to gain some understanding of the enduring power and popularity of the novel.

In addition to its vividly dramatic dialogues, its deep psychological insight into persons and processes, the narrative is also girded at all times by a keen sense of social history. It registers crucial societal transitions, even as they take place, from known patterns of life to new, untried ones. One transition is of that from the country to the city; many of the central

---

sometimes deviates from Snehal Shingavi's more literary version, since I am making points that need to remain close to the Hindi, at the expense of some awkwardness of idiom. The glossary at the end of the present work has been compiled with the generous help of Vasudha Paramasivan.

characters undertake or undergo this traumatic passage. After her marriage, Suman is transported from her well-to-do home in a rural district to the stench of the narrow lanes in the inner city and the claustrophobia of the small dark rooms in which she houses with her elderly husband. Sadan, in running away from his landowning village home, finds himself filled with fear and foreboding as he dashes across field and wood to catch his night train to Benares. Two miles outside the village there is a *pipal* tree, its dense foliage filled with ghosts which appear in all shapes and forms to hinder the wary traveller. Sadan freezes into inaction and can cross its dark presence only when he hits upon the idea of singing verses from Tulsidas' Ramayan at the top of his lungs to fend off the evil spirits which lurk there.

The city itself is changing rapidly. In the second decade of the new century, it continues to be dominated by the old time *rais* or gentry, the great landowners of the district residing in their town homes, and the equally powerful merchant aristocracy with its widely spread kinship networks. But alongside the gentry, the colonial government has allotted some public space to the new professionals whom it has nominated to the municipal board, which has newly been granted some autonomy in civic government. The rhetoric of social reform, as yet thinly represented by these new professionals, is beginning to gain ground and provide unexpected twists to matters long considered settled. But even social reform is a double-edged sword, which can be used to further various ends, especially when it is directed at women. For, at the centre of the novel, as also of Benares, is yet another crucial transition: the courtesans of the city are no longer to be allowed to practice their art publicly. The social reformers have taken up the cause of fallen women. This touches the heart of the relationship Suman and Sadan could have with each other. Suman's private problems become linked to the city's problems and its changing face. Private and public are thus inextricably intertwined.

The Courtesans of the City and the New Novel in Hindi

The courtesans of the city had long occupied a central place in public life. Their reputation went back many centuries; there are references to them in Jataka tales and in Sanskrit works of different genres and periods.[4] The

---

[4] See Motichandra ([1962] 1985: 46, 89, 145).

gentry had ever flocked to the best known among them, in search not only of the more obvious pleasures but also to enjoy the best in the arts: music, dance, poetry, and to luxuriate in an atmosphere radiating refinement in matters of aesthetic taste and judgment. Once a courtesan had acquired a reputation for beauty and mastery of the arts, she could attain high social standing. She would be asked to appear not only at the court of the Benares Maharajas, in the mansions of the rich and the powerful, but also in the most prominent temples and on the banks of the holy river on important religious occasions. The number of these women was small, though their power was often staggering, as the sober voice of James Prinsep, the first British census taker of the city, informs us in the second quarter of the nineteenth century:

If, however, beauty and high vocal skill are comparatively rare, the witching influence of the arts and graces of these women is as much acknowledged and as powerful as ever. Examples are not wanting of large accumulations of wealth from the successful exercise of the skill and accomplishment of the profession: some of the best houses and the handsomest temples of the city have been erected by ladies of dancing notoriety.

According to the census taken in 1827, there were 264 Hindooee and 500 Mosulmanee professional *Nach* girls in the town, not a very large proportion to the population. There were, however four times the number of *khanehgee-kusbees*, who do not profess the accomplishments of singing and dancing.[5]

Prinsep spoke prudishly of 'dancing notoriety', dancing fame would have been the more adequate expression. The city was proud of the beauty of its leading courtesans and of their mastery of the arts.

Bharatendu Harishchandra (1850–85), acknowledged father of modern Hindi literature, old-style merchant aristocrat and modern-style publicist who seldom spent a night at home, had confessed that he visited these women in order to acquire cultivation and knowledge of the arts.[6] He was to note their all-pervasive presence in Kashi and the power they exercised on men, and to eulogize them in one of his short plays, *Prem Jogini*, the *yogini* of love (1874–5), which provided vignettes of the city at its most

---

[5] (1833: 33).

[6] Harishchandra is reported to have told a friend, when he was moved to write a poem after the visit to a courtesan: 'It is for this that I cultivate intercourse with them. Tell me, how else could this true motif have been obtained?' For further details, see Dalmia (1997: 128).

pious but also at its most raucous.[7] He captioned the scenes, when they were published in book form, *Kashi ke chayachitra ya do bhale bure fotograf*, reflections of Kashi or a couple of good and bad photographs. In choosing the word 'photograph', he indicated both the modern character of his undertaking—he was considered a good amateur photographer—as well as the reality of the individual in social situations that the photograph as a medium sought to capture and hold fast. In seeking to ground the reality of city life, he placed the value of these public women at the top of the social spiral and thus of Kashi's claims to fame.

The city as a whole clearly had two sides, the exalted and the seamy. In fact, with the exception of Babu Ramchandra, the central protagonist and his *musahib*, or agent, Sudhakar, the characters in the play consisted almost in their entirety of the rogues and charlatans of the city. At least half of the city, at least as the rogues and charlatans saw it, was run over by prostitutes of all hues and classes:

Adhi kashi bhat bhanderia bahman aur sanyasi
adhi kashi randi mundi rand khangi khasi. (333)

Half of Kashi is run over by bards and *bhanderias*, brahmins and ascetics
The other half with whores, widows with shorn heads, and very special harlots.

But even on the grander map, which offered the more representational face of the city, and which Sudhakar was to go on to offer as the corrective to the seamier version, the courtesans were placed at the pinnacle of the social order. Sudhakar's depiction of the city was mythical and modern at the same time. He waxed eloquent on the beauties of the riverside landscape, the well laid-out ghats, and the high mansions—five- to seven-storied—towering on one side of the river, interspersed with the temples of Gopallal and Bindu Madhav, of Vishvanath and Annapurna. It was a city graced by the presence of other godly beings as well. He eulogized the various rungs of the city's hierarchical order, beginning with the Maharaja, who was the religious and cultural head of the city, backed by the civic and military authority of the British commissioner, the collector, and the magistrates.

---

[7] The play was published, *Premyogini* subsequently as *Premjogini*, in three installments in *Harishchandra chandrika*, the literary journal Harishchandra edited, between August 1874 and April 1875. The text is also accessible in the first volume of his Complete Works, *Granthavali* I (319–54), whence the following quotations.

There were many wealthy merchants, there were scholars, the learned in Sanskrit and the servants of Hindi, and there were the able craftsmen. There were educational institutes and a number of public libraries and monuments. There were the famous ancient ruins of Sarnath. There were people from all parts of the country, and ascetics of the most diverse orders who, in their diversity, encapsulated and encompassed all parts of the incipient nation. There was wealth, trade, textiles, handicrafts. The city blossomed and glowed. And finally, as almost a climax:

> The youthful *barabilasini*, courtesans, exotically dressed and ornamented, with fragrant betel leaves in their mouths, sauntering on the royal paths on the flimsiest pretext, whether it is going to the temples, to sing or to roam in parks, in order to dupe and ensnare men, poor, dim-witted men.
>
> What more can I say? Kashi is Kashi. There is not another city like Kashi in the three worlds. You'll believe it when you see it. It is useless to say more (342).

Kashi was the pinnacle of all cities in the subcontinent, wherein all regions and crafts were represented, and atop this pinnacle were perched the courtesans of the city. This exalted reputation of the women of the city was to continue unabated into the first half of the twentieth century. The best-known courtesans exercised great social power; they played a central role on most public occasions, as even the most puritanical retrospective accounts are constrained to admit:

Nevertheless, there is no doubt these women musicians and dancers made a substantial contribution to the music centre of Varanasi. Furthermore, on certain occasions, such as the worship of the Ganga, the songs of these women formed an essential part of the rituals.

Fees were taken by tawaifs for performing, excepting in certain religious places and on certain occasions that were attended by commoners. They sang free in the *akhada* of Sadhu Kinaram, in the Vagishwari Temple on the occasion of Saraswati Puja, in front of the Shitala Temple in the month of Chaitra, near Panchaganga Ghat in the month of Kartik, in the akhada of Naga Baba near Gai Ghat, near Panchaganga Ghat, near the Kali Temple on the Dashashvamedh Ghat; and also on the various Ghats of the Ganga during worship of the river.[8]

When the well-known Hindi writer Amritlal Nagar set out to document the power and presence of the courtesans of north Indian cities after their profession was banned by law in independent India, Ramchandra Varma,

---

[8] Medhasananda (2001: 668).

The House of Service or the Chronicle of an Un/holy City xiii

one of the many *rasikas* or connoisseurs he interviewed in Benares, spoke once more of their musical talent and of the importance of their role in the ritual life of the city:

The assembly that takes place on the Lolark sixth of Kartik is quite famous here. At Baba Kinaram's place, the entire city's courtesans would perform. 'Adi Vishveshvar', the older Vishvanath, was visited by courtesans every Monday. Each year, they held a *mela* there on the day of Gopashtami. That's why the trendy youth of the day called Adi Visheshvar 'randhibaz Mahadev' or courtesan-addict Shiva.[9]

New poetic compositions gained wide circulation if they were taken up and performed by courtesans. A vital nerve thus connected the performing art with literary composition and its informed appreciation and circulation. The connection would continue to be operative well beyond the era of early moderns such as Bharatendu Harishchandra. It is explicitly evoked in Premchand's novel by Kumwar Aniruddh Singh, powerful Hindu zamindar, involved in the controversy surrounding the eviction of the courtesans from their quarters at the centre of the city. Aniruddh Singh saw the paucity of literary works in modern Hindi as being directly linked to the decline of Indian musical culture. *Navin* or new Hindi Literature could at most lay claim to a couple of plays by Harishchandra, to the popular novel *Chandrakanta*,[10] and for the rest, there were translations from the English, made not even directly but via Bengali and Marathi. There was a great dearth of novels. This meagre production was the direct result of the decline of musical tradition and artistic sensibility which was coupled with it:

Yes, it's true, I like the sitar. I start feeling queasy when I hear the harmonium or the piano. These English instruments have destroyed our own music, which is barely discussed today. And if there were something left to be destroyed, theatre has come forward to complete the task. Whoever you see harps on and on about the *ghazal* and *qawali*. In a while, our music will disappear altogether, like the art of archery. It is music which gives birth to pure thoughts. With the disappearance of music, we have become devoid of these and the worst impact of this loss has been on literature. How sad is it that in the country where an invaluable work like the Ramayan was

---

[9] Amritlal Nagar (1994: 154).

[10] Written by Devakinandan Khatri (1861–1913), the novel (1888), a modified version of the Urdu *tilasm* or thriller, proved to an all-time bestseller, inspiring Khatri to write several follow-ups, amongst them, the 11-part *Chandrakanta Santati* or the progeny of Chandrakanta.

composed, where a work as delightful as the *Sursagar* was created, we have to take recourse to translation, even for the simplest novels.

But the indigenous music which was now being invoked as essential to the survival of the arts, performative as well as literary, had begun to change its contours and context. Aniruddh Singh spoke of Tulsidas' Awadhi Ramayan and the Brajbhasha devotional verse of Surdas in connection with the musical tradition he wished to see regenerated. Clearly, in being projected as national heritage, music was being entirely severed from its original performers in the bazaar of beauty.

It was the Hindu, middle class and respectable, as indeed the new novel in Hindi that was sought to be situated within the city, which was also losing some of its mythical status. The new voices in the city were seeking to create an image of Kashi which was far removed from the one which was socially and ritually centred around the courtesans. In the public disputes about the location of the courtesans, the city's ill reputation was seen as reflected in the sad fate of the nation, of its music, and also that of the Hindu woman. For, provocatively enough, Premchand had chosen to cast Suman as a Brahmin woman who had deserted her husband, rather than as Muslim, and at least nominally single. Suman's move to the bazaar of beauty challenged the status of Hindu marriage as an inviolate social institution and in portraying the psychological motivation of her move with more than a measure of sympathy, the author seemed, at the least, to be also querying its self-evident claim to inviolate sanctity.

Wife and Courtesan in the Changing City

Suman's father had been a district-level subinspector of police, who had brought up his two daughters to expect the best in life. He had indulged them by buying all manner of beautiful clothes and expensive baubles for them and arranged that they receive some education from a Christian lady who tutored them at home. But he had laid no money aside for the considerable sum he would be expected to expend as their dowry, and various disasters overtook the family when it came to finding a suitable match for them. Suman's mother was finally able to marry her off with little expenditure to an elderly bridegroom, relatively poor but with high standing within their own caste group. Confined within the narrow walls of her new home in the city and initially humoured and pampered by her husband Gajadhar, Suman managed to lead an exemplary life as a dutiful housewife for the first two years of her married life. But she was bored and frustrated at the same time and just opposite her lived the plump Bholi, luxuriating in the comfort of her well-lit and well-aired home and visited nightly by the town gentry. Bholi would beckon to her to come over, though Gajadhar reacted with disapproval and censure, when Suman finally succumbed to the temptation to go over to her house. Money did not make the men who visited Bholi great by any estimation, he explained. In the arrogance of their being, the rich chose to ignore religion but Bholi was not purified by their coming, and he quickly forbade Suman to visit her. Suman then tried to become pious in her ways. She bathed daily in the holy river and recited the Tulsi Ramayan to the women of the neighbourhood. If this did not bring peace to her soul, it gave her the satisfaction of being morally more elevated than the likes of Bholi. On the occasion of Ramnavami, the celebration of the birthday of Rama, Suman visited a great temple in the company of her friends. The temple was beautifully decorated, it glittered with electric lighting and so crowded was it, that there was no space in its overfilled courtyard even for the proverbially tiny sesame seed to be accommodated in it. The sound of sweet music wafted in the air and her neighbour, Bholi, sat at the centre of all this festivity, each gesture she made observed eagerly by the most prominent citizens of the city—the rich, the learned, and the pious, many of whom she had seen at the riverfront. Suman stood there as if struck by a thunderbolt, her pride shattered to bits. Not only did wealth bow at Bholi's feet, even religion sought her favour:

The very prostitute whom I wanted to humble with my pious ways is the recipient of esteem and honour in this assembly of great men, in this pure abode of the lord, while I find not even standing space.

Suman abandons religion thereafter. Gajadhar's earnest arguments regarding the ultimate worthlessness of the men who crowded around Bholi fail to convince her. The city's public spaces are reserved for public women, not for poorly dressed creatures like her, as a second incident brings home to her with painful clarity. She accompanies her friends to Beni Bagh, which houses a small zoo and an aviary. Her peace is rudely shattered when she attempts to sit for a moment on a bench. The park watchman immediately unseats her. Just then, two finely dressed women arrive in a carriage, one of them her neighbour Bholi. The watchman not only seats them on the bench, he even offers them a hastily plucked bouquet of flowers. Once they depart, Suman upbraids him for his unseemly behaviour. His words sting her to the quick: 'Do you aspire to be their equal?' He manhandles her when she tries to sit on the bench again. She is rescued by a well-to-do couple passing by in their carriage. The house of her benefactors, the lawyer Pandit Padamsingh and Subhadra, his cultivated wife, becomes a refuge for her. But not for long. Padamsingh is elected as a member of the powerful Municipal Board of the city, and to celebrate the event, he allows himself to be persuaded to hold a *mujra* one evening. It is here that the second key event in Suman's city life takes place. The focalization of the scene is entirely through Suman. From behind the curtain, she and Subhadra watch Bholi bai perform. Bholi is neither as pretty as Suman, nor does she sing particularly well. Suman has both a good ear and a quick memory. She would not need more than a month to learn to sing better than Bholi. She can also cast sidelong glances and knows how to smile demurely:

Suman sat there for a long time, trying to disentangle cause from effect. Finally she came to the conclusion: Bholi is independent while my own feet are in shackles. Her warehouse (*dukan*) is open and there is a rush of clients, while my warehouse is shut, so no one stands and waits. She has no thought for barking dogs, I am scared of social censure. She is outside purdah while I am inside it. She chirps freely as she hops from branch to branch, while I cling to one branch. It is shame, the fear of ridicule, which makes me the servant of others.

Suman's deeply reflexive and dry conclusions, her estimation of marriage as prostitution, though with a single client, can be regarded as none other than revolutionary for her times. Wives are easily acquired and easily disregarded. Social esteem is reserved for the very public women each married man would be quick to condemn at home. Men are fickle, easily swayed, and when it comes to taking quick, bold action to retrieve a situation, they are usually found to be wanting. If they come to the rescue at all, it is usually much after the event.

Suman is beautiful and talented; she aspires to be free, to be admired and respected, to live in luxury, to be rid of her tyrant. The mujra at Padamsingh's house gets over very late; by the time she gets home, it is well past midnight. Gajadhar refuses to let her in, he tells her that she has been afflicted by the water of the city (*shahar ka pani*). His insane jealousy, her own extreme dissatisfaction, and her pride lead to a violent exchange between the two, which bars her further entry into her own house. Just as Nora in *The Doll's House*, Suman picks up her suitcase and departs, into an unknown and uncertain future.

She seeks refuge with Padamsingh and his wife, but her stay at their house is painfully brief. Padamsingh fears for his reputation once word about her putative relationship with him begins to spread in the bazaar. Only Bholi welcomes her warmly and takes her in. Bathed with perfumed soap, expensively clad, Suman views herself in the mirror and is struck by the radiance and beauty of her own person. It does not take her long to learn how to sing, for as Bholi tells her, there is no need to labour at *dhrupads* and *tillanas* any more, nowadays a few catchy *ghazals*, some *thumris* and a couple of popular theatre tunes can do the trick. Suman is an instant hit. Word of her beauty and her talent spreads quickly, for Dalmandi, the bazaar of beauty, thrives on scandal and sensation. Sadansingh, young nephew of none other than Padamsingh, seduced by the wares of Dalmandi, is just one of the many ardent suitors who linger at her door. And Suman cannot help being gratified by his wooing.

But the winds of change are also blowing in the holy city: theosophy, the Arya Samaj, new education, and public lectures have all made an impact. If the narrative sets out to explicitly affirm the need for social reform, it also makes clear that at times it has a very blunt edge, if indeed it is not a double-edged weapon. For, once again, the author works with dual perspective. We are introduced to Vitthaldas, intrepid social reformer and zealous missionary in the cause of public weal. Vitthaldas' endeavours are viewed with some scepticism and not a little irony by the author. We find, as so often in Premchand's work, that the speech surrounding the characters creates 'highly particularized character zones. These zones are formed from the fragments of character speech, from various forms for hidden transmission of someone else's word, from scattered sayings belonging to someone else's speech, from those invasions into authorial speech of other's expressive indicators (ellipses, questions, exclamations). Such a character zone is the field of action for a character's voice, encroaching in one way or another upon the author's voice.'[11] We find reflected in the author's words of introduction not only Vitthaldas' own estimation of his worth, but also a suggestion of the response of his sorely tried wife and the gratitude almost forced out of the recipients of his relentless service:

Babu Vitthaldas was the life and soul of most civic-minded institutions in the city. No task could be accomplished without his help. This personification of manly vigour (*purushartha*) carried his heavy burden gladly. Even if now and then he was pressed down by it, he never lost heart. He had no time for meals, found no leisure to sit at home, his wife complained of his affectionless behaviour. But in his obsession

---

[11] Bakhtin (1981:316).

to serve the nation (*jati*), Vitthaldas had forgotten to look out for his own happiness and self-interest. He roamed around with single-minded intent, raising funds for orphanages or arranging tuition fees for poor students. And if some calamity befell the nation, he brimmed over with his love for it. In times of famine, he could be found going from village to village, bearing a load of flour on his head. The extent of his selfless service during cholera and plague epidemics simply amazed people. When just recently the Ganga was in flood, he did not look into his house for days at end; he had donated his entire wealth to the cause of the nation, but he showed not a trace of pride in this deed. He had not received higher education. His powers of oratory were also not above the ordinary. Often his thinking lacked maturity and far sight. He was neither particularly skilled in manoeuvre, nor clever or wise. But his patriotism was his virtue; this won him the respect of all and sundry in the city.

Vitthaldas inspires grudging respect, for he rushes in where angels fear to tread. He finds simple remedies, he eradicates social ills, even if the people he sets out to help could themselves be eradicated in the process. He is not one to wallow in doubt. He makes up his mind to rescue Suman, though it is he who had spread word in the bazaar about Padamsingh's putative relationship with her in the brief period she could stay at his house. He knocks at her door and takes her to task immediately. The dialogue which ensues is a classic case of two people talking well past each other, one hellbent on social reform, the other equally relentless in her dry and caustic analysis of the social processes of which she herself has been the victim:

Vitthaldas: Now that our much revered Brahman ladies are treading this disgraceful path, there will be no stopping our decline. Suman, you are causing the head of the Hindu jati to be lowered.

Suman answered very earnestly: *You* may think so, no one else does. A few gentlemen have just left after listening to the mujra, all were Hindus, but none of them seemed to have lowered heads. They are very glad that I have come here. And then, I am not the only Brahmani in the Mandi; I could name a couple of others of very high families to you straightaway, whose *biradaris* were not prepared to take care of them; they were left feeling so helpless, that they came here. If the Hindu jati is not ashamed of itself, how long can frail women like us continue to protect it?

Vitthaldas responds by admitting that the Hindu jati had indeed fallen very low. But its moral repute (*maryada*) had always been held aloft by Hindu women. It was their truth and their stainless reputation which saved it from further decline. It was to protect Hindus that lakhs of women burnt to ashes in crackling flames. They chose to bear pain themselves in order to protect others. And if ordinary women did not shrink from doing so, the expectations of Brahmin women could be higher still. It was only the lower caste woman who refused to bear up to suffering of any kind, who ran to her natal home if she took offence at her husband's behaviour. And if she did not get along even there, she ran off to the brothel. He ends with the ringing words: 'Suman you have lowered the head not only of the Brahman jati but of the entire Hindu jati.'

Suman has to correct him repeatedly when he insists that people don't respect her. The highest in the city bow at her feet. There is not one in the city who does not go wild with delight when she deigns to cast a gracious look at him. But Suman is also on the defensive, Vitthaldas' words have stung her to the quick. She had resolved, she tells him, that she will dance and sing but have no sexual contact with the men who surround her.[12] Vitthaldas, never at a loss for remedies, recommends work at home, cottage economy, to her. But even he can respond only evasively to Suman's query: 'Does a single lover of the Hindu jati exist anywhere, who would be willing to spend fifty rupees a month for my upkeep?'

Vitthaldas shows little understanding for the predicament in which Suman finds herself; he is more occupied with her as a symbol of respectable Hindu womanhood. As a once-married Brahmin woman, she has to be extracted from the moral filth in which she finds herself presently mired. When he offers to find a place for her in a home for widows, she is extremely sceptical about the welcome she would receive there. Is she expected to give up her life of relative security and comfort only to be regarded as a barely

---

[12] Premchand thus finds a route to preserve a measure of respectability for Suman; she is the courtesan who manages to remain physically unscathed by the profession she practices. This is the escape route also taken by Bhagavaticharan Varma (born 1913) in his ever-green novel *Chitralekha* (1934) which is set in the Gupta period and also focuses on a Brahmin woman, this time a young widow, who rises to fame as a dancer in the city of Pataliputra.

This sexual abstinence allows for a reading of Suman's character as an 'angelic victim' and makes for a peculiar kind of relationship to the society which has victimized her. Alok Rai has spoken of 'the cult of the angelic victim. This fecund genre, particularly in writings dealing with the question of women, may be considered a sub-set of the cult of the ennobled poor. Here, also, the game consists of representing the woman-victim as being simultaneously damaged and undamaged, wronged but essentially unharmed, both needing salvation and deserving of it. The fact that such representations are necessarily ambiguous in the fashion just indicated, interacts curiously with the confusion regarding the proper relation between wrongs and rights. The consequence is a muddled valorization of victimhood which, curiously, works to soften and make manageable the critique of victimizing societies and institutions' (1991: 201).

tolerated object of charity in a pleasureless abode? But Vitthaldas has yet larger goals in mind. He wants to remove prostitution from public places and do away entirely with mujra, the social custom of song and dance on festive occasions.

In focalizing primarily through Suman on the one hand and Sadansingh and Padamsingh on the other, the author seems to be propelling the reader to view the action through at least three perspectives which seem diametrically opposed to one another and often at odds with the professed auctorial stance. Sadan seeks to situate himself in the city as a man of some affluence and influence. He needs financial resources in order to woo Suman and he manoeuvres to come by them. Later he goes through a spell of enthusiasm for social reform, and we share his reflections. But he finds short cuts and takes morally dubious decisions, finding a measure of stability only at the end. Padamsingh sees through the falsity of many social situations but seldom finds the courage to act boldly when directly challenged to do so. Once again, we are privy to his thought processes. His marriage, troubled as it is, comes nearest to representing marital bliss, and his social reform endeavour comes nearest to being well-reasoned and reflected. But we see him falter in his actions and seek shelter behind self-justification. If the author approves of marriage as a social institution, if he expressly supports social reform, in the action of its proponents, we see these aims questioned if not contradicted. Of the three, the most empathetically portrayed character is that of Suman, and it is her speech that is psychologically more persuasive as also more convincing in its analysis of societal ills and of the resolutions she herself is compelled to seek. Suman's reasoned reflection, her spirited exchange with Gajadhar, and her decision to accept Bholi's offer rather than seek reconciliation with her husband through the mediation of Subhadra, seem entirely comprehensible, given her particular situation. It is then the speech that surrounds Suman which most consistently refracts professed authorial intention.[13]

---

[13] As Bakhtin has shown: 'The language used by characters in the novel, how they speak, is verbally and semantically autonomous; each character's speech possesses its own belief system, since each is the speech of another in another's language; thus it may also refract authorial intentions and consequently may, to a certain degree, constitute a second language for the author. Moreover the character speech almost always influences authorial character speech (and sometimes powerfully so), sprinkling it with another's words (that is, the speech of a character perceived as the concealed speech of another) and in this way introducing into it stratification and speech diversity' (1981: 3/4).

As Suman's reflections bring home to the reader, marriage is a commercial transaction, particularly when negotiated on the basis of dowry. It is not unlike prostitution, which deals more blatantly with the financial exchange involved in buying sexual and other services. Society officially sanctions marriage while at the same time virtually imprisons the woman concerned in cheerless domestic servitude. It does not explicitly sanction prostitution but at the same time it elevates the woman concerned, if she possesses the required talent and beauty, to a position of glamour and relative autonomy, celebrating her charms in lavish public display. Suman makes a radical statement when speaking of both arrangements, the ones in which she and Bholi respectively find themselves, in terms of *dukan*, or warehouse. In what ways is one institution morally more elevated than the other? The social conduct of the men who patronize the warehouse would contradict their public stand on the issue.

Then there is the vexed issue of social reform which sets out to change the older social order, elitist and decadent, while attempting to put into its place a more middle-class morality, itself often flawed and feelingless. Those who advocate social reform, in self-promotion or in bouts of self remorse, seem more concerned with their own public and private ends than with the fate of individuals such as Suman, who are caught in these winds of change and buffeted about, compelled to believe in a public cause rather than in their own hard-won comfort and sense of well-being. The Hindu jati that Vitthaldas speaks of seems to be a caricature of its own projected image, and the social reform being called for, no more than one more measure of social hypocrisy. Out and out social reformers such as Vitthaldas are often callous and unfeeling, or those such as Padamsingh are narcissistic and noble in turns. The author seems to regard them with some aversion and suspicion, though his ostensible sympathies are reserved for the cause they represent.

The rhetoric of social reform, as the author proceeds to show us, seems particularly amenable to misuse for communal purposes. Though Suman is Hindu, many of the courtesans are Muslim and the leading members of Hindu society are not slow to attribute the moral responsibility for the evils of this profession on Muslim culture. The clientele is mixed, but most shops around the Chauk are Hindu owned, and it is the Hindu merchants who stand to suffer the greatest financial loss if the women are made to shift to another part of town. Could this be a ploy of the Muslim faction in the Municipal Board to use this opportunity to harm Hindus? The communalization of the debate seems inevitable.

Social Reform and the Communalization of the Dalmandi Debate in the Municipal Board

Most north Indian cities underwent radical structural transformations in the years after the 1857 uprising. Not only was there a major reshuffling of social hierarchies, space itself was differently allocated and distributed. At the centre of most cities of any size or splendour, was situated the Chauk or town square, and somewhere near it if not located right there, were the courtesans of the city, the *tawaifs* or *bais*. In the cleansing operations which followed in cities such as Lucknow and Delhi, whole *mohallas* were uprooted, though, in spite of widespread damage and destruction, the famous Chauk in Lucknow was saved, and with it, its equally renowned courtesans, sustaining and surviving the loss of their old clientele.[14] In most cities, they would be driven out finally only after 1956.[15]

The civic administration of the city also underwent rapid change after 1857. The Acts of the preceding decades regarding city government had called upon the inhabitants to take the initiative to restore civic order and administer it, for the system of mohalla or neighbourhood control and administration had begun to dissolve in the early decades of the nineteenth century. But these pre-1857 measures to put a civic government in place had been desultory and half-hearted. However, once the Army Sanitary Commission (1861) painted a dismal picture of the hygiene observed in Indian towns, more directives were issued to look after water supply, lighting, and sanitation under a more comprehensive policy laid down by the Government of India. Between 1864 and 1868, three further Acts were passed for Lucknow (1864), Punjab (1867), and the North West Provinces (1868). The municipal administrative body was no longer to be voluntary, it was henceforth to be a nominated body, though still expected to cater primarily to the needs and interests of the British. If the nominated members consisted largely of those prominent citizens—the bankers, merchants, and members of the aristocracy who had remained loyal in 1857—willy-nilly it

---

[14] See Oldenburg (1984) for an account of the changes in the city landscape of Lucknow, following the violence perpetrated by the British in the wake of the 1857 uprising, particularly the havoc wrought in the lives of the courtesans.

[15] Amritlal Nagar has recorded the reactions of the courtesans of Lucknow to this final ousting from the city and their profession (1994).

also ended up including the new professionals.[16] The North West Provinces Act IV of 1868 provided municipal committees with one-third official members and two-thirds elected members. This coincided with the building of the Benares town hall. According to this Act, the District Magistrate was to be president of the municipality, members of the Council were to be appointed on the recommendation of the District Magistrate. Clearly, there was little effort made to extend the system of popular election. Municipal Committees were, thus, highly centralized and bureaucratic. Powerful administrators, such as Sir Charles Wood and Sir Henry Maine, continued to advocate nomination rather than election of the non-official members. According to them, respectable Indians did not wish to be put in a position where they would choose those who were to rule over them; they preferred to avoid contest. However, Lord Ripon's government issued a resolution in 1882 advocating election, the number of official members was now not to exceed one-third. The North West Provinces and Oudh Municipalities Act of 1883 further provided that official members be restricted to one-fourth of the total membership. Boards were empowered to elect their Chairman and Vice-Chairman, but the Commissioner or the District Magistrate continued to be invested with the power of control over the municipal body as a whole. Under the Acts of 1883 and a further Act of 1900, the legislative and executive functions were vested in the Board which was now entirely responsible for the administration of the city, though still under the control of the Commissioner or District Magistrate as before.

Far-reaching change was only to come about in the second decade of the twentieth century when the United Provinces Municipalities Act No. 11 was passed to give effect to the reforms recommended by the Royal Commission on Decentralization (1909) and the Resolution of Government of India (1915). Accordingly, the number of non-official members was increased and a non-official chairman appointed in every council. The details of the administration were delegated to a number of sub-committees. In larger municipalities, a new post of executive officer was created; he was appointed by the Board, subject to the prior approval of the state government. However, the state government and the District Magistrate continued to control, dissolve, or supersede a municipal board. A power

---

[16] See the pioneering study by Narayani Gupta (1981) for the changes brought about by the British in the imperial city of Delhi, once they took charge. On the politics of the municipal boards they created, see pp. 115–22 and 213–16.

tussle was almost preprogrammed. 'The attraction for chairmanship to the intelligentsia was its executive power and the bureaucracy was unwilling to be divested of the influence of the board chairmanship.'[17] It is necessary to recall this long history of power constitution within the city, and the tussle it involved, in order to gain some idea of the privilege it meant to be nominated or elected as a Board member. The stakes could not but be high.

Once the Municipalities Act of 1916 came into force, the non-official members jostled for power amongst themselves, as the *East India Progress and Condition of India During 1917–1918* report put it,

A review of the whole subject of local self-government in India at the present moment would seem to indicate that in the immediate future important developments may be expected. Hitherto the control which government exercised over municipalities and district boards, while unquestionably preventing the commission of serious errors arising from inexperience, has done much to prevent the growth of a real feeling of civic responsibility (185).

But this 'real feeling of civic responsibility' was a euphemism for power long withheld and now allocated and distributed to factions which were known to be oppositional. The Report chided the municipal boards for the prevalence of fissures, though they had almost certainly also been fostered by the imperial government. It complained of the 'spirit of faction' which prevailed on several boards, it admitted, surely not without a smirk, that the 'maintenance of a double record of proceedings was not unknown'.

Benares in the second decade of the twentieth century was also undergoing these changes which were restructuring the very social fabric of the city. Hindus and Muslims now saw themselves as having to band together in their religion-based groups in order to defend what they saw as their common interest. But the views held by individual members of the respective groups within each faction were anything but uniform. The merchants differed from the landed gentry in the interests they represented, while the new professionals, who came into more contact with modernizing trends, were likely to be the ones who were most earnest about social reform. However, even they could ill afford to ignore group loyalties and were thus

---

[17] This account of the evolution of municipal government of cities is based on the first chapter, 'Historical Perspective of Urban Local Government in India', of Debidas Nanda's book (1998). The citation is from page 15. This Municipalities Act of 1916 continues to govern Uttar Pradesh even today.

automatically sucked into the respective Hindu and Muslim factions. What kind of changes did the different social strata desire and with what rationale? As Alok Rai puts it, '(t)he early 1900s were a time of considerable ideological ferment in India. A sort of damaged modernity seemed available under colonial aegis, a modernity at once embryonic and addled.'[18]

Premchand followed these developments with much interest. In a remarkable fictional representation of these debates and the vested interests which sought to control city spaces for financial and social ends, he showed, in precise detail, how in the matter of the displacement of the courtesans, communalism itself was a construct, a public face which masked commercial and political agendas and sought validation through it.[19] The professed concern for the welfare of the courtesans was an issue which was bandied about in a power battle between the communalized Hindu and Muslim factions in the Municipal Board in a manner which made the courtesans seem more like victims of social reform than its beneficiaries.

If Vitthaldas' indefatigable efforts had not galvanized people into action, once Padamsingh took up the challenge, the movement to save the courtesans, while banishing them from the city centre, gathered unexpected momentum. Padamsingh was the son of a landowning family and a lawyer of repute; he was part of the old gentry, but also one of the new professionals who was liberal in his views, in spite of the mujra he had permitted to be held in his house. Propelled ever forward by his guilty conscience, for he realized that he had allowed Suman to be cast out of his house too hastily, he brought the matter to the attention of the Municipal Board.

The Municipality officials had hesitated all along to bring up the matter of the courtesans of the city, for they knew that they would be stirring a hornet's nest:

They used to think, who knows what tumult would occur in the city by just raising the issue. They were so many ra'is, so many government officials, so many merchants,

---

[18] 1991: 197.

[19] The move to oust the courtesans from the centre of the city was apparently a real consideration at the time, though it was not ever effected. Premchand's is therefore a fictional account, which Professor Anand Krishna attributes to his Arya Samaj indoctrination (personal interview, 7 January 2003). The famous courtesans of Benares continued to operate in Dalmandi till well into the early 1950s. According to Professor Anand Krishna, there was a *majlis* or assembly in Girija bai's *kotha* which was situated just opposite Chitra cinema hall.

who had a connection to this market of love (*mandi*). One was a client, another a connoisseur (of the arts), who had the courage to risk antagonizing them? The municipality officials were puppets in their hands.

Premchand records the Municipal Board debates on the issue of the courtesans and the cleansing of the city centre with some earnestness and some outright satire. Once again, the members of the Board, introduced individually within their own factions both the Hindu and the Muslim, enter the stage under the spotlight of slanted speech which forms veritable character zones, integrating the speech of the characters themselves in invisible quotation marks, as also the public appraisal of them. The Board has eighteen members, eight Muslims and ten Hindus, the majority well educated. Within each camp there are social reform enthusiasts but also dissidents who take shelter behind communal verbiage, for entirely different ends, as we shall see.

The various interest groups represented in the Muslim and Hindu camps consist of merchants and shopkeepers, religious leaders, landowners (zamindars), retired civil servants, and the new professionals. By and large, both the Hindu and the Muslim members are equally unwilling to lose the income the courtesans generate for them and, at any rate, do not wish to seal their own source of pleasure and enjoyment. However, they choose their words carefully, for the new professionals give the tone, and all subscribe to it publicly.

The operations of the Muslim camp are presented first. Haji Hashim Sahib exercises a great deal of influence on the populace and is generally considered the leader of the Muslims. He is against the removal of the prostitutes. Maulana Teg Ali is the Vali of the Imam Bara. Munshi Abulwafa is the owner of a perfume and oil factory. He owns a chain of oil and perfume stores in several big cities across north India. Munshi Abdul Latif is a big landowner, an absentee landlord who resides in the city. He loves poetry and is considered a good poet himself. Shakir Beg and Sharif Hasan are lawyers. They have very progressive social views. Sayyid Shafakat Ali is a pensioned Deputy Collector and Khan Sahib Shohrat Khan is a famous *hakim*. These last two stay away from meetings and assemblies, but they do not lack generosity and deeper reflection. Both are religiously inclined and command great respect in society.

Haji Hashim makes of the matter a communal challenge. He asks: 'Are you aware of this new ruse employed by our brothers of the same native land?'[20] And Abulwafa, the oil and perfume factory owner, pointing out that ninety per cent of the *tawaifs* are Muslim, proclaims that this is an attempt by the Hindus to reduce the number of Muslims in the city. The Hindus are out to claim as large a number of the populace as they can, including the Doms.

The two gentlemen who generally stay away from meetings are the most sweeping in their condemnation. Sayyid Shafakat Ali, the pensioned Deputy Collector, wants the prostitutes to be removed altogether from the city. They are contagious, they spread immorality around them. Hakim Shohrat Khan goes a step further and wants to remove them altogether from Hindustan. They are black serpents with poison in their eyes. He views it as a matter of great misfortune that most tawaifs call themselves Muslims.

The new professionals are more charitable. Sharaf Hasan, the lawyer, says that he sees no harm in the fact that they call themselves Muslims. The problem is that no one tries to help them rectify their ways. Once a woman falls, Islam becomes indifferent towards her. Surely these women also repent of their ways, but they have to continue in their profession because they know no better and because they have to consider the future of their children. Now, if grooms could be found for their daughters, the situation would improve considerably. He does not want to reject the suggestion on political grounds, that is, merely because it comes from the Hindus. When Teg Ali, the Vali of the Imam Bara, taunts him, Shakir Beg, the other lawyer, asks people to calm down and offers instead a more moderate suggestion. The tawaifs should be removed from the centre to some corner of the city.

The landowning gentry are not unlike the merchants in their aversion to this change, though their reasons are very different. Thus Abdul Latif, the zamindar, does not want to let go of the pleasure of the courtesan's cultivated company. His views will be echoed by his Hindu counterpart. He speaks in jest but means it seriously: there are all kinds of shops in the Chauk, soaps, leather, oil, textiles, pots and pans—why not the warehouse of beauty? This kind of levity provokes sharp responses. Haji Hashim persists in regarding it as a Hindu-Muslim matter and has no hesitation in proclaiming that he will resist it precisely because it comes from the Hindus.

---

[20] As Harish Trivedi points out in his review of the English translation of the Urdu version of the novel (2004), Haji Hashim uses the term *biradaran-e-vatan*, brothers of the same native land, when speaking of the Hindus and the more intimate *biradaran-e-millat*, brothers in religious faith, when addressing his Muslim compatriots.

Abulwafa, the factory owner, agrees, for the merchants on both sides are in any case against the move. But they present their arguments in communal terms.

But Sayyid Shafakat Ali is a genuine social reformer. He says that if the Hindus are doing something which is advantageous for all, he has no hesitation in joining them. He is against opposition for opposition's sake. There is no conclusive agreement on the matter and the assembly disperses.

Though the Hindus and Muslims regard themselves and each other as homogeneous groups, they are actually split into different interest groups which have almost parallel interests, which cut across the religious divide. The Hindu camp in its agreements and disagreements presents thus almost a mirror image of its Muslim counterpart. Those who are financially and socially most powerful are against the move. The financial losses the Hindu merchants incur will be regarded as political victory for the Muslim group. Seth Balbhadradas, a wealthy merchant, is the chairman of the Board and Lala Chimanlal and Dinanath Tiwari are also important leaders of the merchant community while Lala Bhagat Ram is a contractor. Seth Balbhadradas and Chimanlal own most of the stores in the Chauk, and Dinanath most of the real estate in Dalmandi. Lala Bhagat Ram's transactions are almost entirely dependent on Dinanath. These four men are decidedly against the removal of the courtesans from the centre of the city.

Only the four professionals are clearly for the removal of the prostitutes from Dalmandi: the two lawyers, Pandit Padamsingh and Rustam Bhai, and two others, Ramesh Datt, college professor and Theosophist, and Prabhakar Rao, editor of the daily *Jagat*. Vitthaldas is not a member of the Municipal Board.

The Vice-Chairman of the Board is Dr Shyamacharan, medical practitioner, and ostensibly the most Anglicized in the group. He fears official disapproval. He wavers in his decision, preferring to shift the responsibility on the larger Municipal Council. And finally, there is Kumwar Aniruddha Bahadur Singh, the biggest zamindar in the district. He is liberal in his views, he knows the best of both cultures, he can appreciate both Surdas and Mozart, but he is reluctant to give up the old style pleasures of the cultivated. Both sides hope to win over Dr Shyamacharan and Kumwar Sahib, for victory or defeat seems to depend on them.

Since Padamsingh, the prime mover in the game, is still away at the wedding of Shanta and Sadansingh (which will not take place, once it is discovered that Shanta is Suman's sister), Seth Balbhadradas calls a meeting at his *susajjit baradari*, ornamental reception rooms. Prabhakar Rao was known to be a fanatic opponent of the Muslims, so Balbhadradas hopes to win him over by giving the debate a communal twist.

Dinanath Tiwari, owner of most of the real estate in Dalmandi, begins the debate in words similar to Haji Hashim's: 'Our Muslim brothers have shown great generosity in this matter. They are operating on the principle of killing two birds with one stone. On the one hand they hope to acquire a good reputation through social reform, on the other, they have found a pretext to damage the Hindus. How can they lose such a good opportunity to gain a good name?'

Chimanlal, who owns most of the stores in the Chauk, says with a straight face:

I have no dealings with politics, nor do I go anywhere near them. But I have not the least hesitation in saying that our Muslim brothers have a vice-like grip on our necks. Most of the real estate in Dalmandi and the Chauk belongs to Hindus. If the Municipal Board accepts this, the Hindus will be wiped out. If one wants to learn how to hurt on the sly, one need only look at the Muslims ... Sadly, some of our Hindu brothers have become puppets in their hands. They don't know what harm they will cause their own jati by this ill enthusiasm.

Prabhakar Rao knows he is being trapped by this logic.

He looked helplessly towards Rustam Bhai, asking to be saved. Rustam Bhai was a fearless and clear-speaking man. He stood up to answer Chiman Lal. 'It grieves me to see you people twist a social matter to give it the appearance of Hindu-Muslim conflict ... It can bring profit to some Hindu merchants to riddle it with conflict, but it is difficult to estimate the harm it does to the cause of the community. There is little doubt that if the proposal is accepted, Hindu merchants will suffer the greater loss, but surely there will be repercussions for the Muslims also. There is no small number of Muslim shops in Chauk and Dalmandi. We should not, moved by the spirit of dispute and opposition, suspect the integrity of our Muslim brothers. They are acting in the interest of common weal; it is another matter if the Hindus are suffering greater losses thereby. I firmly believe that even if the Muslims were hit by the greater loss, they would take a similar decision. If you agree, truly, that the proposal has been made with view to the reform of an evil social custom, there should be no hesitation in accepting it, whatever the financial loss. Money should play no part when it comes to a matter of social conduct.'

Prabhakar Rao is much reassured by this clear analysis of the matter—it transcends the communal. The issue is to be decided on moral and social grounds. One takes financial losses in one's stride, if one is to act for the welfare of the populace at large. He gives the example of the loss the government agreed to accept in view of the moral rectitude of giving up the opium trade with China. This seems to be explicit social satire. Kumwar Aniruddha Singh points out dryly:

> Sir, you remain engrossed in the editorial work of your journal. When do you find the time for the pleasures of life? But we, who are free of such anxieties, need to have some amusement ... Today, you bring the proposal of ousting the prostitutes of the city, tomorrow you will say that no one within the municipal district should dance, sing, perform mujra without permission; it will become impossible for us to live.

When Prabhakar Rao suggests that he take up reading as a pastime, Kumwar Sahib answers with obvious pleasure: 'We are forbidden to read.' He knows the dance steps of France and Spain, he can play so well on the piano as to put Mozart to shame, he has full knowledge of English social customs. He knows when to don a solar hat and when the turban. He reads, has cupboards full of books, but he has no need to remain glued to them. He also seeks other refined pleasures of the senses. 'We will be wiped out, if this proposal of yours comes through.' Dr Shyamacharan, the other undecided member, remains evasive in his response. He first wants to put these questions to the Legislative Council.

Now follows some delicious social comedy. Seth Balbhadradas is convinced of victory, he expects the proposal to be rejected. Now he could afford to remain impartial, which was the prerogative of the Chairman. He analysed the proposal in a weighty speech and said:

> I do not believe in social upheaval. It is my belief that the society which needs change takes care of it naturally, in the course of things. Foreign travel, caste difference, the useless restrictions on commensality give way when faced with the changes wrought by time. I want to let society operate freely in this regard. Once there is full consensus that people do not want to see prostitutes in the Chauk, what power in the world would be able to remain deaf to it?

In conclusion, Sethji spoke in very moving tones:

> We are very proud of our music. Even those who are acquainted with the music of France and Italy acknowledge the *bhava*, *rasa*, and blissful peace of Indian song. But such is the wheel of time, that the very institution which our reformers are straining to rip out by its roots, holds the proprietorship of this divine store of riches. Do you really want to destroy this institution and cruelly turn into dust this priceless gift of our ancestors? Did you know that all the national and religious feelings that remain to us are due entirely to our music, otherwise, no one today would even know the

names of Rama, Krishna, and Shiva? ... No ill custom is eradicated by neglect or cruelty. It can only be destroyed by education, knowledge, and compassion. There is no direct path to heaven. We will have to cross the Vaitarani. Those who think they can spring directly into heaven by the good graces of some Mahatma are not more laughable than those who think that by banishing prostitution, all the poverty and sorrow of India will be eradicated and a new sun will rise in the East.

In order to appreciate the irony of these words, we need to recall that in the second decade of the twentieth century, Indian music had come increasingly to be projected as Hindu music with an ancient, Sanskritic past; its Muslim component, in production and performance, had been almost entirely sidelined. This classification had been set in motion in the last decades of the nineteenth century at both ends of the subcontinent. In Calcutta, Sourindra Mohan Tagore had begun to write treatises on Hindu music; in the Bombay Presidency, the Parsis, followed by like-minded citizens in Pune, had begun to found musical societies which made this heritage available to middle-class boys and eventually also to girls. The dissemination of this music through the towering figures of Vishnu Narayan Bhatkhande (1860–1936) and Pandit Vishnu Digambar Paluskar (1872–1931) completed the process in the following decades. Bhatkhande wrote its history, set up a standard notational system, and codified the vast storehouse of ragas and raginis for teaching purposes. Paluskar evolved new modes of music pedagogy and set up a chain of schools, the hugely successful Gandharva Mahavidyalayas. A series of national conferences, convened severally by both men, further propagated the ancient genealogy of Hindu music as also its contemporary respectability.[21] However, public singing by women continued to be the domain of courtesans till well into the 1920s. It was only in 1924, and thanks entirely to the efforts of Paluskar, that it became possible for a female performer to *sit* on stage while performing. 'Till then, female performers, who were mostly prostitutes, were supposed to stand on the stage when they sang. It is significant that Paluskar's school was the first to break this custom.'[22]

Seth Balbhadradas, to serve his own ends, uses precisely this newly won status of music as national heritage to eulogize the courtesans and the monopoly over music that they still hold. In order to save the national

---

[21] See Bakhle's forthcoming monograph on the nationalization of Indian music, whence also the above information.

[22] Bhagwat (1987:112).

heritage, as he pleads so eloquently, these women must be allowed to practise their art publicly, till such future date when others can come forward to relieve them of their burden. To be effective, social change has to be gradual. It cannot be brought about by putting ill-conceived notions of social reform into operation.

Unfortunate Suman

In the final run, however, it is the social reformers who prevail. Padamsingh returns to the scene and the matter is taken up again with renewed energy. The Municipal Board meets, all its members are present on the occasion, and Padamsingh presents the proposal. It has three sections: (i) the prostitutes should be removed from the central part of the city to some settlement far away from it, (ii) they should be forbidden to move about in the central parts and parks of the city, and (iii) those who arrange for their performances should be heavily taxed and all such festivities should be banned from public places. Kumwar Aniruddha Bahadur Singh had feared just this.

After some debate, whereby the same kinds of opinions are aired once again, Seth Balbhadradas calls for a vote. The first section of the proposal is passed with the provision that those who marry within nine months or learn some craft to earn their livelihood, be allowed to remain where they are. When Padamsingh accepts the provision, the reformist members who had thus far supported him, desert him. Nine members vote for it, and eight against it. Thus it is passed with the majority of one vote, that of Seth Balbhadradas. The social reformers, in spite of being in actual minority, and in spite of their last minute split, have won a narrow victory by virtue of their moral stand, which not all feel free to oppose publicly. There is much acrimony after this is brought to pass, for most are unhappy with the outcome and Prabhakar Rao blocks all further activity. Once the dust settles, the other two sections are also passed. The prostitutes leave to be resettled on the outskirts of the town, repentant almost all of them, of their lives. They now find themselves in Alaipur, the first station after Benares Cantonment on the *choti* or narrow gauge railway line. Have all social problems connected to prostitution been resolved? One need only recall Seth Balbhadradas' passionate words appealing for the retention of the women at the centre of the city: 'Those who think they can spring directly into heaven by the good graces of some Mahatma are not more laughable than those who think that by banishing prostitution, all the poverty and sorrow of India will be eradicated and a new sun will rise in the East.'

Meanwhile, pushed by events in the public sphere, matters have also moved on in the private sphere. When Suman and Shanta were cast out of the widow's home where they had initially found refuge, Sadan had happened to meet the two sisters. Through a series of coincidences and chance encounters, it becomes possible for Shanta and Sadansingh to be united as a married couple. A now-pregnant Shanta is reminded incessantly of Sadan's former attachment to Suman and she watches each move Suman makes with suspicion and dislike. Engrossed in their vision of the future, Shanta and Sadan, now backed by his family, pay little positive heed to *abhagini Suman*, unfortunate Suman. She finds herself increasingly unwelcome in their house.

On her way to drown herself in the river, Suman meets Sadhu Gajanand, who is none other than Gajadhar, now turned secular *sadhu* and social reformer. He is at the centre of a movement to found a house for the education of the daughters of former prostitutes, and he invites her to head that ascetic institution, set up somewhere on the outskirts of the city. The little girls will learn how to perform domestic chores effectively, sew, tend the vegetable patch, and sing patriotic songs. Suman is a wan, wry figure at the end of the novel, educator of prostitute's daughters, who have no future in respectable society as wives or mothers. It is this pious, if sorry, end which seems to have made not only for the respectability of the novel but also its contemporary popularity.

A review by Kalidas Kapur in *Saraswati*, the leading Hindi literary journal of the era, proclaimed that *Sevasadan* filled a yawning gap in Hindi literature which, to date, had been forced to make do with little other than translations from the English, often through the medium of Bengali or Marathi.[23]

The good and bad plants of the entire world are here at hand. If you glance this way, you'll see the grafts of Bankimchandra Chatterjee and Tagore. If you glance that way, you'll see the creeper of *Saraswatichandra* from Gujarat. At other places, there are efforts to implant the grafts taken from the historical novels of Hugo and Dumas. At yet other places, you'll see some gentlemen trying to adorn the flower garden with the garbage of English literature. Here and there, tucked away in some small corners, can be seen a tiny number of literature lovers sowing the seeds of true service to literature.

---

[23] I am grateful to Sujata Mody for drawing my attention to the review.

Sevasadan was obviously one such novel. Could it compare to the classics of world literature? Each novel, the reviewer felt, was grounded in its own *desh kal*, place and time, what Bakhtin would call chronotope. Novels were appreciated primarily in the place where they took birth. 'This is why it is so difficult to translate social novels, it is in any case a useless enterprise. This is why it is so difficult to compare them and also so inappropriate. Their good and bad qualities depend on the depiction of their own society.' According to the reviewer, it was this successful depiction of contemporary society that *Sevasadan* had achieved. It had managed to depict the vice rife at the times without indulging in sensationalism, and in such a way that while understanding how it came about, it could still be seen as despicable.[24] Further, the novel even managed to show the way to slip out of the grip of this vice. 'That is the chief aim of this novel.' The crowning achievement of the work, however, was the character of Suman:

Do not consider it hyperbole if I say that it is the depiction of Suman's character which makes for the grandeur of the novel. She is the life breath of the novel. The novel would have been of no use, if her character were to have been slurred in any way ... What saves Suman's character is the fact that she is an Indian woman (*bharatiya nari*). She is faithful to her husband; she strays from her path because she seeks social prestige (*gaurav*) and bodily comfort. She has in the meantime seen that society has little respect for faithful wives ... In a second scene we see her in a room in Dalmandi ... She is saved by the interventions of Vitthaldas. There are many ups and downs, many traps for the unwary, many temptations, but she remains unscathed ... But the author saves her from all sides and in the end even awards her the position of the Director of Seva Sadan. Suman has saved not only herself from falling, but also the novel.

The reviewer closes with the hope that there will be 'many more good novels from the author's pen. If God wills, there will soon come a time when we

---

[24] As the reviewer further explained: 'Take the instance of Dickens and Reynolds. The poor of England have earned the kindness of both, both have sketched a picture of their endless misery, both have tried to show with compassion the vice that their poverty generates. Both harbour hatred for the characters of the rich in their country. But their procedure/mode is different. It is said of Dickens that if anyone has helped to ameliorate their lot, it is he. This is why his novels count amongst the literary jewels of that country. The less said about how far Reynolds has profited his country, the better. By God's grace we hope to remain deprived of Reynold's kind help in this regard. It is a matter of great good fortune that *Seva Sadan* had not made it to this rank' (1920: 104).

also will have the good fortune of being able to proclaim that Hindi literature does not lack a Thackeray, Dickens and Scott.'

In this puritanical period at the beginning of the twentieth century, a novel which dealt with vice without sinking into it, which made a prostitute, who did not prostitute herself, into its central protagonist, had found a way to legitimize its intent, while capturing the reader's attention with its sensational subject matter and deep psychological insight. And this, in fact, was Premchand's great achievement. He conveyed several messages at once, making for surprising turns and twists in the plot, for people behaved unexpectedly, motivated by complex needs and desires.

On the one hand, beautiful, passionate, and headstrong Suman had been tamed and this could be seen as the triumph of virtue. But on the other hand, she was also a tragic figure, the victim of a social system that first failed to accord her the respect she claimed as a virtuous wife, then made much of her as a beautiful courtesan. But the moment she stepped out of that role, the same social system proceeded to regard her as little more than a social outcaste who could only be accommodated as one who looked after others of her kind. In the final run, very few were left to support her in the virtuous role allotted to her. Padamsingh did not even get down from the carriage—out of a mixture of shame, embarrassment, and unwillingness to get involved—when in the last pages of the novel Subhadra, his wife, visits Suman at Sevasadan, the exemplary institution located somewhere on the outskirts of the town. The dialogue between the two women, with which the book closes, is provided without any further narratological intervention. And it is in citing this conversation that I too should like to close this analysis of a remarkable novel. It is a dialogically particularly poignant moment, saying one thing, while also indicating several others.[25]

For one, the author shows us that the usefulness of Sevasadan, the institution, is itself contestable, for it continues to be regarded as a house of

---

[25] For as Bakhtin has said of the art of the novel: 'The novelist does not acknowledge any unitary, singular, naively (or conditionally) indisputable or sacrosanct language. Language is present to the novelist only as something stratified and heteroglot. Therefore, even when heteroglossia remains outside the novel, when the novelist comes forward with his own unitary and fully affirming language (without any distancing, refraction or qualifications) he knows that such language is not self-evident and is not incontestable...' (1981:332).

ill repute. The little girls have an uncertain future; it is unlikely that any man will come forward to marry them, as Suman tells Subhadra. For another, even its benefactors shun it. It is clear that Shanta does not consider visiting her sister there. Suman fears also that Padamsingh will not let his wife come for another visit, though Subhadra assures her that, in fact, she intends to drag him along to visit with her the next weekend. But Subhadra herself is suspicious. Does Sadan still visit Suman? Suman's denial and closing words of gratitude speak more of her loneliness and isolation, and her need to be connected to the world she once knew, than of any real satisfaction derived from being there.

When Subhadra was leaving, Suman said piteously—I will be waiting for you this Sunday.

Subhadra—I shall definitely come.

Suman—Shanta is well, isn't she?

Subhadra—I just received a letter from them. Doesn't Sadan come here?

Suman—No but he sends a few rupees each month in donation.

Subhadra—It's time for me to leave, but you don't need to see me off.

Suman—I am deeply grateful that you came here. Your devotion, your affection, your extraordinary efforts—which shall I praise first? You are a true jewel in the community of women. [With moist eyes] I shall consider myself your servant. As long as I live, I will remain grateful to you. You held my arm and saved me from drowning. May God's grace always grant you good fortune.

It is this level of realism, I would suggest, which asks to be read against the grain, which accounts for the novel's enduring claim to fame. The story of Suman's decline, rise, and decline—the questions it raises about the social institutions fostered by the modernizing middle class still operating under the benign/malignant aegis of British imperial rule, about the self-cleansing undertaken by the city and of the marginalization thereby not only of the courtesan but also of the wife—has lost neither its poignancy nor its significance in today's India.

References

Bakhle, Janaki. Forthcoming. *Two Men and Music: Nationalism and the Making of an Indian Classical Music*, New York: Oxford University Press.

Bakhtin, M.M. 1981. *The Dialogic Imagination: Four Essays*. Austin: University of Texas Press.

Bhagwat, Neela. 1987. 'Vishnu Digambar Paluskar', *Journal of Arts and Ideas*, 14/15, July–December.

Harishchandra. 1975. *Bharatendu granthavali: Pahla khaand* (cited as *Granthavali* I), ed. Shivprasad Mishra 'Rudra' Kashikeya, 2nd rev. edn, Banaras: Nagaripracharini Sabha, (first edited by Brajratnadas, 1950).

Dalmia, Vasudha. 1997. *The Nationalization of Hindu Traditions: Bharatendu Harischandra and Nineteenth Century Banaras*. Delhi: Oxford University Press.

East India Progress and Condition of India During 1917–1918, London, 1919.

Gupta, Narayani. 1981. *Delhi Between Two Empires 1803–1931: Society, Government and Urban Growth*, Delhi: Oxford University Press.

Kapur, Kalidas. 1920. 'Sevasadan Samalochana', in *Sarasvati*, 21/2, February.

Oldenburg, Veena Talwar. 1984. *The Making of Colonial Lucknow, 1856–1877*, Princeton: Princeton University Press.

Medhasananda, Swami. 2001. *Varanasi at the Crossroads: A Panoramic View of Early Modern Varanasi and the Story of its Transition*, Kolkata: The Ramakrishna Mission Institute of Culture.

Motichandra. [1962] 1985. *Kashi ka Itihas*, Banaras: Vishvavidyalaya Prakashan.

Nagar, Amritlal. 1994. *Ye Kothevalian*, Allahabad: Lokbharati Prakashan.

Nanda, Debidas. 1998. *Municipal Administration in India*, Varanasi: Ganga Kaveri Publishing House.

Premchand. [1927] 1999. *Nirmala*, translated, and with an Afterword by Alok Rai, Delhi: Oxford University Press.

Prinsep, James. 1831–1. *Benares Illustrated, A Series of Drawings*, third series, Calcutta: Baptist Missionary Press; London: Smith, Elder and Company; Reprinted by Vishwavidyala Prakashan, Varanasi, 1996.

Trivedi, Harish. 2004. 'The Power of Premchand' in *The Hindu Literary Review*, 2 May.

Verma, Bhagvaticharan. [1934] 1993. *Chitralekha*, Delhi: Rajkamal Prakashan.

1

Eventually, everyone tastes the bitter fruit of remorse. While most blame their shortcomings for their misfortunes, subinspector Krishnachandra blamed his virtues. Even though he had been working as a policeman for twenty-five years, he had never been tempted by the corruption around him. In his youth, when he still wanted the finer things in life, he performed his job dutifully, without ambition. But now, after all this time, he was reduced to wringing his hands over his honesty and his naiveté. His wife, Gangajali, had been a straightforward woman and a faithful wife. She had been able, before, to steer her husband away from temptation and corruption. Now, however, she was deeply worried. She feared that a lifetime's worth of good deeds were about to go down the drain.

Subinspector Krishnachandra was a refined, generous, and decent man. With his subordinates, he acted with brotherly camaraderie. His underlings, however, valued material rewards over kindness. To each other they complained that they could hardly make a living here. What are we supposed to do with his good intentions? Trade them for food? Bitter discipline at work would have been better than this, if their bellies were full. Dry bread served in a silver platter doesn't transform into a dessert, they argued.

The subinspector's superiors weren't too happy with him either. At other police stations, where even the accountants, clerks, and orderlies could afford to throw money around, they were treated handsomely. When the accountant received a bribe, the orderly would receive his share, and the superiors would also be paid in kind. But Krishnachandra's station could not afford any ceremonial welcome for high officials. Krishnachandra took nothing and therefore could not give anything away. People mistook the subinspector's reserve for arrogance.

Despite these constraints, however, there was not a trace of tight-fistedness in the subinspector's nature. He wasn't a self-indulgent man, but he felt it was his duty to keep his family comfortable. There were three other members in his family: his wife and two daughters. The subinspector loved his daughters more than life itself. He would buy them the finest clothes and ever so often order a variety of trinkets from the city. If he saw something in the latest fashion in the bazaar, he would immediately buy it for his daughters. He had a real fetish for furniture as well. The whole house was filled with chairs, beds, and cabinets. And if he saw fancy inkstands, carpets from Jhansi, or silks from Agra, he could not pass them up. Even stolen goods, perhaps, did not elicit such excitement. He had hired a Christian lady to educate the girls and teach them sewing and embroidery and would, occasionally, test them himself.

His wife, Gangajali, was a shrewd woman. She had tried to convince him to exercise more restraint in spending money. If nothing else, he would have to arrange his daughters' weddings one day. Where would he go begging then? You deck them out in velveteen slippers now, but what of the future? she argued. The subinspector would laugh away her fears, maintaining that that too would sort itself out as did everything else. At other times he would become irritated and tell his wife not to burden him with worries, and so the days passed. The girls blossomed like lotus flowers. The older daughter, Suman, grew up to be beautiful, flighty, and arrogant; the younger one, Shanta, was innocent, quiet, and polite. Suman expected to be treated better than those around her. If similar saris were bought for both sisters, Suman would sulk. Shanta was content with whatever came her way.

Gangajali, in the traditional manner, wanted to be free of her obligations towards her daughters as quickly as possible. But the subinspector maintained, that they were not yet ready for marriage. He said that according to the Shastras, it is a sin to marry a girl off before she is sixteen. This is how he rationalized his passivity. When he read leading articles in the newspapers, criticizing the dowry system, he would be thrilled. He would tell Gangajali that in a year or two this barbaric custom would be eradicated, so that there was no cause for worry. In the meantime Suman turned sixteen.

Krishnachandra could no longer delude himself. His lack of worry had not been due to his confidence in his ability to find a husband for his daughter; it sprang from his passivity. Like a traveller who has slept under a tree all day, only to find a huge mountain confronting him in the evening, the subinspector, too, lost all courage. He began to search frantically for a bridegroom for his daughter and asked for horoscopes from many places. He wanted a groom from an educated family, hoping they would be too liberal to ask for a dowry. So he was quite surprised to learn that the size of the dowry was directly related to a groom's education. After the astrologer had been consulted and the stars had been examined, talk would turn to dowry, and Krishnachandra's heart would inevitably begin to sink. Some would ask for a thousand rupees, some for five thousand, and some for even more. The poor man would return home completely dejected. Now, six months later, the subinspector is still sunk deep in worry. The whole thing seemed like a cruel riddle to him. There was no doubt that educated people sympathized with him but each one of them would come up with such unique explanations that he was left dumbfounded. One of them said, 'Sir, I myself detest this awful custom, but what can I do? Just last year I married off my daughter. The dowry alone was two thousand rupees, not to mention another two thousand for the wedding expenses. Tell me, how shall I recover my losses?'

A second man offered an even more irrefutable argument. He said— Darogaji, I have spent a considerable amount of money on my son's education. Your daughter will benefit from this as much as my son will. So, tell me. Is it fair that I should have to bear the entire cost by myself?'

Krishnachandra began to regret ever having been an honest and truthful man. Once he had been proud that he had never cheated or taken a bribe, but no longer. He thought to himself—If I hadn't been so afraid of corruption and sin, I would not have had to suffer this humiliation today. Both husband and wife were extremely troubled. After a long silence, Krishnachandra turned to his wife and said—See? This is the reward for righteousness. If I had been like the others, and taken bribes people would have fallen over themselves to get close to me. But look at me now. No one even treats me with decency or respect. This is the justice in God's kingdom. We have only two options. Either we marry off Suman to a pauper, or I find a goose that lays golden eggs. The former is unlikely. I will have to settle for the latter. Morality and righteousness do not take you far. Now I will show them. I, too, will use corruption to my advantage. That is the only option I have. It is clearly the way of the world. Perhaps it is God's way as well. From today, I will be like all the others.

Gangajali listened to her husband with her head drooping, deeply distressed by his words. She had nothing to say as her eyes welled with tears.

2

MAHANT RAMDAS LIVED in the area which was under the subinspector's jurisdiction and was the head of a sect of monks. All their financial transactions were conducted under the symbolic auspices of 'Shree Bankebihariji' (and Ramdas was his sole representative). Shree Bankebihariji was the divine moneylender and therefore nothing less than 32 per cent interest would be accepted on loans sanctified by him. All rents were paid to him and all deeds for land sales and mortgages were made out in his name. No one had the courage to withhold offerings to Shree Bankebihariji, nor did anyone ever dare to challenge his holiness for money that was due to him. It was impossible to live in the region after having denied Shree Bankebihariji his due. After all, Mahant Ramdas had a permanent reserve of well-armed monks, who wielded the staff in their congregation, drank fresh buffalo milk, consumed *bhaang* prepared in milk in the evening, and never let their hemp bowls grow cold. No one dared to stand up to this intimidating gang.

Mahant Ramdas commanded great respect and influence among the police officers. Shree Bankebihariji fed them fine *laddu*s and *ghee*-laden *halva*. Besides, who could refuse the *prasad* of his holiness? It was clear to all that once His Holiness Shree Bankebihariji had set foot on the earth, it was only appropriate that he follow the ways of the world.

Whenever Mahant Ramdas went on an inspection of his district, he would move in procession, in regal style. At the head of the procession, an elephant carried an icon of Shree Bankebihariji, while the Mahantji followed in a palanquin. Then came an army of monks on horseback bearing the standards of Lord Ram in all their exotic variety. And behind them, camels carried camp supplies and tents. Every village this group passed through was left smarting.

This year, Mahant Ramdas had been on a pilgrimage. Upon returning, he organized a large sacrificial fire that burnt continuously for an entire month. The pots were never off the fire, as ten thousand holy men had been invited for the customary feast. In order to finance these rituals, a five-rupee plough tax was collected from each tenant in the village. Some villagers gave happily, others had to take out loans, and those who didn't have money were forced to write promissory notes. Shree Bankebihariji was too powerful to challenge. The only man who dared to defy him was a poor peasant named Chetu. For the last several years, Chetu's fields had not produced a good harvest. And earlier this year, Bankebihariji had filed a lawsuit to increase the rent on Chetu's land. Chetu was already sinking under the weight of his debts when the plough tax was announced. So he refused to pay the new tax and even refused to sign a promissory note. His holiness could not ignore this act of defiance. His gang of monks apprehended Chetu, took him to the temple, and beat him up in the courtyard. Chetu fought back. Even though they tied up his hands, they could not shut his mouth and he would not stop cursing them while there was life left in him. By nightfall, however, he had been silenced permanently. The next day, the watchman filed a report at the police station.

When the subinspector heard what had happened, he realized that it was the miracle that he had been waiting for. He immediately began an inquiry into the matter. The Mahantji had so much control over the district, however, that the subinspector was unable to find any witnesses. He received a number of reports off the record, but no one was willing to make a formal statement.

Three or four days passed. At first the Mahantji remained stand-offish, confident that he could not be charged. But when he learnt that a number of men had squealed, he began to bend and, appealing to Kubera, the god of wealth, sent a representative to negotiate with the subinspector. The talk inevitably turned to how the matter could be settled with some give and take.

Krishnachandra—You know me. For me, bribery is like a venomous snake.

Representative—Yes, I know, but you have to show mercy towards saints and monks.

Then the two began to whisper to each other.

Representative—No my lord! Five thousand is too much. You know the Mahantji; once he has made up his mind, then not even the threat of the gallows can make him budge. Let us settle on a sum that will not pinch the Mahantji and still see you through.

In the end, they agreed on three thousand rupees.

But there is a great gap between buying the ingredients, preparing a bitter concoction, and swallowing it. After the representative returned to the Mahant, Krishnachandra began to wonder at himself.

On the one hand was the lure of money and the hope that his worries were over but on the other was the fear of losing his soul and having to face the consequences. He could neither go forward nor turn back. He didn't know what to do.

Having been an upright man all his life, Krishnachandra was deeply troubled at having to throttle his conscience now. He thought that if he was going to end up a corrupt man, he might as well have started twenty-five years ago. By now he could have built himself a mansion and bought villages. After having enjoyed the fruits of virtue for so long, committing this crime in his old age didn't make sense.

But then his inner voice asked—You haven't done anything wrong. You managed as long as you could. And you aren't doing this for your own gain. When the nation, the age, the custom, and concern for your family are leading you down the primrose path, how are you to blame? Your soul is still pure. And in God's eyes, you are still innocent. Arguing thus, Krishnachandra managed to convince himself.

Still, he couldn't get over his fear of the criminal consequences. He had never had the courage to take a bribe before, and now, when the moment arrived, he didn't know what to do. He was like a pacifist who has been conscripted to be a general. A simple mistake could get him caught and, then, he would surely end up in jail with his reputation completely besmirched. He could quieten his conscience with arguments but he couldn't argue away his fears. The subinspector kept things as secret as possible. He gave the representative strict instructions not to let the slightest word of it get out to anyone. He even kept things closeted from the staff and the constables at the station.

It was nine o'clock at night. The subinspector had sent all three of his constables away on an errands. He even sent the watchman all over town to gather supplies so that he could be alone at the station while he waited for the representative. There was panic on his face as he looked out the window. The representative hasn't arrived yet. What could he be up to? If the sentries came back and witnessed the goings on, there would be real trouble. And I specifically told him to come early. But what happens if the Mahant doesn't agree to three thousand? No, I won't take less than that. I can't pay for the wedding with less than that.

In his head, the subinspector began calculating how much money he would have to spend on the dowry and how much that would leave him for food and drinks.

Half an hour later, he heard the representative arrive. His heart began to beat faster. He got up from the cot and opened the *paandaan* to put together a *paan* for himself. In the meantime, the representative stepped in.

Krishnachandra—Well?

Representative—The Mahant ...

Krishnachandra looking at the door, asked—Have you brought the money?

Representative—I have it with me, but the Mahant ...

Krishnachandra looking around cautiously once more, said—I won't accept a penny less.

Representative—Ok. But you'll let me have my share, won't you?

Krishnachandra—Get your share from the Mahant.

Representative—I customarily get 5 per cent.

Krishnachandra—You won't get a paisa from me. I am selling my soul. This isn't just some petty crime.

Representative—As you please, but you are depriving me of my share.

Krishnachandra—You will have to come with me.

Immediately, a bullock-cart was hailed and both men got in and drove off. There was a group of watchmen around the bullock-cart. Krishnachandra wanted to get home as quickly as possible. He repeatedly scolded the driver to make him hurry—*Arrey*, are you sleeping? Move faster!

It was eleven by the time they reached home. The subinspector took the representative into his room and closed the door. The representative took out a bag. There were some guineas, some notes, and some rupee coins. Krishnachandra grabbed the bag and, without examining it, put it in his trunk and locked it up.

Gangajali had been waiting for him. Krishnachandra sent the representative on his way and came out of his room. Gangajali asked—Why are you so late?

Krishnachandra—A tough assignment and that too far away.

After dinner, the subinspector lay down, but couldn't sleep. He was afraid to tell his wife about the money. Gangajali also could not sleep. She kept watching her husband's face trying to decipher the signs and see if they had drowned or would survive.

Krishnachandra couldn't take it any more. He said—If you were standing on the bank of a river and a tiger leapt at you, what would you do?

Gangajali understood. She said—I would jump into the river.

Krishnachandra—Even if you were to drown?

Gangajali—Of course. It's better to drown than be devoured by a tiger.

Krishnachandra—And what if your house were on fire and all the doors were locked? What would you do then?

Gangajali—I would climb on to the roof and jump.

Krishnachandra—Do you know what I am getting at?

Hurt, Gangajali looked at her husband and said—I'm not stupid.

Krishnachandra—I have jumped into the river, but I don't know if I will swim or drown.

3

SUBINSPECTOR KRISHNACHANDRA DID not know how to cover his tracks after he had taken the bribe. He was still an amateur at deception. He didn't know that you could not consume stolen goods by yourself. The Mahant's representative thought to himself, I was the one who took all the trouble, now I am being short-changed. Why should I have got involved in this squabble or spent my days and nights flattering this monk? I was the one who saved the Mahant from being arrested. It wasn't my life that was at stake. His freedom and his capture depend entirely on me. And what do I get out of this? If I did all this work, it was in the hope of getting something in return.

On leaving the subinspector, he went directly to the police station and filed a report.

The staff at the police station said—Cheating us, is he? The traitor has been amassing a fortune under our noses. Doesn't he know? We are supposed to be agents of the government. We'll see exactly how he intends to embezzle this money. The hypocrite deserves to be taught a lesson.

Krishnachandra, however, was completely immersed in preparations for the wedding. The bridegroom was handsome, good-natured, and well educated. He came from a high-caste family and was wealthy. Both sides were busy negotiating when the government officials received a confidential communiqué in which the entire episode had been narrated in great detail and with convincing evidence. The legal points had been presented with such precision that the officials were worried that there were no grounds for doubt. A secret investigation was conducted which confirmed their worst fears. Everything was out in the open.

An entire month had passed. Tomorrow was the auspicious *tilak* ceremony. In the evening, the subinspector was lounging against a cushion at the police station, when he saw the English police superintendent approaching. Two officers and some constables followed behind him. Krishnachandra stood up nervously. One of the officers stepped forward and handed him a warrant for his arrest. Krishnachandra turned pale. Silently, he stared at the ground. There was no fear on his face, only shame. These were the same two officers who worked at his station. He had always considered them beneath him. But now his arrogance was shattered and he stood before them, humiliated. A lifetime's good reputation had been ruined in an instant. The staff at the police station murmured, 'This is what comes from keeping bribes to yourself.'

The English superintendent spoke in broken Hindustani—Well Krishnachandra, do you have anything to say in your defence?

Krishnachandra thought to himself—What should I do? Shall I say that I am completely innocent, that this is all happening because of my enemies, that the members of this police station were jealous of my reputation and have framed me?

But Krishnachandra did not know how to mask his guilt from himself. He felt overwhelmed in the face of his own crimes. He had fallen even in his own estimation. It is true that only rarely are crimes punished. But most forget that almost always one has to pay for one's noble deeds. Krishnachandra's face, his eyes, his body, all of them turned into tongues and began testifying against him. His soul presided over him like a magistrate. He was a simple man used to walking a simple path. This complicated moral maze confounded him.

Krishnachandra's conscience turned against him—Here, taste the fruit of your actions. I told you not to place your hand in a den of cobras. But you didn't heed my advice. Now face the consequences.

The superintendent asked once again—Do you have anything to say in your defence?

Krishnachandra said—Yes, all I want to say is that I have committed a crime and that I should be given the most stringent punishment. My face should be painted black and I should be paraded through the town. I committed a sin—for pride, greed, and vanity—and now I deserve to be punished for it. The shackles of conscience and religion could not dissuade me, so I deserve the shackles of the law. Let me inside for a while and when I return, I will go with you willingly.

Krishnachandra's words contained both defeat and arrogance. He wanted to tell the two officers that—I might be a criminal, but I am willing to suffer the consequences like a man. I won't act like a crook and lie about it.

As they heard his words, the two officers looked at each other as if to say—He has lost his mind. If he wanted to be known as honourable man, why take a bribe in the first place? This fool doesn't know the first thing about corruption.

The superintendent took pity on Krishnachandra and allowed him to go home.

Gangajali was decorating a silver plate for the tilak ceremony when Krishnachandra came to her and said—Ganga, the secret's out. I am being arrested.

Gangajali couldn't believe her ears. The colour drained from her face and she began to weep hysterically.

Krishnachandra—Stop crying. This is exactly what I deserve. I'm being punished for things that I have done. They are going to bring criminal charges against me, but there is no need for you to worry. I am prepared to face everything. Don't hire lawyers or attorneys and waste money. Perhaps my penance will make that ill-begotten money pure again. Spend the money on Suman's wedding. Don't spend a single paisa on the court case, or else it will all have been in vain. My reputation has been ruined and I can't save my soul. Let me at least have the satisfaction of knowing that I will have paid my debt to our daughter and that she is settled.

Gangajali began to wail and beat her head with both hands. She couldn't believe that she had been so short-sighted. She wanted the earth to split open and swallow her. It was as if a wave of pain and ache split her heart, like lightning piercing a cloudy sky. Hopelessly, she looked up to the heavens—Hai! If I had known that I would have to live through a day like this, I would have married my daughter off to a pauper, or I would have poisoned her myself. Then she jumped to her feet, as if she had been startled out of her sleep, and grabbed Krishnachandra's hands and said—Burn this money! Take it and throw it back at that murderer, Ramdas. My daughter can stay unmarried. Dear God! Why was I so stupid. I will approach the officers. Why worry about honour or shame now?

Krishnachandra—Whatever had to happen has happened. Nothing can be done now.

Gangajali—Take me to the English officer. I will fall at his feet and say, 'This is your money, take it, and you can give me whatever punishment you want.' I am the poisonous seed. This is all my fault.

Krishnachandra—Be quiet. They can hear you outside.

Gangajali—Why won't you take me to the Englishman? He will have to take pity on a helpless woman.

Krishnachandra—Listen, this is not the time to cry. I've fallen into the clutches of the law and cannot be rescued. But don't lose heart. God willing, we will meet again.

As soon as he said this and went outside, his two daughters ran up to him and clutched his feet. Gangajali clutched him with both hands. All three women began to wail and scream.

Krishnachandra was terrified. He thought to himself—What will happen to these women? God, you are the protector of the weak. I leave them to your mercy.

In an instant, he freed himself and went outside. Gangajali flailed her arms to try and stop him, but failed. Her arms stayed outstretched, like a bird that has been shot and falls to the ground with outstretched wings.

4

KRISHNACHANDRA WAS GENERALLY liked in his district. The news of his arrest spread quickly and caused quite a commotion. A few wealthy men offered to pay his bail, but the English official refused to accept it.

A week later, Krishnachandra was charged with accepting bribes. Mahant Ramdas was also arrested.

Both the cases dragged through the month. The government had them committed to sessions. That took another month. In the end, Krishnachandra was sentenced to five years in prison. The Mahant was sentenced to seven and two of his disciples were sent to the backwaters in the Andamans.

Gangajali had a brother named Umanath. Krishnachandra had not got along with him at all. He had called him a cheat and a hypocrite and made fun of his long tilak. Consequently, Umanath did not visit often. But on hearing the news of Krishnachandra's arrest, Umanath rushed to his sister. He brought his sister and his two nieces back with him. Krishnachandra did not have any brothers who the women could turn to. His uncle had two sons, but they were not close. They hadn't even asked about him.

When he was leaving, Krishnachandra had told Gangajali not to spend a single paisa of Ramdas' money in his defence for he was certain that he would be convicted. But Gangajali was unwilling to acquiesce; she opened her heart and her wallet. The lawyers assured her till the very end that her husband would win the case.

The judge's decision was appealed against in the high court. The Mahantji's sentence was not reduced, but Krishnachandra's sentence was reduced from five to four years.

Gangajali returned to her natal home, but even here she could find no comfort. It was no longer the home where she had played with dolls as a young girl, where she had made clay houses, and had been safe in her parents' lap. Her parents were dead, and she no longer recognized the people in the town. It had changed so much that there were fields where there had been trees and trees where there were once fields. She recognized her own home with difficulty and the worst part was that she found neither love nor respect in it. Her sister-in-law, Jahnvi, couldn't stand her and remained in the house as little as possible. She would go to the neighbours and cry over the pain that Gangajali caused her. She had two daughters. They were cold towards Suman and Shanta.

Gangajali no longer had any of Ramdas' money. She only had the four or five hundred rupees that she had struggled to save. As a result, she never spoke to Umanath about Suman's wedding. Six months later, the family into which Krishnachandra had arranged Suman's wedding no longer wanted anything to do with her.

Umanath could do nothing but think of Suman's marriage. Whenever he got a few days off, he set out to one of the neighbouring villages in search of a potential husband. And wherever he went, there would be a commotion. The young men would dress up in the fancy clothes that they normally saved for weddings. They would borrow rings and necklaces and put them on. Mothers would bathe their children, put *kajal* around their eyes, and dress them up in newly washed clothes and send them out to play. Older men still seeking brides would get their moustaches trimmed by barbers and pluck out any gray hairs. The barbers and water carriers of the town would be called from the fields, so that there would be extra servants in the village. If someone wanted to show off his status, he would have one of them give him a massage, or he would have one of them fold a *dhoti* for him. As long as Umanath was in town, there would continue to be a pretence of leisure. The women would not emerge from their homes; no one would fill his own glass with water; no one would go to work in the fields. Umanath, though, couldn't imagine Suman living in any of these homes. Suman was beautiful and educated; her life would have been wasted if she had to live amongst these rustics.

In the end, Umanath decided to look for a groom in the city. A husband worthy of Suman would not be found in the villages. He had heard much talk of city men and had been quite impressed. He had heard office workers and clerks bragging of making thousands a year, so he didn't even think to consider the wealthier men. When they saw him coming, people would get excited. Some were overjoyed at the thought of arranging a match when they heard about Suman's caste and family, but with some of the men the horoscopes did not match and with some Umanath was unimpressed. He would not settle for a low-caste husband for Suman.

A year later, Umanath still hadn't found a husband for Suman. He had become frustrated running around in vain. He had begun like a man handing out advertisements for medicines to people he thought could afford them, but at the end of the day, realizing that he still had a heavy bundle of pamphlets ended by unloading them on paupers. He had begun to overlook prestige, education, looks, and moral qualities and was holding out only for someone of a high caste. That was one requirement he would not give up on.

It was the month of Magh. Umanath had gone to the river to bathe. As soon as he returned home, he went straight to Gangajali and said, 'Look, your wish has been granted. We've found a suitable boy in Banares.'

Gangajali—Finally your work has paid off. The boy is educated, isn't he?

Umanath—He's just a servant, a fifteen-rupees-a-month clerk in a factory.

Gangajali—Does he own a home?

Umanath—Who can afford a home in the city? Everyone rents.

Gangajali—What about his family?

Umanath—His parents are dead, and in the city, who has relatives?

Gangajali—How old is he?

Umanath—Around thirty.

Gangajali—Is he handsome?

Umanath—He's one in a million. Besides, no one is really ugly in the city. Everyone has a nice haircut and clean clothes. He's an incredibly smart and pious man. When he speaks, flowers bloom. His name is Gajadharprasad.

Gangajali—He must be a widower.

Umanath—Sure, but it doesn't matter. In the city no one is old. The youth are like boys and the old men, youths; there, youth is long-lived. He has the same fresh humor and the same fashionable indulgence in hair oil as the younger men. In the city, people are forever young and die young.

Gangajali—And his caste?

Umanath—Very good. He is two ranks higher than we are. What do you think?

Gangajali responded with resignation—I like him if you do.

5

Suman was married in Phagun. Gangajali wept profusely when she saw the groom, almost as if Suman had been killed.

On arriving at her new home, Suman discovered that it was in much worse shape than she had imagined. There were only two small rooms and a shed, and vines covered all four walls. The stench from the sewers seeped into every corner of the house, which had neither heat nor light. And for this, they paid three rupees every month in rent.

The first two months passed easily for Suman. One of Gajadhar's old aunts did all of the housework. But in the summer, there was an outbreak of cholera and the aunt died. And now things became complicated. The maid they wanted to hire wouldn't do the dishes and clean the kitchen for less than three rupees a month. For two days the hearth didn't burn. Wanting to keep his new wife happy, Gajadhar bought *puris* from the market on both days. He was completely taken by her beauty and her charm. On the third day he got up in the middle of the night and did the dishes, cooked, and brought in the water. When Suman awoke, she was shocked to find the housework done. She knew that Gajadhar had done all the work, but out of embarrassment, didn't say anything. That evening, she did the housework herself. She cried as she washed the dishes.

In a few days, however, she became accustomed to it. She even began to find some joy in it. Gajadhar felt as though he had conquered the world. He bragged about his wife to all of his friends. She wasn't a woman, she was a goddess, a girl from a wealthy family who did even the smallest chores around the house herself, who cooked so well that even simple *daal* and *roti* tasted rich. When he got his wages the following month, he handed her the entire amount. And for the first time Suman felt free; she no longer had to ask for small sums of money. She could spend it as she pleased. She could eat and drink whatever she wanted.

Suman had never handled household accounts before and she couldn't distinguish between essential and inessential expenses. And with ten days in the month still to go, She had exhausted Gajadhar's salary. She hadn't been trained to be a housewife, but only to be a consumer. Gajadhar didn't know what to say when Suman told him so. How will we survive the month? he thought. A mountain of weight descended on his shoulders. He spent the whole day wandering around town, wondering where he could find money in the middle of the month.

Even though he had made Suman the mistress of the house, Gajadhar was by nature a stingy man. The *jalebis* at breakfast tasted like poison. And seeing real butter in his daal gave him a sharp pain in his chest. And while he was eating he would look over to the kitchen to make sure that she hadn't made extra food. Seeing rice and daal wasted made his body shiver.

It was strange, though, that Suman's enchanting figure had tamed him. He couldn't say a word to her.

But today, after several men had refused him loans, he became nervous. He came home and said—You spent all the money, so you tell me, where am I supposed to find more?

Suman—I didn't waste any of it.

Gajadhar—Maybe you didn't waste it, but you knew that we only had so much for the whole month. You should have spent accordingly.

Suman—It's not like we've been living luxuriously on your salary.

Gajadhar—But what are we supposed to do now?

And so, they began to quarrel. Gajadhar said some harsh things. In the end, Suman gave him her necklace to pawn and he left muttering to himself.

Suman's life had been spent in comfort. She was accustomed to finer things. She couldn't hold herself back when she heard the call of street vendors at her door. She used to eat with Gajadhar, but now she ate alone. To satisfy her palate, she began to deceive her husband.

Slowly news of Suman's beauty spread through the locality. Neighbouring women came to visit her. Conducting herself with the natural ease of a woman from a good family, Suman would look down on them and try to avoid meeting them. But her neighbours were quick recognize her status and treated her like a queen. It appealed to her proud nature, and to retain her newfound authority, she began to exaggerate wildly before these women. They cried over their fates, while Suman commended her own. They would complain and gossip about other women and Suman would try to make them see each other's perspectives. She would greet them draped in the silk saris that she had brought from her mother's home. She would hang her silk jackets on the wall. Her new friends liked watching her showy performances more than listening to her talk. And they highly regarded her opinion on ornaments. When they bought new jewellery they would consult Suman, and would ask her opinion before buying new saris. Out of pride, Suman would give them advice in a disinterested manner, but it hurt her deeply. She thought—these women buy new ornaments and new clothes, and in my house we can barely afford roti. Am I the most unfortunate person in the world? As a child, she had been taught only to please herself and enjoy life. She had not learnt the moral lesson nor acquired the religious education that plants the seeds of contentment in one's mind. She became desperate with disappointment.

Gajadhar was working harder these days. After working at the factory during the day, he would keep accounts at another store, and finally return home at eight o'clock at night. This work earned him five extra rupees. But he couldn't see any real difference in his financial situation. His entire earnings only managed to keep them from starving through the month. The miser in him couldn't bear this situation. Seeing Suman cry over her wretched situation made him even more dejected. He could clearly see that Suman was becoming increasingly alienated from him. He didn't understand that Suman received greater pleasure from rich sweets than from his love-filled words. Not finding any satisfaction in either love or labour, he tried to get what he wanted by exerting his authority. And so a kind of tug-of-war began between the two of them.

No matter how confident we may be in our own selves, the company we keep inevitably has an effect on us. Suman may have educated the neighbouring women, but she learned much more from them. We are so stupid when it comes to starting a family; we do not consider preparation or training for it important. A child who plays with dolls, a young girl who frolics with her friends are considered to be qualified enough for marriage. But marriage places a heavy yoke on a carefree child. And under such conditions, we should not be surprised to find dysfunctional families. The women with whom Suman spent her time saw their husbands as the instruments of material pleasure. A husband, no matter what, should give his wife beautiful jewellery and the best clothes, should feed her the most delicious food. If he wasn't able to do this, then he was worthless, he was disabled, and he had no right to marry anyone. He was not worthy of respect or love. Suman learned this well and when Gajadharprasad got angry over her housework, he would have to endure a lengthy sermon on the duties of a husband.

There was no shortage of young men and flirts in the neighbourhood. Returning from school, young men and dandies would knock on Suman's door and run away. They would pass by her house singing romantic songs of Radha and Krishna. Even if Suman was busy, glimpses of her could be caught through the curtain. Her innocent heart received endless pleasure from this kind of flirting. She played these games not out of wickedness, but to show off the lustre of her beauty, to win over the hearts of others.

6

Across the street from Suman's house was a brothel that belonged to a courtesan named Bholibai. Every morning, Bholibai would sit out on her balcony, all dressed and made up. Through the night, Suman could hear the most beautiful music coming from her apartment. Sometimes Bholi would drive around in her carriage. Suman couldn't help but be jealous.

Suman had never met any courtesans, but she had heard that courtesans were the worst kinds of women—wicked and depraved. With their skill, they could ensnare the hearts of young men in their web of worldly illusion. No respectable man would speak to them openly, but rogues would sneak into their brothels at night. Bholi had seen Suman standing behind the screen to her door several times and gestured her over, but Suman couldn't imagine speaking to her. She was, after all, better than Bholi, she thought—I may be poor and miserable, but at least I still have my virtue. There are no rules preventing me from associating with honourable men. None of them would think that I am beneath them! She can enjoy her luxuries as much as she wants, but she will never be respected. All she can do is sit in her brothel and savor the fruits of her shamelessness and her immorality. But Suman slowly realized that no matter how much she considered Bholi to be beneath her, Bholi was much better off.

It was the month of Aashaadh. The heat made Suman restless. No matter what she did, the evening was unbearable. She lifted the screen and sat in the doorway, fanning herself. She could see the preparations for some festivity being carried on at Bholibai's door. A water carrier was sprinkling water. In the courtyard, a canopy was being stretched out, and flower petals scattered about as decoration. Glasswares were being carried in on a cart and a carpet was being laid out. Scores of people were running around when Bholi's eyes fell upon Suman. She walked up to Suman and said—Tonight there is a concert at my place. If you want to come, I can put up a *purdah*, so that you can attend.

Suman replied disinterestedly—I can watch from here.

Bholi entreated—You might be able to see, but you won't hear anything. What's the harm, shall I put up a purdah?

Suman turned away and said—I'm really not that interested.

Bholi looked at her tenderly and thought—who knows what this simple country girl has been thinking. Fine. See for yourself what kind of woman I really am. And without saying another word, she left.

Night fell. It was cool outside and Suman had no desire to go and sit near the hearth. There was already a fire burning in her body, and she didn't want to have to deal with another flame. Still mindful of her duties, she got up to light the hearth. She set some *khichri* to boil and came back to watch the festivities. As the clock stuck eight, the lights under the canopy came on and the entire place was illuminated with the most beautiful lights. The delicate floral arrangements made the spectacle seem even more elegant. Spectators began arriving from all directions—on bicycles, in open horse buggies, on foot. A little later, two or three carriages arrived carrying several well-known gentlemen. In an hour the entire courtyard had been filled. There must have been a hundred men gathered there. Then, the *maulana* arrived with his entourage. The light of education and wisdom shone from his countenance. He placed a pillow on the ornamented seat at the head of the courtyard, sat down on it, and signalled for the festivities to begin. Several men had been stationed at the door to greet guests. Some were sprinkling rose water and some were offering *khus*. Suman had never seen such a group of refined and aristocratic men before.

When Gajadhar arrived at nine o'clock, Suman laid out dinner for him. When he was finished with his dinner, Gajadhar got up and went to the concert as well. Suman was so enrapt in the event, that she forgot to eat her own dinner. She sat there, listening, until the *maulud* came to an end and it was already midnight. When she looked up again, she saw that sweets were being distributed and that people was dispersing. When Gajadhar returned Suman asked him—Who were all those people?

Gajadhar replied—I don't know most of them. There were all kinds of people, respectable and otherwise. There were also some nobles from the city.

Suman—Don't these people consider it dishonourable to go to a brothel?

Gajadhar—Would they have come if they thought it dishonourable?

Suman—You must have thought twice about going, though.

Gajadhar—There were so many respectable men sitting in the courtyard. I was in good company. The man I work for in the evenings, the Sethji, he was there, too.

Suman was confused. She thought for a moment and then said—I had always thought that people looked down on courtesans.

Gajadhar—Some men hold those views, but not many. This English education has made men more liberal. People no longer have that same contempt for courtesans. Besides, Bholibai has a marvellous reputation in the city.

Clouds had gathered in the sky. The wind had stopped and not even a leaf stirred.

Gajadharprasad was tired from the day's work. As soon as he reached his *charpoy* he fell into a deep sleep, but Suman couldn't fall asleep for quite some time.

Next day, when she lifted the screen and sat in the doorway, she saw Bholi sitting on her balcony. She stepped out onto the verandah and said to Bholi—There was quite a celebration at your place last night.

Bholi knew that she had won Suman over. Smiling, she said—Shall I send some *shirini* for you? The confectioner made it and a brahmin brought it.

Suman hesitated for a moment. Then she said—Have it sent over.

7

IT HAD BEEN almost a year and half since Suman had come to live with her husband and in that time she had not been able to go home or visit her mother. She did receive letters from her family, though. At first, she would comfort her mother, writing that there was nothing to worry about, that she was content. But now, her replies were lengthy tales filled with sorrow and pain. 'My life is being swept away in tears,' she wrote. 'What did I ever do to you that you sent me into this hell? I don't have a house to live in, clothes to wear, food to eat. I am living like an animal!'

She stopped bragging about her natal home to her neighbours. Where once she used to praise her husband, she now complained about him interminably. And she had even harsher words for her mother and sister,

'No one cares. My family treats me as if I am dead. They have everything they need at home, but of what use is that to me? They probably think that I am sleeping on a bed of flowers, but they don't know how much I suffer. I'm the only one who knows.'

She even been began to be rude to Gajadharprasad, blaming him for her unhappiness. These days, she slept late, and for a few days now she had not cleaned the house. Sometimes Gajadhar would have to leave for work without breakfast. He didn't understand what was going on, why she had changed suddenly.

Suman hated her house. She grew dejected with each hour that she was forced to spend in that hovel, so she began spending her days at her neighbours'.

One day, Gajadhar returned home at eight o'clock and found the front door locked. It had already become dark. He wondered where Suman could have gone at that hour. He started banging on the door so that if she were nearby, she would hear him and come back. Tonight, he was determined to get some answers from her. At that moment, Suman was sitting in Bholibai's rooms, talking with her. Bholi had been quite insistent that she visit her today, and Suman could not refuse any longer. When she heard the banging on her door, she quickly got up and ran home. Chatting with Bholibai, she had completely lost track of time. She hurriedly opened the door, lit a lamp, and began to light the fire. She was already feeling guilty when Gajadhar said to her angrily, 'What were you doing sitting over there this late at night? Don't you have any shame or self-respect?'

Suman replied meekly—She has invited me over several times, so I went. Change your clothes. Dinner will be ready soon. You are home early today.

Gajadhar—Dinner can wait. I'm not hungry. First tell me why you went there without my permission. Do you take me for a fool?

Suman—I can't bear to sit alone in this cage all day.

Gajadhar—Is this why you have decided to make friends with prostitutes? Do you care at all about your honour or your chastity?

Suman—What's the harm in going to see Bholi? The most respected people come to her house; my going there can't possibly make a difference.

Gajadhar—I don't care whether nobles visit her or not. You've humiliated me by going there. I can't stand by and watch my wife associate with courtesans. What do you know about the respectable people who go to her house anyway? People don't earn respect just because they have money.

Duty and honour are far more important than wealth in these matters. It seems as though you have really been taken in by the things that you saw at the concert that night, so listen carefully. There was not a single honourable man in the entire audience. My boss may be quite wealthy, but I would never let him cross the threshold of my house. These people are so caught up in their own greed that they forget about duty. Bholi hasn't suddenly become pure or chaste just because those men go to visit her. I am warning you. Don't ever go there again, or else ...

Suman understood—he must be right. What do I know of those people? The rich are always running after courtesans. Bholi said so herself. I am a fool.

But instead of feeling humiliated, Suman was secretly overcome with joy. After all, those men had not gone to see Bholi because she was more beautiful or talented, but because they were lascivious by nature. Her poverty seemed bearable now that she had found a basis from which to declare herself superior to Bholi.

Suman turned religious. To secure her spiritual capital and be better than Bholi she started observing a number of rituals. As soon as she woke, she went to bathe in the Ganga every morning. She also ordered a copy of the Ramayan and would occasionally read it to her friends. Sometimes she would read it to herself in a high voice. She may not have found inner peace, but it did bring her some kind of satisfaction.

It was the month of Chait. For Ramnavmi, Suman went with her friends to the main temple to watch the *Janmotsav* celebrations. The temple had been ornately decorated. The electric lights made it as bright as day. And it was very crowded; the courtyard of the temple was completely packed. But over the din of the crowd, one could hear an extraordinary melody coming from inside. Suman peeked in through a window and saw Bholi, singing. In the audience, she saw men of high repute. Some wore a Vaishnav tilak; others had smeared holy ashes on their foreheads; some had beads around their necks and were draped in *Ramnami* sheets; some wore ochre. Since she had seen several of them bathe in the Ganga, she was certain that they were all religious and scholarly men. They now appeared to be in the throes of some divine intoxication induced by Bholi. Through her performance, Bholi glanced around the room seductively, stopping on a face or exchanging glances with one of the men. Every man who locked eyes with Bholi seemed like he was looking into the eyes of God himself. Suman couldn't believe what she saw. The ground on which she was standing began to slip from under her feet. It was one thing when Suman believed that only wealth bowed its head at Bholi's feet; but now Suman realized that religion had become her devotee as well. Even the most religious men respected her—I had hoped to beat that courtesan with religion and piety, but look at her. She is the epitome of respect and honour in god's home, in this assembly of great men, and yet there isn't even a place for me to sit anywhere in this temple. Suman could not stay there for another instant.

She came home and tied up her copy of the Ramayan and put it away. She decided to forego her bath in the Ganga and her religious vows. Like a boat without a helmsman, she began to drift.

8

GAJADHAR FELT TRAPPED, like a man holding a bag full of gold coins in the middle of a den of thieves. Suman's beauty, which had drawn him like a moth to the flame, now seemed like a blaze. His own desire threatened to swallow him whole, so he kept his distance. The real source of a woman's beauty is her love for her husband. Without that, her beauty is merely the nectar derived from the fruit of the senses, poisonous and deadly.

Gajadhar did everything he could to keep Suman happy, but it was never enough. He realized that it was beyond his power to bring the stars down from the heavens for his wife.

These days, Gajadhar was mostly preoccupied with trying to find a new home. The fact that his current house did not have a courtyard was the source of much bitterness between husband and wife. Whenever Gajadhar forbade her from sitting near the doorway, she would reply sharply, 'Do you want to me to suffocate within this prison?' Finding a house with a courtyard would mean that she couldn't complain anymore. He also hoped that moving would mean that Suman would no longer meet with the women in the neighbourhood who, he was convinced, had turned Suman against him. He looked high and low for a new house, but as soon as he heard the outrageous rents he would return home dejected.

One day he came home from work at eight o'clock at night. He saw Bholibai sitting on his charpoy, laughing and talking with Suman. His lips began to quiver with rage. As soon as she saw him, Bholi came out and said—Had I known that you worked for the Sethji, I would have had you promoted by now. I only just learned this from your wife. The Sethji is quite taken with me, you know.

Her words stung Gajadhar, like salt on a wound. Furiously, he thought—what kind of man does she take me for? I would never use her recommendation to get myself a promotion. I spit on such promotions.

He didn't say a word to Bholi.

Suman saw the expression on his face, and she could tell that he was boiling over with anger and spoiling for a fight, but she was ready for him. Gajadhar also made no attempt to hide his displeasure. As soon as he sat down on the charpoy he said—Why do you still associate with that woman? Haven't I forbidden it?

Suman was ready for a quarrel. The words that she had rehearsed came spilling from her lips—She isn't contagious. In her character and conduct, she is anyone's equal. Everyone can see that she has dignity and respect. So what harm is there in talking with her? If she wanted, she could hire the likes of us as servants.

Gajadhar replied—You have turned everything upside down again. Dignity and respect are not acquired through wealth.

Suman—But they are acquired through religiosity, right?

Gajadhar—What? Do you think that she is some kind of saint?

Suman—God knows, but saintly people do offer her respect. Just the other day, during the Ramnavmi festival, I saw her singing to an audience of famous pundits and holy men. None of them despised her. Everyone's eyes were fixed on her face. People were not only kind and generous towards her, they considered themselves lucky to be able to speak with her. They may have hated her in their minds, only God knows for sure, but it seemed as if Bholi was the centre of everyone's attention. We can only see what people do; no one really knows what goes on inside their minds.

Gajadhar—So, you saw the long tilaks on their foreheads and assumed that they were holy men, did you? These days, religion has become a hiding place for villains. A gentle stream filled with crocodiles. They make their living by swallowing simple-hearted devotees. People are easily deceived by their long matted locks, their long tilaks, and their long beards, but they are all hypocrites, who bring religion a bad name, who trade the glory of religion for money. They are the sinners who live for excess and luxury. If Bholi weren't respected amongst these people, where would you expect her to be respected?

Suman asked frankly—Are you telling me the truth, or just playing games?

Gajadhar looked at her compassionately and said—No Suman, this is how things really are. There are not too many honourable men in this country, but it is not completely devoid of them either. There are a few men who are merciful and righteous, who remain devoted to charity. Even if Bholi had been an angel, such men would not look at her.

Suman became quiet. She was pondering over Gajadhar's words.

9

From the next day, Suman stopped sitting near the doorway. The street vendors would shout and then leave without selling anything. The dandies would sing their love songs and leave without attracting her attention. Now, they couldn't see anyone inside. Bholi invited her over several times, but Suman would complain that she wasn't feeling well. Occasionally, Bholi came to see her, but Suman would not meet with her openly.

It was now two years since Suman had been living in this house. Her silk saris had become tattered and torn. Her silk jackets were threadbare. And her declining status was felt in the neighbourhood as well. She was no longer the queen she had been. Her advice was no longer sought and her influence was being whittled away. Without her superior fashions, Suman could not retain her throne. That was why she no longer visited her neighbours and they no longer visited her. She would spend the whole day locked up in her cell of a house, passing her time reading or sleeping.

Trapped indoors all day, her health began to deteriorate. She had severe headaches. Fevers became frequent, as her heart raced. There were also symptoms of ulcers. Simple work would exhaust her. Her body became feeble and her lotus-like skin began to wither.

This concerned Gajadhar. Sometimes he would get irritated with Suman and say—Whenever I see you, you are lying about. If you can't even cook a decent meal for me, what is the point of your living here?

But soon afterwards he would feel sorry for Suman and regret his selfishness.

He slowly began to realize that Suman's bad health was the result of a miasma. Earlier, he had forbidden her from standing near the doorway, going to fairs, or bathing in the Ganga, now he would open the door himself and insist that she bathe in the Ganga. As a result, Suman went to bathe in the Ganga several mornings in a row, and her health improved noticeably, so she made a habit of going every morning. The withering plant began to flourish now that it had been watered.

It was the month of Magh. Suman and several of her neighbours were on their way to the Ganga. They passed an interesting park called Beni Park on the way to the river, especially since it housed a number of small animals. The city had even constructed a large dome of thin wire to keep a variety of birds. On the way back, everyone wanted to stroll in the park. Usually, Suman would return home immediately, but today her friends insisted that Suman accompany them to the park and she couldn't refuse. Suman stared at the fascinating creatures for quite some time. After a while, she sat down on a bench to rest. Suddenly she heard a voice. 'Arrey, who does this woman think she is, sitting on that bench? Get up from there! Has the government made this bench for you?'

Embarrassed and afraid, Suman turned around to see who was yelling at her. She saw the watchman rushing towards her, flashing his teeth.

Suman got up from the bench and went over to the birdhouse to get over the insult. She wished that she had never sat down on that bench. In the meantime, a rented carriage pulled up in front of the birdhouse. The watchman ran up to the carriage and opened the door. Two women got out. One of them was none other than Suman's neighbour, Bholi. Suman took cover behind a tree and watched as the two women began strolling about the park. They fed chickpeas to the monkeys, scattered seeds for the birds, stood on the backs of tortoises, and then went to watch the fish in the pond. The watchman followed them around like a servant. From the bank of the pond, they watched the fish dart around; in the meantime, the watchman made bouquets of flowers and presented them to his two guests. After a little while, the two women came and sat down on the same bench that Suman had been forced off. The watchman politely stood to one side. As she took all this in, sparks of anger began to flash from her eyes and she was consumed by rage—sweat spilled out from every pore, her limbs quivered like straw, her heart raced as if it were on fire. She grabbed the folds of her sari and started to cry. As soon as the two courtesans left, Suman pounced like a lioness and stood face-to-face with the watchman. Trembling with anger, she said—What is this? You made me get up from the bench, as if it belonged to your father, but you didn't say a word to those two whores.

In a condescending voice, the watchman replied—Are you their equal?

These words were enough to kindle Suman's ire. She bit her lip and said—Shut up you fool. You carry the slippers of prostitutes for pennies and feel no shame. Just wait and see if I don't sit on this bench. What will you do then?

At first the watchman was a little scared, but as soon as Suman sat on the bench he jumped at her and grabbed her arm and pulled her off. Suman got up like a lioness with fire in her eyes, ready to attack. But she was so angry that she couldn't find the words to speak. Her friends, who had walked all over the park and had met at the birdhouse, stood at a distance watching the scene unfold. Not one of them said anything in Suman's defence.

In the meantime, a buggy pulled up in front of them. The watchman was still wrestling with Suman when a gentleman got out and ran towards the watchman and gave him a strong shove. He said—What is going on here? Why have you grabbed her? Leave her alone!

Stammering, the watchman stepped back. He was mortified. He said—My lord, is this woman from your household?

Angrily, the nobleman said—What difference does that make? The real question is why are you harassing her? I could have you fired for this.

The watchman began pleading with him. At the same time, the woman who was still sitting in the carriage beckoned to Suman with a gesture. She said—What was he saying to you?

Suman replied—Nothing. I was sitting on this bench, and he wanted me to get up. Just a while ago, there were two courtesans sitting on that bench. Does my being poor mean that he can treat me worse than a courtesan?

The woman tried to calm her—He is a small, unimportant man, who earns four paisas, the slave of courtesans. Don't trouble yourself with the likes of him.

The two women introduced themselves. The woman's name was Subhadra and her husband was a lawyer. She lived in Suman's neighbourhood, but at some distance from Suman's house. The two of them had been returning after bathing in the Ganga. As they were passing by, her husband saw the watchman arguing with a woman from a respectable home, so he alighted from the carriage and intervened.

Subhadra was so drawn to Suman's beauty and her voice that she invited her to ride with them. Her husband sat out, with the driver. The carriage took off. Suman felt as if she were riding in an aeroplane on her way to paradise. Although Subhadra was not very beautiful and her clothes were rather ordinary, she was so modest, and her manner was so simple and quiet, that Suman was immediately drawn to her. On the way, when she saw her friends walking along the road, she opened the window and looked at them with this immense pride, as if to say—you will never be this lucky. But alongside this pride, she also felt fear—will Subhadra think less of me when she sees my house? Of course that's what will happen. She doesn't know how raggedly I live. What a fortunate woman she is! What a god-like man her husband is! If they hadn't come, who knows what that heartless watchman might have done to me? He is so noble that he let me sit inside while he went to sit next to the driver. She was completely immersed in her own thoughts when they arrived at her house. Embarrassed, she said to Subhadra—Please stop the carriage, this is my house.

Subhadra had the carriage stopped. Suman glanced over at Bholibai's house quickly. She was strolling on her balcony. Their eyes met, and it was as if Bholi had said—what a spectacle! And Suman replied in the same way—Take a good look at the kind of people these are. Even if you die, you will not be lucky enough to sit next to this goddess.

Suman got up. She looked at Subhadra tenderly and said—After all that you have done, please don't forget me. I will keep you in my thoughts.

Subhadra said—No sister, I still have things that I wasn't able to talk to you about. I will call you tomorrow.

The carriage left. When she went inside her house, Suman felt like she had just woken up from a blissful dream.

Gajadhar asked—Whose carriage was that?

Suman—It belongs to a lawyer from around here. I met his wife in Beni Park. They insisted that I ride back with them. They wouldn't take no for an answer.

Gajadhar—So, you sat with the lawyer?

Suman—Do you hear yourself? That poor man sat next to the driver.

Gajadhar—That's what took you so long.

Suman—They are both models of nobility.

Gajadhar—Fine, light the stove, there's been enough praise for one day.

Suman—You know Vakil Sahib, don't you?

Gajadhar—There is a lawyer in this neighborhood named Padamsingh. Are you talking about him?

Suman—He is a fair and tall man. He wears eyeglasses.

Gajadhar—Yes, that's him. He lives just east of here.

Suman—Is he a wealthy lawyer?

Gajadhar—I don't keep track of his accounts, you know. I see him occasionally, in passing. He is a good man.

Suman could tell that Gajadhar didn't relish this discussion about Vakil Sahib. She changed her clothes and began to cook dinner.

10

THE NEXT DAY, Suman did not go to bathe in the river. Since morning, she had been mending one of her old saris.

In the afternoon, one of Subhadra's maids came for her. Suman had hoped that a carriage would come for her, but when it didn't, She felt small and insignificant again. She had been afraid that this might happen.

She went with the maid to Subhadra's house, and stayed with her for two or three hours. She couldn't tear herself away. While she described every little detail of her natal home for Subhadra, Subhadra only spoke of her husband's home.

The two women were fast becoming friends. Whenever Subhadra would go to bathe in the Ganga, she would take Suman along with her. And Suman wouldn't let a day pass without going to visit Subhadra. Like a fish that has been squirming on the sand begins to play as soon as it reaches the water, Suman forgot her miseries in Subhadra's care and became a playful child again.

If Subhadra were working on something, Suman would drop everything to help her. Occasionally, she would cook Pandit Padamsingh's dinner, or perhaps make a paan and have it sent to him. And she never considered doing these things a chore or a bother. In her eyes, there was no one as good-natured as Subhadra or as noble as Padamsingh in the entire world.

Once, when Subhadra had a fever, Suman would not leave her side. She went home for a few minutes, prepared something for dinner—she didn't even check to see if it was undercooked or overcooked—and then raced back. Gajadhar, though, couldn't stand this. He didn't trust Suman. He would try and keep her from going to meet Subhadra, but Suman would not pay any attention to him.

It was the month of Phagun. Suman was beginning to worry about how to get new clothes for Holi. Gajadhar had not been working for the Sethji for over a month, so now he only received a salary of fifteen rupees. She had repeatedly asked Gajadhar for a Tanzebi sari and a silk-velveteen jacket, but Gajadhar would always find some way to avoid the issue. Suman, though, worried that she would have to wear her old saris to the Holi celebration at Subhadra's.

In the middle of all this, Suman received a sad letter about her mother's death. Suman was not as upset as she might have been, because her mother had broken her heart. But for the moment, it provided an excuse for not getting new, fancy clothes for Holi. She said to Subhadra—Bahuji, now I am an orphan. I no longer have the heart to look at new clothes and jewellery. I have worn enough of them in my time. This pain makes it impossible to think about dressing up and fashion. My soul is a wretched thing. I can't force it out of my body. And it forces me to bear an unspeakable pain in my heart. She repeated the same sorrowful words to her friends. Each and every one of them praised her devotion to her mother.

One day she was sitting next to Subhadra reading the Ramayan when Padamsingh entered the house excitedly and said—I struck it rich today.

Subhadra was overjoyed and said—Really?

Padamsingh—Arrey, why do you have doubts?

Subhadra—Well, at least give me my money. You won yours, so now you can give me my share.

Padamsingh—Yes, yes, you will get your money. Just be patient. My friends have been insisting that we have a festive celebration.

Subhadra—Well, we will have to organize something.

Padamsingh—I suggested a banquet, but no one was terribly keen on it. They insisted on seeing Bholibai dance.

Subhadra—So, let's do what they want. It won't cost thousands of rupees. And besides, it's almost Holi, so you can have it on the same day. We can kill two birds with one stone.

Padamsingh—Money is not the issue. It's a matter of principle.

Subhadra—Maybe we can disregard these principles just this once.

Padamsingh—Vitthaldas will not agree under any circumstances. He will get on my case.

Subhadra—Let him babble. The majority of the people in this world do not pay him any attention.

After years of fruitless effort, Pandit Padamsingh had successfully become a member of the municipal council. This is what they were getting ready to celebrate. He wanted to have a simple banquet, but his friends were pressurizing him into having a performance with singing and dancing. Although he was an extremely principled man himself, he didn't have the resolution to remain fast to his principles. Partly on account of his civility, his gentle nature, and his fear of sarcastic taunts from his friends, he could not hold his ground. Babu Vitthaldas was a close friend and a bitter enemy of these singing and dancing acts performed by courtesans. He had started a reform movement to eliminate this awful vice. Pandit Padamsingh was amongst his few supporters. That was why the Pandit was afraid of Vitthaldas. But in the end, Subhadra's encouragement alleviated his anxieties.

He finally gave in to his courtesan-loving friends. The plans were finalized; he would host Bholibai's performance.

Four days later, it was Holi. That night, Padamsingh's sitting room took on the shape of a dance hall. A group of his friends sat on beautiful, multi-colored carpets, and Bholibai sat in the middle of the room with her entourage and sang in a melodious voice and danced with expressive gestures.

The room was lit up with bright electric lights. The smell of perfume and roses filled the air. With laughter and amusement, the bazaar of pleasure came alive.

Both Suman and Subhadra were watching the performance through holes in the lattice screen. Subhadra thought that Bholi's singing was flat and bland. She was astonished—why were people listening to the song so intently? Much later, she understood what the song was about. The flowery language had charmed the audience. Suman was a much more accomplished connoisseur of music. She understood the poetry and had a keen sense of rhythm and melody. As soon as she heard a song, it would be permanently imprinted in her memory. Bholibai sang—

Ah, the flames of Holi burn inside me,
My lover is gone,
I wait at the door,
How can I find the strength to be calm?
The flames Holi burn inside me.

Suman began to hum along, and as she sang the song, She was charmed by her own abilities. She only had trouble with the vibrato. But all of her attention was focused on the performance. She saw hundreds of eyes fixed on Bholibai. There was such desire in those eyes! Such respect, such longing! Bholi's every glance and gesture made their eyes dance, shine. When her gaze fell upon a man he brimmed over with bliss, and when she laughed with another or said a few words to a third, they felt as if they had all the wealth of Kubera. The entire group would stare at that lucky man with respect. The group was filled with respectable men, each more wealthy, educated, and handsome than the other, but each one of them was ensnared by the amorous designs of this courtesan. Each face was the epitome of desire and longing.

Suman thought to herself—what kind of magic does that woman possess? Beauty! Yes, yes, she is attractive. There is no doubt about it. But I am not ugly either. She is dark. I am fair. She is plump. I am slender.

There was a mirror in Panditji's room. Suman stood in front of the mirror and examined herself from head to toe. She compared each limb with the image of Bholibai she had etched in her memory. Then, she asked Subhadra—Bahuji, can I ask you something if you won't think less of me? Is that heavenly fairy that much prettier than me?

Subhadra looked at her curiously. She smiled and said—Why are you asking me this question?

Suman hung her head in embarrassment. She said—No reason. Just tell me.

Subhadra said—She has a body indulged in pleasure, that's why she blossoms, but in form and figure she is not your equal.

Suman started thinking again—so are people so captivated just by her make-up and her hairdo, her clothes and her jewellery? If I wore make-up and did my hair like her, wore clothes and jewellery like hers, wouldn't my beauty become more elegant, wouldn't my youth sparkle even brighter? But where can I get these things?

Why are people so impressed with her voice and grace? Her voice has no range. My voice is much better than hers. If I had even a month's training, I would sing much better than her. I know how to flirt. I know how to look coy and smile.

Suman sat there for a long time deliberating over the cause and effect of these things. In the end, she concluded—she is free; there are shackles on my feet. Her warehouse is open, that's why there is a crowd of customers; mine is closed, that's why no one is standing in line. She doesn't care whether or not the dogs bark about her, but I am afraid of what people will say and think. She can go outside of the purdah, while I am cloistered in it. She can swing freely on branches, while I have to hang on for dear life. This shame and this fear of derision have made me the servant of others.

Halfway through night, the group dispersed. People went to their respective homes. Suman also headed home. There was darkness all round. There was also a darkness of despair in Suman's heart. She was walking towards her home, but very slowly, like a horse walking toward a bomb. She wanted to run away from her house, just as pride wants to remain at a distance from depravity.

Gajadhar arrived home at nine o'clock as usual and found the door locked. He was confused—where could Suman have gone at this hour? There was an elderly seamstress in the neighbourhood. He went over to ask her about Suman. He found out that she had gone on an errand to Subhadra's house. He got the key, opened the door, and saw that dinner had been set for him. He sat at the door to wait for Suman to return. At ten o'clock, he sat down to eat, but he was so angry that he had lost his appetite. He picked up all of the food and tossed it outside. He went back in, locked the door from the inside, and tried to sleep. He was resolved: 'I don't care how hard she bangs her head, I won't open the door. We'll see where she goes now.' For a long time, he stayed wide awake. At the slightest noise, he would pick up his stick and stand near the door. If Suman had returned home then, she would not have been safe. By eleven o'clock, the god of sleep had cast a spell over him.

When Suman reached her door, she heard the clock strike one. The sound buzzed through each one of her veins. She was under the impression that it was only ten or eleven o'clock. The colour drained from her face. She looked through the gap in the door and saw a lamp still burning. She saw that the smoke from the lamp had filled the entire house and that Gajadhar was lying there, holding a stick, snoring loudly. Her heart skipped a beat. She didn't have the courage to knock on the door.

Where can I go at this hour? Padamsingh's door has probably been locked, and his gatekeeper has probably gone to sleep. If I shout and scream a lot, I am sure they will open the door, but who knows what Vakil Sahib will think. No, it's not a good idea to go back there. Why don't I just sit here? It's already one o'clock. In three or four hours, it will be morning. She thought about it and sat down. But she was concerned—what if someone sees me sitting here like this, then what? He will think that I am a thief, lurking in the shadows. The truth of the matter was that Suman had become a thief in her own house.

In Phagun, the night winds are cold. Suman only had a torn silk jacket to cover her body. The wind pierced her bones like arrows. The joints in her hands and feet grew stiff and painful. And to top it all, the sewers below gave off such an awful stench that it was difficult to breathe. From all four directions, dark clouds cast their shadows; only dim rays of light from Bholibai's brothel shone upon the dark street like the loveless eyes of pity.

Suman thought—I am so unlucky. There are women who get to sleep in comfort, with pillows and servants to massage their feet, and here I am crying over my fate. Why must I suffer? I sleep on a broken cot in a small hut, eat dry bread, and have to listen to insults everyday. Why? To maintain my honour and my dignity? Does the world care whether I have my honour and dignity? Does the world place any value on such ideals? Is there some mysterious significance that I can't appreciate? In the festival of Dashera, in the festival of Mohurrum, in the gardens, everywhere, I can see the world operating on a different system of values. Until today I thought that only degenerate people consorted with these prostitutes, but today I discovered that men with good moral standing and piety are equally attracted to them. Vakil Sahib is a very noble man, but today even he went crazy over Bholibai.

She thought these things over for a while and then got up to knock on the door—let things take their course. It's not worthwhile standing out here and being miserable, because I will be as miserable inside. Am I fed bites of gold, or made to sleep on a bed of flowers? I tear at my chest all day working so hard, and only then do I get something to eat. And on top of that, I have to live with this threat. She saw Gajadhar, holding his stick, and her heart began to tremble. He no longer looked human, but like an animal—wild and vicious. Suddenly, Suman spied two constables with sticks on their shoulders coming this way. In the darkness, they appeared quite terrifying. Suman's blood turned cold. There was no place to hide. She leaped to her feet and began violently banging on the door. She screamed—I have been shouting for two hours. Can't you hear me?

Gajadhar got up startled. He was just beginning to fall into a deep sleep. He got up and opened the door. In her voice, he could hear some fear, some desperation. She pretended to be angry and said—Well, sleepyhead! You're fast asleep as if you do not have a care in the world. I have been shouting for two hours, but you didn't even notice. My hands and feet have become stiff from the cold.

Fearlessly, Gajadhar said—Don't play games with me. Tell me, where have you been all night long?

Suman replied bravely—What do you mean all night? I went to Subhadra's at nine o'clock. There was a celebration. She invited me. I left their place at ten o'clock. I have been standing at your door for two hours yelling. It must be twelve o'clock. Can you remember anything in your sleep?

Gajadhar—You came home at ten?

Annoyed, Suman responded—Yes, yes, at ten.

Gajadhar—You're lying. I heard the clock strike twelve before I went to sleep.

Suman—Sure you did. You don't even know where your head and your feet are when you sleep, and you want me to believe that you were counting the chimes?

Gajadhar—I won't tolerate this disrespect. Tell me straight, where have you been? I have been keeping a close eye on you these days. I am not blind. I understand feminine wiles. You had better tell me everything, or else I won't take any responsibility for whatever happens.

Suman—I already told you that I came back at about ten or eleven o'clock. If you don't believe me, then don't. Don't buy me the jewellery that you were going to. It might upset me, but at least I will have saved this worthless marriage! Whenever I look at you, you are ready to strike, with your sword out of its scabbard, for no apparent reason.

Suman surprised even herself with these words. She realized that she was overstepping her limits. She had forgotten all the things that she had thought and that she had resolved to do while sitting at the doorstep. Our habits and all of the feelings that we have suppressed in our hearts cannot be changed overnight.

Gajadhar was flabbergasted. This was the first time that Suman had ever spoken back to him. He was enraged—What, do you want me to stand by and let you do whatever your heart desires? Who knows where you were the whole night, and when I ask you, you say that I have no regard for you, that I don't give you anything? Now I see that you have been affected by the modern ideas in the city, and you have picked up the bad habits of your friends. Fine. Things cannot go on like this. I have tried to make you understand that you shouldn't talk to these witches, shouldn't go to fairs and festivals, but you don't listen. Fine. Until you tell me where you have been tonight, I won't let you set foot in this house. If you won't tell me, from this day, you no longer matter to me. You can go wherever you want, do whatever you please, but you will never set foot in this house again.

Timidly, Suman said—I didn't go anywhere except the Vakil Sahib's house. If you don't trust me, just go and ask him. I don't know how long I was there. There was singing and Subhadra wouldn't let me leave.

Gajadhar began accusing her—Oh, so you have grown fond of Vakil Sahib. Why didn't you say so? Then why would you ever care about labourers like me?

These false accusations pierced Suman's heart like an arrow. She was enraged—Do you hear yourself? You are slandering the reputation of a gentleman without any proof! I was late today. You can say whatever you want to me. You can beat me, strike me. Why do you have to drag Vakil Sahib into this? That poor man doesn't even set foot in the women's quarters while I am there.

Gajadhar—Listen girl, you can't deceive me. I have seen several such gentlemen. If he is a god, then go to him. This hut is no longer fit for you. You are becoming too headstrong. This no place for you any more.

Suman could only watch as the situation deteriorated. If she could have taken back her words in any way, she would have, but how you can retrieve an arrow that has been shot? Suman began to cry—May my eyes explode if I even so much as look at him. May my tongue fall out if I even said a word to him. I went to see Subhadra to ease my mind. If you tell me not to go any more, I won't.

Once a suspicion has taken root in a man's mind, it is nearly impossible to weed it out. Gajadhar thought that Suman was humouring him just to calm him. He was extremely bitter—No, why won't you go? They have tall garrets to stroll in, you will get to eat the finest foods, you can sleep on a bed of flowers, and every day will be a parade through paradise.

Sarcasm and anger react like oil and fire. Sarcasm lacerates the heart like a chisel that breaks ice into tiny pieces. Suman was overwhelmed with anger—Watch what you say. Things are getting out of hand. For the past hour, you have been spewing out whatever nonsense comes into your head. I have even had to stand here listening to it all. Do you think that I am some kind of a whore?

Gajadhar—That's exactly what I think.

Suman—You are accusing me falsely of sin. You will have to answer to God.

Gajadhar—Get away from my house you slut! Stop cursing!

Suman—Why don't you just say that you don't want me any more? Why do you have to accuse me of these sins? Do you think that I cannot survive without you? I will find work, and will be able to fill my belly.

Gajadhar—Are you going to leave, or just stand there insulting me?

Suman was too proud to bear such injustice. The threat of eviction made her most dangerous wishes come true.

Suman—All right. I am leaving.

As she said this, she took a step towards the door, though she didn't intend to leave for certain.

Gajadhar thought to himself for a minute. He said—Take your clothes and your jewels. They are of no use to me.

These words blew out the flickering flame of hope. Suman was now certain that this was no longer her home.

Suman picked up her box and went out of the door. However, hope wouldn't die and she thought—Gajadhar will come and make peace with me. So she stood silently outside the door. The folds of her sari were drenched with her tears. Suddenly, Gajadhar loudly slammed the doors to the house shut. Those were the doors of Suman's hopes, which were now permanently closed to her. She thought—where will I go? Instead of feeling remorse and regret, she was furious with Gajadhar. In her mind, she hadn't done anything to deserve so harsh a punishment. So, she was late getting home. Two or three harsh words would have been a sufficient punishment. This expulsion was a gross injustice. What hadn't she done to calm Gajadhar? She had begged, she had pleaded, she had cried, but he had not only dishonoured her, he had also accused her falsely. Even if Gajadhar tried to make up with her now, Suman would not relent. As she was leaving, he had said—Don't show your face here again. These words stuck in her mind—if I am so depraved that he doesn't want to see me any more, why should I show my face here again? Do all women have husbands? Are there no single women? Now I am single as well. There is a big difference between the cool breeze of spring and the harsh wind of summer. One is joyful and invigorating; the other is harsh and lacerating. Love is the spring breeze; hatred the summer wind. The flower that blossoms in the spring breeze can wither at the slightest touch of the summer wind. There was an open courtyard not too far from Suman's house. She went there and lay down, using the box as a headrest. It was three o'clock. She had spent two hours trying to figure out where to go. Among her friends was a dreadful woman named Hiriya at whose house Suman could have stayed, but she didn't dare go there. She still had some self-respect left. In one respect, she was free to do all of those self-indulgent things that she had wanted to do but her conscience had kept her from doing. Now there was nothing to prevent her from fulfilling those dreams. But like a small child that is overjoyed seeing a cow or a goat from a distance, yet hides from it out of fear as soon as it approaches, Suman could not take that final step through the doorway to her desires. Shame, regret, hate, disgrace—all of these had placed a sort of shackle around her ankles. She decided to go to Subhadra's house—I can cook for them, do small chores for them and stay with them. Beyond that, my fate is in God's hands.

She hid her box in the folds of her sari and arrived at Pandit Padamsingh's house. A couple of his clients were washing their hands and faces. Another had laid out a prayer mat and was meditating—I hope that my witness doesn't ruin things. Another was counting his rosary, but at the same time was calculating how much money he would spend during the day with each bead that he counted. The sweeper was collecting last night's bread.

Suman hesitated before going inside, but as soon as she saw Jeetan, the *kahaar*, approaching, she sped inside. Subhadra was surprised to see her—What brings you here this early in the morning?

Slowly, Suman replied—I have been thrown out of my house.

Subhadra—Arrey! Why?

Suman—Because I was late returning home from here last night.

Subhadra—He got so angry over such a small thing? Look, I will call him over. He is a strange man.

Suman—No, no, don't call him over. I cried, wept, and begged for forgiveness. But that heartless man didn't show the slightest mercy. He grabbed me by the hands and dragged me out of the house. He is arrogant enough to believe that I cannot live without him. Well, I will break his arrogance.

Subhadra—Listen, don't talk like that. I am going to call him.

Suman—I don't want to see his face again.

Subhadra—Have things gone so far?

Suman—Yes, this is how things stand. He and I no longer have a relationship.

Subhadra thought to herself—we won't solve anything while she is this upset. She will calm down in a few hours. She said—Alright, go wash your face. Your eyes are bloodshot and you look like you haven't slept. Sleep for a little while, then we'll talk.

Suman—If it had been my fate to sleep peacefully, would I have been married to such a good-for-nothing man? Now I have come to seek your asylum. If you will have me, I will stay. Otherwise, I will blacken my face with soot and drown myself. I only need a little space in some corner; I can stay there. And whatever I am able to do, I am willing to do in your service.

When the Panditji came inside, Subhadra told him what had happened. Panditji was extremely concerned. It was improper to keep an unrelated woman in one's house without her husband's permission. He decided to invite Gajadhar over and calm him down—it is best for this woman to leave here as soon as possible, he thought.

He went outside and immediately sent a messenger to call Gajadhar, but he was not at home. When he came back from the courthouse, the Panditji again sent for Gajadhar, but he was still not home.

As soon as Gajadhar learned that Suman went to Padamsingh's house, his suspicions were confirmed. He began marching through town slandering Padamsingh. He first went to see Vitthaldas. Vitthaldas absorbed the story as if it were a Vedic truth. This man—a patriot and an activist against social evils—was a strange mixture of generosity and conservatism. His trusting heart sympathized with the entire world, but he didn't have an iota of sympathy for his enemies. And hatred had blinded him. Ever since Padamsingh decided to invite courtesans into his home and hold a concert, Vitthaldas began to count him among his enemies. So on hearing Gajadhar's news, he was beside himself with joy. He went to Sharmaji's friends and collaborators and repeated the story. He would say to people—see? Didn't I say that this concert would have consequences? He has taken a brahmin woman out of her home and brought her to live with him. The poor husband is wandering all over, cursing his fate. And he considers himself the paragon of higher education! I have always suspected there was something amiss when I saw the woman at his house. But I didn't realize what kind of main course was being cooked up inside.

What was surprising was that even people who were intimately acquainted with Sharmaji believed this story.

The next day, Jeetan went to run some errands in the market. He heard this gossip coming from all directions. The shopkeeper asked him—Well Jeetan, how is the new mistress? Jeetan became anxious. He ran back home and said—Brother, since Bahuji has allowed Gajadhar's wife to stay here, the family name is being dragged through the mud in the market. It seems she had an argument with Gajadhar before she came here.

Vakil Sahib couldn't believe his ears. He was preparing to go to court and was putting on his coat; one arm was in the sleeve, the other was out. He didn't even remember to dress properly. Things were taking just the course he feared. Now he had the missing piece to the puzzle of Gajadhar's seeming lack of concern. He stood still for a while and thought—now what do I do? There is no other alternative but to send her away. Whatever will be, will be; it cannot be my responsibility. The important thing is that I save myself from this scandal. He was furious with Subhadra—why did she have to let her stay here? She didn't even ask me. All she has to do is sit at home; I am the one who will have to go outside and hang my head in shame in front of others. But if I force her to leave this place, where will the poor woman go? She doesn't seem to have anywhere to go. And Gajadhar will probably not let her come back. Today is the second day, and he hasn't even asked about her. He is certainly planning on leaving her. She will think that I am cruel and merciless. But this is the only way to save myself from humiliation. Nothing else that can be done. After he had rationalized his actions, he said to Jeetan—Why didn't you tell me earlier?

Jeetan—Sir, I only just found out. I swear my life on it, brother; I couldn't sit by without telling you.

Sharmaji—Alright, go inside and tell Suman that her presence is ruining my good name. She should make whatever arrangements she needs in order to leave today. Speak to her with civility. Don't be cruel. Be sure that you explain clearly that it is not my fault.

Jeetan was thrilled. He despised Suman in the same way that servants despise those small people who get too close to their masters. He didn't like Suman's attitude at all. Old people regard even the simplest fashion with suspicion. He thought like a man from the village. He called black things black, and bright things bright; he didn't know how to call black things bright. Even though Sharmaji had told him to speak to her with restraint, he began to shout for her as he walked in her direction. Suman was making a paan for Sharmaji. She was startled when she heard Jeetan's voice, and she looked at him timidly.

Jeetan said—Why are you staring at me? Vakil Sahib has ordered that you leave today. You have ruined his reputation in the entire city. You may have no shame, but have some regard for his reputation. You are like a calf that runs away with four lengths of rope, without any honour.

Subhadra heard what was going on. She came up to Jeetan—What is it Jeetan? What are you saying?

Jeetan—Nothing. Master has ordered that she leave immediately. Your reputation is being smeared everywhere.

Subhadra—Go and send him in.

Suman's eyes filled with tears. She stood up—No Bahuji. Why are you sending for him? No one can force one's way into another's home. I will leave immediately. I will never take a step inside this threshold again.

In times of crisis, people become extremely sensitive. In such moments, inhumanity seems like the worst kind of injustice and sympathy, infinite kindness. Suman hadn't thought that Sharmaji could ever do such a thing. With the licence that a heart has in moments of crisis, she was convinced that Sharmaji was actually a wicked, cowardly, merciless, and irresponsible man—Today you are afraid of slander; you value your honour dearly. Just yesterday you were overjoyed sitting with a courtesan, you were head over heels in love with her, and then, you had no concern for your honour. Today your honour has become a cheap trinket.

She picked up her box with cautious deliberation, bowed to Subhadra, and walked out the door.

11

SUMAN WAS OVERCOME with worry as she left. Where will I go now? Even Gajadhar's cruelty seemed less painful than the torment she now found herself in. She thought to herself—I was a fool to leave home. I was gambling on Subhadra's kindness. I even believed that Panditji was an honourable man, but now it's clear that he is a spotted jackal, just like the rest. And now, the only place I can turn to is my mother's home. How could I turn to strangers for help? Why didn't I just go to my mother's in the first place? Did they really think that I would spend the rest of my life at their house? After a few days, when Gajadhar had calmed down, I would have gone back home on my own. Oh dear God! Anger makes it impossible to think straight. I should never have come to their house, even by mistake. I have fallen into my own trap. Who knows what they must be thinking about me?

Suman walked ahead, trying to move on, but after a few moments her thoughts took an about turn—where do I think I am going? He will never let me enter that house. I begged and pleaded, but he wouldn't have any of it. When it was only a matter of being a few hours late, he was so suspicious. And now, it's been twenty-four hours and I, unlucky wretch that I am, went to the very place I should never have gone to. Now, he won't even come near me, not even to shout at me. And why should I endure his scoldings? All I need is a place to stay. I will manage to earn enough to feed myself. I can earn enough to keep body and soul together if I become a seamstress. So why should I tolerate anyone's threats? What kind of happiness did I ever find with him? I had these useless shackles around my ankles, and even if they did protect me from the scorn of the world, they mocked me every time I got up or sat down. I just need to find a place to stay. Won't Bholi do this little favour for me? She is always calling me to her place. Won't she have a little mercy?

Can I go to Amola? But who misses me there? Mother is dead. There is Shanta but she has enough trouble herself, who will care for me? My aunt won't let me live. She will tear me to shreds and kill me. I will go ask Bholi and see what she says. If nothing else, I can always find a permanent home in the Ganga. Having come to a decision, Suman went to Bholi's, looking over her shoulder to make sure that Gajadhar was not around.

As she came up to Bholi's door she began to have second thoughts. Why should I go to her place? Couldn't I go to a neighbour's house? In the meantime, Bholi spied her and called her up with a gesture. Suman began to climb the stairs.

Suman couldn't believe her eyes. She had been to Bholi's once before, but she had only managed to see the courtyard below before she left. Bholi's room was decorated with carpets, pillows, pictures, and glassware. There was a silver paan-box on top of a small table. On a second table, there was a silver plate and a silver glass. Suman was spellbound.

Bholi asked—Where have you been today with that box in your arms?

Suman—I will tell you my sad story later. For now, I need a favour from you. Can you set up a small room for me somewhere? I wish to stay there.

Bholi was shocked—Why, have you had a fight with your husband?

Suman—No, who said anything about a fight? I can do what I want.

Bholi—Look me in the eyes. Yes, I can see it on your face. What's the matter?

Suman—Honestly. Nothing's the matter. Why should you stay where you are not welcome?

Bholi—Arrey, why won't you tell me the real story? Why did he get so upset?

Suman—There was no reason for it. But once he became upset, what could one do?

Bholi—You don't have to tell me if you don't want to, Suman. I give up. If you won't be upset, I'll tell you something. I knew that sooner or later there would be trouble between the two of you. Can an Arabian horse and an ass be yoked together to the same carriage? You should have been the queen in a royal family. But you have fallen in with a wretched man, who doesn't deserve to even wash your feet. Only you could put up with him; anyone else would have kicked the husband and left a long time ago. If God had given me your face and looks, I would be a rich woman by now. But I don't know the details of your situation. Perhaps you didn't get a good education.

Suman—I was tutored for two years by a Christian lady.

Bholi—If only you had put in two or three years more. If you had studied longer, perhaps you would not be in this situation. You would have learnt what it means to live, how to extract the pleasure out of living. We are not farm animals that our parents can sell to anyone who turns us into his property. If God had wanted you to endure misery, why would he have given you the face of an angel? This uncivilized custom of treating women as if they were second class citizens persists only in this country. In every other country, women are independent. They can marry according to their own wishes and if there is no love left in their marriages, they can divorce their husbands. But we still follow the old traditions.

Suman thought about it. She said—What shall I do, sister? No one wants to live in misery, but it's this fear of what society will say that keeps us where we are.

Bholi—And these are the consequences of this stupidity. My mother and father married me off to some decrepit old man. He had money and lived in all kinds of comfort, but I couldn't stand his looks. I somehow managed to stay with him for six months, but eventually I had to get out. Life is a blessing that cannot be wasted in crying one's days away. If you aren't getting any pleasure out of life, what is its use? At first, I was afraid that people would say horrible things about me and think me the worst kind of woman. But I should have left sooner, because before long I was so sought after that the richest people were begging for me. I had already learned to sing at home, but I learned a little more, and suddenly I was the talk of the town. Today, is there any nobleman, any gentleman, any *maulvi*, any *pandit* who doesn't consider it an honour to be able to rub my feet? My performances are held in temples and in the homes of wealthy landlords. I get requests for appearances all the time. Why I should I consider this dishonour? If I wanted, I could send a messenger and have that Mahantji from the Krishna temple come running. What do I care if anyone thinks that this is dishonour?

Suman—How long will it take me to learn to sing?

Bholi—You will pick it up in six months. No one really asks for elaborate songs here. You don't really need to know classical forms and *raags*. Popular *ghazals* are fashionable here. If you learn a few short tunes and a few popular songs from the theatres, that will be good enough. Here, all you need are good looks and elegant conversation, and God has given you enough of both. I swear to you Suman, just break the chains around your feet, and you will see, men will run after you like madmen.

Anxiously, Suman said—I am just worried about ...

Bholi—Yes, yes, go ahead. You want to say that you are worried about having to do indecent things with all kinds of strange men. In the beginning I was afraid of such things as well. But later I learned that these were all imaginary fears. Strange men don't have the courage to come here. Only noblemen come here. And all you have to do is to keep them ensnared. If he is a gentleman, you won't have any trouble getting along with him and there won't be any talk of indecency. But if you don't like him, then keep him hooked with conversation, plunder him as long as you can. Eventually, he will become frustrated and leave by himself, and then his brothers will come to be trapped by you. Of course, everyone is shy at first. Weren't you shy with your husband? You'll get over your fear, just like you did with your husband.

Suman smiled—At least get a room ready for me.

Bholi could tell that the fish had taken the bait. Now, it was only a matter of driving in the hook. She said—You are more than welcome to use these chambers. You can live here comfortably.

Suman—I will not stay with you.

Bholi—Why, will your reputation be ruined?

Suman (choking)—No, it's not that.

Bholi—Will your household fall into disrepute?

Suman—Why are you being sarcastic?

Bholi—Then what, will Pandit Gajadharprasad Pande become angry?

Suman—Is there anything left for me to say?

Suman had no arguments left with which to respond to Bholi's questions. By making fun of her inhibitions, Bholi had weakened them. And although she possessed the natural human aversion to wrongdoing, Bholi's words seduced her. She couldn't put her feelings into words. She was like a man in a garden who upon seeing a ripe fruit craves it, but even though the owner is not around, cannot steal it.

In the meantime, Bholi said—How much rent can you afford to pay? I can call my uncle and make the arrangements.

Suman—Two or three rupees.

Bholi—What else can you do?

Suman—I can sew.

Bholi—And will you stay by yourself?

Suman—Yes, who else is there?

Bholi—You are talking like a little girl. Don't be so naïve! You can see everything but you are still blind. Well, will you be able to stay in a place all by yourself? Hyenas will ravish your chastity. It's a thousand times better for you go back to your husband.

Suman—I never want to see his face again. I can't hide it from you any more. The day before yesterday, you performed at Vakil Sahib's house. His wife and I are close friends. She invited me to the performance and wouldn't let me leave until about twelve or one o'clock. When you were done singing, I returned home. That's it. He got so upset over such a small matter that he said whatever came into his head. He went so far as to accuse Vakil Sahib of sin. He said—Get out, don't show your face here again. Sister, I swear to God that I made every attempt to appease him. I cried, I fell at his feet, but he still forced me out of the house. Even being thrown out of my own house wasn't a crisis. I went to Vakil Sahib's house thinking that I could stay there for four or five days. But that wretch began slandering Vakil Sahib. And then Vakil Sahib sent his servant to tell me that I should leave. Sister, I was miserable, but at least I had the hope that God would be pleased with my honour and virtue. Now, my face has been blackened with the soot of sin. It doesn't matter what fate has in store for me, but I will not go back to that house.

As she spoke, her eyes filled with tears. Bholi consoled her—Go and wash your face. Eat something. Then we can decide what to do. It looks as if you haven't slept the whole night.

Suman—Can I find water here?

Bholi smiled—Everything will be taken care of. I have a Hindu water carrier. Several Hindus come here. That's why I keep a Hindu water carrier.

Bholi's elderly aunt took Suman to the washroom. She bathed with soap. Then the aunt braided her hair. She brought her a new silk sari to wear. When Suman came back upstairs and Bholi saw her, smiled and said—Go and look at yourself in the mirror.

Suman stood in front of the mirror. It seemed as if the idol of some beauty stood before her. Suman had never realized she was so beautiful. Shame-free pride had made her lotus-blossom face bloom and there was something absolutely intoxicating about her eyes. She lay down on a couch.

Bholi said to her aunt—What do you think Jahuran, we will trap Sethji now, won't we?

Jahuran—He'll massage the soles of her feet—the soles of her feet!

After a while, the water carrier brought some sweets. Suman prepared her dinner. She ate a paan and stood in front of the mirror. She said to herself—why should I leave this happiness and go back to that dark hovel?

Bholi asked—What shall I say if Gajadhar asks me about you?

Suman—You can say that I am not here.

Bholi's wish had been fulfilled. She was certain that Seth Balbhadradas, who had been avoiding her, would hover around Suman's beauty like a bumblebee.

Suman was like a greedy doctor who, on visiting a sick friend, won't accept payment directly. Hesitatingly, he says, 'There is no need for this,' but when the money is placed in his pocket, he smiles with joy and returns home.

12

PADAMSINGH HAD AN older brother named Madansingh. He handled the affairs at the family home. He owned some property, and was an occasional moneylender. He had an only son; his name was Sadansingh. His wife was called Bhama.

An only male child is a lucky creature. He eats plenty of fancy food, and he never has to taste bitter reproaches. In his childhood, Sadan was rambunctious, headstrong, and quarrelsome. When he became older, he was lazy, arrogant, and spoiled. His parents did not seem to mind. No matter how badly he behaved, they could not think any less of him. They could not bear being separated from him for even a day. Padamsingh had repeatedly asked his brother to send Sadan to stay with him—I can get him enrolled in an English school. But his mother and father would not agree to it. Sadan studied Hindi and Urdu in the local school. Bhama felt that he had no need for any further education. There is plenty to eat at home, why break leaves off trees, one by one? Even if he doesn't get an education, he still has his own eyes with which to see.

Sadan, however, wanted nothing more than to go to the city with his uncle. He was fascinated with his uncle's soap, oil, shoes, slippers, wristwatch, and collar. He had everything he needed at home, but he had none of these fashionable things. He wanted to be like his uncle. I, too, will dress up nicely and ride around in a buggy, just like uncle. He respected his uncle very much. He would do anything that he asked him to but wouldn't pay attention to anything his parents said; he would even talk back to them. But in front of his uncle, he became the very paragon of good behaviour. His uncle's refinement had won him over. Every time Padamsingh came back to his village, he brought Sadan fine clothes and shoes. Sadan looked forward to those gifts eagerly.

Padamsingh always returned for Holi. This year, he had sent a letter just a week before Holi to say that he would come. Sadan was already dreaming of silk coats and varnished shoes. Madansingh sent a greeting party to the railway station the day before Holi, both in the morning and in the evening. The next day, horses were sent both times as well, but Padamsingh had already arranged for Bholibai's performance at his house, and had forgotten all about his village. This was the first Holi that Padamsingh had ever missed. Bhama was in tears. And there was no end to Sadan's disappointment—no clothes, no outfits, how can I celebrate Holi? Madansingh was too disappointed to be festive. A sad cloud descended over all of them. The village women came to celebrate Holi. Seeing Bhama's tears, they consoled her, 'Sister, you can never make a stranger your relative. The two of them are probably enjoying the celebrations in the city. They would be bored in the country.' Even after the singing and the dancing, Bhama felt no better. Madansingh would drink a lot of bhaang at Holi. Today, he didn't so much as touch the stuff. Sadan moped around the whole day, shirtless. In the evening, he went to his mother and said—I want to go and see uncle.

Bhama—Is anyone expecting you there?

Sadan—What do you mean? What about uncle?

Bhama—He is no longer your uncle. No one there will even ask after you.

Sadan—I am still going.

Bhama—I have told you once. Don't test my patience. I won't let you go there.

But Sadan insisted on doing the very thing that Bhama forbade. In the end, she walked away in frustration. Sadan also walked out. Obstinacy cannot be tackled head-on; it has to be attacked from the flanks.

Sadan decided to run away to his uncle's house—these people will never have silk coats made for me. I have to get out of here. At best, they will get me a muslin kurta, and who knows what I will have to do in return. When they bought me a gold chain, they acted as if they had conquered the world. And when they gave me a bracelet, they made me show it off all over town, as if I was supposed to wear it all the time. I am going to leave. No one can stop me.

He had made his decision and now he looked for an opportunity to carry out his plan. At night, once everyone had gone to sleep, he sneaked out of the house. The distance from his house to the railway station was about three miles. Darkness had set in, as the fourth-day moon had already set. On the outskirts of the village, there was a hut for water buffaloes. As he approached it, he heard a 'chu-chu' like noise. His heart skipped a beat. But then he discovered that it was merely a buffalo chewing its cud. A little farther ahead was a mango tree. A few months back, the son of a farmer had fallen from that very tree and died. As he drew nearer to the tree, he thought that he saw someone standing in front of him. His hair stood on end; he felt dizzy. But when he had calmed himself down and looked more closely, he discovered that there was nothing there. He walked on cautiously, barely realizing that he had left the village behind.

Two miles from the village was a *pipal* tree. It was common knowledge that this tree was the meeting place of various spirits. They were all rumoured to live in that tree. A certain blanketed ghost was their leader. It was believed that the ghost would stand before travellers, with his blanket draped around him, wearing his wooden shoes, and wave his hands asking for something. As soon as the traveller extended his arm to give it to him, he would disappear. No one knew why the ghosts concerned themselves with this game. At night, no one came here alone, and any man brave enough to walk past the tree was sure to see some supernatural spectacle or other. Some said that they heard singing. Others, that they saw a village tribunal meeting. This was Sadan's ultimate fear. He had already calmed himself down once, but as he approached the tree, his courage melted like ice. When he was still a furlong away, he couldn't move his feet. They wouldn't come off the ground and he began to worry. What shall I do? He looked in all directions, but couldn't see another human being. If he could spy even an animal, he might have gained courage. For half an hour he stood there waiting as if for someone to arrive, but no one walks on village roads at night. He thought to himself—how long can I stay here like this? The train comes at one o'clock. If I am late, my plan will be ruined. Finally, he got up enough strength and started to walk reciting verses from the Ramayan as loudly as he could. He tried to keep thoughts of ghosts and demons as far from his mind as possible. But at moments like these, thoughts are like summer flies that won't go away even when swatted. Before long, he found himself standing in front of that treacherous tree. Sadan looked at it carefully. Half the night had passed, and the light from the stars lit up the ground. Sadan couldn't see anything at all. He began to sing even louder. At that moment, every hair on his body stood on end. He kept looking in both directions; he could see various kinds of animals, but as soon as he looked carefully they would vanish. Suddenly, he thought that he saw a monkey sitting to his right. His blood went cold. In a short while, though, the monkey turned out to be a heap of dirt. And when Sadan reached the tree, his voice began to tremble. He couldn't speak. By now, he had no strength to fight off his thoughts, as it had taken all of his mental and intellectual faculties just to get this far. Suddenly, he saw something running towards him. He was startled. When he looked closely, he saw that it was a dog. But he had heard that sometimes ghosts take on the shape of dogs. He was petrified. He stood at attention, like a man waiting to fight a great warrior in battle. The dog hung its head and quietly slunk away. Sadan shouted at the dog, which ran away with its tail between its legs. Sadan chased him for a while. Once he had crossed the frontier of fear, however, there was only courage left. Sadan was certain that it was only a dog. If it had been a ghost, he would have certainly performed some trick. He was less afraid, but he didn't run away. He stood next to the pipal tree in order to shame his timorous heart. Not only that, he also walked around the tree and clutching it with both his hands, tried to shake it with all his might. This was a strange display of bravery. He didn't seem to realize it, but earlier even the slightest noise, the slightest rustling of leaves, would have scared him to death. Having passed this test, Sadan walked on with his head held high.

13

Once Suman left, a sense of guilt pervaded Padamsingh—I didn't do the right thing. Who knows where she has gone. If she has gone to her own house, then there is nothing to worry about, but she probably hasn't gone there. What won't a desperate man do? Perhaps the woman from the Coolie Depot has ensnared her, and then it will be impossible to save her. These wicked people are most treacherous at times like this. Who knows if she has fallen victim to an even worse group of people. When the brave have no one to help them, they survive by stealing. When the cowardly have no one to help them, they beg to survive. But when a woman has no one to help her, she is forced to abandon her virtue. Kicking a young woman out of the house is just as good as condemning her. I made a terrible mistake. Worrying about honour, now, will not fix anything. That woman is drowning; I should save her.

He began to dress to go to Gajadhar's house. When he was done, he set out. But soon he began to have second thoughts—what if someone sees me at his door? Who knows what Gajadhar will think of me. A confrontation would be scandalous. He had already come out of the house, but he went back and took off his clothes.

When he sat down to dinner at ten, Subhadra spoke to him angrily—Why did you get after Suman's life this morning? If you wanted to kick her out, you could have done so properly. You sent that awful Jeetan; he blurted out whatever nonsense came into his head. The poor woman didn't utter a single word. She left quietly. I was so embarrassed that I couldn't even look her in the eye. You could have told me; I would have explained it to her. She isn't a rustic; she would have left as soon as she was able to. But you didn't do any of this. You simply handed down your tyrannical edict. So afraid of scandals! Will there be any less of a scandal if she doesn't head straight home? Who knows where she will end up, and then whose fault will it be?

Subhadra had her say, but she was still seething. Padamsingh, like a sinner confessing to his sins, hung his head and listened quietly. He had been thinking the very thing that Subhadra had pointed out. He ate quietly and went off to court. Three days had passed since the party. The people at the courthouse thought that Padamsingh was an upright man and respected him. But for the past three or four days, lawyers he had never met before would sit next to him talking obliquely at him.

One said—Sharmaji, have you heard that a courtesan from Lucknow is in town. She is a famous singer. Won't you invite her to perform?

Another—Pardon me Sharmaji, have you heard the news? Seth Chimmanlal is terribly fond of your Bholibai.

Others said—Friend, people are going to bathe in the Ganga tomorrow, there will be much rejoicing on the river. Why don't you have a party? You can invite Saraswati. She doesn't sing all that well, but her beauty is matchless.

Sharmaji hated having to listen to these things. He thought to himself—what gives them the right to talk to me this way? Am I a pimp?

Sharmaji noticed that the way that the employees of the courthouse behaved towards him had changed. Whenever they had a break, they would smoke cigarettes and sit next to Sharmaji and talk about the same kinds of things. It had become so bad that Sharmaji would make excuses to shake them off and then hide behind a tree for an hour. He began to curse the inauspicious day when he had decided to have that party.

He couldn't stay long in the courthouse today either. He grew weary of the same loathsome conversation and came home around two o'clock. As soon as he reached the door, Sadan came forward to touch his feet.

Sharmaji was surprised—Arrey Sadan, when did you arrive?

Sadan—I came on the last train.

Padamsingh—All is well at home, I hope

Sadan—Yes sir, everything is fine.

Padamsingh—When did you leave? On the one o'clock train?

Sadan—No, I left at nine o'clock last night, but fell asleep on the train and woke up in Mughalsarai. I came from there on the twelve o'clock stagecoach.

Padamsingh—Quite a story! Have you eaten?

Sadan—Yes I have.

Padamsingh—I wasn't able to come this Holi. Did Bhama say anything?

Sadan—People started looking forward to your visit two days before Holi. Father even sent a palanquin to the station on both days. Mother cried a lot. I couldn't bear it, so I ran away and came here.

Sharmaji—So you didn't ask if you could come?

Sadan—Of course I asked, but you know what kind of people are. Mother wouldn't have it.

Sharmaji—They must be worried. If you were bent on coming, you could have brought someone with you. No matter. I am glad to see you as well. Now that you are here, we may as well get you enrolled in a school.

Sadan—Yes, that's what I was thinking as well.

Sharmaji sent a telegram to Madansingh—Don't worry. Sadan is here. I am going to enrol him in a school.

After he had sent off the telegram, he asked Sadan to tell him every little detail about the village. There was no *kurmi*, no kahaar, no *lohaar*, no *chamaar* about whom Sharmaji didn't ask a question. There is an affection among people in a village community that is missing in the city. It is a kind of love that binds all people, from the smallest to the most important, together.

As evening fell, Sharmaji took Sadan for a walk. But he went towards the Durga temple and the Krishna *dharamshala* instead of Beni Park or Queen's Park. He was consumed with anxiety, and his eyes constantly searched for Suman. He had come to a decision—if I find her now, I won't let her go, no matter what happens to my reputation. I won't let it go so far that her husband files a lawsuit against me. When Suman wants to, she can go back to him. I will go to Gajadhar's. Maybe she has already returned by now. As he finished the last thought, he arrived home. Some clients had been waiting for him. He looked over their files, but his mind was elsewhere. As soon as he was done with them, he went over to Gajadhar's house, but he kept looking over his shoulder to make sure that no one saw him or followed him. Pretending to walk aimlessly, he arrived at Gajadhar's door. Gajadhar had just come back from the store. He had heard this afternoon that Sharmaji had kicked Suman out of his house. But he suspected that this was all a ruse to hide her somewhere. And when he saw Sharmaji at his doorstep, he was unable to show him any hospitality. He got up from his cot and said Namaste. Sharmaji stopped. Feebly, he asked—So Pandeji, has your wife returned?

Some of Gajadhar's doubts vanished—No, since she left your house, I have been unable to find her.

Sharmaji—Haven't you been asking around? Still, what was it that made you so angry?

Gajadhar—Sir, kicking her out was only an idle threat. In actuality, she wanted to leave. The wicked women in this neighbourhood turned her against me. For the past few months she has been troubled. She came home at one o'clock at night on Holi, so I began to wonder. But she was eager to leave.

Sharmaji—But if you wanted to bring her back, you could have picked her up from my home. Instead, you began slandering me. And friend, who wants to be slandered? I kicked her out of my house. Tell me, what else could I do? Everyone places a high value on his honour. In this case, I am only responsible for the party that I had at my house. Had I known the consequences, either I would never have had that party or I would have let her stay the night at my house. And for these small mistakes you have ruined my name in the entire city.

Gajadhar began to weep. All his doubts had been removed. He cried and said—Sir, you can punish me as you want for this crime. I am a stupid idiot, who believes whatever he is told. You know that Babu from the banking house, with that noble name—Vitthaldas. I was fooled by his lies. The day before Holi he came to my store, bought some clothes, took me aside and said ... how can I repeat his words? I became suspicious upon hearing him talk. I thought that he was a noble man. He walks around the town instructing people to do good to others. If such a pious man says something, you tend to believe him. I don't know what he has against you. He has ruined my family for certain.

Gajadhar began to cry again. He was no longer suspicious. He cried and said—Master, you can punish me for this crime in any way that you desire.

Sharmaji felt as if someone had taken a hot iron stake and branded his chest. Beads of sweat formed on his forehead. He could fight someone with a sword attacking him directly, but he was unprepared to be stabbed in the back. Vitthaldas was his best friend. Sharmaji respected him greatly. Even though they had differing ideological positions, he appreciated his pure goals. But when such a man intentionally smears mud across your face, what else can you say about him except that despite his good intentions he is a cruel man? Sharmaji understood now that Vitthaldas had engineered this whole thing after he heard about his Holi party. He is falsely accusing me just to ruin my good name, just to spoil my reputation in the community. Trembling with anger, he said—Will you say this to his face?

Gajadhar—Yes, what harm is there in telling the truth? Let's go, I will say it to his face now. We'll see if he is able to deny it.

In a flurry of anger, Sharmaji felt ready to go and confront Vitthaldas. But in a short while, the force of the storm died down. He controlled himself. Things would only worsen if they went to see him. He thought to himself and then said—Fine. Come when I call for you. But don't sit here waiting idly. Keep searching for your wife, the times are bad. Send me the bill for your expenses.

Sharmaji returned home. Vitthaldas' treacherous blow had left him powerless. He thought that Vitthaldas had conspired against him out of spite. Sharmaji did not stop to think that Vitthaldas might have done so with the best of intentions and with complete faith in his actions.

14

The following day, Padamsingh tried to enrol Sadan in school. But every school he approached plainly replied—No seats available. There were twelve schools in the city but none had room for Sadan.

Sharmaji became frustrated and decided to teach Sadan himself. He couldn't tutor him in the mornings because he was tied up with clients. So he began to teach him after he came home from court, but after a week the task seemed overwhelming. Before he took on the task of Sadan's education, Sharmaji used to come home and read the newspaper or play the harmonium, but now it felt like he was futilely teaching an old parrot to repeat everything he said. And this made him furious. He decided that his nephew really was an idiot. If he asked Sharmaji about something that he had already been taught, Sharmaji would become incensed. He would turn the pages of the book angrily to show Sadan where he had first come across the concept. Then he would ask him questions until Sadan came up with the definition of the word by himself. This meant that little was accomplished, and the task remained incredibly complicated. Several hours were wasted in covering four lines of the lesson. Teaching exhausted Sharmaji. He didn't even have the strength to go out for an evening walk. He was certain that he didn't have the stamina for this work. Sadan, too, became afraid every time a book was opened in front of him. He was miserable—what was I thinking of, coming here? I was better off in the village.

There was a teacher in the neighbourhood. He agreed to teach Sadan for twenty rupees a month. Now Sharmaji had to figure out where to get the twenty rupees from. Sharmaji was a 'fashionable' man, and so his finances were always strained. 'Fashion' was an expensive burden, but they never buckled under the weight. He sat by himself for a long time and could come up with no answers. So he went to Subhadra—The teacher has agreed to twenty rupees.

Subhadra—Are there no other teachers? Teachers are plentiful, money is not.

Sharmaji—God will give us the money somehow.

Subhadra—In all my years, I have never seen God grant extra wishes. He only gives you enough to fill your belly. That's what God does.

Padamsingh—Then you must come up with an alternative.

Subhadra—You can stop giving me whatever little you have been giving me so far. Alright?

Padamsingh—I doesn't take much to upset you.

Subhadra—Then don't upset me! There's no secret. You know what we spend. Where do you want me to find the money to save? There are no rivers of milk and honey in your house. There are no piles of jams and sweets either. The work won't get done without a servant, and we need to have a maid. What expenses do you want me to cut down on?

Padamsingh—You can stop buying milk.

Subhadra—Sure, we'll stop. It might be fine for you, but Sadan still needs to drink milk.

Sharmaji began to think. Paan and tobacco cost at least ten rupees a month, and other such small luxuries could be cut out to save money. But he did not want to bring up the matter fearing that Subhadra would be angry. From the way she was talking, he could tell clearly that she had no sympathy with him. He began calculating the inessential expenses in his head. Finally he said—Well, could we do without spending so much on electricity for the lights and fans.

Subhadra—Of course we can. Why do we need lights? We can start going to bed early. If someone comes to visit, he will go away after calling out a few times if no one answers. And when we return at nine o'clock from our walk, we can even fan ourselves. Before we had electricity, people did survive the heat, didn't they?

Padamsingh—Should I spend less on feed for the horse?

Subhadra—Well, you have been blessed with foresight, haven't you? Why should we buy feed at all? There is grass aplenty. So what if his hipbones begin to show through his skin. He will get you to the courthouse somehow, even if he barely survives. At least no one will be able to say that you don't have the means to get to work.

Padamsingh—We pledge two rupees to the girls' school every month, another two rupees in club fees, and three rupees to the orphanage. What will happen if we stop paying these?

Subhadra—It will be great. It is the law of the land that you should first burn a candle in your own home before you light one in a mosque.

Padamsingh grew angrier as he listened to Subhadra's sarcastic responses, but he kept his patience—I can manage to come up with fifteen rupees a month, you have to come up with the remaining five rupees. I won't ask about the specific details, but you have to balance our expenses somehow.

Subhadra—Sure. I can manage. It's not that difficult a thing to do. We can eat only once a day. Why should we cook meals twice a day? There are millions of people in this world who only get one meal a day and never get sick or weak.

Sharmaji was stupefied. He usually shied away from these domestic squabbles, but he couldn't let this insult passs. He said—Do you want Sadan not to have a teacher so that he can waste the rest of his life as a consequence? You should have been trying to help me out, but you are bent on making things difficult. Sadan is my brother's son, the very brother who carried bundles of flour and gram on his head when he came to get me admitted into a school. I have never forgotten that day. I will never forget his love; sometimes I want to fall at his feet and cry for hours. It might seem intolerable to you to cut back on lights and fans, on paan and tobacco, on horses and grooms, but my brother went barefoot so that I could have freshly polished shoes to wear. I wore silken clothes while he managed with a torn kurta. I owe him so much for all that he has done for me that I will not be able to repay him in this lifetime. I would do anything for Sadan. I don't mind walking to the courthouse, fasting, or even cleaning his shoes myself—I would do all of it, and more, for that boy. If I didn't, I would be the most ungrateful person on earth.

Subhadra's face withered with humiliation. Even though Sharmaji had spoken from the bottom of his heart, Subhadra felt that he had said these things only to shame her. She hung her head—I never said don't hire a teacher for Sadan. If you have a debt that needs to be paid, you should pay it. We will manage somehow. Since your brother went through so much trouble for you, it is only proper that you do whatever you can for Sadan. I will do whatever you tell me to do. You never told me how important this was to you, that's why I felt that it was not a necessary expense. You should have made arrangements for a teacher on the very day that Sadan came to town. Why did you lose so much time? He might even have learned something by now. He's already wasted so much of his life. You shouldn't have wasted a single day in starting his education.

Subhadra had exacted immediate revenge for her shame. Panditji had to acknowledge his mistake. Had Sadan been his own son, it would never have taken him this long to figure something out.

Subhadra was sorry for what she had said. She made a paan and gave it to Sharmaji. It was a peace offering. Sharmaji took the paan and peace was restored.

As he was leaving, Subhadra asked—Have you heard anything of Suman?

Sharmaji—Nothing. Who knows where she has gone. I couldn't find Gajadhar either. I have heard that he has abandoned his house and left the town.

The very next day, a teacher arrived to tutor Sadan. He would teach Sadan and then leave at nine o'clock; then Sadan would bathe, eat, and go to sleep. He was restless all by himself. He had no friends or comrades. There was no laughter or happiness here. How was he supposed to feel like he belonged? Of course, in the mornings, he would exercise a little, as he did in the village where he had made a little gymnasium for himself. There was no gymnasium here, so he would do push ups in his room. In the evenings, Sharmaji would have the phaeton prepared for him. Then, Sadan would put on his suit and his vanity and go out in the phaeton. Sharmaji would go around on foot. He would walk either towards the cantonment or the park, but Sadan wouldn't go in those directions. What did he know of the pleasures of walking in the fresh air? The pleasant coolness of a fresh breeze, the dreamy loneliness of a lush meadow, and the blissful appreciation of a charming, bright vista—he did not know how to savour these pleasures. He was young, and possessed by the demon of fashion. He was extremely handsome, strong, and had a good build. While he lived in the village, where he didn't have to worry about reading, writing, and teachers, and when he had no anxieties about exams, he would drink seers of milk. His family owned a few buffaloes, and he could down cupfuls of ghee. He was also fond of exercising. It had given him an athletic physique. His chest was wide and his neck was straight; it was as if his body were made of iron. His face had neither the maturity nor the refinement that comes from education and wisdom. He looked masculine, arrogant. His eyes were intoxicated, bright, fickle. He was not a sapling cultivated in a park; he was a strong tree from the forest. Who would appreciate him in an isolated park or garden? Who would admire his youth or beauty? That's why he would set out towards Dalmandi or the Chauk. Everyone, young and old, noticed his looks and his mannerisms. The young looked at him with envy, the elderly with affection. People walking along would stop in their tracks just to get a better look at him. The shopkeepers thought that he was the son of a nobleman.

Situated above the shops were the brothels, veritable bazaars of beauties. As soon as Sadan was seen walking in the bazaar, a bustle would ensue. The courtesans would run out onto their balconies and, flirting, try to capture his attention—let's see whose rooftop this lost pigeon flies to, which trap will catch this golden sparrow. Sadan didn't have the maturity that helps moral men in such situations. He didn't even possess the strength of will that would have kept his eyes from wandering upwards. As a consequence, his phaeton made its way through the bazaar very slowly. His eyes remained fixed on the young women. When we are young, we take great pride in our rebellions and our defiance of morality; later in life, in our demonstrations of conventional kindness. Sadan wanted to show that he was romantic and bold; but more than love, he desired something scandalous. If Sadan had had a close friend then, he would have told him tall tales of his imaginary, star-crossed love.

Over time, Sadan became so distracted that he gave up studying altogether. The teacher would come, teach, and leave, but Sadan couldn't be bothered. He was constantly daydreaming about the bazaar, the same scene dancing before his eyes, the transfixing recollection of the beauty and the gentle smiles of those temptresses. After wasting away the day, he would dress up and head towards Dalmandi as soon as it was evening. Ultimately, his vice bore the same fruit that it always does. After three or four months, he lost all his inhibition. In the phaeton, he was constantly hounded by two groomsmen who watched his every movement like spies. That's why he didn't dare to pick the sweet flowers from the forbidden garden. He began plotting ways to rid himself of these two spies and finally came up with a suitable stratagem. One day he said to Sharmaji—Uncle, buy me a good horse. I hate riding around in a phaeton like an invalid. Horseback riding will give me exercise and time to practice my riding.

Since the day Suman left, Sharmaji had been sick with worry. His clients said—Who knows what is wrong with him these days? He gets upset over every little detail. And how will he argue our cases if he doesn't pay attention to us? As long as we are paying for services, why should we act as if he is the only lawyer around? There are several others wandering around looking for work. As a result, Sharmaji's earnings declined. And so, when he heard Sadan's demand, he was more than a little concerned—Why not saddle up the horse we already have? He could be trained in a few days.

Sadan—No sir, he is very skinny and he won't survive being ridden. He doesn't even have a proper gait; he can neither pace nor gallop. And how can I ride him when he returns from the courthouse exhausted and defeated?

Sharmaji—Fine, I will look around, and I'll buy a good animal when I find one. Sharmaji had hoped that this would stall him. Even cheap horses cost between two and a half to three hundred rupees, and on top of that, it would take fifty rupees a month to feed it. He couldn't afford such expenditures now, but he didn't think that Sadan would ever understand. Every morning, he repeated his demand to Sharmaji, going so far as to press him at every available opportunity. Sharmaji would take one look at his face and melt. Had he openly explained his condition to Sadan, Sadan would have stopped asking, but he didn't want to burden his nephew with his worries.

Sadan had asked his two grooms to let him know if they heard of a horse for sale. With the greed of middlemen, they poured all their energies into this search. And they found a horse. A gentleman named Digby was leaving the country. He had put his horse up for sale. Sadan went to see the horse himself; he examined it, rode it, paid close attention to its gait. He was completely taken by the animal. He went to Sharmaji and said—You must come and see the horse. I like him very much. Now, Sharmaji had no means of escape. He was forced to see the horse, meet with Digby Sahib, haggle over the price. Digby Sahib asked for four hundred rupees and not a paisa less.

Where would they get that kind of money? If there were any money in the house, one or two hundred rupees, it would be in Subhadra's possession, and Sharmaji had not the slightest hope that Subhadra would be sympathetic to his plight. The loan manager of the bank, Babu Charuchandra, was a friend of his. He thought about asking him for a loan, but so far Sharmaji had never needed to ask for a loan. Repeatedly, he resolved to go to the bank, but each time, his courage failed him. What if he says no? He felt daunted by the painful fear of rejection. He had no idea of the kind of faith that people have in members of the nobility. He even took out his pen and inkstand to write a promissory note a couple of times, but he couldn't figure out what he should write. In the meantime, Sadan had brought the horse home from Digby Sahib's place. The saddle and harness had cost an extra fifty rupees. He had promised to deliver the payment the next day. And now there was only the span of a night to arrange for the money. It wouldn't have been difficult for a man of Sharmaji's status to find that kind of money. But he only saw darkness in every direction. For the first time he became aware of his own insignificance. A man who has never climbed a mountain becomes dizzy atop a small hill. In his helplessness, he had no saviour other than Subhadra. She saw his troubled face and asked—Why are you so upset today? Are you all right?

Sharmaji looked towards the floor—Yes, I am all right.

Subhadra—Then why do you look so sad?

Sharmaji—What can I say? There's nothing to say. Sadan has me nonplussed. He has been begging for a horse for days. He bought a horse from Digby Sahib today. Wasted four hundred fifty rupees for it.

Subhadra was startled—Well, and when were you planning on telling me.

Sharmaji—I was afraid to tell you.

Subhadra—Why were you afraid? Do you think that I am Sadan's enemy? Did you think that I would burn and sizzle with rage? ... He will have only one chance to enjoy his youth. It's not that much money. May God protect you, four or five hundred rupees are always falling into our laps, you know. At least the boy will be happy. He is, after all, the son of your brother, the one that raised and fed you until you became the man you now are.

Sharmaji was prepared for her sarcasm. That was why he had begun by criticizing Sadan. But in fact, Sadan's insistence didn't cause him as much grief as his wretched poverty. In order to make Subhadra sympathize, it was necessary to reach her heart. He said—Regardless, I was afraid to tell you. I am speaking from my heart. We all like seeing boys well-fed and happy, but only when there is money in the house. I have done nothing but worry about this all day. I haven't been able to think straight. Digby Sahib's agent will come in the morning. What shall I say to him? If I were to fall sick, I would at least have that excuse.

Subhadra—We can arrange that. In the morning, just stay wrapped up in your blanket, and I will tell him that you are not feeling well.

Sharmaji couldn't keep from laughing. This sarcasm was so devoid of mercy, so filled with contempt. He said—I'll assume that we can delay him for a day, but Digby Sahib is leaving the day after next. We will have to come up with something or the other tomorrow.

Subhadra—Then why didn't you deal with it today?

Sharmaji—Look, don't hassle me. If I could come up with a solution, why would I come to you? Wouldn't I have fixed everything by myself? Because I haven't been able to come up with anything, I have come to you. Tell me, what should I do?

Subhadra—What do you want me to tell you? You have studied law. I haven't even passed middle school. Of what use is my brain? All I know is that your rivals' hearts will start to race as soon as they hear the horse neighing at the door. As soon as you see Sadan sitting on the horse, you will be content.

Sharmaji—That's what I am asking: how can I fulfil my wish?

Subhadra—Have faith in God. He will contrive something or the other.

Sharmaji—Now you're joking.

Subhadra—What else can I do? If you think that I have money, you are mistaken. I don't know how to bargain. Here's the key to the box. There might be a hundred or a hundred and twenty five rupees in there. You can take them. You will have to come up with some other arrangement for the rest. You have many friends. Won't they be able to loan you a few hundred rupees?

Although Padamsingh had expected this response, as soon as he heard it, he became anxious again. The situation hadn't improved. He began to stare quietly at the sky, like someone drowning in an endless sea.

Subhadra was prepared to give him the key to the box, but instead of a hundred rupees, there were a full five hundred rupees tucked away in her wallet. This was all that Subhadra had saved in the past two years. She used to fantasize about her savings. Sometimes she would think—when I go home, I will take back a beautiful bracelet for my sister-in-law and a new sari for every girl in the village. At other times she would think, if this money can be useful and Sharmaji needs it, then I will immediately give it to him. Won't he be pleased. He will be shocked. Generally, young women do not have such generous fantasies. When they save money, it is for their own jewellery. But Subhadra was the daughter of a wealthy family, and she had had her fill of jewels.

She was not in the least bit attached to the money. Of course, she hesitated about handing it over for such a frivolous thing, but Panditji's distraught expression brought on feelings of pity. She said—You didn't have to assume the entire burden yourself. It is a simple matter. You could have said, listen, I don't have any money, and could have solved the problem by now. What's the point of worrying yourself like this? Today he wants a horse. Tomorrow it will be a motorcar. What will you do then? I know that your brother has done countless things for you, but you can only do what is within your means. Your brother will not be pleased when he hears what you have done.

She got up quickly and took the money out of the box. She took out five bundles of notes and dropped them in front of her husband. She said—Here's five hundred rupees. Do whatever you will. Had I held on to it, it would have only been to help you. But take it. At least you will have peace of mind. Now, not a single cent remains in the box.

Panditji was confused. He viewed the money agitatedly, but he wasn't won over by the gesture. Certainly, his worries decreased, and lines of calm began to appear on his face, but the lightness, the excitement that Subhadra had hoped for, were not visible at all. And in an instant, those lines of calm disappeared without a trace. Shades of shame and sorrow appeared in their place. He felt awkward as he reached for the money. He thought—I don't know how much hard work it has been for Subhadra to save this money. Who knows what trouble she has endured for it.

Subhadra said—You don't seem too pleased with the free money?

Sharmaji looked at her with compassion—How can I be pleased? It wasn't necessary for you to give me this money. I am leaving. I will return the horse. I will say that it is unlucky or I will find some other fault with it. Sadan will not be happy, but I can't do anything about that.

If Subhadra had made the same suggestion earlier, Sharmaji would have been furious. He would have thought her uncivilized and would have been quite harsh with her, but Subhadra's selflessness had subdued him. After all, should one show civility inside the home or outside it? He decided that it was necessary in the home, but when have we ever worried about our family members in maintaining our status in the eyes of others?

Subhadra was shocked—What is this? You have changed your mind so quickly! What will you solve by returning the animal? Digby Sahib might even take it back, but that would still be an enormous injustice towards him. That poor man is about to leave the country. This will only upset him. No, this is a small matter. Take the money and give it to him. Money is saved for days like this. I have no use for it. I give it to you gladly. If you want, think of it as a loan that you can pay back.

The situation had not changed, but the terms were different. Sharmaji was content—Yes, I will accept it on that condition, I will pay you back in monthly instalments.

15

THE ANCIENTS HAVE prescribed two methods to control the senses—hedonism and asceticism. The first is extremely dangerous and unattainable. And yet our society has decided to travel down this dangerous road by placing Minabazaar at the centre of the town. It is determined to turn households into muddy lotuses.

At each different stage of a man's life, his desires also differ. Childhood is the time for sweets, and old age for stinginess, but youth is the time for love and longing. And a young man, walking through Minabazaar in this condition, can easily be overwhelmed. The fickle, shameless, and wicked fare well enough. The rest trip and fall.

We try to keep liquor stores away from our neighbourhoods, and we despise gambling houses, but we gladly display brothels in the most elegant buildings in the Chauk. This is nothing but a recipe for disaster.

Even ordinary things in the bazaar are so fascinating! We go crazy over them and buy them for no apparent reason. So what kind of person would be able to keep himself from these beautiful, priceless jewels? Are we really this naïve?

The opposition claims that it hardly matters. Thousands of young men roam through the streets daily and scarcely any of them fall victim to such things. They want visible proof of the depravity of men. But they don't understand that weakness, like wind, is an invisible thing whose presence can only be felt in its ramifications. Why are we so shameless, so deficient in resolve? Why do we no longer possess nobility in our souls? What is the cause of our stagnation? These are all symptoms of mental weakness.

That's why it is necessary to keep these venomous serpents away from the population, in a separate location. Then, we will have to think twice before going near such loathsome places. As long as they are kept away from the population and there are no good excuses to wander off there, fewer shameless men will dare to set foot in that relocated Minabazaar.

Several months had passed. The monsoon had arrived. The excitement of fairs and picnics was in full swing. Sadan, dressed like a dandy, would boldly ride through the town on his horse. His heart burned with desire and longing. He had become so cavalier that he would get off his horse in Dalmandi and sit by the paan vendors chewing on a paan. To the people there he seemed to be the fallen son of some nobleman. They would tell him all the news from the brothels, and intense discussions would commence about who was the best singer and who the most beautiful. The bazaar was always full of such talk, and Sadan listened to every word enthusiastically. Such discussions refined his sensibilities. At first, ghazals didn't mean anything to him. But now, when he heard them, they made his heartstrings vibrate like a sitar. He was enchanted by the melodious voices. It took every ounce of his strength not to ascend those stairs to the brothel.

Padamsingh wanted Sadan to be fashionable, but he couldn't bear to see him all slicked up like a dandy. He went for a walk every day, but he never saw Sadan in the parks or gardens—where does he go every day? I hope he hasn't fallen into the trap of Dalmandi.

He had seen Sadan in Dalmandi on two or three occasions. Whenever he saw his uncle, Sadan would duck into a store and pretend to be buying something or the other. But Sharmaji had seen him. He could only stare at the ground and walk away. He wanted very much to keep Sadan from returning to the place, but was too embarrassed to say anything.

One day, Sharmaji was going for a walk when he ran into two gentlemen, both members of the municipal council. One was named Abulwafa, and the other Abdullatif. The pair was going for a ride in a phaeton. They stopped as soon as they saw Sharmaji.

Abulwafa said—Well, look! We were just thinking about you. Come. Ride with us for a while.

Sharmaji replied—You will have to forgive me. I am on my walk.

Abulwafa—I have something important to discuss with you. We were going to stop by your house in any case.

Sharmaji was powerless against the conventions of polite behaviour. He climbed into the buggy.

Abulwafa—Do you want to hear some good news?

Sharmaji—Please.

Abulwafa—Your servant has become 'Sumanbai'.

Abdullatif—By God, you have a discerning eye. She has been performing in Dalmandi for only three or four days now, and already she has been declared the most beautiful. You can't call the rest beautiful, in all honesty. There is a constant crowd of admirers in front of her balcony. Her face is like a rose and her skin glows like gold. Sir, I swear to you that I have never seen such an intoxicating face.

Abulwafa—Brother, I am prepared to humble myself before anyone who claims to be able to control himself around her. It requires a person of your refinement to find such a diamond in the rough.

Abdullatif—She is a sight for sore eyes. It isn't more than five or six months since she left your place, but I was completely overwhelmed by her singing. In this town, no one can equal her. No other voice has the same range or delicacy.

Abulwafa—And listen, everywhere I go, I hear people talking about her. Everyone seems bewitched. I have heard that Seth Balbhadradasji has been visiting her. Come, you must renew your old friendship with her. And by your grace, we will also receive her favour.

Abdullatif—We will drag you along with us. You will have to oblige us on this one.

Panditji hung his head as if the weight of sorrow, shame, and regret were too much for him to bear. This was exactly what he had feared would happen. He wanted very much to sit by himself and analyse the situation and figure out how much of a part he had played in all of this. He was exhausted by their intransigence. He said—You must forgive me. I won't be able to go.

Abulwafa—Why?

Sharmaji—Because I can't bear to see a woman from a good household in such a condition. You can think whatever you like, but the only thing that was ever between us was that she and my wife were friends.

Abdullatif—Dear Sir, save these excuses for someone else. I have grown up in these streets, and I understand these situations rather well. You can put in a good word for us with her.

Panditji could no longer stay calm. Excitedly he said—I have already told you that I won't visit her. Let me out.

Abulwafa—And we have told you that we will take you with us. You will have to bear a little inconvenience for our sakes.

Abdullatif whipped the horse once more. He began to gallop. Sharmaji said angrily—Do you want to ruin me?

Abulwafa—Sir, you owe us an explanation. We are almost there. Look here, this is the street.

Sharmaji knew that these men would not listen to him. He would rather be pushed down a well than face Suman. So he took his fate into his hands and jumped from the speeding phaeton. He tried to steady himself, but he couldn't keep his balance. He tripped and stumbled for about fifty paces. Several times he almost managed to steady himself, but in the end, he slipped and fell. He bruised the joints in his hand badly and he completely lost his wind. Drenched in sweat, dizzy, and seeing stars, he sat down on the ground. Abdullatif stopped the phaeton, and the two men ran back to him. They took out their handkerchiefs and began to fan him. After some fifteen minutes, Sharmaji regained his breath. Both men felt guilty and ashamed; they began to apologize profusely. They insisted that he let them drive him home, but Sharmaji wouldn't hear of it. Leaving them behind he began to limp home. Yet, when he thought about it now, he didn't know why he had jumped out of the phaeton—if I had asked them sharply to stop the phaeton, they would have stopped it, and if they had still refused, I could have taken the reins myself. However, it is over. If those two had distracted me in conversation and taken me to Suman's, it would have been difficult. How would I look her in the eyes? Perhaps I could have run away as soon as I got out of the phaeton, and run into the market like a madman. I can watch a cow being slaughtered, but I can't bear seeing Suman in this condition. The worst nightmares haunt me every day.

Repeatedly, he asked himself the same question—who is responsible for this tragedy? Again and again, he went over what had happened—if I hadn't kicked her out of my house, she would not have fallen like this. She had no one to turn after I kicked her out of my home, and angry and desperate, she was compelled to act this way. This is all my fault.

But why was Gajadhar so upset with Suman? She wasn't a cloistered woman. She used to go out to parties and fairs. Gajadhar should never have given her such a harsh punishment for being a little late on one occasion. He could have scolded her; he could have even slapped her a couple of times. Suman might have begun to cry. But eventually Gajadhar would have calmed down and would have made up with Suman. The argument could have been resolved. But that's not what happened, because Vitthaldas had already made the situation explosive. There is no question that it is entirely his fault. I only kicked Suman out of the house because of him. Having been slandered across town, I had no choice but to behave callously. Having fixed the blame on Vitthaldas in this manner, Sharmaji saw clearly once more. This clarity put out a flame that had been burning in his heart for months. He now had an opportunity to discredit Vitthaldas. As soon as he reached home, he began composing a letter to Vitthaldas. He didn't even stop to change his clothes.

Dear Sir,
Namaste! You will be infinitely pleased to hear that Suman now resides in a brothel in Dalmandi. You will remember that on Holi, she came to my house out of fear of her husband, and I thought it appropriate to give her aid in an honest manner for a few days until her husband calmed down. But in the meantime, several of my friends, who are not completely unaware of my character, began to disparage me and gossip about me until I was forced to remove that poor woman from my home. Ultimately, she fell into the very realm of sin that I was afraid of. And now you will be able to answer two questions: who is to blame for this tragedy, and was I wrong to help her?

Yours,
Padamsingh

Babu Vitthaldas was the driving force behind most of the town's public associations. No job could be completed without his assistance. This paragon of industry would undertake each difficult task with pleasure. Occasionally he would buckle a little under the pressure, but he never gave up. He barely had time to eat, and he never had the luxury of relaxing at home. His wife constantly complained about his uncongenial behaviour. Vitthaldas forgot his own pleasure and needs while serving the community. Sometimes he would run around collecting donations for the orphanage. At other times, he would focus on arranging scholarships for the poorer students. Whenever there was a crisis in the community, his love for the nation would swell up inside him. When famine struck, he carried bags of flour on his head to various villages. When the cholera and plague epidemics spread, people were amazed by his dedication and selflessness. And just recently, when the Ganga had flooded over, he didn't go home for months. He spent all his wealth for the nation, but he never bragged about it. He had never been to college. He had a very simple oratorical style. His schemes usually lacked foresight and planning, and he wasn't especially diplomatic, clever, or smart. But he had a certain kind of patriotism that made him popular throughout the city.

Sharmaji's letter was a slap on his face. It wasn't the letter's overwhelming sarcasm that bothered him. Nor was he troubled in the least by the fact that he had slandered one of his best friends. He didn't know how to worry about things that had already happened. For now, one had to think about potential solutions, and he immediately came up with a plan. He was not an indecisive or ambivalent man. He put on his clothes and went straight to Dalmandi. He found out where Sumanbai lived and intrepidly walked up the stairs and knocked on her door where Hiriya, Suman's servant, opened it.

It was nine o'clock. Suman had just finished her concert. She was getting ready for bed and was consequently startled to see Vitthaldas. She remembered seeing him at Sharmaji's house on several occasions. She quickly stood up, bowed her head, and said—Sir, how did you lose your way and come here!

Vitthaldas sat down carefully on a cushion. He said—I haven't lost my way. I came here for a reason, which I was unwilling to believe until I saw for myself. Today, when I read Padamsingh's letter, I thought that someone had deceived him, but how can my eyes be deceived? When our respectable, Brahmin women begin to walk down this sinful path, there can be no limit to our devastation. Suman, you have shamed the entire Hindu race.

Suman responded calmly—You might think so, but no one else shares your opinion. Just a while ago several gentlemen came to hear me sing. They were all Hindus. And yet none of them seemed embarrassed to be here. They were delighted to see me. Besides, I am not the only Brahmin woman in this part of the town. I can tell you the names of a few others who are also from a high caste. They, too, were forced to come here when they couldn't find a way to survive in the Hindu community. When the Hindu race itself has no shame, how can members of the fairer sex like me defend it?

Vitthaldas—Suman, you are right. The Hindu race has certainly reached a crisis, and by now it would have been destroyed had Hindu women not been protecting its dignity all along. It has survived only because of their honesty and virtue. Thousands of women have thrown themselves into the fire just to save the honour of the Hindu race. This is an extraordinary land, where women endure all kinds of hardships, tolerate dishonour and disrespect and do not mimic the cruel barbarism of men, and thus preserve the honour of the Hindu race. And these are merely the qualities of ordinary women—can we even begin to speak of the qualities of Brahmin women? But the sad thing is that these very goddesses have begun to forsake their dignity. Suman, I know that you suffered greatly in your home. I will concede that your husband was poor, violent, and mean. And I will even concede that he kicked you out of his house, but Brahmin women endure such pain for the sake of their race and clan. It is the true duty of Brahmin women to remain firm in tragedy and to endure hardship. But you have done what low-caste whores do, who run to their parents' homes after a fight with their husbands, and when they cannot settle down at home, find shelter with prostitutes. Just think how sad it is that thousands of women live their lives happily in circumstances similar to yours, while you spit on your reputation and your dignity and take on this wicked lifestyle. Haven't you seen women who are worse off than you were? But such awful thoughts do not even approach these women; else this heavenly land would have turned to hell long ago. Suman, your actions have forced not only the Brahmin caste but the entire Hindu race to bow its head in shame.

Suman's eyes began to well up. Out of shame, she could not lift her head. Vitthaldas spoke again—There is no doubt that you get plenty of wonderful things here, that you live in a beautiful and noble building, that you sit on soft cushions, that you sleep on a bed of flowers, or that you eat all kinds of delicious foods! But think about the price that you have had to pay for such things. You have sold your honour and dignity. You were once very respected. People used to anoint their foreheads with the dust from your feet. But now they consider it a sin even to look at you ...

Suman interrupted him—Sir, what are you talking about? I am a hundred times more respected now than I ever was before. Last Janmotsav, I went to Seth Chimmanlal's temple to see the festivities, but I had to stand outside all night, drenched in the rain. No one let me inside. But last night, I sang in that very temple, and it felt as if I cleansed that temple with my presence.

Vitthaldas—But have you thought about the character of these people?

Suman—They could have any kind of character for all I care, but they were certainly leaders of the Hindu community of Benares. And what difference does it make what kind of men they are? From morn to night, I see thousands of men walking down this road. The educated and the uneducated, the foolish and the wise, the rich and the poor—I see all kinds of people, and I see each and every one of them stare at me, whether openly or secretly. There isn't one of them that wouldn't go crazy at a kind look from me. What do you call that? It is possible that a few men in the city find me contemptible. You are certainly one of them and so is your friend, Padamsingh. But when the world worships me, why should I concern myself with the contempt of a few men like you? Besides, whatever problem Padamsingh has, it is with me, not with others like me. During Holi, I saw him laughing with Bholi with my own eyes.

Vitthaldas could not come up with a reply. He felt trapped. Suman spoke again—You might even think that I took up this evil profession to seek pleasure and luxury, but that's not the way it happened. I am not so blind that I cannot recognize the difference between right and wrong. I know that I have done many sinful things. But I was helpless, I had no alternative. If you will suffer to listen, I will tell you my tragedy. You will grant that everyone in this world has a different disposition. Some can endure dishonour, others cannot. I am from a noble family. Because of my father's stupidity I was married off to an idiot and a pauper, but being poor did not mean that I could tolerate being insulted. Those who should have been beneath contempt received the highest honours, and as I saw this happen, the worst kinds of feelings arose inside me. But I let this fire consume me from the inside. I never let anyone know what I was feeling. This fire might have extinguished itself with the passage of time, but Padamsingh's party re-ignited the flame. You know what terrible things happened to me after that. After I was kicked out of Padamsingh's house, I sought refuge with Bholibai. But even then, I tried to avoid this path of evil. I thought that I could earn a living sewing clothes, but the villains harassed me so much that, in the end, I had to jump into this well myself. Even though it is difficult while living in a brothel, I have vowed to protect my chastity. I will sing. I will dance. But I will never let my body be polluted.

Vitthaldas—Sitting here is enough to pollute you.

Suman—So tell me, what am I supposed to do? How else am I supposed to live happily?

Vitthaldas—If you think that you can live happily here, you are gravely mistaken. If not today, then soon, you will realize that you will never find happiness here. Happiness is procured through contentment, never through excess or luxury.

Suman—Maybe I won't find happiness, but at least I am respected here! At least I am not anyone's slave.

Vitthaldas—This is another of your delusions. Even if you are not anyone's slave, can you deny that you are a slave to your senses? Being a slave to one's senses is much worse than any other slavery. You will find neither respect nor happiness here. Sure, you might enjoy luxury for a while, but in the end you will have to wash your hands of this as well. Just think: for a few days of pleasure, you are committing a grave crime against your soul and against society.

Suman had never heard anyone say such things before. She had thought that sensory pleasure and respect were the prime objectives in life. She realized for the first time that happiness was born out of contentment, and respect out of service.

She said—I am willing to forsake happiness and respect, but I will have to find some way to earn a living.

Vitthaldas—God has given you wisdom. There is no reason for you to live in Dalmandi and earn a living as a prostitute. There are so many jobs that you can perform from your own home.

Suman could not come up with a single response. Vitthaldas' enthusiasm left her utterly speechless. You cannot deceive an honest man. His honesty inspires a higher morality in our hearts. She said—Sitting here, I suddenly feel ashamed. Tell me, what alternative can you find for me? I have a skilled voice; I can teach singing.

Vitthaldas—There are no such schools here.

Suman—I have also studied a bit. I would make a good teacher for girls.

Vitthaldas responded with concern—There are many girls' schools, but I doubt that people will accept you.

Suman—Then what would you have me do? Is there some lover of the Hindu race who will agree to give me fifty rupees a month to live on?

Vitthaldas—That's not so easy.

Suman—Do you want me to grind flour? I won't be content doing that.

Vitthaldas said with embarrasment—I can arrange for you to live in a home for widows, if you will agree to it.

Suman responded thoughtfully—I will even agree to that but if I see the women whispering about me to each other I won't stay another instance.

Vitthaldas—That's an unreasonable condition. I can't keep people from talking. Anyway, I don't think that the committee will accept you.

Suman spoke sarcastically—If the Hindu race is so heartless, why should I suffer to save its reputation, why should I give up my life? When you can't get the community even to help me, when the race itself has no shame, why should I feel guilty? I will make one more demand and if you cannot fulfil it, then I will not bother you anymore. You must send Padamsingh to see me for an hour. I want to speak to him privately and then I will leave that same hour. I only want to see if the man you claim to be the leader of the community values my remorse in any way.

Vitthaldas responded happily—Yes, I can do this. When would you like to me arrange it?

Suman—Whenever you want.

Vitthaldas—You won't go back on your word, will you?

Suman—I haven't sunk that low.

16

Babu Vitthaldas could not have been happier if he had just inherited a fortune. He was certain that Padamsingh would not refuse him this little favour. It was only a matter of going to see him. The last time he had seen

Sharmaji was a few days before Holi. Even though he hadn't spared any efforts when he spread rumours about Padamsingh, and perhaps he was even sorry about it now, he didn't think twice about going to see him. He started walking towards Padamsingh's house. It was ten o'clock at night. There were dark clouds in the sky and it was pitch dark all around. Everywhere except in the brothels, where the lights still danced in the bazaar of pleasure. The upper quarters scattered rays of light on the streets below. Dulcet tones could be heard coming from one direction; sweet laughter, from another; and from still another direction, romantic whispers could be overheard. In every direction, sex and longing revealed their naked forms. As soon as he left Dalmandi, Vitthaldas felt as if he had arrived in a deserted town. But there were still people on the road. And when Vitthaldas saw a man he recognized, he wasted no time in giving him a report of his endeavours!—do you have any idea where I am coming from? I went to save Sumanbai. I cast such a spell on her that she couldn't look me in the eye. Now, she is prepared to go to a widow's home. This is how hardworking people get the job done.

Padamsingh was lying on his charpoy, awaiting the arrival of the goddess of dreams, when Vitthaldas came to the door and called out to him. Jeetan kahaar was sitting in his room and counting his day's earnings when he heard the voice. He quickly gathered up the money and placed it in his belt. He said—Who is it?

Vitthaldas said—Listen, it's me. Has Panditji gone to sleep? Go inside and wake him up, tell him it's me, and that I am waiting outside. It's very important. Go quickly.

Jeetan was annoyed. He hadn't finished counting his money—who knows how much more money I had left to count? He got up drowsily, opened the door, and gave Panditji the message. Panditji knew that it must be something important for Vitthaldas to come this late at night. He immediately went outside.

Vitthaldas—Look, I know that I have caused you much grief. Please forgive me. Do you have any idea where I am coming from? I went to see Sumanbai. As soon as I read your letter, I raced over to see if it was possible to bring her back onto a moral path. After all, she is not just dishonouring herself; she is ruining the reputation of the entire race. When I got there, I was stunned by the spectacle of her lifestyle. That innocent woman is now the queen of the courtesans. I don't know how she became so skilled so quickly. For a while, she listened to me in silence, and then she started to cry. I thought that it was best to strike while the iron was still hot. Now, she is in our grasp. At first she was scared when I mentioned a widow's home. She said—Give me fifty rupees to live on. But you know as well as I do, that there is no one in this town who will give fifty rupees. I didn't agree to that. In the end, after listening to her, I agreed to one of her conditions. It will be your job to see that it is fulfilled.

Padamsingh looked at Vitthaldas anxiously.

Vitthaldas—Don't worry. It's a very simple condition. All you have to do is go and see her for a while. She wants to say something to you. Since I was sure that you wouldn't have any problem with this, I agreed at once. So tell me, when do you plan to go? I think that morning would be best.

Padamsingh, however, was a reflective man. He couldn't come to a decision without thinking it over for hours. He began to wonder—what is her motive in all of this? What does she want to tell me? Couldn't she just as well write me a letter? There is something suspicious about this. Abulwafa has probably told her about my jumping out of the buggy. She must have thought, since he doesn't want to come near me, I will devise this plan, and then I'll see how he refuses. She only wants to see me dishonoured. All right, even if I do go and see her, what will happen if she decides to go back on her promise? He thought this last argument would be a useful stratagem to get himself out of this mess. He said—Okay, and what if she decides not to fulfil her obligation?

Vitthaldas—Why would she do that? Is that even possible?

Padamsingh—Well, it's not entirely inconceivable.

Vitthaldas—So, do you want her to sign some kind of contract?

Padamsingh—No, I just have my doubts about her desire to leave her luxury and the willingness of the committee members to accept her.

Vitthaldas—It's my job to win over the committee members. If they won't let her in, then we will have to find her some other place to live. But first things first. Let's assume that she does go back on her word, what do we have to lose? We will have done our duty.

Padamsingh—Yes, but even so, I do not trust her. She will eventually deceive us.

Vitthaldas became impatient and annoyed—Even if she does deceive us, it is not as if you are losing some enormous investment!

Padamsingh—In your eyes, I may not have much honour, but I don't consider myself worthless.

Vitthaldas—So in short, you won't go, right?

Padamsingh—My going won't accomplish anything. It's another matter entirely, although, if you wish to see me completely ruined.

Vitthaldas—It is very sad, indeed, that you are coming up with such excuses for social work. Shame! You can see with your own eyes that a woman from our Hindu race has fallen into trouble, and you, one of the most intelligent people of this race, are haggling over details. You are only good for sucking the blood of stupid peasants and landowners. You can't do anything else.

Sharmaji didn't respond to this insult. In his mind, he was ashamed of his indecision and he thought that he deserved to be insulted! But it was extremely offensive to hear these words from a man who was the root cause of this tragedy. It took much effort to resist the temptation to say what he thought of him. He sincerely wanted to help Suman, but discretely. He said—She must have more conditions, surely?

Vitthaldas—Yes, she does, but will you be able to meet her demands? She wants fifty rupees a month to live on. Can you provide that?

Sharmaji—I can't give fifty, but I am prepared to give twenty rupees.

Vitthaldas—Sharmaji, don't joke around. You couldn't bear the smallest of burdens, but you want me to believe that you will provide twenty rupees a month?

Sharmaji—I swear to you that I will continue to give twenty rupees a month, and if my earnings increase even slightly, I will come up with the entire sum. Yes, I can't do it now. I will only save twenty rupees by selling my horse and phaeton. I don't know. It seems as if my business is failing these days.

Vitthaldas—Ok, even if you put up twenty rupees, where will the rest come from? You know how others are. I already have great difficulty in obtaining donations for the widow's home. I am going. I will make every effort, but if this work is not done, it will be your fault.

17

It was evening. As Sadan rode his horse he stared into the balconies and windows on both sides of the streets in Dalmandi. Ever since Suman had arrived, Sadan would regularly find some excuse to loiter in front of her window for a while. This new blossom had aroused such desire and longing in his heart that he no longer had a moment's peace. Her beauty and elegance had a certain captivating simplicity which seduced him and drew him towards her. It was his deepest desire to offer his love to this idol of simple beauty but he could never find the right moment to do so. Everyday, there would be a flood of admirers at Suman's door. Sadan was afraid that one of them might turn out to be a friend of his uncle's, and so he had never been able to work up the courage to go upstairs. Hiding his overwhelming desire in his heart, he left everyday in the same way, frustrated. But today, he had resolved to meet her, no matter how long it took. He could no longer bear the thought of being away from her. He arrived in front of her brothel. He could hear the melodious notes of an evening *raag*. He walked on and spent two hours circling the park and garden until it was nine o'clock. Then he went towards Dalmandi.

The bright rays of the moon in the month of Ashwin looked like a silvery blanket thrown on high roofs of Dalmandi. Once again, Sadan stopped in front of Suman's brothel. The singing and music had stopped, and he couldn't hear any voice. He was certain that Suman was alone. He got down from his horse, tied it to a pole in front of a shop downstairs and walked up to Suman's door. He was out of breath and his heart was racing.

Suman had just finished singing and a fatigue had overcome her like the calm that follows a tempest, the after-effect of indulgence in pleasure and entertainment. It was a kind of warning that the soul offers a mind lost in pleasure. In this state, our heart becomes the playground of memories. For a little while, we are flooded with knowledge. Currently, Suman's attention was turned towards Subhadra. In her mind, she was comparing herself to her friend—can I ever find the peaceful bliss that she has? Impossible! This is an ocean of desire; where can you find peace and happiness here? When

Padamsingh used to return home from the courthouse, Subhadra would joyfully prepare a paan for him, make him some fresh halva. And when he would come inside, how she used to run to him with the impatience of love. Oh! I have even seen her embrace him. How emotionally! How truly! Do I have such happiness? Here, either blind men come to see me, or talkative men come to listen to me. Some spread out the nets of their wealth, others, of their pretentious ideas. Their hearts are dull, insipid, shallow.

Just then, Sadan stepped into her room. Suman was startled. She had seen Sadan on several occasions. She thought that his face resembled Padamsingh's. Except that instead of gravity he had a kind of wilfullness. He had neither the pretence nor the cruelty that are the primary markers of the lovers that flooded this place of illusions and tricks. He was a straightforward and simple young man with a natural disposition. Suman had caught him spying on her brothel earlier today. She could tell that this pigeon was balancing on a wire, ready to descend on someone's rooftop. Seeing him here gave her a sense of vanity, as that of a wrestler after a victory in a wrestling match. She smiled and extended her hand towards Sadan.

Sadan blushed out of shame and his face turned pink. His eyes dropped. A sense of terror overcame him. He couldn't utter a word.

A man who has never tasted wine will still hesitate to bring it to his lips, even when he is longing to become intoxicated.

Even though Sadan didn't give Sumanbai accurate information about his background, he did tell her that his name was Kumvar Sadansingh. But he couldn't hide his secret for very long. Ever since Suman sent Hiriya to find out exactly who he was, she was in a serious dilemma. She couldn't bear not seeing Sadan. Day by day, her heart was drawn towards him. And while he was with Suman, it was difficult for even the wealthiest nobleman to get an audience with her. But she still thought this love was improper and illicit, and she tried to hide it. For no apparent reason, her mind thought that this love and longing would be a terrible treachery—what will Subhadra and Padamsingh think of me if they find out about this? What kind of grief will they suffer? In their eyes, how base and contemptible will I have become? Whenever Sadan talked about love, she would change the subject. And when his fingertips would roam daringly, she would look at him with coy eyes and gently move his hand away. At the same time, she wanted to ensnare Sadan. She didn't have the strength to forsake this longing for love.

But because Sadan didn't know how to read her behaviour, he thought that her lack of interest was caused by his poverty. His simple, straightforward heart had fallen deeply in love. Suman had become a necessary part of his life. But the curious part of it is that despite this desperate longing, he managed to suppress his sinful intentions. He was cavalier no longer. He only wanted to do what made Suman happy. The lust that penetrates sinful love can mutate into gentleness when it obeys true passion. But seeing Suman's reluctance grow each day, he felt that pure love had no value here. This goddess, he thought, is not pleased through prayers, but through gifts. But where would he get the money for gifts? Whom could he ask? In the end he wrote a letter to his father—I am not eating well here, and am too shy to ask uncle. Please send money.

When this letter reached his family, Bhama began nagging her husband—You had so much faith in your brother and your pride kept your head in the clouds. Well, are you still proud of him now? Even Sadan was completely taken with his uncle, but now he sees the truth. In this day and age, no one thinks about kindness. They are lost in selfishness. I did everything for that boy; I gave him the milk from my breasts. This is what I get in return. It's not that poor man's fault, I know him well enough. This is the handiwork of that princess. The next time I see her, I will give her a piece of my mind.

Madansingh knew that Sadan was up to something. He had complete faith in his brother. But now that Bhama was insistent that he send the money, he had no choice. Sadan made daily trips to the post office and frequently interrogated the mail clerks. On the fourth day, a twenty-five rupee money order arrived. The mail clerk knew him well, and he had no trouble in getting the money. Sadan was overcome with happiness. That evening, he bought an expensive silk sari from the market. But he began to have doubts. Would Suman like it? He had already told her that he was a Kumvar, the son of a noble, so he couldn't offer her common trinkets. He carried the sari with him on his horse and wandered around for a while, procrastinating. Earlier, when he had been to see Suman, he had not hesitated to arrive empty-handed. But today, with a gift in his hand, he hesitated. When it was quite dark, he steadied himself and walked up to Suman's brothel. He quietly took out the sari and placed it on her dresser. Suman had been worrying about what was taking him so long. When she saw him, she blossomed like a flower. She said—What's this?

Sadan nervously said—Nothing. I saw a sari that I liked and so I brought it for you. It's a gift.

Suman smiled—I waited a long time for you tonight, is this to make up for that?

She looked over the sari carefully. Considering Sadan's actual financial state, the sari could be called priceless.

Suman thought to herself—where did he get so much money? He didn't steal it from his home, did he? Since when did Sharmaji begin giving away this kind of money? Or maybe he cheated someone or stole it from somewhere? She thought that she should return the sari, but she was afraid of hurting his feelings. On the other hand, she was worried that he might get the wrong idea if she kept the sari. Ultimately, she came to a decision—I will keep it this time, but I will warn him about bringing more in the future. She said—I am pleased by your generosity, but I am in no need of such gifts from you. That you burden yourself to come here each day is enough for me. I only want your kind regard.

But when the gift didn't have the desired effect and when he didn't see any change in Suman's behaviour towards him, he felt that his effort had been wasted. He felt small—I gave her an ordinary gift and hoped for an enormous reward, I tried to steal the stars from the sky while standing on the ground. And then he became obsessed with trying to come up with an adequate expression of his love. But for months, he couldn't come up with anything.

One day when he went for his bath, he found that there was no soap in the bathroom. He went to the other bathroom to get some soap. As soon as he set foot inside, his gaze fell upon a bracelet that had been left on the shelf. Subhadra had just finished bathing. She had taken off the bracelet and left it on the shelf and had forgotten to pick it up when she finished. It was time for Padamsingh to go to work, and so she was in a hurry to prepare breakfast. Sadan picked up the bracelet as soon as he saw it. At the time, he had no bad intentions. He thought—I will give it to her after I harass her for a while, it will be great fun. He hid the bracelet in his towel, came outside, and hid it in his trunk. Subhadra was lying down, exhausted from the cooking. She was sleepy. She dozed off and got up only at three o'clock. Then, when Panditji came home and they began talking about this and that, she completely forgot about her bracelet. Sadan went inside a couple of times—let's see if they are worried about it or not, but he didn't hear them even mention it. In the evening, when he was getting ready to go out, he felt suddenly compelled to put the bracelet in his pocket. He thought—Why don't I show this bracelet to Sumanbai? No one will think that I stole it, and if they ask, I'll just say that I don't know anything about it. Aunt will think that the servants took it. These wicked thoughts helped him make up his mind. He went out for a ride, but his heart wasn't in it. He was anxious to give Suman this gift. Earlier than his usual time, he turned his horse towards Dalmandi. There, he bought a small velveteen box, placed the bracelet in it, and went to Suman's place. He wanted to present her with this priceless gift as if it were an ordinary trinket. Today, he sat silently for a long time. She always set the evenings aside for him. But today, his heart wasn't even in the talk of love. He was worried about how he would present her this bracelet. When it was quite late, he got up quietly, took the box out of his pocket, left it on her bed, and turned towards the door. Suman saw it and asked—What's in this box?

Sadan—Nothing, it's empty.

Suman—No, wait. Let me see.

She grabbed Sadan's hand and opened the box. She had seen this bracelet on Subhadra's hand. It had a beautiful design. She recognized it, and her heart became heavy. Concerned, she said—I have already told you that I have no desire for such things. You are needlessly embarrassing me.

Sadan replied disinterestedly, as if he were some great prince—You should accept the gifts of the poor.

Suman—For me, your grace is the most priceless gift. May I always have it. Give this bracelet to your new wife as a gift from me. I only feel pure love towards you, devoid of such desires. It seems, from your actions, that you still think me a common whore. You are the only man to whom I have given my love, given myself completely, but you still haven't understood the value of any of it!

Sadan's eyes filled with tears. He thought to himself—what have I done? To think that a priceless jewel like her would desire these meaningless gifts. In trying to capture beauty with my hands, I have committed a serious offense against this woman. Is there anyone in this town who wouldn't hand over his entire wealth for one flirtatious glance from her? Extremely wealthy men come here, but she doesn't even look at them. I, on the other hand, am that unredeemable fool who tried to buy her jewel-like love with trinkets. These self-lacerating thoughts made him cry. Suman thought that her words had hurt him. Tenderly, she asked—Are you angry with me?

Sadan—Yes, I am.

Suman—Why are you angry?

Sadan—Because you torment me with arrows. You think that I want to buy your love with these meaningless baubles.

Suman—Then why do you bring them?

Sadan—Because I want to!

Suman—No, please don't do it again.

Sadan—Well, we'll see.

Suman—I will keep this gift for your sake. But I will consider it a loan. You are not independent yet. When you become the lord of your estate, I will consider it mine. But not till then.

18

Babu Vitthaldas never left a job half-done. Getting nowhere with Padamsingh, he began to worry—where will I get fifty rupees a month for Sumanbai? The organizations that he had set up all ran on donations, but it was an enormous challenge to collect funds for them. He had handled the construction of the widow's home, but even after two years, he couldn't come up with the money to put a roof over the walls. The books for the free library had only provided food for the termites. There was a shortage of material to make the cabinets. And despite these impediments, he couldn't come up with any other way to collect money, save donations. Seth Balbhadradas was the town's chief politician, the honorary magistrate and the chairman of the municipal council. Vitthaldas sought his aid first. Sethji was relaxing in an armchair in his bungalow and smoking a hookah. He was a pale skinny man, with a refined and indulgent sensibility. He entered into each project only after considerable deliberation. He listened to Vitthaldas' proposal and said—This is an excellent proposal, but tell me, where are you planning to keep Suman?

Vitthaldas—In the widows' home.

Balbhadradas—The home's reputation will be sullied throughout the town, and it is likely that many widows will leave.

Vitthaldas—Then we will keep her in a separate place.

Balbhadradas—And the youth in the town will fight duels over her.

Vitthaldas—Then you suggest an alternative.

Balbhadradas—I think that it is best for you not to become involved in this matter. No force can save a woman who is not afraid of social scorn. It is standard procedure that if gangrene strikes a limb, it must be amputated, so that the disease doesn't spread to the rest of the body. We should apply the same rule to our social practices. I can see that you don't agree with me, but I have told you exactly what I think. I am one of the members of the board of directors of the widows' home! I will never let that courtesan into the widows' home.

Vitthaldas was furious—In short, you won't help me at all in this. When a great man like you says this, what hope can I have of other men? I have wasted much of your time. Please forgive me.

Vitthaldas got up and left to seek aid from Seth Chimmanlal. Seth Chimmanlal was a dark and ugly man. He was extremely fat; in his flabby body, there was meat where there should have been bone, and air where there should have been meat. His ideas were as ugly as his body. He was the president of the Rishi-Dharma Assembly, the chairman of the Ramlila Committee, and the manager of the Ramlila Council. He thought of politics as a venomous cobra and of newspapers as its den. He only wanted to meet with the highest officials. He was neither generous nor kind. He made his decision to donate only after scrutinizing the list of those who had already donated. In English societies, he was particularly respected. They heavily praised his natural talents. He had one great quality that hid all his weaknesses—he was incredibly good humoured.

He listened to Vitthaldas's proposal and said—You, sir, are a terribly dull man! You have no sense of enjoyment at all. After a long time, something in Dalmandi has caught my attention, and you are bent on removing that as well. At least wait until the Ramlila festival is over. She is performing on Coronation Day. It will be spectacular! Usually, Turkish women are employed to corrupt the temples, so it shouldn't make any difference that she is a Brahmin woman. But please forgive me and don't pay me any attention to my words. I should congratulate you; it is only by your efforts that such noble deeds are done. Where is the list of donors?

Vitthaldas scratched his head—I have only been to see Seth Balbhadradas, but you know him. He is so socially adept. He talked about all sorts of things to buy time.

If Balbhadradas had donated a rupee, then Chimmanlal would certainly have donated two. Had he put down two, Chimmanlal would definitely have put down four. But when the multiplier was zero, the product could only be zero as well. But what excuse could he come up with? Immediately he thought of a plan. He said—Sir, I am completely sympathetic to your cause. But Balbhadradas must have thought about it before he refused. And the more I think about it, the more it stinks of politics. I am certain of it. You may not see it that way, but I can clearly see backroom politics in this matter. The Muslims will definitely be outraged at this. They will complain to the government officials about this. And you know the government—it doesn't have eyes, only ears. They will immediately suspect a conspiracy.

Vitthaldas was annoyed—Why don't you just say that you don't want to donate anything?

Chimmanlal—You can think so if you like. I haven't taken all of the world's problems upon myself.

Vitthaldas' project hadn't succeeded here either, but this wasn't anything new for him. He encountered such frustrations daily. From here, he went to see Doctor Shyamacharan. The gentleman doctor was a very wise and educated man. He was the city's chief political leader, and his practice was quite successful. He considered each word carefully before he spoke. His silence was considered to be proof of his sober thoughtfulness. He was a devotee of peace, and that's why his opposition harmed no one, and his agreement provided no help. People from every walk of life considered him their friend as well as their enemy. He represented his commissionary as a member of the province's advisory board. He listened to Vitthaldas and said—I will help you in any way that I can. But we should endeavour to reform these bad customs that prevent us from completing our projects. If, at this time, you only help one person, what will that change? Such terrible things happen here on a daily basis. We should try to fix the root causes of these problems. If you like, I could ask the council about this.

Vitthaldas sat up—Yes, that would be wonderful.

The doctor immediately prepared a list of questions—

1. Can the government inform us about the precise increase in the number of courtesans in the last year?

2. Has the government determined the cause of this growth and what does the government intend to do to stop it?
3. To what extent is this increase caused by mental disorders, financial troubles, or social ills?

After this, the doctor began attending to his patients, and left Vitthaldas waiting for a half hour. In the end, Vitthaldas grew impatient and said—What would you like me to do?

Shyamacharan—Be patient. I will certainly draw the government's attention to this matter at the next council meeting.

Vitthaldas wanted to be rude to the doctor, but after thinking it over, decided to remain silent. After this, he didn't have the heart to visit other important men. But this single-minded worker did not shy away from challenges. Every day he approached some gentleman seeking his help. And his hard work was not completely unfruitful. He received promises totalling a hundred rupees and another hundred rupees in cash, but the additional thirty rupees a month he needed would not be found in such a meagre sum. After three months of hard work, he was only able to come up with ten more rupees a month.

When he was convinced that he could not find any more aid, he went, one morning, to see Sumanbai. She was a little troubled to see him. She said—Well sir, what can I do for you?

Vitthaldas—Do you remember your promise?

Suman—If I have forgotten it after so many days, it's not my fault.

Vitthaldas—I really wanted to arrange things quickly, but people seem to be under a spell that has completely destroyed social conscience. Nevertheless, my efforts have not been entirely unsuccessful. I have arranged for you to receive thirty rupees a month, and I am certain that I will be able to find the remaining money. I hope that you will accept it now and leave this hellish place today.

Suman—Were you unable to bring Sharmaji?

Vitthaldas—He was unwilling to come under any circumstance. But he has donated twenty of these thirty rupees a month.

Suman was surprised—Well! He turned out to be generous. Did you get any help from the Seths?

Vitthaldas—Don't even talk about the Seths. Chimmanlal would have been happy to give a thousand or two for the Ramlila festival. Balbhadradas would have given even more to reward the officers, but in this matter, they were unwilling to give anything.

At this moment, Suman was trapped in the web of Sadan's love. She had never felt the joy of love before, and she was unwilling to let go of that rare gem. Even though she knew that this affair could only end badly, her heart told her to enjoy it as long as possible—who knows what will happen in the future? Who knows what whirlpool the boat of my life will encounter, where it will drift? She wouldn't let herself think about material things, because there was nothing there for her but terrible darkness. Suddenly, the desire to improve her situation, to which she had succumbed and made promises to Vitthaldas, had evaporated. Now, she would not be satisfied even if Vitthaldas had promised her a hundred rupees a month, but all the same, she was ashamed of going back on her word. She said—I will give you my decision tomorrow. Let me think for a while.

Vitthaldas—What is there to think about?

Suman—Nothing, but give me until tomorrow.

It was ten o'clock at night. The golden moonlight of the month of Sharad spread over the city. Suman was staring out her window at the clear blue sky. In the moonlight, the light from the constellations was dim. And in the same way, the moonlike good intentions in her heart outshone the anxiety-constellated stars.

Suman was faced by a huge problem—what do I say to Vitthaldas?

This morning she had delayed him by promising to give him an answer tomorrow. But after thinking about it the whole day, she had changed her mind.

Although Suman had all the fineries of life here, she still had to regularly meet with men whose sight made her cringe, whose words made her nauseous. Her moral upbringing had not been completely destroyed yet. She hadn't fallen into that kind of misery in which evil completely destroys the good qualities of a heart. She didn't doubt that she loved luxurious things, but obtaining those things required shameless acts, which she couldn't bear and which would cause her, when she was alone, to compare her present condition with her previous one. There had been no luxury then, but her community had regarded her with respect. She could take pride in her nobility with her neighbours; she could gain dignity through her piety and her faith. She didn't have to hang her head in shame before anyone. But here, her pride had to take a beating at each step. She felt as if she was not even worthy of looking a common prostitute in the face. And because she had to endure disrespect and dishonour daily, the romantic conversations and the love-crazed glances that she received only caused her more pain and struck her sensitive heart like an axe. That was when her troubled heart resented Padamsingh the most—if that heartless man had not scorned me out of fear for his reputation, I might have gone home, or if even Gajadhar had apologized and brought me home, we would have fought for the rest of our lives in the usual way. That was why she had wanted Vitthaldas to bring Padamsingh to her.

But today, when Vitthaldas informed her that Sharmaji was desperate to help her and was prepared to donate money generously, instead of resentment, she began to admire him—He is a very kind man. I was wrong in placing the blame for my sins on him. He has been merciful towards me. I will go to him and fall at his feet and say, 'You have done this unfortunate woman a favour, may God bless you.' I will return the bracelet as well, so that he will have proof that the soul he has helped is not completely unworthy. Enough. Then I will leave this web of delusion forever.

But how will I make myself forget Sadan?

She was angry with herself for being so fickle—I would be a fool to give up this rare opportunity to reform myself for this criminal love. Will I endure the darkness of sin everyday in exchange for few days of moonlight? Will I destroy a simple boy's heart with my own hands? And against the noble man who is responsible for my salvation, can I commit such a fraud? Such deception? No, I will remove this corrupt love from my heart. I will forget Sadan. I will tell him as well, 'Let me leave this web of delusion.'

Oh! I am such a fool! This place looks so beautiful and attractive and blissful from a distance. I thought that it was a flower garden, but what is it really? A horrible jungle, filled with carnivorous animals and poisonous insects!

From afar, this river appears to be so beautifully covered by a blanket of moonlight. But what do you find underneath? A playground for enormous and awful sea monsters! Suman was lost in a wave of anxiety. She was feeling uneasy at the thought of the morning, when Vitthaldas would arrive—how can I escape from this place? Half the night had passed and she still couldn't sleep. Slowly, she began to wonder what would happen if Vitthaldas didn't come in the morning—will I again have to endure the flattery of admirers all day long? Will I have to show respect to and welcome these vicious puppets? It wasn't even six months since Suman had arrived here, but in this short span, she had become familiar with every detail of the place. There was a constant crowd of admirers at her doorstep. They would proudly tell her stories of their crimes, frauds, and wicked deeds. Some were clever pickpockets, some excellent gamblers, others were skilled con artists, and others were really good at housebreaking. But each one of them was proud of his cowardice and weaknesses. The neighbouring women would also visit. They were beautiful, all dressed up, glowing like candles, yet they were merely gold pots filled with poison—there was so much pettiness in them! So much deceit! So much sin! With what pleasure they would narrate the stories of their shamelessness and their sins! Not one of them possessed an ounce of shame. They were all bent on cheating and lying, and their minds were lost in craving. Upstanding members of the community were, here, regularly derided and made the subject of ridicule. They were called 'stupid' and 'cowardly' and the like. The whole day, all she heard was tales of stealing and looting, of abortions and adultery, of failure and deception. She now saw the true nature of the 'respect' and 'love' one received in this place. It was not respect, was not love, it was only seedy lust. Until now, Suman had courageously endured these misfortunes. She thought—if I have to spend the rest of my life in this hell, how long can I keep running from these things? Living in hell necessarily meant following a demonic religion. When Vitthaldas had first come to see her, she had thought little of him. But then, she had been unaware of the things that went on in this place. But now that she could see the door to freedom open before her, she couldn't bear to remain in this prison for another instant. Just as the human desire for evil awakens at an appropriate time, the desire for goodness also awakens at the right time.

It was three o'clock at night. Suman was still tossing and turning. Against her will, her thoughts were drawn towards Sadan. And as dawn drew nearer, she became more anxious. She was trying to reconcile contradictory thoughts in her head—why are you so taken with this love? Don't you know that it is only about beauty and attraction? It's not love; it is only a longing for love. No one comes here to find true love. No one comes here to make promises of love, just as no one goes to a temple with honest prayers. People only come here to entertain themselves. Don't fall under the spell of such love.

At dawn, Suman fell asleep.

19

It was evening. Suman had waited for Vitthaldas the entire day, but he still hadn't come. Suman's doubts had begun to grow stronger—Vitthaldas won't come now. Something is certainly wrong. Either he is busy with some other work, or the people who had promised to help have changed their minds. Still, he should have been here by now. At least I would know what was going on. If people refuse to help me, let them. I can help myself. I only need the protection of one kind man. Can Vitthaldas not even accomplish this much? I will go and tell him that I don't want financial assistance, that he shouldn't trouble himself over it. I only need him to arrange a place for me to stay and to give me some work, from which I can earn enough to survive. I don't want anything else. But I don't know where he lives and how I will find his place without an address.

I will go towards the park. People go there for walks, and it is possible that I will run into him. Sharmaji used to go there for a walk every day; it's possible that I will run into him as well. I will give him this bracelet and use it as an excuse to talk to him for a while.

Suman hired a phaeton and went for a ride by herself. She covered both windows, but she peeked through the lattice screens all the way through. She looked towards the distant cantonements in both directions, but she didn't spot either man. She was about to tell the driver to take her to Queen's Park when she saw Sadan racing his horse, coming towards her. Her heart began to pound. It seemed as if she hadn't seen him in ages. Changing circumstances occasionally inject a new enthusiasm into love. She wanted to call out to him, but she didn't. She watched him with longing, with love-filled eyes, until he disappeared from sight. She had never been so enamoured with Sadan's incredible beauty.

The buggy went toward Queen's Park. The park was at a distance from the city and only a few people went there. But Padamsingh's love for solitude had drawn him here. He would sit on a cushioned bench in the large garden and be lost in thought for hours. When the buggy passed through the gate, Suman saw Sharmaji sitting alone in the garden. Suman's heart began flickering like a candle. Had she known that she was going to be this frightened, she would never have come. But it would have been silly to leave and not do anything after having come so far and having seen him. She had the buggy stop at a distance and got out. She walked toward Sharmaji much in the same way that words travel against the wind.

Sharmaji had been watching the buggy with curiosity. He didn't recognize Suman. He was perplexed—who is this woman coming towards me? He thought that it might be some Christian lady, but when Suman came closer, he recognized her. At first he squinted in her direction, and then he stared at her as if he were paralysed. And when Suman came and stood in front of him with her head bowed, his ashamed and distressed eyes began to search for a place to hide. Then, he suddenly got up, turned around, and started walking quickly in the opposite direction. Suman felt like she had been struck by lightning—I came here hoping for one thing and am witnessing something else entirely. God! He thinks that I am so base and low that he is even scared of my shadow! The faith that she had in Sharmaji vanished in an instant. She said—I have something to say to you. Please wait. At least do me this one favour.

Sharmaji began walking even faster, like a man chased by a ghost. Suman couldn't tolerate this insult. In an angry voice she said—Why are you so afraid? I didn't come here to ask you for anything. I came to return this bracelet. Take it. I will leave you alone.

She took out the bracelet and threw it towards Sharmaji.

Sharmaji was taken aback as he looked at the bracelet lying in the grass. It was Subhadra's. Suman turned and began to walk toward her buggy. Sharmaji came up to her and said—Where did you find this bracelet?

Suman—I hope you won't be offended if I don't listen to you and just keep walking.

Padamsingh—Sumanbai, don't embarrass me. I am not worthy of showing my face to you.

Suman—Why?

Padamsingh—I keep thinking that if I hadn't forced you out of my house that day, things wouldn't be the way they are.

Suman—Why should you be embarrassed about it? You did me a favour by kicking me out of the house. You fixed my life.

Sharmaji was taken aback by her sarcasm. He said—If it was a favour, then Gajadhar Pande and Vitthaldas are responsible. I don't want the credit for such favours.

Suman—You are being modest, following that old adage about 'doing good and casting it into the well,' but I consider you a great help. Sharmaji, don't make me say things, let my thoughts remain private. It's just that I never expected such heartlessness from a kind man like you. Perhaps you think that only noblemen are hungry for respect and honour, but people in poverty are even hungrier because they don't have the means to obtain such things. They steal, lie, cheat, and do all sorts of things for respect. Respect produces a contentment that pleasure and luxury do not provide. Every day, I worried about where I would find this respect. I found several answers, but the answer that I got at your Holi party rid me of all delusions. I could now see the path to honour and respect. If I had never seen that performance, I would be living contentedly in that hut today! I thought that you were an extremely noble person, and that was why your nobility had an even greater influence on me. Bholibai sat before you arrogantly, and you became a paragon of respect and devotion before her. Your friends danced like puppets at her command. Can you imagine the kind of impact that such a scene can have on a simple heart, on a woman longing for respect? But what's the use of talking about the past? What's done is done. How can I blame you? It was all my fault. I ...

Suman wanted to say more, but Sharmaji, who had been listening to this story gravely, interrupted her and asked—Suman, are you saying these things to make me feel ashamed, or do you really mean them?

Suman—I say them to make you feel ashamed, but they are true as well. It has been a long time since I thought about these things, but when you tried to run away from even my shadow, the memories came flooding back. But now I only feel regret. Please forgive me.

Sharmaji didn't look up. He was again lost in thought. Suman had come here to thank him, but the conversation had deteriorated rapidly and she hadn't got a chance to thank him, and after such harsh words, she felt that talk of mercy and kindness would have been awkward. She walked towards her buggy. Suddenly Sharmaji asked—And the bracelet?

Suman—I found it yesterday at a pawnshop. I had seen Bahuji wearing it; I recognized it and immediately bought it.

Sharmaji—How much did it cost you?

Suman—Nothing, the lender actually owes me more now.

Sharmaji—Can you tell me his name?

No, I've promised him not to—Suman said and left. Sharmaji remained sitting for a while, and then he lay down on the bench. Each one of Suman's words echoed in his ears. He had become so lost in thought that he would not have noticed if someone had walked up and stood in front of him. His thoughts left him paralysed. It was as if he had suffered a serious wound in his heart. His body seemed comatose. He was a sensitive man. If Subhadra even jokingly said something harsh to him, he would ruminate upon it for days. He took great pride in his behaviour, his conduct and ideas, and the way he did his duty. Today, that pride had been ground to pieces. The injustice which he had blamed on Vitthaldas and Gajadhar thereby giving himself peace of mind, had today returned a hundred times heavier as a burden on his own head! He felt that he was being crushed under the weight of his crimes. His thoughts became alive and personified. He heard a distant voice in his ears—if that performance had never happened, I would have been happy in my hut today. Then the wind blew, the leaves rustled, and the trees shook their dark and terrible tops as if to say—You are the cause of Suman's misfortune.

Sharmaji got up frightened. It was late. A bell was ringing in a church with a tall steeple. The melodious notes of the bell were saying—you are the cause of Suman's misfortune.

Sharmaji repressed his powerful emotions and stepped forward. He looked up at the sky. Bright celestial characters appeared on the dark screen, which read, *You are the cause of Suman's misfortune.*

Like a man in a barren field who sees dark clouds surging ahead and so runs towards a distant tree, Sharmaji was talking large steps away from the park towards the town, but how could he stop his nightmares? Suman was following him. Sometimes she would stand in front of him and block his path and say—You are the cause of my misfortune. Sometimes she would appear from the left, sometimes from the right, but always repeating the same words. Sharmaji made it home with difficulty, went straight into his room, and covered his head. When Subhadra called him to dinner, he complained of a headache and refused to eat. The entire night, Suman haunted his dreams, cursing him—you are educated, you are proud of your wisdom and foresight, but you light firecrackers near straw houses. If you want to waste your wealth, then go to the garden and waste it. Why must you burn down the houses of the poor and downtrodden?

In the morning, Sharmaji went to see Vitthaldas.

20

In the evening, Subhadra remembered about her bracelet. She ran to the bathroom. She was fairly certain that she had left it on the shelf, but it wasn't there. This made her nervous. She looked in every shelf and cabinet in her room and everywhere in the kitchen, and she became more worried. Then she looked in every box, in every corner, as if she were looking for a needle, but she still couldn't find it. She asked her maid, but she swore on her son's life that she didn't know. She then called Jeetan and asked him.

He said—Mistress, don't accuse me of such things in my old age. All my life, I have worked for wealthy men, but I have always been honest. I don't have enough days left to ruin my reputation.

Subhadra was at a loss—whom do I ask now? Restless, she opened up every box and every bundle of clothing in search of the bracelet. She even scoured the bins of flour and daal, and put her hand into the water pot and splashed around in it. In the end, she sat down on the charpoy, frustrated. She had seen Sadan walking out of the bathroom. She wondered—maybe he has hidden it as a joke, but she didn't have the courage to ask him. She thought—I will tell Sharmaji when he sits down to breakfast after his walk. As soon as Sharmaji came home, Subhadra gave him a report of the situation. Sharmaji said—Look harder, it must be here. Who would take it?

Subhadra—I have been over every inch of this house.

Sharmaji—Ask the servants.

Subhadra—I have. Both of them swear to not having seen it. I clearly remember leaving it on the shelf in the bathroom.

Sharmaji—Did it grow wings and fly off by itself?

Subhadra—I don't suspect the servants, though.

Sharmaji—Who else could have taken it?

Subhadra—If you want, I can ask Sadan. I saw him coming out of the bathroom. Maybe he's hiding it in jest.

Sharmaji—Listen to yourself! Wouldn't he have told you if he had hidden it?

Subhadra—So what's the harm in asking him? Maybe he plans to tease me before giving it back.

Sharmaji—What do you mean, what's the harm? If he hasn't seen it, he will think that we are calling him a thief.

Subhadra—I know he went into that bathroom. I saw it with my own eyes.

Sharmaji—And so, he went there to take your bracelet? You are not making sense. Don't you dare ask him about it. He probably didn't take it, and even if he did, he will return it sooner or later. What's the hurry?

Subhadra—Where will I find another heart like yours? I need to measure myself.

Sharmaji—It doesn't matter. Just don't ask him.

Subhadra was silent for a while. But when uncle and nephew had sat down to dinner in the evening, she couldn't stop herself. She said to Sadan—Lala, I couldn't find my bracelet. If you have hidden it, please give it back. Why are you teasing me?

Sadan's face became pale and his heart began to race. After having stolen, he didn't know how to cover his tracks. He had a bite of food in his mouth. He forgot to chew it. He became so silent it was as though he hadn't heard a thing. Sharmaji looked at Subhadra with fiery eyes that made her blood run cold. She didn't have the courage to open her mouth after that. Sadan quickly swallowed two or three more mouthfuls and hurried out of the kitchen.

Sharmaji said—This is a bad habit of yours: I ask you not to do something, but you deliberately do it.

Subhadra—Didn't you see his face? He took it. If I am wrong, you can punish me as you would the real thief.

Sharmaji—When did you learn to read minds?

Subhadra—You could see it on his face.

Sharmaji—All right, suppose he did take it. What is the big bother about the bracelet? Everything I have, even my body, is, after all, for his protection. I would give him my life if he asked for it! Everything I have is his, whether he asks for it or steals it.

Subhadra became upset—If you are contracted to being his servant, that's one thing, but I won't stand by while someone steals my things.

Next day, when Sharmaji returned from his walk, Subhadra went to call him for dinner. He threw the bracelet in front of her. Subhadra was surprised. She ran over, picked it up, and recognized it—Didn't I tell you that he had hidden it? Isn't that what you discovered?

Sharmaji—Again that nonsense! I found it in a pawnshop in the bazaar. By accusing Sadan, you hurt him and embarrassed yourself.

21

VITTHALDAS WAS NO longer sure about how things would turn out—thirty rupees a month is not enough for Suman; perhaps that's why she made up that nonsense about giving me an answer tomorrow. So, he didn't go to see her the next day. All he could do was worry about how he would come up with the rest of the money. Sometimes he thought of organizing a delegation to a neighbouring town; at others he thought about acting. If he had his wish, he would have packed all the wealthy men of Benaras onto a ship and sent them to the notorious black hold of the Andamans. In town, there lived a noble and liberal-minded man named Anirudhsingh. But Vitthaldas turned back after having walked up to his doorstep because he heard a *tabla* playing inside. He thought to himself—of what use will an aesthete be to me in solving real problems? In Vitthaldas's mind, those who helped him were virtuous and those who opposed him, the worst sinners. He was still debating with himself whether or not he should go to see Suman. In the meantime, he saw Pandit Padamsingh walking towards him. He had bloodshot eyes and dull face, and Vitthaldas could tell that he hadn't slept all night. He was the epitome of anxiety and depression. Vitthaldas had not been to see him for three months. He no longer considered him a friend! But when he saw Sharmaji in this condition, his heart melted and he shook his hand lovingly and said—Brother, you look troubled. Is everything all right?

Sharmaji—Yes, of course, everything is fine. I haven't seen you for months, and I had so wanted to see you. What have you decided about Suman?

Vitthaldas—I think about nothing else all day and all night long. This is such a big town, but I can't put together thirty rupees a month for Suman. I think I don't know how to ask people. Perhaps I don't have the ability to make people sympathize. I blame other people, but it's really my own fault. Till now, I have only been able to come up with ten more rupees a month! All of the rich men are cold and heartless. Well, that is not all that surprising, but Mr Prabhakar Rao refused to help me as well. If you read his articles, you think that he is full of nationalist feelings and kindness. Months after your Holi party, he was still launching insults at you, but yesterday, when I went to ask him for help he said, 'Am I the one who owes the greatest debt to society? I have a pen, and with it, I can help the community. And a man with money can help with his wealth.' I didn't know what to say. He is having a new house built, and he has recently bought shares in a coal manufacturing company, but he won't involve himself in this social work. Other people merely shy away a little. He, on the other hand, started attacking me.

Sharmaji—Are you certain that Suman will go to the widows' home if she gets fifty rupees?

Vitthaldas—Yes, I am sure. It's another matter entirely if the Ashram committee won't let her in. Then, I will have to come up with some other arrangement.

Sharmaji—Well, then, I will end your worries. I will give fifty rupees a month, and God willing, till the very end.

Vitthaldas looked at Sharmaji with surprise and gratefully embraced him—Brother, you are remarkable! You have done something so amazing that I want to fall at your feet and cry. You have saved the reputation of the Hindu race and you have put all the millionaires to shame. But how will you bear this burden?

Sharmaji—Everything will be taken care of. God always shows the way.

Vitthaldas—Is your practice doing better these days?

Sharmaji—My earnings are turning to stone. I can sell my horse and carriage, and that will save me thirty rupees, and I can stop using electricity, and that will save another ten rupees. I will squeeze out an additional ten rupees from somewhere or the other.

Vitthaldas—I feel bad about placing this entire burden on you, but what can I do? I could get nowhere with the wealthy men in this town. If you sell your carriage, how will you get to the courthouse? Will you have to rent a carriage everyday?

Sharmaji—No, don't be silly. I don't need to rent a carriage. My nephew just bought a strong brown horse. I can ride it to work.

Vitthaldas—Arrey, isn't he the one who wanders around in the Chauk in the evenings?

Sharmaji—It could be him.

Vitthaldas—He looks a lot like you. He wears a pinstriped jacket—very strapping and fair. He has these really big eyes and looks athletic.

Sharmaji—Well yes, it sounds like him. It must be him.

Vitthaldas—Don't you try to stop him from going to the bazaar?

Sharmaji—I don't keep a track of his wanderings. It's possible that sometimes he goes out toward the bazaar. But he's a good boy, and that's why I've never worried about him.

Vitthaldas—You are making a terrible mistake. It doesn't matter how a good a boy he used to be—he's developed some bad habits. I have seen him repeatedly in places where I should not have seen him. It seems as if he has fallen under the spell of Sumanbai.

Sharmaji was dumbstruck. He said—This is terrible news! He is the torchbearer of my family. If he has fallen into immoral ways, I may as well be dead. How will I ever look my brother in the face?

Sharmaji's eyes welled up. Then he said—Look, you have to help me with him. If my brother gets even the slightest inkling of this, he will never look at me.

Vitthaldas—No, we will work to bring him back onto a moral path. I didn't know, until today, that he was your nephew. I will start working on him immediately. Besides, if Suman leaves tomorrow, he will straighten himself out.

Sharmaji—But just because Suman leaves, the bazaar won't be empty. Another woman might seduce him. What should I do? Should I send him home?

Vitthaldas—There's nothing in the village for him any more. First of all, he won't go back, and even if he does, he will come running back the next day. Such desires are strong in young men. It's all because of the immoral attitude that has miraculously infected this city's public institutions. It's criminal—instead of banning the places that cause such emotional turmoil we decorate them lavishly and encourage immoral behaviour in our innocent youth. Who knows how this awful custom started? Perhaps it started during the reign of sensual Muslim *badshah*s. We have set up a marketplace of sex where there should be libraries, religious assemblies, and public institutions. Aren't we encouraging licentious behaviour? We are intentionally pushing our youth into a ditch. Pity!

Sharmaji—You started a movement about this, didn't you?

Vitthaldas—Yes, I did. But several sympathizers have turned a deaf ear in the same way that you did after you had agreed to help me, and well, a single chickpea cannot break an oven. I don't have money, or influence, or an important title. Who listens to me anyway? Everyone thinks I am a blabbermouth. There are many able and educated men in this city who live comfortably and indulge themselves. No one will hear me out even by accident.

By nature, Sharmaji was a temperate man. He needed a strong catalyst before he would take up a cause. Not even the praise of his friends, which would be enough to wake an ordinarily sleepy man was enough for him. And he wasn't sleeping; he was awake. He was only lying down because of inertia. And that was why an urgent cause was more effective than screaming and shouting to get him moving. It is strange but true that it is easier to wake a sleeping man than a man who is already awake. A sleeping man jumps out of bed when he hears his name called; a man who is awake thinks—whose voice is this? What does he want with me? Will it really make a difference? He gets up only when he receives satisfactory answers to his questions. Otherwise, he stays in bed. Padamsingh was in a similar state. He had heard the cries of the community on several occasions, but he still hadn't risen. But the cry that he heard this time violently brought him to his senses. He would do anything to save his nephew, whom he loved more than if he were his own son, from sin, and to lessen his brother's pain. He didn't need any more proof of the horrible consequences of this social evil to align himself with the forces that would root it out. Even the fiercest enemies of child-widow-marriage have changed sides in a similar way. There is no more solid proof than visible evidence. Sharmaji said—I am prepared to help you in any way that I can.

Vitthaldas was pleased—Brother, if it were up to me, I would move heaven and earth, but forgive me, I don't think that you really believe in this cause. You sound excited now, but tomorrow you will become uninterested again. Such work requires genuine commitment.

Embarrassed, Sharmaji said—God willing, you won't have this complaint much longer.

Vitthaldas—In which case, we will definitely succeed.

Sharmaji—Everything is in God's hands. I don't know how to speak or write persuasively, but I will follow you blindly wherever you lead.

Vitthaldas—Look, things will work themselves out. We just need to have faith. Firm belief can move mountains. Your speeches will be so powerful that people will be overwhelmed. You just have to remember not to lose your courage.

Sharmaji—You will keep me strong.

Vitthaldas—Good, so now listen to my plan. First, the courtesans must be removed from public places, and second, the custom of singing and dancing by courtesans must be stopped. Do you agree with me or not?

Sharmaji—Do you still doubt me?

Vitthaldas—You didn't think this way about dancing, did you?

Sharmaji—I have already ruined one family, I won't ruin another in the same way. I don't know what came over me then. I am now certain that my party was the reason that Sumanbai was kicked out of her house! But I do have one question. After all, people like us have lived in the city all our lives. Why haven't we been tempted? And the dances have been going on in this city much before we arrived, but only a few cases end in horrible tragedy. We can only conclude that the most important factor in this matter is an individual's nature. You can't change an individual's nature with your plan.

Vitthaldas—That was never my intention. I only wanted to reform those who feed on weak minds that don't know better. Some people are born fat, and you don't need to find special foods for them to eat. There are other people who eat their fill of butter and milk and become fat, and others who remain skinny all their lives, who would not become fat even if they lived inside containers of butter and milk. We are only concerned with the second kind of person. You and I are not the kind of people who are easily seduced; we have never been able to stop worrying about filling our bellies, and so we never thought that we could find ourselves in this marketplace of sex. The rich, the handsome, the generous, the refined—they are susceptible. If God gives a woman beauty, He should make certain that she has money as well. A penniless, beautiful, and clever woman easily falls under the spell of evil.

22

As Suman returned from the park, she regretted what she had done—Why did I say such hurtful things to Sharmaji? He has been so generous to me, and this is how I repay him? In all honesty, I have been blaming him for the sin of my own weakness. Dancing and singing performances happen in houses all over the world, and everyone—the nobles, the ordinary people, the poor—they all watch happily and are content. If I jumped into this fire because of my own foolish notions, then why blame Sharmaji or anyone else? Babu Vitthaldas went to see the nobles in this town, and he talked to men who come here as well. But not one of them helped him. Why? The only reason is that they don't want me to be free of this place. If I leave, they won't be able to satisfy their lust. They are merciless tigers, slashing my chest and then watching me suffer. There was only one man who tried to save me from this darkness and I insulted him.

He will think me so ungrateful. He even ran away when he saw me. I should have mended my ways out of shame but instead, out of fear of sin, I have insulted him. And I welcome into my world the very men who are ruining my life with their profanity! A hunter can't stand to see an animal escape from his trap. And a dirty child can't help but smear dirt on all the other children so that they will be dirty as well. Am I the greedy hunter or the stupid child?

Ask any author if he values thoughtless praise over the harsh criticism of an impartial reviewer. Suman appreciated Sharmaji's anger much more than the endless flattery of her lovers.

She spent the night thinking about these things. She decided that she would go to see Vitthaldas in the morning and ask him to help her—I don't want your money; I only want a safe place to stay. I will grind flour. I will sew clothes, and somehow I will manage to keep body and soul together.

Morning came. She got up and was getting ready to go to Vitthaldas' home when he himself arrived. Suman was elated, like a devotee before his God idol. She said—Please come in. You've disappointed me, you know. I waited for you all day yesterday. And now, I was getting ready to visit you.

Vitthaldas—I couldn't come yesterday because I was held up by some work.

Suman—So, have you found a place for me to stay?

Vitthaldas—I wasn't able to do anything, but Padamsingh managed to keep my promise to you. He has managed to fulfil all of your conditions. He came to see me and vowed that he would give you fifty rupees a month as long as he lives.

Shocked, Suman's eyes filled with tears. Sharmaji's incredible generosity ignited the devotion, faith, and pure love of her soul. She was terribly embarrassed about the harsh things that she had said. She said—Sharmaji is an ocean of mercy and compassion. I won't be able to repay his debt in this lifetime. May God protect him always. But I only said those things to test you. I wanted to see if you really wanted to liberate me or if you were just preaching. Now I know that both of you gentlemen are god-like. I don't wish to trouble you unnecessarily. I was hungry for sympathy, and I have got that. I won't burden you with my problems any longer. Just find a place for me to stay, where I can be safe from harm and abuse.

Vitthaldas was taken aback. His eyes shone with a sense of racial pride. He thought to himself—even the fallen women of this country have such noble thoughts. He said—Suman, I can't tell you how happy it makes me to hear you say such noble things. But how will you survive without money?

Suman—I will work. There are thousands of unfortunate people who have no one but God to help them. I won't ask you to pay for my indecency.

Vitthaldas—Will you be able to endure such hardship?

Suman—I wouldn't have been able to before, but now I can endure anything. This place has taught me that indecency is the most unbearable thing of all. Other hardships trouble the body, but this one wreaks havoc on the soul. I thank God that He sent people like you to help me.

Vitthaldas—Suman, you are truly a wise woman.

Suman—So when should I leave here?

Vitthaldas—Today. I haven't talked to the Ashram Committee, but there shouldn't be a problem. You can stay there. We will worry about the committee making trouble when it comes to that. You must remember not to tell anyone about yourself, or else the widows will create trouble.

Suman—I am prepared to do whatever you think best.

Vitthaldas—You will have to leave this evening.

Just after Vitthaldas left, two courtesans came to visit Suman. Suman said to them—I have a headache.

Suman used to cook her own meals. Even though she was a fallen woman, she took the trouble to cook her own food. She decided that she would fast today. Even prisoners can't stand food on the day of their release.

In the afternoon, two groups of people came to see her. Suman sent them away with an excuse. She couldn't stand the sight of their faces. Seth Balbhadradas sent a basket of Nagpuri tangerines, which Suman promptly returned. Chimmanlal sent his buggy at four o'clock so she could ride around. She sent it back as well.

Like the moment of dawn that follows darkness, when the birds begin to chirp and the calves are lost in play, Suman was feeling mischievous. She ordered a pack of cigarettes and a bottle of varnish, which she placed on a shelf, and she broke off one leg of a chair and propped it against the wall out on the balcony. As the clock struck five, Munshi Abulwafa arrived. His Excellency smoked cigarettes all the time. Today, Suman was different towards him and after talking about this and that, she said—Come, I have some cigarettes that you will never forget.

Abulwafa—Courtesy and respect!

Suman—Look, I bought these at an English store especially for you. Take them.

Abulwafa—I will have to count myself amongst the fortunate. Lucky me—that I have such close friends.

Abulwafa placed the cigarette between his lips. Suman took out a box of matches and lit a stick. Abulwafa bent forward to light his cigarette, and somehow the match managed to light his beard instead of the cigarette. More than half of his beard was burnt, as if it were made of straw. He threw the cigarette away and began rubbing his face with both hands. The flame was extinguished, but his beard was ruined. He ran to the mirror to look at his face. The charred hair looked like the boiled skein of a rope. Suman spoke apologetically—May my hand burn! Why oh why did I light that match?

She tried hard to contain herself, but she couldn't keep herself from laughing. Abulwafa was horrified, as if he had just been orphaned. Suman stopped laughing. His ugly face was a bizarre spectacle of terror and bitterness. He said—What have I done to deserve this?

Suman—Munshiji, sincerely, may both of my eyes fall out if I intentionally set fire to your beard. And even if I was upset with you, I had no enmity with that poor beard.

Abulwafa—A lover's playful mischief is pleasing, but not enough to warrant burning my face. It would have been better if you had just cremated me. How will I show my burnt face to anyone? Allah! You have ruined me.

Suman—I am sorry. What do you want me to do? I would give you my own beard if I had one. Can't you find a fake beard?

Abulwafa—Suman, don't pour salt on my wounds. If anyone else had played such a trick on me, I would have spilt his blood.

Suman—Arrey, it's only a few burnt hairs, nothing else. They will grow back in a month or two. Don't get upset over such a small matter.

Abulwafa—Suman, don't antagonize me. I am liable to say things right now I might regret later. I am not in my right mind.

Suman—Narayan, Narayan. Going crazy over a little beard! All right, suppose I did plan to burn your beard. Everyday, you set fire to my soul, my religion, and my heart. Are these worth less than your beard? A beard does not make a man a lover. Go home and don't come back again. I don't need immature men.

Abulwafa stared angrily at Suman as he took a handkerchief out of his pocket. He hid his burnt face in its folds and sneaked out quietly. This was the same man who wasn't even slightly embarrassed to be out in the market openly laughing and flirting with courtesans.

It was now time for Sadan to arrive. Suman was anxious about tonight's meeting. This would be their last encounter. The curtain would soon fall on this romance. She would never see that charming boy again. Her eyes would forever more long to see him. She would never again hear his beautiful words filled with pure love. Her life would become stale and loveless again— It might have been sinful, but it was true love. God, grant me the strength to endure being away from him. No, it's best if Sadan doesn't come tonight. It's best if I don't see him. Who knows if I will be able to hold myself back when I see him? But if he comes, I will speak to him from my heart. I will try to save him from drowning in this ocean of lies.

In the meanwhile, Suman saw Vitthaldas getting out of a rented carriage. Her heart began to race.

In a few minutes, Vitthaldas came upstairs. He said—Arrey, you haven't packed yet.

Suman—I am ready.

Vitthaldas—Aren't you going to pack your bedding?

Suman—I won't take anything from this place. I want to forget all this.

Vitthaldas—What will happen to all of this stuff?

Suman—Sell it and give the money to charity.

Vitthaldas—Good, I will lock the place up. Come, the carriage is waiting downstairs.

Suman—I can't leave before ten o'clock. I have to say goodbye to my admirers tonight. I have to listen to the things they say, and I have some things to tell them as well. Why don't you wait on the terrace until then. Don't worry, I am ready to go with you.

Vitthaldas didn't like this at all, but he decided to be patient. He went upstairs and began pacing on the open roof.

It was seven o'clock, but Sadan still hadn't arrived. She waited for him until eight o'clock. After that, she gave up hope. This was the first time he hadn't come since they had started seeing each other. Suman felt like she was lost in a desert. Her heart palpitated with a strong but simple, painful but beautiful longing. She asked herself—What could be keeping him? What omen has scared him?

At eight o'clock, Chimmanlal arrived. As soon as she saw his buggy, she went out onto the balcony. Sethji climbed the stairs with great difficulty and was panting when he reached upstairs. He said—Where are you my goddess? Why did you send the buggy back this morning? Have I done something wrong?

Suman—I am out on the balcony. It was warm inside. I had a headache today. That's why I didn't feel like going out.

Chimmanlal—Why didn't you send Hiriya to see me? I could have had the doctor prescribe something for you. He has some wonderful medicines.

Sethji sat down on the chair, but the three-legged chair collapsed, and Sethji fell over, face down on the ground like a bundle of clothes. He mustered up enough strength to say 'Arrey' and then he couldn't say another word. His body had defeated his consciousness.

Suman was afraid that he had suffered a serious injury. She got a lantern to examine him more closely, but she couldn't keep herself from laughing. Sethji was lying incapacitated on the floor as if he had fallen off a cliff. Prostrate on the floor, he said—Dear God, I think I have broken my back. Go call my driver. I want to go home.

Suman—Have you hurt yourself badly? You pulled the chair out. Had you left it against the wall, you wouldn't have fallen. Please forgive me, I should have warned you about the chair. But you didn't even try to stop yourself. You just fell down.

Chimmanlal—My back might be broken and you are cracking jokes.

Suman—It's not my fault. If you were thinner, I could have picked you up myself. If you try to support some of your own weight, I might be able to help you up.

Chimmanlal—Now it will be impossible for me to get home. *Hai*! I must have come in at an inauspicious moment. I won't be able to make it down those stairs without dying. Baiji, what did I do to deserve this?

Suman—I am so sorry.

Chimmanlal—Please, don't pretend to be hurt. You planned it so that I would fall.

Suman—Why should I be angry with you? It was an accident. And even if I were angry with you, your poor back didn't do anything to me.

Chimmanlal—There is a curse on all who come here.

Suman—Sethji, there is no reason to get so upset. And suppose I did plan it so that you would fall, so what?

In the meanwhile, Vitthaldas had come downstairs. The Sethji was quite shocked to see him, as if he had been hit by pail of water.

Vitthaldas kept himself from laughing and said—Tell me Sethji, how did you happen upon this place? I am quite surprised to see you here.

Chimmanlal—Don't ask me any questions now. May there be a curse on me if I ever come here again. You have to help me get downstairs somehow.

Vitthaldas supported him by one of his arms, and the driver held him by the waist. In this way, they managed to get him downstairs and put him in his buggy.

Vitthaldas went back upstairs and said—The driver is still waiting downstairs. It's ten o'clock. Don't delay any further.

Suman said—I still have one more task to perform. Pandit Dinanath should be on his way. Let me finish things with him, and then I will go. Please bear with me.

As soon as Vitthaldas went back upstairs, Pandit Dinanath arrived. He was wearing a Benarasi turban and a shimmering silk jacket. His black-trimmed fine *dhoti* and polished black pumps suited him well.

Suman said—Come in, my lord and bless me.

Dinanath—Blessings! May your youth be long, may you capture many blind and wealthy men, forever and always.

Suman—What kept you yesterday? I kept my dancers waiting for you till quite late last night.

Dinanath—Don't ask. I got stuck in a heated debate yesterday. Doctor Shyamacharan and Prabhakar Rao dragged me to a colloquium on *Swaraj*. They were ranting and raving all night. Everyone wanted me to say a few words. I said, 'Do you take me for a fool?' I finally got away. That's why I couldn't come.

Suman—It's been several days since I asked you to varnish the doors. You said that you couldn't find varnish anywhere. Look, I bought a bottle of varnish today. Be sure to do it tomorrow.

Pandit Dinanath was sitting against a pillow. His forehead was directly beneath the shelf with the bottle of varnish. Suman picked up the bottle, and no one knows how the top fell off the bottle and Panditji was covered in varnish. It was as if he had fallen into a vat of syrup. He leaped to his feet. He took off his turban and began to wipe his forehead with his handkerchief.

Suman spoke—I don't know what happened. Perhaps the bottle was broken. Now all the varnish is wasted.

Dinanath—You are worried about your varnish! All my clothes are drenched. Now it will be impossible to get back home.

Suman—Who could possibly see you at this hour? You can sneak out quietly.

Dinanath—Please, just stop. You have ruined my clothes and now you want to offer me advice? I won't be able to clean these.

Suman—Do you think that I spilled it on purpose?

Dinanath—Who knows what was going on in your head?

Suman—Fine, leave. I spilled it on purpose.

Dinanath—Well, What did I say? You can spill some more if you like.

Suman—Your clothes must be expensive. Here is some money for you.

Dinanath—Why are you so angry, *Sarkar*? I was just saying that you probably did me a favour by spilling varnish all over me.

Suman—You're saying that as if you are doing me a big favour.

Dinanath—Suman, don't embarrass me.

Suman—You are getting all upset about a few ruined clothes. So much for your love. And I am tired of listening to your stories over and over again. Now the secret's out. I am no longer under your spell. You have awakened me at just the right moment. Now do me a favour and go home. Don't come back here again. I have no use for yes-men like you.

Vitthaldas observed the whole scene from upstairs. He knew that the performance was over now. He went downstairs. Dinanath took one look at him and recoiled with shocked. He picked up his cane and went downstairs quickly.

After a while, Suman descended from her quarters wearing only a bright sari; there weren't even any bracelets on her wrists. She looked sad, not because she was leaving this luxury behind, but because she had come to such a pass. There was no impropriety in her sorrow, only a kind of temperance. This wasn't the shadow of passionate sorrow that falls on an intoxicated visage. There was only resignation and thoughtfulness.

Vitthaldas locked up the place and sat on the coachbox of the carriage. The carriage left.

All the shops in the bazaar were closed, but the streets were still alive. Suman peeped out the window. She saw a beautiful chain of lanterns in front of her. But the string of lights moved farther away as the carriage approached them. They would reach individual streetlights soon enough, but that chain of lights kept slipping away like her dreams.

The carriage was moving fast. Suman's destiny took off with the same speed, like a boat in the ocean of her thoughts; it shook, wavered, and eventually became entangled in the constellations as it moved forward.

23

W<small>HEN</small> S<small>ADAN WENT</small> home the next day, he saw the bracelet on his aunt's wrist. He was so embarrassed that he could only stare at the ground. He ate his breakfast quickly and left. He thought to himself—how did she ever get that bracelet back?

Is it possible that Suman sent it back here? How did she know whose bracelet it was? I didn't even tell her where I lived. It's possible that it's a different bracelet of the same style, but it could never have been made so quickly. Suman must have had me followed and returned the bracelet to my aunt.

Sadan deliberated this extensively, but he always came to the same conclusion. He thought some more—fine, let's suppose that she knows where I live. How dare she return to them something that I gave to her? This is treachery. She's betrayed me.

If Suman knows about my background, then she must think me a fraud, a hypocrite, and a cheat. And if she returned the bracelet to my aunt, she must also think me a thief.

That evening, Sadan couldn't muster up enough courage to go see Suman—how can I go there now that she thinks that I am a thief, a traitor? His heart was heavy, but he couldn't bear to sit at home. By evening, he was quite depressed. He was like a man recovering from an illness, who is sad and laconic, who doesn't want to speak to anyone, for whom each step is like climbing a mountain so he doesn't move once he has sat down.

In the end he became restless. On the eighth day, he saddled up his horse and went to see Suman. He wanted to explain everything to her— how can I hide something from the woman I love! I will fold my hands and say, I may be bad, I may be good, but whatever I am, Sarkar, I am still your servant. You can punish me however you see fit, as I stand here with my head bowed before you. I stole, I lied, but I did it all for your love. Forgive me.

Morality, wisdom, or conscience cannot overcome lust. Its intoxication renders us entirely helpless.

Impatiently, he left at five o'clock, and he wandered around until he reached the bank of the river. The cool, light breeze felt good against his burning body, and the fish jumping out of the clean, dark, golden waters seemed to him like the seductive eyes of a beautiful woman sparkling beneath her veil.

Sadan alighted and sat down on the riverbank; he was absorbed in the idyllic scene. Suddenly, he saw a *sadhu* with matted locks walking towards him from the shade of the trees. He had rosaries around his neck and his eyes were bloodshot. Instead of the brilliance of knowledge and meditation, his face exuded a kind of simplicity and compassion. As he came up to him, Sadan got up and offered his respects.

The sadhu grabbed him by the wrist as if he knew him well and said—Sadan. I have wanted to talk to you for several days now. I need to tell you something for your own good. You must stop going to see Sumanbai, or you will be completely ruined. Do you know who she is? In the stupor of love, you cannot see her flaws. You think that she loves you. But you are mistaken. How can a woman who has forsaken her own husband continue to love others? You were going to see her just now. Listen to the advice of a saint and go home. That's the best thing for you to do.

The sadhu left the way he had come, and before Sadan had a chance to ask him any questions, he had vanished.

Sadan thought—who was this great soul? How does he know who I am? How does he know my secrets? Partly because of the silence around him, partly because of his state of mind, and partly because of his sudden arrival and his insights, the sadhu seemed like an oracle. Sadan feared some predestined calamity. He couldn't go see Suman now. He got back on his horse and went home, thinking about this strange encounter all the way back.

Ever since Subhadra had suspected Sadan of taking her bracelet, Padamsingh had been angry with her. That was why Subhadra no longer felt comfortable in her own home. Sharmaji was also concerned about finding a way to send Sadan back to his parents. And even Sadan was becoming increasingly uncomfortable, staying on. He wanted to go home as well, but no one was willing to broach the subject. Next day, however, a letter from Pandit Madansingh arrived, solving everyone's problems. He had written that arrangements for Sadan's wedding were underway. Sadan and Subhadra were to come at once.

Subhadra was ecstatic at the news. She thought—there will be visitors for a month or two, there will be music, and the days will pass easily. She couldn't keep her joy to herself. And when Sharmaji saw her insensitivity, he became even more irritated. He thought—she doesn't think about anything other than her own happiness. She will be back here in a few months, but look at how happy she is for the moment.

Sadan made preparations to leave. Sharmaji had thought he would surely want to stay longer, but no such thing happened.

It was eight o'clock now. The train left at two o'clock every day, so Sharmaji decided not to go to the courthouse. He went inside several times, helplessly in love, but he never even got a chance to speak to Subhadra. She was absorbed in packing her clothes and jewellery and in braiding her hair. Some of her jewellery was packed away, and the maid was cleaning the rest. The paandaan was being washed. Women from the neighbourhood were visiting. Subhadra was so happy, she had no time to eat. She made puris and sent them to the table for Sadan and Sharmaji.

Things went on like this until it was one o'clock. Jeetan had brought the buggy around to the front door. Sadan put his trunk and his bedding in it. At that moment, Subhadra thought of Sharmaji, so she said to the maid—Go and find him. Call him for me.

She went outside to look for him. She looked in his room and downstairs, but Sharmaji was nowhere to be found. Subhadra became upset. She said—I won't go until he comes for me.

But Sharmaji hadn't gone anywhere. He was merely sitting on the roof. When the clock struck one and Subhadra still hadn't come out of the house, he got annoyed and went inside. He said to Subhadra—What are you still doing here? It's one o'clock.

Subhadra began to cry. And as he looked at her, Sharmaji's stern demeanour evaporated. He regretted being so bitter. He wiped Subhadra's tears; he put his arm around her and took her to the buggy.

When they finally arrived at the station, the train was just about to leave. Sadan ran and got into his boxcar. Subhadra had hardly climbed on when the train started moving. She stood near the window and watched Sharmaji. She didn't move until he disappeared from view.

The train arrived at its destination that evening. Madansingh had brought a horse and a palanquin with him to the station. Sadan ran to his father and touched his feet.

As they got closer to the village, Sadan became more excited; and when it was still half a mile away and it was difficult for the horse to run on the edge of the rice paddies, he got down and started running towards the village. Today, his village appeared lonely, quiet, deserted. The sun had set. The peasants were shouting at their oxen, leading them back from the fields. Sadan didn't say a word to anyone; he went straight to his mother and touched her feet. His mother hugged him and gave him her blessings.

Bhama—Where is she?

Sadan—She's on her way. I ran through the fields.

Bhama—Have you had your fill of your aunt and uncle?

Sadan—Why?

Bhama—I can see it on your face?

Sadan—I know. I've got fat.

Bhama—Liar. Your aunt mustn't have fed you well.

Sadan—She's not like that. I was more comfortable there than I was here. They have very rich milk there.

Bhama—Then why were you asking for money?

Sadan—I was testing your love. In all the days that I was gone, I only asked for twenty-five rupees! I got seven hundred from uncle. He also bought me a horse for four hundred rupees. He had fancy clothes made for me so that I could walk through the city like a nobleman. In the mornings, aunt would make fresh halva and I would get a seer of milk. There were dried fruits and sweets in the afternoon. I will never forget how happy I was living there. I thought to myself, I have enjoyed all the things that I could afford on my own, so why miss this opportunity for lack of money—I indulged every desire.

Bhama no longer understood the way her son spoke. She could sense a kind of city-ness in his speech. Sadan told her all about his city life with a characteristically youthful enthusiasm. Bhama's simple heart warmed towards Subhadra.

Next day, the respected members of the village community were invited for a feast, and Sadan's engagement ceremony commenced.

Sadan's desire and longing were now so strong that even the thought of the rigid religious shackles of marriage did not worry him. The love that he had felt for Suman was born of desire. Even though Suman had lived in his heart, she could not have become his partner in life. If Sadan had Kubera's wealth, he would have handed it over to Suman. He could offer her all the happiness in his life, but he could never let her see his pain, his misfortune, his struggles, or his desperation. He could enjoy the bliss of comfort with her, but not the solace of pain. Suman didn't have that kind of fidelity that love requires. Now he would be free of the web of that false love. Now there would be no need for disguises. Now he could behold love in its true form and display that true love for others. And in marriage he would acquire that priceless thing, which he would never have been able to find with Suman. These thoughts made Sadan covet his new love even more. He was only worried about what would happen if his fiancée was not attractive. Beauty and elegance are natural qualities. Personality is an acquired characteristic; education and intelligent conversation can improve it easily. Sadan decided to ask the barber sent by his in-laws about these things. He got him drunk and fed him many sweets. He even gave him one of his own dhotis. Intoxicated, the headman sang a lengthy paean to the young woman, and he drew such a beautiful picture of her that Sadan was no longer worried. The picture resembled Suman quite a bit. And so, Sadan was even more excited about meeting his bride for the first time.

24

It is true that God provides for everyone in some way or the other. But Pandit Umanath seemed to be enjoying his worldly life without any such assistance. His was a celestial condition. He had neither cows nor buffaloes, yet rivers of butter and milk flowed through his house and even though he himself was not a farmer, the grain containers in his house were always full. If a fish was caught, a goat slaughtered, a mango picked, a festival celebrated anywhere in the village, Umanath would get his share without asking. Amola was a large village. There must have been two and half or three thousand people in the village, and still nothing was done without Umanath's consent. If women wanted jewellery made, they would tell Umanath. And the weddings of young men and women were all arranged through Umanath. Land sales, mortgages, and deeds would all be written with Umanath's counsel. All legal business was filed with him, and the ironic part of it all was that his influence and his honour were not the result of his refinement. Whenever he was with the villagers, he was dull and dry. He would get right to the point and didn't know how to be diplomatic, but people drank in his criticism like milk. No one could describe it precisely, but there was something magical about him. Some said that he was naturally gifted and others that luck favoured him, but I think that it was because he had unique insight into human nature. He knew when to bend and when to be strong. With the villagers, he got things done by being stern, and with the officers, by bowing. In matters of law and money, from the servants up to the tax collector, everyone treated him with respect. He had a horoscope prepared for the tax collector, and he regularly informed the deputy of the progress of his destiny. Record keepers and court officials did not need invitations to be his house guests. He would provide magical charms to some, read passages of the *Bhagvad Gita* to others, and for those who didn't place much faith in such things, he fed them sweet pickles and *navratan* chutney and kept them happy. The police commissioner considered him his right hand man. Panditji could get things done where the commissioner was unable. Was there any reason, then, that the villagers should not have worshipped him?

Umanath loved his sister Gangajali, but a few days after she arrived, she discovered that her brother's love was nothing compared to her sister-in-law's contempt. Umanath regretted ever having brought his sister home. In order to please his wife, he would agree to everything she said with a 'yes dear'. What right did Gangajali have to wear new clothes? It didn't matter how Shanta had been raised, what right did she have to compare herself to Umanath's daughters? Umanath listened to his wife's jealous taunts and kept quiet. To make matters worse, whenever Gangajali became angry, she took it out on her brother. She thought that he was putting her down in order to appease his wife—and even if he scolds her, she will probably still be angry at me. Whenever Umanath got a chance, he would take Gangajali aside and try to calm her down. But first of all, Jahnvi never gave him a chance to talk to her, and secondly, Gangajali was no longer comforted by his sympathetic words.

And in this way, a year passed. Worry, concern, and desperation had made Gangajali ill. She began running a fever. First Umanath tried ordinary medicines, but when they had no effect, he became anxious. One day, when his wife had gone to see a neighbour, Umanath went into his sister's room. She was lying unconscious, her bedclothes were tattered, and her sari was threadbare. Shanta was sitting next to her and fanning her. Umanath wept when he saw this pathetic scene—this is my sister, who once had two maids to attend to her every need, and now this? He felt extremely guilty at his own helplessness. He sat at the head of the bed and said with tears in his eyes— Sister, it was a mistake to bring you here. I didn't know that it would come to this. I will get a doctor immediately. God willing, you will be well soon.

In the meantime, Jahnvi had returned. She heard what Umanath said and taunted—Oh sure, run! Go and get the doctor, otherwise Shanta will become an orphan! When I had fever that lasted a month, you never called the doctor. Maybe if I had wrapped myself up and stayed in bed all day, too, you would have been concerned about me, but I have never had the luxury of lying around. Who would have ground the flour? Is happiness too much for me to ask of fate?

Umanath gave up. He didn't have the courage to go to the doctor. He knew that if he called the doctor, Gangajali would not be able to live out in peace the two or three months left to her.

Gangajali's condition worsened day by day, until finally the fever made her delirious. Everyone lost hope that she would survive. How could a belly that could not digest tapioca handle barley? In the end, her diseased body could not bear this suffering any longer. Six months of illness ended with a mournful eclipse.

Shanta was now absolutely alone. She had written two letters to Suman, but she hadn't received any reply. She thought that her sister had disowned her. There are no friends in times of tragedy. While Gangajali was alive, Shanta could hide her face in the folds of her sari and weep. Now she no longer had even that support—like a cane continually slipping from the hands of a blind man. For now, Shanta hid and cried in the corners of her room, but there was a huge difference between this and her mother's sari. One was a soothing ocean of water; the other, a desert.

Shanta could not find peace anywhere. Her heart burnt constantly like a flame; she considered her aunt and uncle to be her mother's killers. While Gangajali was alive, Shanta made every effort to save her from their harsh words; she would run at the slightest gesture from her aunt, so that she wouldn't have an excuse to complain about Shanta to her mother. Once, Gangajali dropped the container of butter. Shanta told her aunt that she had dropped it. She had to bear many insults because of it, but she knew that her mother's heart wouldn't have been able to bear the wounds of sarcasm.

But now, Shanta was no longer afraid of these things. Now that she was alone, she became rebellious. She was no longer as patient as she had once been and would get angry very easily. She even began responding with insults of her own. She had readied herself to endure the worst. She listened to her uncle, but never to her aunt, and she answered her cousins with viciousness. She was like a cow that grazes on other people's land, unafraid of death.

And so another year passed. Umanath tried very hard to make arrangements for her wedding, but nothing could be managed within the small amount of money that he was willing to spend. He wheedled two hundred rupees out of his friends at the police station and the collector's office. But who could find a groom for so little? If Jahnvi had her way, she would have married Shanta off to a beggar so that she could be rid of her, but for the first time in his life Umanath stood up to her and set out to look for a worthy husband. Gangajali's sacrifice had emboldened him.

25

EVEN PUBLIC INSTITUTIONS need influential men. Even though Vitthaldas had no shortage of followers, they were mostly simple men. Important men generally avoided him. Padamsingh breathed new life into the organization as soon as he became involved in it. This drying riverbed soon overflowed with water. He began to be talked about in important circles. People had a newfound confidence in his leadership.

But Padamsingh didn't come alone. Usually, even when we believe a cause is important, we are afraid to get involved, afraid of losing face, so we await the approval of important men. As soon as someone leads the way, we become certain of ourselves, and we no longer fear ridicule. Sometimes we are even afraid to be alone in our own homes, but when we find someone to accompany us, we can stay in jungles fearlessly. Professor Ramesh Datt, Lala Bhagatram, and Mister Rustambhai used to assist Padamsingh secretly. Now they did so openly. The number of sympathizers grew daily.

Vitthaldas did not believe in flowery rhetoric when it came to matters of reform; as a result, his speeches were never very interesting. People who had always been disinterested found his caterwauling unbearable but Vitthaldas did not worry about such things.

Padamsingh was a driven man. Zealously, he took up the movement to remove courtesans from the center of the town. Some members of the municipality were followers of Vitthaldas. But they were not optimistic about the project's viability. The issue itself was so complex that people were afraid to even think about it. They would argue—this resolution will cause chaos in the city. Countless nobles, colonial officials, and merchants have visited this love-market. Some as customers, and some as admirers—who would dare stand up to all of them? The members of the municipality were like puppets in their hands.

Padamsingh repeatedly met with each member to draw his attention to the resolution. Prabhakar Rao's biting editorials also helped him greatly. Pamphlets were printed and lectures were organized to raise public awareness. Ramesh Datt and Padamsingh had experience in these things. They took responsibility for all the details. Now the movement had a more organized look to it.

Even though Padamsingh had drafted the resolution, the more he thought about it, the more confused about the issue he became. He wasn't convinced that evicting the courtesans would produce the desired effect. It was possible that it would make matters worse instead of improving them. Honesty is the best cure for pessimism. It's impossible to succeed without it. Sometimes thinking about the issue demoralized him. But, since he was now a proponent of the resolution, he couldn't reveal to anyone that he still had his doubts. Being a social reformer in public was no problem, but in private, with his friends or other gentlemen, he had a hard time remaining firm in his principles. Sometimes it was incredibly difficult for Sharmaji to face them. Someone would say—Why are you doing all of this? Have you been listening to Vitthaldas, too? Enjoy your self. Why do you waste your time with such matters? Someone else would say—It seems, my friend, as if a woman has scorned you, and so you've decided to go after the courtesans. It was an exercise in futility to talk about ideals and reforms to such friends.

And while giving lectures, when Sharmaji turned to emotional subjects, he would try to paint a touching scene, but he wouldn't find the words, and even when he found the words, he was embarrassed to say them. Actually, he wasn't much versed in this art. When he thought about his dispassionate speeches, it seemed to him that his heart was devoid of love and affection.

After he finished a speech, Sharmaji was not as interested in knowing the effect it had on the audience, as he was in knowing whether his speech was considered elegant, sound, and powerful.

But despite these problems, the movement grew larger each day. And the success made Sharmaji's enthusiasm and confidence grow.

There were still two months to go before Sadansingh's wedding. With his wife gone, Sharmaji devoted all his energies to the movement. His heart was not in his legal work. Even in court, he worried about the same things. Such intense meditation on a single subject cannot but endear a heart towards it. Slowly, this endearment dawned in Sharmaji's heart.

But as the wedding drew close, Sharmaji became was increasingly anxious. He worried—my brother will certainly ask me to invite courtesans, and then what will I do? The party will be lifeless without a performance. People come from afar just to see these dances; they will be annoyed if they don't see a dance, and my brother will be upset. What am I to do? I should stop my brother from continuing this awful custom! But how? It is inappropriate to talk about justice and ideals before one's elders. My brother has grand plans; he will be hurt if they are not realized. But whatever happens, my duty is to uphold my beliefs.

Even though there were more people who would be offended by his beliefs and few who would be pleased, still, Sharmaji thought it best to keep the minority happy. He decided that he wouldn't invite the courtesans—if I cannot reform my own family, then it would be hypocritical to try to reform others.

Having made up his mind, Sharmaji began putting together the things necessary for the wedding. He didn't think it right to economize at times like this. And he wanted other excesses in the wedding to balance the deficit of the dance, so that he couldn't be accused of being cheap.

One day, Vitthaldas said to him—How much have you spent on preparations for the wedding?

Sharmaji—That will be worked out only after I return.

Vitthaldas—Still, it can't be less than two thousand.

Sharmaji—Yes, perhaps it is even more than that.

Vitthaldas—You have wasted all that money. Wouldn't it have been better if you had spent it on a worthy cause? If a progressive man like you is going to throw money away like this, how can we expect others to behave differently?

Sharmaji—I don't agree. A man who has been blessed by God should spend money openly during such festivities. Well, not by getting into debt or by selling one's house, but by staying within one's means. There are only a few opportunities to display the depth of one's feelings.

Vitthaldas—Do you think that Doctor Shyamacharan can afford to spend ten thousand rupees?

Sharmaji—Even more than that.

Vitthaldas—But when his son was just married, he spent a lot less on music and dancing.

Sharmaji—Yes. He might have spent less when it came to music and dancing, but he made up for it and spent even more on the dinner party. And what was the result of his economizing? The money that would have gone to poor musicians, florists, and the men who prepare the fireworks has ended up in the hands of the 'Murray Company' and the 'White Way Company.' I don't call this economizing. I call it injustice.

26

It was nine o'clock at night. Padamsingh was sitting with his brother discussing the wedding plans. The wedding procession would leave tomorrow. The *shehnai* played at the door and there was singing going on inside.

Madansingh—Will the cars you hired reach Amola by tomorrow evening?

Padamsingh—They should get there by the afternoon. Amola is near Mount Vindhyachal. I made sure that they left this afternoon.

Madansingh—So what will we have to take with us?

Padamsingh—We will need to take some food. I have made arrangements for everything else.

Madansingh—How much did you spend on the dance? There are two troupes, right?

Padamsingh knew that there was no way to avoid talking about the dance any more. His head bent low in shame when he heard the question. Meekly, he said—I didn't make arrangements for the dance.

Madansingh was shocked, as if someone had punched him. He said—Wonderful! You managed to sink the boat after all. Well, then what did you get for the wedding party? Could you not find the time or were you just afraid to spend the money? That's why I wrote to you four days in advance. A man who invites a holy man to dinner always keeps something to offer him as *dakshina* or parting gift. If you were concerned about the expenses you should have told me straight out and I would have sent you the money. Thank God, I am not wanting for anything right now. Tell me, what can we possibly do now? You have blackened all of our faces. You are going to a respectable man's home; what will he think? He has probably invited relatives from afar; people will have come a long way to join in the bridal procession; what will they all think? Dear God!

Munshi Bejnath, who owned 50 per cent of the land in the village, looked at Madansingh with empathy and said—They won't just think it, *Janab*, they will say it to your faces and insult you. Everyone will say that you have fat wallets but small hearts. And they will gossip about you everywhere. What's a groom's party without a dance? I have never heard of such a thing myself. Perhaps Bhaiya just forgot about it, or perhaps the wedding preparations have not been managed properly.

Padamsingh responded nervously—It's not that ...

Madansingh—Then what is it? Maybe you thought that you were going to have to pay for everything, but I can honestly say that's not why I wrote to you. I don't want charity.

Padamsingh was deeply hurt by his brother's harsh words. Tears welled up in his eyes. He said—Bhaiya, for God's sake, please don't talk like that. I would gladly give up my life if it could be of some use to you. I have always tried to help you in any way that I could. I only did what I did because people in the city have begun to disapprove of this custom of having dances. The educated classes are speaking out in opposition to it and I have joined their ranks. I couldn't go against my principles.

Madansingh—Oh, so that's what it is. Well, at least people's eyes have opened. I think that it's an awful tradition myself, but I don't want to be a non-conformist. I will stop when everyone else does. Why should I be a trendsetter? I have only one son, and I want his wedding to be just as I have dreamed it to be. After the wedding, I will also take up your cause. But let me walk my old walk for now, and if it's not too much trouble, can you take the morning train tomorrow, settle everything, and head for Amola from there? I am only asking you to go because the people in the city know you. Anyone else would be robbed blind.

Padamsingh bent his head in worry. Seeing him silent, Madansingh furrowed his brow and said—Why are you quiet? Don't you want to go?

Padamsingh replied wretchedly—Bhaiya, if you will forgive me …

Madansingh—No, no. I won't impose on you. Don't go if you don't want to. Munshi Bejnath, I know that it will be some trouble for you, but will you go on my behalf?

Bejnath—I have no objections.

Madansingh—You can leave for Amola from the city. You will be doing me a big favour.

Bejnath—There's no need to worry. I will take care of everything.

For a while, the three men sat in silence. Madansingh couldn't understand why his brother was being so stubborn. Bejnath worried that he might have offended Padamsingh by supporting Madansingh, and Padamsingh remained quiet, fearful of his brother's ire. He could barely lift his head. There was no way out for him. On the one hand, he would upset his brother, and on the other hand, he would be forced to sacrifice his principles and morality. He was caught between a dark precipice and a steep hill. Ultimately, he managed a few words—Bhaiya, you have forgiven me on many occasions. Please forgive my last stubborn insistence. I don't understand why you insist on having courtesans at the wedding when you know that the custom is so wrong.

Madansingh was annoyed—You talk like you weren't born and bred in this country, like you are a real foreigner. This isn't the only bad custom we have; there are several that are followed even though people know they are wrong. Who thinks that cursing is a good thing? Who likes dowries? But people point fingers when you don't follow the custom of the world. If we don't have courtesans, people will say that we are just stingy. We will lose honour. No one will notice my principles.

Padamsingh said—Fine, but if you were to take the same money and spend it on something else, no one could call you a miser, now, could they? You want to hire two dance troupes. These days people really take notice of the wedding ceremonies; it will cost you at least three hundred rupees. What if you spent five hundred rupees instead on buying blankets for the poor of Amola? At least two hundred men will give you their blessings and as long as those blankets remain, they will sing your praises. If you don't like this idea, you could spend two hundred rupees and build a working well in Amola. You will become a legend. I can make arrangements for the money.

Madansingh's argument about being insulted couldn't stand up to these suggestions. He was still thinking of a response when Bejnath who, though afraid of alienating Padamsingh, still desired to show off the magnitude of his intellect said—Bhaiya, there is a proper occasion for everything. You should give gifts when it is the time to give gifts, have a dance when it is appropriate to have a dance. No one appreciates bad timing. And it would be another thing entirely if we were talking about the educated people from the city. If you offer blankets to the uneducated peasants from the village, they will look at you and laugh.

Madansingh had been quiet, but Munshi Bejnath's explanation animated him. He looked at him gratefully and said—Yes, of course. Who likes to hear funereal dirges in the spring? Bad timing ruins everything. That's why I say you should leave in the morning and hire those two dance troupes.

Padamsingh thought—these men will do whatever they want, but let's see what arguments they use to justify their decision. Bhaiya trusts Munshi Bejnath completely. This last fact worried him a little. So, without hesitation, he said—But how can you say that a wedding is just a celebration? I think that there is no better opportunity for generosity and kindness. Marriage is a religious ritual, a spiritual vow. When we enter into marriage, when the burden of life and its worries falls upon our heads, when we bow our heads before our worldly obligations, when the shackles of duty tighten around our ankles, we should proceed with care. Are we so heartless that when a young man from our family is entering into something so important and serious we are off celebrating? He will be crushed under the weight of his obligations while we enjoy ourselves in the festivities. Why should we follow this backward custom just because it persists today? We are educated; at least we should know better than to let the pleasure of fools guide us in our moral decisions.

Madansingh became frustrated again. He knew that Padamsingh's argument was justified, but he also knew that justice, truth, and principles all meant nothing when it came to tradition. He suspected that Bejnath had been rendered speechless, but Munshiji was not ready to admit defeat yet. He said—Brother, you are a lawyer. I don't have the skill to argue with you. But I do know that there is only shame in destroying the traditions that have been handed down from our ancestors, whether they are proper or not. After all, our ancestors were not complete fools. They must have thought about these customs before passing them on.

Madansingh hadn't thought of this argument. He was very pleased. He looked at Bejnath with new respect and said—Truly. The customs that we have inherited all have some hidden logic behind them, even if we no longer understand them today. These days, people with modern notions consider it their personal mission to do away with customs. They don't understand the things that stare them in the face. They don't understand that all the knowledge, wisdom, education, and manners that we possess have been handed down to us from our ancestors. Some say—What is the point of the sacred thread? Some are bent on eliminating traditional education, and some are even convinced that the lower castes should be treated like Kshatriyas. Some are singing the praises of widow remarriage, and there are even fools who want to do away with the system of caste and kinship entirely. This is not for me. People who want to accept these things are free to do so. I prefer the traditional way of doing things. If I live long enough, I will see the consequences of these European ideas. Our ancestors knew the value of agriculture, but these days, people mimic the Europeans and race to put up factories and machines. Just wait and see. There will come a time when the Europeans will come to their senses and will replace their mills and machines with fields. Which is better—being a slave to a factory or being an independent farmer? And then these countries starve because they cannot import enough food. Countries that follow such backward ideals cannot possibly become models for us. These bastions of technology and industry will only last as long as there are weak and feeble races in the world. The Europeans force cheap goods down their throats and live in luxury. But as soon as these races awaken, the superiority of Europe will come to an end. I won't say that we have nothing to learn from the Europeans. Of course not. They are the lords of the world today and have many admirable traits. Take their good qualities and avoid their bad ones. But our customs and traditions are appropriate for our situation. There is no reason to change or get rid of them.

Madansingh spoke these words with pride, as if he were some learned scholar offering an original argument, but in reality these were things that he had heard before, whose meaning he didn't fully understand himself. Padamsingh took these arguments quite seriously, but he didn't respond to them. He was afraid that the matter would get out of control if he disagreed. When a debate begins to look like an argument, it always misses its target.

In the end, modesty and decorum have more influence than even a strong man. So he said—Then I will go myself. Don't trouble Munshi Bejnath. If he goes, a lot of things will be left unfinished here. Come Munshiji, let's you and I go outside. I have some things to discuss with you.

Madansingh—So, why don't you talk here? If you want, I will leave.

Padamsingh—No, no. It's not that. I just want to talk to Munshiji to allay my fears. So, Bhaiya, tell me. How many people from Amola will we be entertaining? Shall we say about a thousand? Of these, how many will be peasants and how many *zamindars*?

Bejnath—There will be more peasants, but there will be at least two to three hundred zamindars.

Padamsingh—Fine. Do you agree that peasants will be happier receiving blankets and dhotis than watching a dance?

Bejnath had many arguments left in his arsenal. He said—No, I don't agree. There are many peasants who would never dream of taking handouts. They will come to see the festivities, and if the festivities are not entertaining, they will return to their homes disappointed.

Padamsingh's head began to hurt. The chain of Socratic questions that he had prepared in his mind had broken down. He realized that Munshiji was on his guard. Now he would have to come up with a different strategy. He said—Do you agree that the bazaar is filled only with goods for which there are customers, and that the supply of goods depends on the demand of the customers?

Bejnath—Yes. I have no problem with that.

Padamsingh—Then it follows that goods enter the market only because there are customers for it. If no one eats meat, then why would anyone need to butcher a goat?

Bejnath knew that he was being taken along a different track, but he hadn't yet figured out where it would lead. Nervously, he said—Yes, that's true.

Padamsingh—Then, if you accept that, you will have to agree that the people who hire courtesans, who provide for their comfort and allow them to live their lives in luxury, are just as guilty as that butcher who puts a knife to a goat's throat. Would I have become a lawyer if I had never seen other lawyers driving around splendidly in their buggies?

Bejnath laughed and said—Brother, you make your argument in a very roundabout way, but what you say is true.

Padamsingh—In which case why is it hard to understand that there are thousands of women who can be seen sitting in their balconies every day, who have sacrificed their honour and their chastity, and whose lives we have destroyed? Thousands of families are being sucked into this vortex of sin everyday and they will pull us in with them when God passes judgment. How can it be right to keep a custom that gives rise to so many evil things?

Madansingh was listening to him carefully. He didn't have the kind of higher education that would have told him that man's desire for free will and independence makes him an enemy of social bonds and traditional principles. No, he was a man of common sense. He couldn't go on arguing once he was convinced of something. He smiled and said to Munshi Bejnath—Well, Munshiji. What do you say now? Is there any way out of this problem?

Bejnath laughed and said—I don't see any way out.

Madansingh—Well, find a loophole.

Bejnath—If I had studied law for a few years, I would have tried that. But now I can't come up with anything. Well brother Padamsingh, what would you say if you were in my place?

Padamsingh (laughing)—I would definitely come up with something or the other, whether it made sense or not.

Madansingh—I will even go so far as to say that these dances certainly tempt men. When I was younger and I came home from a dance, I would ramble on about the courtesan's beauty and her grace for months.

Bejnath—Brother, let Padamsingh have his way and let us hand out blankets.

Madansingh—If we dig a well, we will be remembered forever. As soon as the rituals round the sacred fire are over, let us start work on the well.

27

THE RAINY SEASON had set in and dark clouds filled the skies. Pundit Umanath was standing on the bank of the Ganga near Chunargadh waiting for a boat. He had visited several villages, and he wanted to reach a village near Chunargadh before it grew dark. He had heard that there was a suitable groom in that village. Umanath had to return to Amola tonight because there had been a petty crime in his village and the constable was going to investigate it tomorrow. But the boat was still stuck on the other bank. Umanath was annoyed with the boatman, but he was even angrier with the passengers who were taking their time getting to this side of the river. They should have been racing to get to the other side so that Umanath could get across. And after he had been standing there for quite some time, Umanath called out loudly to the boatman. But his voice didn't really try to reach the boatman's ears. It played with the waves and got lost in the river.

In the meantime, Umanath spied a sadhu walking towards him. He had matted locks, a string of rosaries around his neck, a long tobacco pipe in one hand, an iron staff in the other, and a deerskin draped over his back. He came and stood on the bank of the river. He wanted to cross the river as well.

Umanath felt as if he had seen the sadhu somewhere before, but he couldn't remember where. A curtain seemed to hide the memory from him.

Suddenly, the sadhu looked over at Umanath, bowed before him and said—Maharaj! Is everything well at home? How did you happen to come by here?

The veil lifted from Umanath's mind and his memory returned. The man looked different but Umanath recognized the voice. It was Gajadhar Pande.

Ever since Suman had got married, Umanath had not been to visit her. He didn't have it in him to face her. But now, Umanath was shocked at seeing Gajadhar dressed like this. For a moment he thought he might have been mistaken. Nervously, he asked—What is your name?

Sadhu—It used to be Gajadhar Pande. Now it is Gajanand.

Umanath—Oh! That's why I couldn't recognize you. I thought I had seen you somewhere, but I must say that I am surprised to see you like this. Where is your family?

Gajanand—I have left that world of illusions.

Umanath—Where is Suman?

Gajanand—In a brothel in Dalmandi.

Umanath looked at Gajanand in amazement but Gajanand had hung his head in shame. After a moment he asked—How did it happen? It doesn't make sense.

Gajanand—The same way that it always happens in this world. My wicked cruelty and Suman's desires together destroyed both of us. Now, when I look back at what happened then, it seems as if I made an enormous mistake in marrying the daughter of a wealthy family and an even greater mistake in not giving her the respect she deserved after we were married. I was poor; that's why it was important to fill up the holes of poverty with love and devotion. But instead of that, I dealt with her mercilessly. I troubled her over every bit of food and clothing. She wasn't very good at housework and could never have been, but I made her do all the work and got upset if she was even a little tardy. Now I know that it was my fault that she left the house. I couldn't dote on her beauty and that's why Suman couldn't love me. But she was definitely devoted to me. But I was blind. A poor man becomes quite full of himself when he comes into a little wealth, and he falls into the same error when he marries a beautiful woman. That's how it was with me. I didn't trust Suman and because I couldn't say so, I hurt her with my cruelty. Now when I think back on all the awful things that I did to her, I feel so bad about the way I behaved that I want to kill myself. I am paying for that crime now. Two or three days after she left, I was still quite angry, but when the anger wore off, I couldn't stand being in that house. I never went back to it. I became a *pujari* in a temple. I was saved the trouble of making my own meals. Everyday, two or three men would come to the temple. I would read the Ramayan and other religious stories to them. Sometimes, even famous sadhus would come to the temple. That gave me a chance to discuss issues with them. In listening to their wisdom, I began to recognize my ignorance for what it was. Honestly, when I became a pujari, I didn't have even a trace of devotion in my heart. I only became a pujari because I couldn't be bothered to work and to taste the flavour of rich foods, but when I read religious texts, devotion and love began to grow in my heart and when I spoke to scholars, that devotion turned to renunciation. Now I wander from village to village helping people as much as I can. Are you coming from Benares?

Umanath—No, I am coming from the village. Suman has a younger sister and I have been looking for a husband for her.

Gajanand—This time, find a suitable man.

Umanath—There is no shortage of suitable men, but I don't have the money to afford them, do I? Didn't I do everything that I could to find Suman a good husband?

Gajanand—How much money do you need to get a suitable husband?

Umanath—The dowry will be at least a thousand rupees, and there are other expenses as well.

Gajanand—Start making preparations for the wedding. God willing, I will get you the thousand rupees. Wearing these clothes makes it quite easy to get money out of people. I now know that I can do a great deal to help people. I will see you at your home in three or four days.

The boat arrived and both got in. Gajanand began talking to the boatman, but Umanath was lost in thought. He felt responsible for what had happened to Suman.

28

PANDIT UMANATH HAD just returned after seeing Sadan and making plans for the engagement. He didn't say a word of Gajanand's offer to Jahnvi. He feared that she would want to keep the money to marry off her own daughters. His dictates never had any effect on Jahnvi. He had to give in to her every time.

He fixed the wedding on the promise of a thousand-rupee dowry. But now he was worried about finding the money to pay for the expenses for the wedding. He still needed at least another thousand rupees. He couldn't see how he would ever get that money. Still, he was happy about the fact that Shanta would be married into a good home, that she would be comfortable, and that Gangajali's soul would be pleased with his efforts.

He knew that the wedding was only three months away—hopefully, I can come up with the money by then. But if not, I will just make a scene with the wedding party. I will get upset at something or the other, and the groom's party will get annoyed and go back. I may be slandered a little, but the wedding will go through. At least Shanta will go to her new home comfortably. All I have to do is be clever while making the scene so that everyone will blame the groom's party instead of me.

It had been a week since Pandit Krishnachandra had been released from prison, but Umanath still hadn't spoken to him about his daughter's wedding. He was ashamed to speak to Krishnachandra face-to-face. There was a noticeable difference in Krishnachandra's behaviour. Instead of gravity, there was now an uninhibited arrogance. His body had withered away, but it seemed as if some strange power flowed through him. At night, he would sigh loudly and moan 'Hai! Hai!' In the middle of the night, when every corner of the house was shrouded in silence, he would toss and turn on his charpoy singing—

A fires a' burnin' the beautiful woods

And sometimes—

When wood burns it turns to coal, when coal burns, to ash.
But when a sinner like me burns he turns neither to coal nor ash!

There was a kind of restlessness in his eyes. Jahnvi couldn't stand to be around him. He scared her.

In winter, the peasants' wives would go to work in the fields. Krishnachandra would also set out for the fields and flirt with the women. Because he was a brother-in-law, he was allowed the liberty of talking to the women of the village, but his words were so bawdy and his stares so sexual that the women would hide their faces out of modesty and go and complain to Jahnvi. In truth, Krishnachandra was being consumed by sexual frustration.

There were several educated men in Amola, but Krishnachandra would not sit with them. Every night he could be seen smoking a hookah with low-class men. He would sit with them and tell them stories of his experiences in prison, a stream of vulgar expressions pouring out of his mouth.

Umanath had a great standing in his village. And so it bothered him to see his brother-in-law's behaviour and he would pray to God that he would simply leave. But even more troubling was the fact that even Shanta was afraid of her father and would think twice before going to see him. When the village women complained to Jahnvi about Krishnachandra's conduct, it hurt Shanta deeply. She couldn't understand what had happened to her father—he used to be such a sober, thoughtful, generous, and good-natured man. Now, he is completely unrecognizable. It is his body, but where is his soul?

And so, a month passed. Umanath was annoyed—His own daughter is about to be married and he is loafing around without a worry. Why should I go through all this trouble for nothing? It's not like he has tried to go out and earn any money. Instead, he is ruining my reputation as well.

29

ONE DAY, UMANATH threatened one of Krishnachandra's companions—If I ever see you sitting and smoking with him again, there is no telling what might happen. I will get each and every one of you. Umanath had connections throughout the village. Krishnachandra's friends were terrified. And the next day, when Krishnachandra went to chat with them, they said—Maharaj, don't come back here. Don't make Pandit Umanath angry with us. If he makes trouble for us, we would be better off dead.

Filled with rage, Krishnachandra went to see Umanath and said—I can tell that you don't want me here.

Umanath—It's your home, too. You can stay as long as you want, but I don't want you to sit with those lowly men and ruin both our reputations.

Krishnachandra—Then with whom should I sit? Do you think that the good people around here would want to associate with me? All of them condescend to me, and I won't tolerate that. Can you point out any among them who has a genuinely moral soul? They are all treacherous, bloodsucking whoremongers, determined to ruin the peasants. I don't consider myself beneath them. I have paid for my crimes. They are still running from their punishments, and that's the only difference between us. They commit countless crimes to a hide a single transgression, and in this respect they are actually worse criminals than me. I won't prostrate myself before these hypocrites. I only mix with people who are willing to respect me even in this condition, who don't think that they are better than me, who know that they are crows and don't pretend to be swans. If my behaviour hurts your reputation, then I won't impose myself on you.

Umanath—As God is my witness, that's not why I asked those men not to sit with you. You know that I have to deal with government officials regularly. I hate having to explain your behaviour to them.

Krishnachandra—Then you can tell them that no matter how awful Krishnachandra may be, he is still better than the likes of you. I was once a government officer and I know something about the character and conduct of such officials. They are all crooks. Krishnachandra will not take orders from villains, thieves, sinners, and immoral men.

Umanath—You may not care about these officials, but my livelihood depends on them. How can I disparage them? You were a police officer once. Don't you know that the local constable watches everything that you do? If he sees you with those rogues, he will surely report on you and we will both be ruined. Such men are true to no one.

Krishnachandra—Who is the local constable?

Umanath—Masood Alam.

Krishnachandra—Oh, it's that cheat, that bastard, that glorified scoundrel! He was head constable in my time and I saved him from going to jail once. Let him come here, and he will never forget what it means to deal with me.

Umanath—Get into trouble if you want, but please don't drag me in with you. You have nothing to lose, but I will be ruined.

Krishnachandra—Why? Because you are an honourable man and I have no place to go? Don't make me curse. Why are you bragging about your honour? You've been a middleman for the police and you still pretend that you are honourable?

Umanath—I may very well be a terrible sinner, but I have been more than generous to you not to deserve such criticism.

Krishnachandra—What have you done for me? You ruined my family. How can you say you've been 'generous' with a straight face? I have seen all I need to see of your generosity. You killed my wife. You married one of my daughters to a heaven knows what kind of scoundrel and you have turned my other daughter into a servant. You tricked my stupid wife into squandering all of our savings on that trial and then you brought her back to your home to die in misery. And now you talk of generosity!

Ingratitude hurts a proud man more than anything else. Even if he has no expectation of a reward or thanks, even if he does good just for the sake of doing good, the thought of helping someone brings with it the hope of at least being respected. Umanath thought to himself—this is a cruel world. I ran around the courts and magistrates for months for this man, I had to ingratiate myself to all kinds of lawyers, I was harassed by government officials, I wasted so much of my own money, and this is the thanks I get. For all these years I have cared for his family. I searched for a husband for Suman for months, and for months I have barely been home just so I could find a husband for Shanta. My feet are covered with blisters, and my body is wasting away trying to find money, and this is the reward that I get! Ha! Cruel world, where you can be destroyed while trying to help others get up. As he thought this, his eyes filled with tears. He said—Bhaiya, whatever I did, I did because I thought it was for the best. But I am ill-fated. If God decides that everything I touch turn to rubble, then so be it. I have stolen from you, and eaten you out of your home. Now you can punish me as you want. What else can I say?

Umanath had wanted to say—what's done is done. Now you take over and leave me alone. Make the arrangements for Shanta's wedding. But he was afraid that in his rage, Krishnachandra might actually take Shanta away. That's why he thought it best to bite his tongue. Witnessing the anger of the powerless arouses feelings of kindness in a generous man. But when a gentleman is cursed by a pauper, what can he do but keep quiet?

Umanath's restraint calmed Krishnachandra as well, but the two were no longer in a state to discuss things further. Both of them sat silently engrossed in thought, like two dogs that sit facing each other after they are done fighting. Umanath thought it best to remain quiet, lest the world think him even more heartless. Krishnachandra felt that he shouldn't have dug out these skeletons. There is a special tenderness to a soul that awakens after it has been deadened by anger. Krishnachandra began to realize what he needed to do. His anger pushed him out of his inertia. In the evening,

Krishnachandra asked Umanath—You have arranged for Shanta's wedding, haven't you?

Umanath—Yes, to Pandit Madansingh's son in Chunar.

Krishnachandra—He sounds like a wealthy man. What kind of a dowry have they settled on?

Umanath—One thousand.

Krishnachandra—We will have that much in expenses too, isn't it?

Umanath—Yes, what else.

Krishnachandra didn't know what to say. He asked—Where will the money come from?

Umanath—God will show us the way. I have a thousand rupees. I am just trying to find the other thousand.

Krishnachandra said in utter helplessness—You know that I have nothing.

As he spoke these words, tears began to stream from his eyes.

Umanath—Don't worry. I will take care of everything.

Krishnachandra—God will surely reward you well for this. Bhaiya, please don't think ill of me because of all of my shortcomings. I have not been myself lately. All that I have gone through has turned me crazy. It has torn my soul to shreds. I am a man without a soul. It wouldn't surprise me if angels turn into demons in this kind of a hell. I didn't have the strength to bear such a heavy burden all by myself. You have rescued me—you have helped me find my way. It isn't right that I turn over this immense responsibility to you while I do nothing. Let me go in search of some money. I will go to Benares tomorrow. I know a few people there though I don't want to stay with them. What area does Suman live in?

Umanath's face went pale. He said—Stay here until the wedding. Then you can go wherever you want to.

Krishnachandra—No, let me go tomorrow. I will come back a week before the wedding. I will stay at Suman's for a few days until I find some work. What part of the city does she live in?

Umanath—I don't remember exactly. I haven't been there for quite some time. And where does one find city people? They change their addresses daily. Who knows what neighbourhood they are in now?

At night, while having dinner, Krishnachandra asked Shanta for Suman's address. Shanta did not see Umanath's gestures. She told him where Suman lived.

30

There were a total of eighteen members in the city's municipal council. Eight of them were Muslims, and the rest were Hindus. Since a majority of the members were well educated, Sharmaji was confident that the municipal council would pass the resolution to evict courtesans from the city. He had personally met with each member and had allayed their concerns about the proposal, but there remained a few gentleman members who, he feared, would vehemently oppose the resolution. These were business-minded, wealthy, and influential men who Sharmaji thought might try to pressurize the rest of the members. The head of the oppositional faction among the Hindus was Seth Balbhadradas, and among the Muslims, Haji Hashim. As long as Vitthaldas led the movement, these men hadn't given it a second thought, but ever since Padamsingh and a few other members of the municipal council had taken up the cause, the Sethji and Haji Sahib had become quite nervous. They knew that this proposal would come before the council before long, so both began to consolidate their allies. First, Haji Sahib sequestered the Muslim members. Haji Sahib had great influence in the community and was considered the leader of the Muslim members. Among the seven other members was Maulana Teg Ali, the trustee of some religious landholdings. Munshi Abulwafa was the owner of a perfume and hair oil factory. He had stores in several large cities. Munshi Abdullatif was a wealthy zamindar, but he spent most of his time in the city. He had a real love for poetry and was himself a good poet. Shakir Beg and Sharif Hasan were lawyers with progressive social ideals. Sayyid Shafakat Ali was a retired deputy collector and the revered Khan Sahib was a famous philosopher. These two men usually didn't associate with the rest of the members but they did not lack in generosity or kindness. They were both religious men who were well respected in the community.

Haji Hashim spoke first—Have you seen this new scheme our countrymen have hatched? They are quite clever. We should learn how to pick pockets from the likes of them. I trust them so little that even if I could attain salvation by putting my faith in their good intentions, I wouldn't.

Abulwafa agreed—But by the grace of God, we are at least able to see the harms and benefits to ourselves. This is an obvious attempt to reduce our population in the city. Ninety per cent of the courtesans are Muslims. They keep their fasts and observe their holy days. We don't have any argument with our fellow Hindu members. God will reward and punish good and evil accordingly. We are only concerned with their numbers.

Teg Ali—But are there so many of them that they could have an effect on our collective vote.

Abulwafa—It will definitely have an effect, but who knows just how much influence they could have. Just look at our fellow country-men. They are trying to ally themselves with the untouchables. They run from the shadows of the untouchables, they say that they are more wretched than animals, but in these political matters, they have accepted them as a part of their bloodlines. And most of the untouchables are criminals. All kinds of untouchables go through our jails. These people are professional cheats, murderers, and robbers. But when we try to separate them from the Hindu community, they become enraged. They begin reciting verses from the Vedas and Shastras. These are things that we should also learn to do.

Thoughtfully, Sayyid Shafakat Ali said—The government knows the whereabouts of these criminals. They are under constant police surveillance. I used to report their forgeries and lies when I encountered them during my rounds. And as far as I know, no responsible Hindu has opposed these governmental regulations. Still, I don't think that stealing and murder are as bad as prostitution. Even a low-caste woman who becomes a prostitute is kicked out of her community. And if an untouchable has a lot of money, then he can easily buy what his heart desires in this open market of bodies. May God never show us the day when we are forced to sink to such depths for political reasons. Even if following the religion of prostitution means that God would turn the entire world into a paradise, I would prefer to go to hell. I wouldn't ever want to regain control of this country if it meant relying on courtesans to increase our numbers. I don't think that they should just be evicted from the centre of town; they should be relocated outside the city limits.

Hakeem Shauharat Khan spoke—Janab, if I had my way, they would be kicked out of Hindustan. We could set up a separate island colony for them to settle in. I have met several patrons of this bazaar. And since they haven't affected my religious convictions, I can say that these courtesans are incarnations of the plague and cholera. Cholera kills you off in a matter of hours and the plague in a few days. But these devilish creatures slowly torture you to death. Munshi Abulwafa thinks that they are some kind of heavenly fairies, but they are cobras, with venom in their eyes. They are fountains that constantly flow with streams of sin. There are countless gentle wives that weep tears of blood on account of them. There are countless good men that are ruined and crushed because of them. It is our misfortune that these shameless courtesans call themselves Muslims.

Sharif Hasan spoke next—The problem isn't that they call themselves Muslims. It's that Islam makes no effort to bring them back to the path of righteousness. Islam has copied the Hindus for so long that it has merely cast these women aside. Islam permanently closes its eyes to a fallen woman. Just watch as Maulana Sahib puts on a new turban, puts kohl around his eyes, rides his motorcar to their brothels, eats delicacies from their tables, smokes their fragrant tobacco, and burns perfumed incense. And that's the end of the religious reforms that Islam offers. It's a virtue to be ashamed of one's crimes. These wayward women may not realize it now, but after the intoxication has worn off they realize their condition. But by then, their repentance is meaningless. They have no way to provide for themselves other than to use their daughters to entrap other men with their love. And thus, this terrible cycle continues indefinitely. If their daughters could have proper marriages and if they were promised financial support alongside then I think that at least 75 per cent of the courtesans would gladly take that option. A person may become a terrible criminal, but he always hopes that his children will be good and decent. It will be impossible to reform the courtesans by evicting them. It is only by keeping that fact in front of my eyes that I have the courage to object to the proposal to evict them. But I cannot oppose it for purely political reasons. I don't make decisions based on a communal perspective that I wouldn't also make for principled reasons.

Teg Ali—For God's sake, be careful about what you say. You wouldn't want to be called a non-believer and have a warrant out against you. These days, everything is communal. It is not even a question of justice and principles. If you are a teacher, you should fail only your Hindu students. If you are a collector, you should tax only the Hindus. If you are a magistrate, punish only the Hindus; a subinspector in the police department, bring false accusations against Hindus, investigates them, and writes down their testimonies incorrectly. If you are a thief, go and rob a Hindu home. If you are a sex-crazed lover, then rape a Hindu girl, and then you will be a servant of the community, a reformer of the community, the captain at the helm of the community—everything.

Haji Hashim muttered to himself. Munshi Abulwafa raised his eyebrows. Teg Ali's words had cut him to the quick. Abulwafa wanted to say something but just then Shakir Beg started—Look; this is not the time for sarcasm or polemics. We were having a friendly discussion. There is a deadly poison in the things that you were saying. I don't think that princely traditions are completely out of place in city life. When we start building a house, we always remember to build gutters. Without those gutters, the foundations of the walls become unsteady. We should look at these women as if they were society's gutters. And like gutters that are not in the main sections of a house, but are concealed from view in some corner, we should evict these women from their elegant abodes in the city and remove them to some corner.

Munshi Abulwafa agreed with the first part of his speech, but didn't at all approve of the gutter metaphor. Frustrated, Haji Hashim looked at Abdullatif, who had so far been sitting quietly, and said—Janab, what do you think about all this? You haven't been washed away in this flood of friendly discussion, have you?

Abdullatif replied—Janab, I do not befriend friendship nor make enemies of enmity. I am just a mediator and am not even sure if I am awake or dreaming. Intelligent men have confounded heaven and earth in order to support this ridiculous proposition. I can't believe what I am hearing. You don't have any problems with soap, leather, and kerosene vendors. There are shops that sell clothes and wares and you don't think that they are inappropriate in the least! Does beauty have no worth in your eyes? Is it necessary that courtesans be confined to some dark and narrow alley? And what good is a park, and I think that it is appropriate to call it a park, which has rows of firs hidden in one corner, which has vines and rosebushes and flower beds tucked away in another corner and where neem and jackfruit trees line the trails but stumps of pipal trees are in the centre and overpruned mangrove trees are at the side? Why should kites and crows on rooftops be allowed to caw their cacophonies but the nightingale be forced to cry her dirges of pain in some dark, secluded corner? I am vehemently opposed to this resolution. I don't even think it deserves such an extended debate.

Haji Hashim smiled, and Abulwafa looked on approvingly. Several gentlemen listened to his ridiculous speech with philosophic smiles, but Teg Ali wasn't so patient. Mockingly, he said—My dear philanthropist, why don't we pass this resolution at the board meeting: the municipal council should spare no expense to beautify Minabazaar and whoever walks through the bazaar should be ordered by the government to put on a cheerful disposition? I think that many people will come out to support this resolution and the secretary who takes the minutes at the meeting will be immortalized in history. After his death, there will be religious celebrations near his grave and he will lie in his coffin, enjoying his dreams of beauty and listening to golden tunes.

Munshi Abdullatif flushed with anger. Haji Hashim, sensing that things had gotten out of hand, spoke—I had believed that principles are important things, but it seems that I was mistaken. It wasn't that long ago that you gentlemen organized a delegation with an Islamic injunction, and were asking Muslim prisoners about their religious conditions, and if memory serves me correctly, you were the same people behind that effort. But today it seems as if there has been a sudden turnabout. Fine. I hope your hypocrisy serves you well. I am not so credulous. I have made it a lifelong principle to oppose each and every resolution that our fellow countrymen devise, because I have no faith that any useful reform will come of it.

Abulwafa said—Ali Haji. I can believe that the sun can shine at night, but I will never believe that the Hindus can be honest.

Sayyid Shafakat Ali replied—Haji Sahib, you have done us a disservice by calling us unprincipled hypocrites. We have the same principles that we have always had and will always have, and that is to promote religious works and to try to improve the condition of our own countrymen in every way possible. If our gain means that our fellow countrymen lose something, we don't have a problem with that. But when a proposal benefits both of us, and doesn't benefit us any less than them, it is wrong for us to oppose it. We don't oppose things just for the sake of opposing them.

It was late at night. The meeting ended. This endless debate didn't yield any surprising results. People left with exactly the same opinions that they had come with. Haji Hashim's hopes of a complete victory were dashed.

31

When the Hindu members who were opposed to the resolution heard about what happened in the Muslim council, they became concerned. Their hopes that the Muslim council would oppose the resolution were dashed to pieces. There were a total of ten Hindu members. Seth Balbhadradas was the chairman of the Hindu council and Doctor Shyamacharan, the vice-chairman. Lala Chimmanlal and Dinanath Tiwari were the leaders of the business community. Padamsingh and Rustambhai were lawyers. Ramesh Datt was a college professor; Lala Bhagatram, a contractor; Prabhakar Rao, the editor of the Hindi newspaper *Jagat*; and Kumvar Anirudh Bahadursingh, the wealthiest zamindar in the district. Most of the shops in the Chauk belonged to Balbhadradas and Chimmanlal. Dinanath also had several stores in Dalmandi. All three of these men were opposed to the resolution. Lala Bhagatram's business depended on financial assistance from Chimmanlal, so he, too, endorsed their position. Prabhakar Rao, Ramesh Datt, Rustambhai, and Padamsingh were in favour of the resolution. Still, no one was certain which side either Doctor Shyamacharan or Kumvar Sahib were on. Both sides believed it was possible to win both men over. The success of either side depended on the two men. And since Padamsingh still hadn't returned from the wedding, Seth Balbhadradas considered it an opportune moment for his faction and invited all the Hindu members into his ornamental reception rooms. His main goal was to win over Doctor Sahib and Kumvar Sahib to support him. Prabhakar Rao was dead set against the Muslims. The men decided to try to explain the resolution in terms of the Hindu–Muslim conflict and thus win Prabhakar Rao to their side.

Dinanath Tiwari said—Our Muslim brothers have shown considerable open-mindedness in their decision, but they are hiding a dark secret. They are trying to kill two birds with one stone. On the one hand, they can appear to be reforming the society, and at the same time, they have an excuse to hurt Hindus. Why wouldn't we expect them to seize such an opportunity?

Chimmanlal—I don't care for politics and I never involve myself in political matters. But I won't hesitate even slightly to say that our Muslim brothers have us by the throat. Most of the property in the Chauk and in Dalmandi belongs to Hindus. If the board approves this resolution, it will ruin us. These Muslims could teach us a thing or two about sabotaging our enemies. It wasn't that long ago that they tried to attack Hindus under the veil of interest rate hikes. Once that plot was exposed, they devised a new strategy. It is quite sad that some of our Hindu brothers are puppets in their hands. They don't understand how much harm their ill-conceived actions will have on our brethren.

When the resolution about interest rates had come up before the local council, Prabhakar Rao had opposed it. Chimmanlal tried to change Prabhakar Rao's mind by recalling the resolution and presenting the current issue from a financial perspective. Prabhakar Rao looked at Rustambhai helplessly as if he to say—these men are tightening the noose around my neck, and you must do something to save me. Rustambhai was a very bold and outspoken man. He stood up to respond to Chimmanlal and said—I am quite disappointed to see that you are viewing a social concern in terms of the tension between Hindus and Muslims. The same trick was tried when the resolution about interest rates came up before us. Reducing national questions to communal conflicts benefits some Hindu merchants, but it hurts national unity immeasurably. There is no doubt that the approval of this resolution will mostly hurt Hindu merchants, but the Muslims will certainly also have to bear some of the burden. There are several Muslim shops in the Chauk and Dalmandi. We shouldn't doubt the honest motives of our Muslim brothers by getting caught up in the heat of debate or argument. Whatever they have decided about this matter, they have done so with public welfare in mind. It's irrelevant whether Hindus are hurt more than Muslims. I am certain that even if Muslims were affected by this resolution more than Hindus, they would have come to the same conclusion. If you truly believe that this resolution has been designed to reform a social evil, then there should be no reason for you not to approve it, no matter how much money is lost in the process. Capital should have no leverage in moral matters.

Prabhakar Rao breathed a sigh of relief. He said—Yes, that's what I was about to say. If it means only a little financial loss to reform a social evil, then we should gladly accept that loss. You know how profitable the opium trade with China was for the British government. It must have brought in more than eighteen crore rupees in revenues. But they didn't even flinch in accepting the loss in order to put an end to the awful opium houses in China.

Kumvar Anirudhsingh looked over at Prabhakar Rao and said—Sir, you spend all your time in editing your newspaper. You don't have the time to enjoy the pleasures of life, do you? But those of us who are carefree need some way to entertain ourselves, don't we? We can spend our evenings playing polo, our afternoons napping, and our mornings in talking to government officials or riding our horses. But what are we to do between the evening and ten o'clock at night? Today you suggest that we should evict the courtesans from the city. When tomorrow you propose that every dance, concert, or party in this district should have approval from this board, it will become quite impossible for us to survive.

Prabhakar Rao smiled and said—Don't you have other ways to entertain yourself other than polo matches and concerts? You should read something.

Kumvar—We are debarred from reading. We don't want to become bookworms. We have already learned all of the things that we need in order to lead a successful life. We know the dances of Spain and France. You may not even have heard of them. You can put me before a piano and I will play a tune that will put even Mozart to shame. We know all about English morals and customs. We know when to wear solar *topis* and when to put on a turban. We read books as well. You will find that my bookshelves are filled with books, but I don't rely on them. This resolution of yours will be the end of us.

The irony and sarcasm in Kumvar Sahib's speech silenced both sides.

Doctor Shyamacharan looked over at Kumvar Sahib and said—I have a few questions to raise before the council about this matter. Until the government answers these questions, I am not prepared to take a decision.

He spoke and then read his list of questions aloud.

Ramesh Datt replied—It is likely that the government will not respond to these questions.

Doctor—Whether or not we get answers is not the point. We will at least have asked our questions. What else can we do?

Seth Balbhadradas was now convinced that his side would win. Apart from the Doctor, out of the seventeen other votes, he counted nine in his favour. That was why he could now remain neutral, as befitted the dignity of a chairman. He gave a pithy speech and analysed the resolution. He said—I don't have confidence in social reform. I think that society implements the reforms that it needs by itself. Taboo against foreign travel, the antagonism between castes, the meaningless dietary restrictions, all of these things fall with the flow of time. I think that we should leave society alone in this matter. When the community speaks unanimously that courtesans be removed from the Chauk, then no force in the world will be able to ignore that demand.

Sethji finished his speech with these emotional words—We are proud of our own music. Those who are familiar with Italian and French music also appreciate the character, melody, and depth of Indian music. But who can stop the march of time? The very institution that some of our reformers are trying to root out is the last vestige of this pure—this heavenly treasure. Will you destroy this institution and cruelly stamp out the priceless treasures that our ancestors have passed down? Do you realize that whatever cultural and religious values remain are due to our music? Otherwise, no one would know the names of Ram, Krishna, and Shiva today! Even our worst enemies couldn't come up with a better plan to erase the feeling of racial pride from our hearts. I am not trying to say that courtesans don't hurt the community. No intelligent man would dare say such a thing. But you rid a disease with medicine, not with silence. A bad custom cannot be erased with indifference or sarcasm. It can only be removed with education, knowledge, and compassion. There is no straight road that leads directly to heaven. You will have to encounter the river Vaitarani at some point. Those who think that the blessings of a saint will secure them a seat in heaven are no less ridiculous than those who think that removing courtesans from the Chauk will remove all of the pain and suffering in India and usher in a new dawn for this country.

32

A MAN WAKES up from his sleep when he hears someone shout, but after he looks around for a bit, he falls asleep again quite easily; similarly, Pandit Krishnachandra forgot his obligations once his fit of anger and frustration had subsided. He thought—how can my staying here possibly trouble Umanath? I only consume half a seer of flour and not much else. Still, he stopped sitting and smoking with low-class men that very same day. He didn't think it was necessary to make a fuss about such a small matter. Now he would sit on the verandah and flirt with the women that passed by. He became Umanath's yes-man, and said a lot of things to Umanath just to flatter him. At dinnertime he would eat whatever he was served, and wouldn't ask for a second helping even if he was still hungry. His spirit diminished.

Whenever Umanath spoke to him about Shanta's wedding, he would respond quite honestly—Bhaiya, do what you think is best. You are her guardian now. He thought that since Umanath was spending the money, he should be free to make all decisions.

But Umanath had not forgotten his brother-in-law's biting accusations. Putting butter on a burn eases the pain for a short time, but before long the pain flares up again. While he quickly forgot Krishnachandra's pleas, his harsh curses continued to buzz in his ears. As he got ready for bed, Jahnvi asked him—Why was Lalaji (Krishnachandra) upset at you today?

He looked at her with sarcasm—He was singing my praises. He was saying, 'You have robbed me blind and killed my wife, you have abandoned one of my daughters and you are turning the other into a slave.'

'Don't you have a tongue in your mouth? You could have told him that you didn't really invite his family over. They didn't have a place to go; they would have wandered around, turned away from every place. We slaughtered a goat for them and now they complain about the flavour. We have done everything we can for them, and this is the thanks we get? He worked in the police station for years, but Gangajali never bothered to send even a bottle of *sindoor* for us, not even by mistake. If he had said that to me, I would have told him off until he had a sour taste in his mouth. He has yoked us to his good-for-nothing daughters, and he still has the nerve to say these things. We have become paupers because of him, and this is the thanks that we get? Why doesn't he take his daughter and go somewhere else now? As if he can't move because he has *mehndi* on his feet, humph.'

'He's talking about leaving now. He even asked for Suman's address.'

'So, now he's going to impose on his own daughter? How shameful!'

'No, he's not like that. He might stay there for a few days.'

'What are you talking about? There's nothing left for him to do. He has no shame. He's going to make himself a burden for her, just wait and see. He won't last a single day.'

Until now, Umanath had kept the story of Suman's fall a secret from Jahnvi. He knew that women could not keep these things to themselves. She would surely tell someone or the other and then the news would spread like wildfire. When Jahnvi was affectionate with him, he wanted desperately to tell her about Suman. The waves would begin lapping in the ocean of his heart, but the moment he thought about the consequences he would stop himself. Today, Krishnachandra's harshness and his wife's tenderness made Umanath ignore his better judgement—he couldn't keep it a secret any longer. It was as if something which has been stuck in a pipe is released, along with much else, as soon as the flow of water catches it from behind. He told Jahnvi everything. When he woke up in the middle of the night, however, he knew that he had made a mistake, but the arrow had already been released from the bow. Jahnvi had promised her husband that she wouldn't tell another soul, but it was as if she carried a heavy weight on her chest. Her heart wasn't in any of her work. She was irritated with Umanath for having confided in her. She wasn't disgusted or angry with Suman. But now she had an interesting story to tell, and a good example of the study of human nature. Jahnvi now had the perfect argument against the education of women. She couldn't cheat herself out of this pleasure for too long. It was impossible. She took two or three neighbouring women, who confided in her every detail about the happenings in their homes, in her confidence. She was also eager to hear what the other women thought about the matter. Still, Jahnvi contained herself for several days.

One day, Kubera Pandit's wife, Subhagi, came to chat with Jahnvi and said—Sister, it's Ekadashi today. Will you come to bathe in the Ganga with me?

Subhagi and Jahnvi were very close. Jahnvi said—I would go, but there is a demon sitting at my doorstep. How can I possibly go out, leaving him there?

Subhagi—Sister, what shall I say about him? It's embarrassing. If my family ever come, to know, they will kill him. Yesterday, he was reading a god-knows-what kind of poem to my eldest daughter. Today I saw the two of them giggling near the well. Sister, I can't keep anything from you. My daughter can't be more than two or three years older than Suman. It would be one thing if she was his sister-in-law. But she is like a daughter to him. And he doesn't even think about that. If Panditji hears about this, there will be bloodshed. I am telling you, you must take him aside and straighten him out somehow.

Jahnvi couldn't restrain herself any longer. She told Subhagi all about Suman's condition and adding spice to the good parts. Sharing secrets, Jahnvi believed, was a two-way street.

The next day, Kubera Pandit sent his daughter to his in-laws and determined to take revenge for this insult.

33

It was Sadan's wedding day. The wedding procession left Chunar and headed for Amola. It would be pointless to describe its composition. It was like a thousand other wedding processions, an extremely touching spectacle of majesty and poverty. The palanquin was draped with a finely embroidered cloth, but the servants wore torn and ill-fitting jackets. Motley staffs and spears in the hands of starving peasants did not make for a comfortable sight.

The road to Amola was some twenty miles. Along the way, there was a river to cross. The wedding procession stopped at the pier. They haggled with the boatmen for hours over the fare before the gates were opened. Madansingh got annoyed and said—It's a good thing that you aren't from my village, else I would show you what real labour is.

But Padamsingh was secretly quite proud of the stubborn boatmen. He could see that they truly loved their work.

The wedding procession reached Amola in the evening. One of Padamsingh's assistants had already set up the canopy. Tents had also been erected, decorated with lanterns, chandeliers, and large vessels. Embroidered cloths, cushions, pillows, and perfume were aplenty. There was some excitement about the fact that a few dance troupes had arrived.

After the *dwar puja* Umanath draped a towel on his shoulders and welcomed the wedding procession personally. The village women stood in the hall singing the *mangalacharan*, while the groomsmen jostled to determine who was the most beautiful amongst them. And the women, too, smiled flirtatiously at the men.

Jahnvi was a bit cut up. She was thinking to herself—it would have been so nice if my Chandra could have been married into that family. Subhagi was eager to find out who the groom's father was. Krishnachandra was performing a *puja* at Sadan's feet and thinking to himself about what an upside-down kind of ritual this was. Madansingh was slyly trying to figure out how much money had been put into the *thali*.

The wedding procession retired to the tent. The dinner was being readied. There was a commotion in every direction. Someone said—I don't have enough butter, and someone shouted out that the dung cakes hadn't been passed around. Lala Bejnath demanded alcohol.

After everything had been distributed, people burnt the fuel cakes and placed the pots on top. The light from the lanterns turned yellow from the smoke.

Sadan was sitting against a cushion. The entertainment had begun. A company of singers from Kashi began to sing tunes from *shyam-kalyan*.

A thousand men standing filled all corners of the tent. Some with jackets and with turbans wrapped around their heads sat on the carpets. People started asking each other about the dancers. Curiously, they peeped into each of the tents and said with great curiosity—What kind of a wedding procession is this which doesn't bring dancers? What kind of beggars are these people? Why even bother to put up such a large tent? Madansingh heard each of these taunts and was infuriated with Padamsingh, while Padamsingh wouldn't go near him out of shame and fear.

In the meanwhile, people began throwing stones at the tent. Lala Bejnath got up and ran to the tents. Some people began cursing the rioters. There was an enormous commotion. People were running all over. Some were hurling insults and others were bent on violence. Suddenly, a tall man, his face smeared with ashes and carrying a trident in his hand, came and stood in the middle of the party. His bloodshot eyes were glowing like candles and a brilliant light emanated from his face. The people grew silent. They began staring at this mahatma with wide-eyed fascination—where did he come from? Who is this sadhu?

The sadhu raised the trident over his head and shouted reproachfully—Fools! There is no dance here, no courtesans. All the old men are sitting around moping. The songs of Krishna are so wonderful, but no one listens to them, no one has ears anymore. Everyone wants to see whores dance instead. You either give them a dance or watch them break your skulls. Well, I will show you a dance. Have you ever the seen the dance of the gods? Look at how the soft moonlight dances on the leaves of that tree. Look at how drops of water dance on the petals of the lotus in that lake. Go in the jungle and you will see how the feathers dance on a peacock. Don't you like the way that the gods dance? Fine, let me show you the dance of the demons. Look at how the wretched peasants in your neighbourhood dance while they are beaten by the zamindars! Look at how your brothers' orphans dance when they are crazy with hunger! Look in you own homes and watch how the tears of sadness and agony dance on the faces of widows! Don't you like watching these dances? Then look in your own hearts, where deception and hypocrisy dance! The entire world is a school of dance, and people dance their own dances in it. Don't you have eyes that can appreciate such dances? Come, let me show you Shankar's *tandav-nritya*. But you aren't worthy of watching that dance. Your lust will not be satisfied with this dance! Ha! Ignorant statues! Ha! Slaves of pleasure! Aren't you ashamed just to say the word 'dance'? If you have any concern for your happiness, get rid of this custom. Abandon these desires. Stop chasing after harlots.

People sat around like statues listening to the mahatma's wild speech when he suddenly vanished, but they could hear him singing from behind the shade of the mango tree just before them. Slowly, even that song vanished into the darkness, just as at night, when imaginary ships get lost in the ocean of our dreams. This crowd of people was like a bunch of street gamblers who become silent when they spy a group of police officers. One of them quickly gathers up the money while another one tries to hide the dice. And so the sadhu's sudden arrival, his brilliant form, and his prophetic warning made the people afraid of an invisible calamity. The rioters quietly returned to their homes and the people who were sitting in the tent and growing impatient, who thought that it was going to be a waste of time, began to sing hymns. Some simple-hearted men ran after the mahatma, but they couldn't find any trace of him.

Pandit Madansingh was sitting in his tent and examining the clothes and jewellery when Munshi Bejnath came running up to him and said—Bhaiya! Everything is ruined! We should never have agreed to this wedding.

Madansingh was startled. He asked—Why? What happened? Is there something wrong?

Bejnath—Yes, one of the men from this village came to see me. He told me everything about these people and I nearly collapsed.

Madansingh—What, are they low caste?

Bejnath—They aren't low caste, but the situation is still quite grave. The bride's father was recently released from prison and her older sister is a courtesan. Sumanbai from Dalmandi is this girl's sister.

Madansingh felt as if he had just fallen out of a tree. His eyes widened in rage and he said—That man you talked to isn't an enemy of that family, is he? People often make false accusations in order to stop weddings.

Padamsingh—Yes, that's exactly what this sounds like.

Bejnath—No, no. He claimed that he would say it all to their faces.

Madansingh—So she's not Umanath's daughter?

Bejnath—No. She's his niece. You remember that time there was a court case against a police officer, well that police officer was Umanath's brother-in-law. He's only been out of prison for a few months.

Madansingh beat his forehead and said—Dear God! Why are you doing this to us?

Padamsingh—We should talk to Umanath.

And as he finished, they saw Pandit Umanath himself coming towards them with the barber. They had come to fetch clothes and jewellery for the bride. As soon as he stepped through the opening of the tent, Madansingh leapt at him, grabbed both of his hands and pulled him toward himself saying—Well, well you tilak-wearing hypocrite! Why did you have to drag me down with you? Couldn't you have found someone else?

Like a mouse caught in a cat's claws, Umanath replied meekly—What have I done wrong?

Madansingh—You have done something so horrible that it would not be a sin for me to kill you. What, was mine the only house to which you could have a sent a girl whose sister is a fallen woman?

Umanath strained to speak—Maharaj, everyone has enemies. You shouldn't believe every aspersion cast on me. Call that man over. He can say whatever he wants to my face.

Padamsingh—Yes. That's the right thing to do. We should call that man.

Madansingh looked at his brother with stony eyes and said—Why are you getting involved in this, huh? (To Umanath) It may be that he is your enemy, but I want to know whether the accusation is true or not.

Umanath—What accusation?

Madansingh—That Suman is the girl's sister.

Umanath went pale and hung his head in shame. His eyes dimmed. He said—Maharaj ..., and then could say no more.

Madansingh roared—Why won't you speak up? Is it true or false?

Umanath tried to respond again, but he could only say—Maharaj ...

Madansingh's suspicions were confirmed. He flew into a rage. His eyes became bloodshot. His body began to shake. He looked at Umanath with fiery eyes and said—If you value your life, get out of my sight. Snake, cheat, heretic! You put on a tilak and parade around like a *pandit*, you untouchable worm! The water you serve is no longer fit to drink. Turn your girl into an amulet and wear her around your neck—he said and walked out. He walked into the tent where Sadan was sleeping and called loudly for the servants.

After he left, Umanath spoke to Padamsingh—Maharaj, please try to calm him down somehow. I won't be able to show my face anywhere. You have surely heard about Suman. That wretched girl has permanently blackened my reputation. It was God's will, but what's the use of digging up buried corpses? Please, tell me. What else could I do but hide this fact from everyone? That girl had to be married. And how could I do that unless I hid the facts? I am telling you the truth. I didn't hear about Suman until after the engagement.

Padamsingh responded with concern—If my brother hadn't found out about it, it would not have been a problem. Look. I will go and talk to him, but it looks like it will be almost impossible to get him to change his mind.

Madansingh was shouting at the servants to pack up so that they could all leave quickly. Sadan was gathering up his clothes, as well. His father had told him everything.

In the meantime, Padamsingh came to plead with him—Bhaiya. Don't be so hasty. We should think it through first. Yes, we have been deceived, but it will be even more shameful if we get up and leave.

Sadan looked at his uncle indifferently, while Madansingh was shocked.

Padamsingh—Let's consult two or three men and see what they think is best.

Madansingh—Do you hear yourself? Do you want me to forget my duty?

Padamsingh—At least there won't be any social embarrassment in it.

Madansingh—You are behaving like a child! Don't you know what is going on here? Go. Get ready to leave. Right now, social embarrassment is the better evil. At least our family won't be ruined for eternity.

Padamsingh—But think about what will happen to that girl. What has she done to deserve this?

Madansingh was enraged—You are a complete idiot. Let's leave this place quickly. If something happens tomorrow, I bet that you will be the first one to point a finger. You can't deal with the ways of the world with your legal arguments.

Padamsingh looked at him sharply and said—I don't have any problem doing what you ask me to, but it is really awful that the life of this girl is going to be completely ruined.

Madansingh—Why do you always make me so angry? Is she my problem? She will get whatever fate has in store for her. Why should I concern myself with it?

Padamsingh was frustrated. He said—Suman doesn't even come here any more. They have cut her off completely.

Madansingh—I have already asked you not to make me angry. Aren't you in the least bit ashamed of yourself for saying things like this? You want me to marry my son to a prostitute's sister? Disgusting! You aren't thinking straight.

Padamsingh hung his head in shame. He knew that he would have said the same things if he were in his brother's place. But he thought of the terrible consequences and mustered the courage to speak once more. Like a student who, despite his disappointment at not finding his name in the newspaper, still rushes to get his marks, Padamsingh deluded himself into believing he could change his brother's mind. He spoke meekly—Sumanbai is now living in a widow's home.

Padamsingh spoke without looking up. He didn't have the audacity to look his brother in the eye. As soon as these words left his lips Madansingh gave his brother a forceful shove and he fell to the ground. Padamsingh looked at him in shock. Madansingh was trembling with fury! He was about to yell insults at his brother, but once he saw Padamsingh on the ground, he was alarmed and controlled himself. Madansingh was like a man about to cut off his nose to spite his face.

This was the first time in his life that Padamsingh had been roughed up by his brother. Through his childhood, even though they had had fights, his brother had never once laid a hand on him. He began to cry like a child, sobbing and choking, though he wasn't angry at all. He was only troubled by the fact that his stubbornness had hurt someone who had always cared for him and who had never said a harsh word to him. This was the flame that was burning in his heart, the invisible reality of shame, dishonour, and lassitude. It was the fury of the waves of grief that were swelling in his heart. Sadan leapt to his feet and picked Padamsingh up. He looked at his father angrily and said—Have you lost your mind?

Just then, a few men had arrived and began asking—Maharaj, what is the matter? Why have you ordered the wedding procession to turn around and go back? Try to find a solution so that both sides can save face. Your honour and his honour are one and the same now. If the dowry is not enough, please just accept whatever he offers. God has given you enough already. You won't become rich by taking his wealth.

Madansingh didn't say a word.

The entire wedding party was in an uproar. Everyone was asking everyone else what was going on. The crowd in front of the tent was growing by the minute.

There were many men from the bride's side in the wedding party as well. They went to Umanath and began asking him questions—Bhaiya, why are they bent on leaving?

When Umanath didn't give a satisfactory answer, all of them went to Madansingh and began pleading with him—Maharaj, what have we done that was so wrong? You can punish us however you see fit, but don't turn the wedding procession around. It will ruin the reputation of the village.

All Madansingh said to them was—Go and ask Umanath. He will tell you what the problem is.

Pandit Krishnachandra was overjoyed once he saw Sadan. The auspicious moment for the wedding was approaching. He was awaiting the groom's arrival when some men came and told him what was going on. He asked them—Why are they leaving? Did they get into an argument with Umanath or something?

The men responded—We don't know. Umanath is still standing there trying to make peace.

Enraged, Krishnachandra went toward the groom's party—Turning the wedding procession back as if this were some child's game. Do they think that this is the marriage of dolls? If they didn't want to have a wedding, why did they come here in the first place? We'll see who dares to call off this wedding. Rivers of blood will flow. That was exactly how Krishnachandra used to speak to his friends. He lengthened his stride and came to the groom's tent and said challengingly—Where is Pandit Madansingh? Maharaj, come outside.

Madansingh heard the threat and came outside. He spoke firmly—Well, what do you want?

Krishnachandra—Why are you calling off the wedding?

Madansingh—I want to! We don't want to go through with this wedding.

Krishnachandra—You have to go through with it. You can't come here and then leave like this.

Madansingh—You can do whatever you want. We will not go through with the wedding.

Krishnachandra—Why not?

Madansingh—Don't you know?

Krishnachandra—If I knew, why would I ask you?

Madansingh—Then ask Pandit Umanath.

Krishnachandra—I am asking you.

Madansingh—Please, let it be. I don't want to embarrass you.

Krishnachandra—Oh I see. It's because I was in prison. That's why you are leaving. My, my. This is fairness now, isn't it?

Madansingh—That would never have been the reason to call off the wedding.

Krishnachandra—Then perhaps Umanath didn't offer you enough money in the dowry?

Madansingh—I am not that base.

Krishnachandra—Then what is it?

Madansingh—Listen. Don't ask me.

Krishnachandra—You have to tell me. Calling off a wedding once you have come to my doorstep, this is not some childish game. Blood will be spilt here. Don't fool yourself about it.

Madansingh—I am not worried about that. I may die here, but I won't allow my son to get married. I haven't come here to throw away my reputation.

Krishnachandra—Why, are we lower than you?

Madansingh—Yes, you are lower than we are.

Krishnachandra—Do you have any proof?

Madansingh—Yes.

Krishnachandra—Then why are you hesitating to tell me?

Madansingh—Fine. Then listen and don't bother me after that. Your daughter Suman, this girl's sister, has become a prostitute. If you want, you can find her in Dalmandi.

Krishnachandra tried to disbelieve him and said—That's a lie!

But just then, he remembered that when he had asked Umanath about Suman's address, Umanath had stalled. He finally understood all those oblique looks that Jahnvi would give him over every little thing. He became convinced and his head hung low in shame. He became unconscious and fell to the ground. Hundreds of men from both parties were watching, but all of them remained silent. No one knew what to say at a moment like this.

In the middle of the night, everything was torn down. Darkness enveloped that little hamlet. The jackals held an assembly and the owls began to talk to each other.

34

VITTHALDAS HAD KEPT Suman's presence in the widow's home a secret. He hadn't give any of the members of the board of directors the slightest hint. He presented her as a widow to the other widows there. But it couldn't be kept a secret from a spy like Abulwafa for too long. He tracked down Hiriya and asked her where Suman had gone. Then he told many of his more aristocratic friends the news, with the result that these gentlemen developed a special kind of generosity towards the widow's home. Sometimes Seth Chimmanlal would visit, at other times Seth Balbhadradas would come, and sometimes Pandit Dinanath would stop by. These benefactors demonstrated a surprising sympathy for the widow's home, its order and beauty, and its financial solvency. They spent their days and nights in doing things for the betterment of the widow's home.

This became an enormous problem for Vitthaldas. Sometimes, he thought about resigning from his duties—am I the only one responsible for this ashram? There are so many other men in the committee who could handle this work. They will do what they think is best. At least I won't have to see this hypocritical behavior with my own eyes. At other times he thought about confronting these licentious men—let whatever happens, happen. But when he calmed down and thought about it, the only solution that he could come up with was to do his duty patiently. Sure, he wanted to speak harshly to these men. He wanted to reject their offers and tell them that he couldn't stand what they were doing. But he could never catch them in the act. Whenever he was around, the two Seths easily turned into paragons of refinement and morality. Tiwariji became so quiet that it was impossible to believe that he could ever become angry. Vitthaldas couldn't think of what to do against this underhand plot.

One morning, while Vitthaldas was thinking about these very things, a buggy pulled up at the ashram. And who could be seen stepping out of it? Abulwafa and Abdullatif.

Vitthaldas was completely taken aback. He thought that the Seths were bad enough and now there was this. He wanted very much to reprimand the two of them, but decided that it was best to keep a cool head.

Abulwafa said—Greetings, we are at your service. Are you not feeling well today? By God, hearing of your work brings joy to my soul. This nation is blessed to have volunteers like you. And then there is our selfish, self-centred community, which can't be bothered to even think about things like this. Even the most virtuous men aren't ultimately pure, don't you agree Munshi Abdullatif Sahib?

Abdullatif—Janab, don't even mention our community. Call it what you want—self-involved, self-interested, self-centred, hypocritical, contrary, and crooked—it's all true. Look at our leaders. They are all spotted jackals, dressed in treachery. May you always be blessed. It is as if God has selected you from the angels and sent you into this lucky community.

Abulwafa—Your generosity definitely has had an effect on our hearts. Aren't there women at the ashram who weave and quilt? I have a friend who has sent me an order for dozens of handmade sheets. Of course, there are several places that produce such sheets in the city, but I think that private contractors should not be given preference over the ashram. If you have some of their work lying around, could you take the trouble to show it to me?

Vitthaldas—Such work is not done at the ashram.

Abulwafa—But it should be. I am sure if you look, you will find that some of these women are already trained. We are not in any hurry. We don't mind coming once, twice, four, or even ten times. You yourself make so many sacrifices. Certainly, I can at least do this, no? I don't think that religious divisions are appropriate in these circumstances.

Vitthaldas—I am grateful for your generosity, but the committee has already ruled against these kinds of transactions. My hands are tied.

Vitthaldas finished and got up. The two men didn't know what else to do other than to leave. They cursed Vitthaldas inwardly and got into the buggy.

But just as the sounds of the buggy were fading away into the distance, Vitthaldas heard Chimmanlal's motorcar drive up. The Sethji got out with much pomp. He shook Vitthaldas' hand and said—Well, Babu Sahib! What have you decided about the play? The play *Shakuntala* is Bharatrihari's best work. The English are very fond of this play. You should definitely put on a production. If the women have memorized some of the lines, I would be happy to hear them.

Sometimes, it is easier to come up with a solution to a problem on the spur of the moment, to which deliberation has provided no answer. Vitthaldas had been trying to find a way to get rid of these Seths, but he couldn't come up with any ideas. But now, he had an inspiration. He said— No, I was advised not to put that play on. I asked the Commissioner for advice about it. He wouldn't hear of it. I don't understand what people mean when they talk of politics. Today, in passing, I asked the Commissioner for an annual donation for the ashram and he said that he wouldn't assist any political group. I was startled to hear him say that. So I asked him why he thought that the ashram was a political institution. And he replied by saying that he didn't want to get into it.

Chimmanlal's face lit up. He said—So the Sahib thinks that the ashram is political as well?

Vitthaldas—Yes, he said so plainly.

Chimmanlal—Well, if he thinks that, then certainly the people that come and go in this place must be watched carefully, no?

Vitthaldas—Yes, what else? But what would that accomplish? Patriots don't fear such things, do they?

Chimmanlal—No, no. I am not like those nationalists. If I had known that these people thought that the Ramlila festival was political, I would have gotten rid of that, too. My hair stands on end at the mention of politics. Come to my house and you will see that there isn't even a single copy of the Bhagvad Gita there. I have given my servants strict orders to get things from the bazaar wrapped in leaves; I won't let those dangerous newspaper wrappings into my house. I used to have a picture of Maharana Pratap in my room, but I took it down and locked it up in my trunk. Now please give me leave to go.

As he finished, he supported his belly with one hand and bounced back to the motorcar. Vitthaldas laughed to himself. What a great trick, he thought and didn't even stop to think about how much he had lied and what ruination he had brought upon his soul as a consequence. This model of service and duty would keep far away from lies and deception in his personal affairs, but in matters of national importance, he didn't hesitate in the least to employ all means at his disposal.

After Chimmanlal had left, Vitthaldas picked up the registry of pledges and set out to collect donations. But he hadn't even stepped out of the room when he saw Seth Balbhadradas approaching in a rickshaw. He fumed with rage, slammed the registry down, and prepared for a fight.

Balbhadradas stepped forward and said—Well sir, about the plant that I sent yesterday. Have you planted it yet? I wanted to take a look at it. If you want, I can send my gardener over.

Vitthaldas spoke despondently—No. You don't have to send your gardener. And that plant can't be planted here.

Balbhadradas—Why not? My gardener will come and fix everything. Plant it immediately, otherwise it will dry up.

Vitthaldas—It may very well dry up, but it won't be planted here.

Balbhadradas—If you didn't intend to plant it, you could have said so at the beginning. I ordered it from Saharanpur.

Vitthaldas—It is sitting in the courtyard. You can pick it up and take it with you.

Seth Balbhadradas was a proud man. Usually, he was the picture of propriety and refinement, but if anyone ever talked back to him, or was condescending, he would burn with rage. He was a fearless, skilled politician and as a result, he was respected in the community. People had complete faith in him and believed that he would never back down on issues of justice or truth, that he would never ever think of misleading society for his personal gain or honour. People didn't trust Doctor Shyamacharan in the same way. They believed that, education, intellect, and talent were not as valuable as a strong character.

Seth Balbhadradas' brows furrowed when he heard Vitthaldas speak so dryly. He stood up and said—Why are you so disgruntled today?

Vitthaldas—I don't know how to talk sweetly.

Seth—You needn't talk sweetly, but at least don't be rude.

Vitthaldas—I don't need you to teach me manners.

Seth—You know that I am a member of the board of directors.

Vitthaldas—Yes, I am aware.

Seth—If I wanted, I could be the head of it.

Vitthaldas—Sure.

Seth—My word is just as important as anyone else's.

Vitthaldas—What's the point of all this?

Seth—I could close down the ashram if I wanted.

Vitthaldas—Impossible.

Seth—In a single day, I could get rid of it without a trace.

Vitthaldas—Impossible.

Seth—What makes you so sure?

Vitthaldas—I have faith in God.

Offended, the Sethji looked over at the ashram as he got back on to his rickshaw. His threats had no effect on Vitthaldas. Vitthaldas was certain that the Sethji wouldn't say anything about the ashram to the other board members. He was too proud a man. It was possible that he might praise the ashram to the other members to cover up his embarrassment but Vitthaldas was sure that his rage would flare up again sooner or later. There was no doubt about it. Men with such pride never forget insults. Despite the risks, however, Vitthaldas didn't show any signs of anxiety that normally beset one after an argument. Instead, he was quite content with the way he had handled the situation. He only regretted that he had waited so long. His self-satisfaction overcame him and on a whim, he began to sing loudly—

> *Dear God, what can shame me now?*
> *Through many births have I wandered*
> *Uselessly and proud.*
> *Dear God, what can shame me now?*

In the meantime, he spied Padamsingh approaching. His face was weighed down with worry and despair as if he had been weeping. Vitthaldas stepped forward to meet him and asked—Have you been ill? I almost didn't recognize you.

Padamsingh—No, I haven't been ill. But I am desperate.

Vitthaldas—Did the wedding go off well?

Padamsingh looked up at the rooftops and said—Don't ask me about the wedding. There was no wedding. We went to destroy a poor woman's life. She turned out to be Sumanbai's sister. As soon as my brother found out, he called off the wedding.

Vitthaldas sighed—This is terrible. Didn't you try to explain things to your brother?

Padamsingh—I did whatever I could, but nothing worked.

Vitthaldas—Look, what is that poor girl going to do now? If Suman hears of this, she will be terribly upset.

Padamsingh—Well, tell me about things here. Have the widows created a problem since Suman moved into the ashram? They must despise her.

Vitthaldas—If they ever find out, the ashram will be cleared out.

Padamsingh—And how is Suman?

Vitthaldas—She is doing very well, as if she had spent her whole life in an ashram. It seems as if she is trying to repent for all of her sins from each one of her lives. She is ready and willing to do any work. Most of the women sleep all day, but Suman cleans out their rooms for them. She has been teaching a few of the widows to sew, and some have been learning how to sing from her. Everyone seeks her counsel in every little detail. She has really taken charge of things inside those four walls. I could never have hoped for this. She has also started reading and well, only God knows what she feels, but she seems a completely changed woman.

Padamsingh—No, she's not a bad woman by nature. She used to come to my house regularly. Everyone in my house thought very highly of her (and suddenly he stopped). There were just some bad elements that forced her into this situation. If you ask me, she has had to suffer for our sins. And yes, have you heard anything about the municipal council? Has Seth Balbhadradas devised another scheme?

Vitthaldas—Of course. He's not the kind of man who sits quietly and lets things happen. These days there is a lot of commotion. And a few days ago, the Hindu council had a meeting. I wasn't able to go, but the other side won out. And with the chair's two votes, they have six votes and we have four. After the Muslims are counted, the vote will be even.

Padamsingh—Then we have to find at least one more vote. Do we have any prospects?

Vitthaldas—I can't think of anyone.

Padamsingh—If you have the time, let's go see Doctor Sahib and Lala Bhagatram.

Vitthaldas—Yes, let's go. I am ready.

35

EVEN THOUGH DOCTOR Sahib's bungalow was nearby, the two of them took a carriage. It wasn't fashionable to go to the Doctor's house on foot. On the way, Vitthaldas told him about all the things that had happened that day and his cleverness in dealing with them.

Padamsingh listened and then responded with concern—Then we need to be even more careful now. In the end, the entire burden of maintaining the ashram may fall on us. Balbhadradas may be quiet for a while, but he will definitely find a way to lash out.

Vitthaldas—What would you have me do? I couldn't stand by and watch these scoundrels. I was infuriated. These men call themselves educated, wise, and courteous, and yet they do such wicked things. Had I known how to tackle them, I wouldn't have had to pick a fight with them.

Padamsingh—It had to happen sooner or later. These are all the fruits of my sins. I can only wait and see what sprouts up now. Ever since the wedding party returned, I have been in a strange mood. I don't feel hungry or thirsty and I spend my nights tossing and turning. I keep worrying about what will happen to that poor girl. And if I have to bear the responsibility of the ashram also, I know it will kill me. I feel I am sinking in quicksand. Every time I try to pull myself out of it, I sink deeper and deeper.

And as they were talking, they arrived at Doctor Sahib's bungalow. It was ten o'clock. Doctor Sahib was in his sitting room playing chess with his elder daughter, Miss Kanti. Two terriers sat on the table watching the game of chess quite intently, and sometimes, when they thought that the players had made a mistake, they would knock over the pieces with their paws. Miss Kanti laughed at their mischief and reproached them in English, 'You, naughty.'

To the left of the table, Sayyid Teg Ali sat in an armchair and in between the moves, he offered suggestions to Miss Kanti.

That's when our friends arrived on the scene. Doctor Sahib got up and shook hands with them. Miss Kanti observed them obliquely and then picked up a newspaper from the table and began to read.

Doctor Sahib spoke in English—I am so happy to see you two today. Let me introduce you to Miss Kanti.

After the introductions, Miss Kanti shook hands with them, laughed and said—Father was just talking about you. I am so pleased to meet you.

Doctor Shyamacharan—Miss Kanti has just returned from Dalhousie. The school has closed for the winter. They have a wonderful school there. She lives in the boarding house with English girls. The lady principal has written such nice things about her. Kanti, show them the letter that your lady principal wrote. Mister Sharma, you will be amazed when you hear Kanti speak English. (Laughing) She teaches me new words every day.

Shyly, Miss Kanti showed Padamsingh her report card. He looked it over and said—You study Latin as well?

Doctor Sahib said—She won a medal in Latin this term. Yesterday at the club, Kanti taught us to play such a wonderful game, even the English-women were delighted. Yes, you weren't present at the last meeting of the Hindu members, were you?

Padamsingh—No. I had gone home.

Doctor—We debated your resolution. I don't think that we should try to force a vote on it in the council too soon. I don't think that it can be passed right now.

Teg Ali—Janab, you will get the full support of the Muslim members.

Doctor—Yes, but there is disagreement among the Hindus.

Padamsingh—With your help, I am sure that the resolution will go through.

Doctor—I am completely in agreement with the resolution, but you are well aware that I am a government-nominated member. Until I find out what the government thinks of this resolution, I can't help you in these social concerns.

Annoyed, Vitthaldas spoke up—If being a nominated member means that you can't think for yourself, then you should resign.

All three men looked at Vitthaldas with derision. He had crossed the line with that remark. Teg Ali responded with sarcasm—Resign? Then what will happen to his honour? How will he sit at the same table as the Lieutenant Governor? How will he be called 'Honorable'? How will he have the pleasure of shaking hands with high-ranking English officials? How will he be able to go to government dinner parties and succeed at swindling the British? How else will he get to tour Nainital? How will he show off the brilliance of his oratory? What about those things?

Vitthaldas was embarrassed. Padamsingh regretted ever having brought Vitthaldas with him.

Doctor Sahib responded gravely—Most people think that these luxuries are the reasons that one seeks to be a civil servant. They don't understand how many responsibilities come with the job. Civil servants are poor, overworked, and have to sacrifice much time and money in the course of their work. And all they really get out of it is the satisfaction that they are helping their communities and their nation. There is no other reason to seek a civil service post.

Teg Ali—Certainly. There is no doubt about that. Those who undertake such splendid work can feel it in their hearts.

The clock struck eleven. Shyamacharan turned to Padamsingh and said—It's time for lunch, so you will have to excuse me. Come back and see me this evening.

Padamsingh said—Yes, of course. Please enjoy your lunch.

He thought to himself—how am I going to get others to support my cause when this one is so worried about getting to lunch on time. People want to help their communities and their nation but are unwilling to sacrifice anything for these worthy causes.

Lala Bhagatram was sitting in a chair sunning himself and smoking his hookah. His youngest daughter was sitting in his lap, trying to catch the smoke as it blew away. Some carpenters and masons sat on the ground in front of him. As soon as Bhagatram saw Padamsingh he got up and bowed.

He said—I heard last night that you had returned. I was coming to see you this morning, but I have been tied up and haven't had the opportunity. Contracting is so tiresome. Get the job done. Put up your money. Spend some more money trying to get clients. These days, the engineer has become irritated with me and doesn't like any of my ideas. I had contracted to build a bridge. He has torn it down three times. Sometimes he says, 'This is not right.' At other times, 'That's not right.' There's no profit in it anymore. I am probably going to lose money. But no one listens to me. You must have heard that the Hindu members have had a meeting.

Padamsingh—Yes. I heard and am a little disappointed. I had placed a lot of faith in you. Don't you think that this resolution is a good idea?

Bhagatram—Not only do I think that it's a good idea, I want very much to support it, but I don't have control over my vote. I have sold myself for self-interest. I have become a gramophone. I can only repeat what others make me sing.

Padamsingh—But surely you know that you have to distinguish between your self-interests and the good of the nation.

Bhagatram—I know this in the abstract, but it's a hard principle to put into practice. You know that all my business depends on Seth Chimmanlal. If I go against him, he will see to it that I am ruined. And my position in this community depends entirely on my business. I don't have an education or even any wisdom. All I have depends on this make believe. If anyone finds out, then there is no doubt that I will be forced out of the society like some annoying insect. Tell me. Is there anyone else in this city who will lend me a thousand rupees, without interest, just on my word? And it's not that I am just worried about myself. I spend at least three hundred rupees a month taking care of my family. I am prepared to give of myself to the nation, but how can I let my children go hungry?

When we want to avoid our responsibilities, we come up with such elaborate excuses to save ourselves from censure that everyone is left speechless. People abandon their inhibitions and say things about themselves that are better left unsaid. This is what was going through Lala Bhagatram's mind. Padamsingh knew that it was useless to argue with him. He said—How can I ask anything of you when you are in such a situation? I only need to find one more vote. Can you tell me where I can find it?

Bhagatram—Go and talk to Kumvar Sahib. God willing, you will get his vote. Seth Balbhadradas has just brought a three thousand-rupee lawsuit against him. The decree was just handed down yesterday. Kumvar Sahib is furious with him. If he had his way, I am sure that he would kill him. I have one more trick you might use to convince him. Make him the head of some committee or the other. He will be putty in your hands.

Padamsingh laughed—Well, well. I will go and see him immediately.

It was afternoon, but Padamsingh was neither hungry nor thirsty. He got into his buggy and left. Kumvar sahib lived in a bungalow on the bank of the Varuna. He got there in half an hour.

The courtyard of the bungalow was barren and unkempt. There were no plants or flowers. A few dogs were chained up in a corner. Kumvar Sahib was fond of hunting and, occasionally, he went as far as Kashmir in search of sport. But now, he was sitting in the hall playing his *sitar*. Spears and rifles stood in a corner of the room. In the other corner, atop a large table, lay a crocodile. As Padamsingh entered the room, he was completely startled to see it. It had been so carefully stuffed with straw that it looked as if it were still alive.

Kumvar Sahib welcomed Padamsingh with great affection—Welcome. It has been so long since I saw you. When did you return?

Padamsingh—I came back yesterday.

Kumvar—You look pale. Are you ill?

Padamsingh—No. I am doing fine, thank you.

Kumvar—Can I get you something to eat or drink?

Padamsingh—No, thank you. Have you been practising?

Kumvar—Yes. I love the sitar. I get nauseated when I have to listen to that awful harmonium or piano. These English instruments have ruined our music. No one listens to the sitar any more. And whatever is left is being destroyed by the theatres. Everywhere you look, people are talking about ghazals and *qawali*s. In a few years, Indian music will be a forgotten art, like archery. Music brings forth the noblest sentiments. Ever since singing has declined in popularity, we have become a completely unfeeling people. And you can see the effect that it has had on our literature. It's really a shame that the country that produced priceless epics like the Ramayan, gave birth to a wonderful poetry like Sursagar, has to rely on translations for even ordinary novels. In Bengal and Maharashtra, where they have a strong tradition of music, they haven't lost their sense of beauty. They still have wonderful imagination and aesthetic sense. I have stopped reading Hindi novels altogether. The translations aside, there is really nothing of worth other than a few plays by Harischandra and a few things such as *Chandrakanta Santati*. This must be the most pitiful literature in the world. And worse, there are some individuals who have translated a couple of English novels with the help of Bengali and Marathi translators and who think that they are prominent literati in this country. One such man generated a word-for-word translation of Kalidasa's plays, and now he considers himself the Hindi Kalidasa. One scholar translated two books by Mill, not himself, but with the help of Marathi and Gujarati translators, and he thinks that he has single-handedly revived Hindi literature. I think that all these translations are ruining Hindi literature. Originality never has a chance to thrive.

Padamsingh was a little surprised to learn that Kumvar Sahib knew so much about literature. He hadn't thought that he cared for anything other than hunting or polo. He didn't know much about Hindi literature himself, and so he was unwilling to reveal his ignorance. He smiled as if he had thought of it all before and said—You are raising an issue that will require endless debate, and I have come to ask for your help on a completely different matter. I have heard that you sided with the Seths in the last meeting.

Kumvar Sahib guffawed and his laughter echoed throughout the room. The brass shield hanging on the wall shook from the vibrations. He said—Tell me the truth. Who told you?

Padamsingh was taken aback by his odd laughter. He knew that Kumvar Sahib was about to catch him in a cleft stick, and he responded with irritation—Everyone. Do you want a list?

Kumvar Sahib let out another hearty laugh and said—And you believed them?

Padamsingh knew that this was all a trick to embarrass him. He responded sternly—I didn't have any reason not to believe them.

Kumvar—The reason would be that it is grossly unjust towards me. I expended all my energy in support of your resolution. I didn't think that the opposition deserved a second thought. I handled it all with a touch of irony. (Remembering) Yes, that possibility exists. I know. (Roaring with laughter again) If that's the case then you must see that the municipal council is filled with simpletons. Surely, you understand my sarcasm. Some people must have misunderstood. It's strange that none of the most learned and respected municipal council commissioners understood my simple irony. Shame! What a terrible shame! Well sir, you have been troubled for nothing.

You will have to forgive me. I support this resolution from the bottom of my heart.

Padamsingh smiled as well. He believed Kumvar Sahib's words. He said—If these men were so easily fooled, they are thick headed. But Prabhakar Rao was fooled as well, and that doesn't make sense. It seems as if his daily translations have worn out his brain.

When Padamsingh left, he was content, as if he had just returned from some pleasant vacation. Kumvar Sahib's kindness and humour had put his anxieties to rest.

36

When Sadan returned home, he was a like a man with a thousand plans for his life's earnings who discovers on arriving that he had been robbed.

The ability to think depends on education, society, and experience, and Sadan possessed none of these advantages. He was at that stage in life when we take a certain pride in religious thought and social customs. We aren't able to examine them critically. We do not have the courage to listen to arguments against them and we do not require answers to the whys and hows. Sadan would rather run away from home than take the women of the house to bathe in the Ganga. If ever he heard women laughing inside, he would find his mother and shout at her. Even Subhadra's mother-in-law hadn't been that harsh with her. He wasn't a liberal philosopher, but a dry ascetic, and he couldn't bear to see this kind of moral decay. He had seen the village boycott a wealthy *thakur* when he brought a dancing girl into his home. Eventually, the man was forced to kick the dancing girl out of his house. There was no doubt that Sadan loved Suman, but he didn't think that loving Suman was as unpardonable a crime as bringing her sister into his home. He hadn't even eaten a paan at Suman's brothel. He valued his family's prestige and social customs far more than he did his own soul.

Even the thought of the disgrace that his family would suffer if he married into the family of that whore was unbearable. When Padamsingh was discussing the issue at the wedding, Sadan had been fidgety. He had been afraid of what might happen if his father became convinced by his uncle's arguments. He couldn't understand what had come over his uncle. If another man had said the same thing, he would have cut off his tongue. But his uncle intimidated him. He had wanted to stand up to his uncle, and if the matter had remained at the level of argument, he would have gladly engaged with him. But Madansingh's insolence turned his eagerness for argument into a desire for compassion.

Frustrated and alone, Sadan's heart turned once again towards memories of Suman. Now that he had tasted the flavour of lust, his fantasy of love became overwhelming. His heart refused to live in darkness after having felt love's warm glow. He returned to Kashi with Padamsingh.

But even after he returned, the problem remained. He wondered whether Suman had heard about what had happened. She wasn't there. Her family has certainly disowned her. But surely they must have told her about the wedding. She won't ever speak to me again. It's possible that she may even hate me. As soon as it was dark, he changed his clothes, saddled his horse, and headed towards Dalmandi. His longing and his hopes melted away his fears. He was thinking about what Suman's first words to him might be and how he might answer them—what if she hasn't heard anything and wraps her arms around me as soon as she sees me and calls me cruel for leaving her? This last thought set his heart on fire and he whipped his horse and raced into Dalmandi. But just like a mischievous boy who is a little scared when he enters the school grounds, Sadan paused a moment before he went any further. His passion had worn off. He quietly stepped on to a platform that allowed him a clear view into Suman's room and peeked in meekly. The door was locked from the outside. A weight lifted from Sadan's shoulders. He was as happy as a penniless father forced to indulge his whining child when he finds the toy store closed.

As soon as he returned home, he began regretting his half-heartedness. His longing for Suman made his anxious. He couldn't sit still. At night, after everyone had gone to sleep, he sneaked out of the house and took off for Dalmandi. It was a wintry night and the cold wind was howling. The moon peeked out through the clouds and retreated quickly like a scared man. Sadan rode to Dalmandi as fast as he could, but as soon as he got there, he froze just as they had earlier. His hands and feet were as frozen as his heart. Suddenly, he felt stupid for returning—what will Suman say if she sees me now? She will be shocked to see me at this hour. Why can't I think straight? He turned around and went home.

He did the same thing the next evening. He had decided that he would go up to see her only if she saw him and called him up. Otherwise, he would ride straight through—I will know if she still cares for me by the way that she calls my name. She wouldn't have any reason to call for me otherwise after what has happened. He advanced but then started to think again—will she be sitting on her balcony waiting for me? She doesn't even know that I have come back. Either way, I have to go and see her once for myself. Suman could never be angry with me and even if she is angry, I can definitely make amends, no? I will fold my hands before her, prostrate myself at her feet, and I will wash away her pain with my tears. It doesn't matter how upset she is with me; she will never be able to erase the sign of my love that is stamped on her heart. Oh! When she looks at me with those gentle, tear-filled eyes, there is nothing that I would not do for her. If she still doubts my love for her, I will give my life for her just to prove her wrong. Surely, she will have to forgive me then. But as soon as he approached Dalmandi, his hopes of love disappeared, just as his doubts would evaporate upon seeing the goddess' image under a neem tree in the evening in his village. He thought to himself—what if she sees me and says, 'There goes that Kumvar Sahib, walking around like an heir to some fortune. What a fraud!' And his feet froze. He couldn't go any farther.

Several days passed in this manner. His daily sand castles of love would be destroyed in the evening with a single gust of underconfidence as soon as he approached Dalmandi.

One day his wanderings led him into Queens Park. A tent had been strung up and people were sitting underneath it listening to Professor Ramesh Datt's spell-binding lectures. Sadan got down from his horse to listen to the speech. Sadan had decided that courtesans were poisonous for the community and really did serious harm to individuals—I was terribly lucky; otherwise, I might have fallen into that trap as well. They should certainly be removed from the city. Had they never been in the marketplace, I would never have fallen for Sumanbai's charms.

The next day he returned to Queens Park. This day, Munshi Abulwafa was delivering an emotional and elegant discourse. Sadan listened to it intently, too. He thought—certainly, courtesans are responsible for our progress. It's true, and if it's not, then there is no one that is fit to offer prayers to the gods. And it is correct that brothels are located in places where Hindus and Muslims meet openly and amicably, where there isn't a trace of enmity, where there is place to rest from life's daily battles, where we can find refuge to lighten our hearts and forget our troubles. Definitely, evicting them from the city would be a terrible injustice not only to them, but to the entire community as well.

After a few days, he changed his mind again. The cycle seemed endless. Sadan didn't have the ability to think for himself. He never tried to examine or evaluate the merits of an issue. As a result, any persuasive individual could easily sway his decisions.

One day he saw a flier for a talk by Padamsingh. He had been getting ready for it since three o'clock and at four, he promptly arrived at Beni Park. No one else was there yet. A few men were laying out mats for the meeting. He got down from his horse and helped them. Around five o'clock, people began arriving and in half an hour, there were thousands. Then he saw Padamsingh approaching in a phaeton. His heart began to beat fast. First, Rustambhai read aloud a poem that Sayyid Teg Ali had penned for the occasion. When he was finished, Lala Vitthaldas stood up. Even though his speech was dry—without elegance or wit—people listened carefully to what he said. His selfless social work had earned him the respect of the community. People listened to his lifeless words zealously, like thirsty men offered a few drops of water. Other drinks would taste bland in comparison to the plain water he offered. Finally Padamsingh got up. Sadan's heart began to race. The speech was teeming with emotion and compassion. The ease and power of his words mesmerized Sadan. Some of the words he used were so emotive that Sadan's hair stood on end. He said—The decision to evict the courtesans from the city is not the result of hatred. Rather, we have no right to hate them. It would be grave injustice towards them. Courtesans are merely a manifestation of our weaknesses, our social crimes, and of our outmoded traditions. Dalmandi is merely a profane reflection of our lives, the visible shape of our demonic acts. How dare we despise them? The courtesans live desperate lives. It is our duty to return them to a virtuous path and help them repair their lives, and that will only happen once they have been removed from the city's terrible influences. Our social crimes are like a flame and these poor women are like straw. If you want a flame to die out, you need to keep it away from fresh kindling. Then it just dies off naturally.

Sadan was completely captivated by the speech. When the men sitting around him paid a compliment or when he heard them applaud the speech, Sadan was overwhelmed. But it seemed a little strange to him that members of the audience left one by one during the lecture. They were mostly men who despised courtesans and who had come to hear sharp polemics against prostitution. They had found Padamsingh's liberal perspective untenable.

37

Sadan became so fond of these lectures that he would go to every single one that he heard about. After listening to both sides for months and thinking carefully about them he began to learn how to make up his own mind about issues. Now, he was no longer immediately charmed by new ideas but would try to evaluate them based on the evidence. Ultimately, he decided that these lectures were mostly pageants of showy language—either there was no meaningful argument being made, or the same old arguments would be dressed up anew and reproduced. He had developed a critical perspective. He had taken up his uncle's position.

But in defending his position, his critical perspective was both one-sided and unnecessarily harsh. He did not possess the generosity to acknowledge that his opponents had good intentions. He had decided that everyone that opposed the resolution was a slave to lust and sex. In fact, these ideas had such an influence on him that he stopped going to Dalmandi altogether. Every time he saw a courtesan sitting in the park or riding in a buggy, he wanted nothing else but to remove her from his sight. If he had his way, he would have razed Dalmandi to the ground. The dancers and the people that watched the dances were now, in his mind, the most depraved individuals in the world. If he was ever alone with one of them, he was simply rude. And even though he still had some doubts, he was not the least bit concerned about being a supporter of the resolution. So he thought it best to ignore his doubts lest they weaken his position by being raised.

Suman still lingered in his thoughts and his heart still skipped a beat at the thought of her love. He could still see Suman's beautiful body every time he closed his eyes. To save himself from these images he tried not to be by himself. He would get up very early to bathe in the Ganga. He would read whatever he could find until ten or eleven at night, but still he could not make himself forget Suman. She would appear in his mind in all kinds of costumes playing, all kinds of characters—sometimes sulking, sometimes consoling, sometimes embracing him lovingly, sometimes smiling shyly at his love. And then Sadan would start, awakening from a kind of sleep, and try to ignore the thoughts that preoccupied him so that he could think of other things—I wonder why uncle is so depressed lately. I never see him laughing any more. Why does Jeetan bring him medicine every day? What's wrong with him? And then Suman would again appear in his imagination and with tears in her delicate eyes she would say—Sadan, I never thought that you could do this to me. You think that I am a whore, but I never behaved like a whore with you. I entrusted you with my heart. Don't you think that's worth anything? Sadan would start again and try to push her out of his mind. He had heard in one of the lectures that man controls his own destiny, can become whatever he wants to become but to do so must keep immoral, base, and lewd ideas out of his head. With all his strength, man should always attempt to keep such thoughts from his mind and keep his heart pure with the most virtuous thoughts and feelings. Sadan never forgot this advice. In the same lecture, he had also heard that man doesn't need higher education to elevate himself, just good thoughts and pure feelings. Sadan liked this idea very much. And so he kept trying to fix his mind on moral things. A thousand men had heard in that very lecture that bad thoughts can not only ruin one's life but can have grave consequences in the next life as well. But most of the people, many with education, listened and then soon forgot. But Sadan, with his simple heart, listened and carried them with him always, like a pauper who comes upon a golden object and then guards it with his life. He was now swimming in the waves of repentance. If he ever saw a young woman while he was walking in the streets, he would immediately censure himself and remember that a moment's pleasure could destroy his soul. And this self admonition would give him peace.

One day while Sadan was going to bathe in the Ganga he saw a group of courtesans walking in the Chauk. The most famous and popular courtesans in the city had just performed an Urs at a religious concert, and were returning from it when Sadan saw them. He was dazzled by the sight for he had never before seen such a spectacle of beauty, gold, and perfume in his life. Sadan had never seen forms, figures, and femininity so remarkable, dresses and ornaments so dazzling. He tried to repress his feelings as well as he could, but he didn't succeed. He stared long and hard at these otherworldly beauties, like a student who indulges in sensual pleasures after the hard labour of months of study is finally over. He wasn't satisfied with just one look, and so he turned around and looked again, but this time, he couldn't tear his eyes away, and he even forgot to keep walking. He stood there like a statue. And when the courtesans had passed, he came to his senses with a jolt and began to censure himself—you fool! You squandered months of effort in a second! Who knows how badly I have ruined my soul? Why am I so weak? In the end, he consoled himself with the fact that it couldn't possibly be a sin just to look at them—I didn't look at them sinfully, after all. It wasn't lust. It is our duty to experience pleasure in God's marvellous creations.

He kept walking, but he couldn't quieten his conscience—why am I deluding myself? Why is it so hard to accept the fact that I made a mistake? Yes, I was wrong. I am not an ascetic or a saint. I am just an ordinary man, and under these circumstances, it is certainly pardonable. I wasn't able to live by the high standards I set for myself. Dear God! But beauty is an amazing thing, isn't it? People say that sin makes the face dark, but sin makes those women even more beautiful. They say that the face is the mirror of the heart, but it seems that is false as well.

Sadan composed himself again and tried to distract himself by looking at the issue from another perspective—yes, those women are exceedingly beautiful and delicate, but they have abused their divine gifts. They have damned their souls. Yes. And for what? For these fine silks and these sparkling jewels. Their eyes are filled with fraud, scorn, and ill-will rather than the light of love. Their hearts, which should bring forth genuine, pure love, are covered instead with a smelly, poisonous mire. What a pity.

Sadan drew some satisfaction from his contempt. He wandered towards the bank of the Ganga. The time that he had spent thinking about these things had made him late, so he didn't go to the spot that he usually went to, to bathe. It would probably already be crowded, and so he ended up at a section of the riverbank near the widow's home. It was usually deserted. Few people went there because it was so far.

When he reached the edge of the water, he saw a woman walking towards the river. He recognized her immediately. It was Suman, but she had changed dramatically. No long flowing hair, no refinement, no laughing rosy lips, no sparkling eyes, no make-up, no dazzling jewels. Now she wore only a plain white sari. He could see the heaviness in her gait and the lines of despair on her face. She was the same poem, but without elegance or rhyme, and therefore meaningful and honest. Sadan was overcome with love when he first saw her and he took several quick steps toward her, but when he saw the transformation that she had undergone, he stopped short, almost as if he didn't recognize her any more, as if she weren't Suman but some strange woman. The spell of love had been broken. He couldn't understand why she had changed. He looked at Suman once again. She had been staring at him, but with concern rather than longing, either because she had already forgotten what had passed between them or wanted to. As if she wanted the dying flames of love in her heart finally to be extinguished. Sadan inferred that perhaps she considered him to be swindling, lowly, and selfish. After a moment he looked back at her—to decide if my hypothesis is false or not. Their eyes met and as suddenly darted away. Sadan arrived at a conclusion about his hypothesis. His pride rose up along with his conclusion. He censured himself—I had just made such progress and in a few seconds, I have fallen back into the same trap of my desires. He didn't look back at Suman. He hung his head and walked away. Sadan saw that his feet were trembling and he wasn't moving, nor did he even make a gesture. In his mind he had already dared Suman—if you run a hundred feet away from me, I am ready to run 10,000 feet away from you. But he didn't seem to realize that he was standing in the same place, frozen. He had become a monument to the very emotions that he had tried to suppress.

After a few minutes, he followed Suman at a distance and just out of sight. He wanted to know where she lived. His longing overpowered his good sense.

38

KRISHNACHANDRA HAD NOT come out of his house ever since the wedding party left. He sat in his room all day, hopelessly dejected. He was too ashamed to show his face anywhere. Even if that wretched Suman had only lowered him a little in the eyes of society, he couldn't bear the sight of himself. He couldn't bear the insult that this had proved to be. He had been in prison for three or four years and still had never sunk so low in his own esteem. He had even drawn some satisfaction from the fact that he had paid for his crimes by going to prison. But this stain completely destroyed his self-respect. He could no longer show his face even to the rogues whom he used to sit and smoke with. He knew that he had fallen even lower than them. He felt as if his name was being slandered throughout the world—people will say that my daughter ... Whenever he started to think about it, he would become lost in an ocean of shame and despair—Hai! I would have slit her throat if I had known that she was going to ruin my reputation this way. I know that she was unlucky, that she deserved to be married into a wealthy family, that she lived for luxury and pleasure. But I never knew that her soul was so weak. Who ever gets what they deserve in this world? Everyone faces misfortune. The wives of the wealthiest men also yearn for various things, but no one can see the slightest trace of concern or want on their faces. They pass their days in tears, but no one ever sees them crying. They never speak of their misfortunes to anyone. They may even die, but they will never trouble anyone for help. They are like goddesses. They live for the honour of their families and die trying to uphold it. But this wicked, this wretched ... And her husband is such a coward for not slitting her throat. Why didn't he strangle her when she first stepped outside the house? It seems as if he, too, is base, cowardly, and castrated. Had he any concern for his family honour, he would never have let things get out of hand. She may not be ashamed of herself, but I am and I will see that she gets what she deserves. These hands that nurtured her, raised her, will also hold the sword that slices her throat. These eyes that delighted in watching her play will now take pleasure in watching her drown in her own blood. There is no other way to restore our ruined reputation. The world will know what punishment they mete out who die protecting their honour.

Having made up his mind, Krishnachandra set out to accomplish his plan. In prison, he had learned dozens of ways to kill a man from the other inmates. That's all they would talk about. He thought it best to slice Suman's throat with a sword and then turn himself over to the authorities—And the testimony that I give before the magistrate will open the eyes of everyone who hears me. In his mind, he was quite pleased with the plan that he had devised and so he began practicing the testimony that he would deliver—first, I will tell them about the sensuality of polite society, then I will expose the corruption of the police force, and then I will talk about the crimes of marriage. I will produce such a scathing critique of the custom of dowry that people will be left speechless. But the most important part will be the one where I announce that we are responsible for the destruction of our own honour. Our cowardice, our fear of social scorn, our false love for our children, our senselessness, our lack of self-respect—we hide these crimes from ourselves and try to veil them. And so weak souls are encouraged to go on.

Krishnachandra had made up his mind to do all of this, but he hadn't thought about what would happen to Shanta. The shame that he felt from this insult had made it impossible for him to worry about anything else. He was like a man who leaves his child's funeral to seek revenge on his enemies; who while sitting in a boat sees a snake in the water and pounces on it to kill it but forgets about the danger of overturning the boat and drowning in the process.

It was evening. Krishnachandra had decided that today he would set out for the murder. And yet, his heart was heavy. It was the same kind of heaviness that weighs down the heart before some awful task. After days of being enraged and overwhelmed by the pace of his rage, today he was more than a little languid, like wind that blows fiercely for a while and then turns into a calm breeze. It was a kind of heaviness that suits the heart in matters like these. It is a glimpse into spirituality, which allows men a little time to examine their lives, and allows memory the chance to play in the heart. Krishnachandra thought back to the days when his life was blissful, when he would take his two daughters for a walk every evening. Sometimes he would hold Suman in his arms, and sometimes Shanta. And when they would return, how Gangajali would run up to the girls and embrace them. No bliss is as wonderful as when it is recollected. The jungle and the mountains, that sometimes seem desolate and treacherous to you, the rivers and lakes whose banks you cross with your eyes closed—after a while, they appear in your mind's eye as beautiful and peaceful and you begin to long for those spectacles again. Memories of his previous way of life had brought Krishnachandra happiness many times. Tears welled up in his eyes—Hai! What a terrible end to such a wonderful life! I am preparing to slaughter with my own hands the daughter that played in my lap. Krishnachandra felt sorry for Suman—That poor girl has really fallen into some misfortune. She was the apple of my eye, I did everything so that she could be happy— can I be so heartless toward my own daughter that I should stone her? But kind thoughts didn't last long in Krishnachandra's heart—The most disgusting part about Suman's crime was that her door was open to any man. Hindu, Muslim, anyone could go there. And as soon as he thought about this, his heart filled with shame and dejection again.

In the meanwhile, Pandit Umanath came to sit with him and said—I just got back from the lawyer. He recommends that we bring a lawsuit against them.

Krishnachandra asked with a little surprise—What kind of a lawsuit?

Umanath—Against them, for stopping the wedding.

Krishnachandra—And what will that achieve?

Umanath—Either they will marry the girl or they will compensate us.

Krishnachandra—But won't there be even more shame in this?

Umanath—We have faced all the insults that we could possibly face. What is there left to be afraid of? I gave him a thousand rupees in the tilak ceremony, spent four or five hundred on food and drinks. Why should I forget about those things? If I had given that money to an honourable but poor family, they would have happily agreed to the marriage. At least we will expose these educated nobles for what they are.

Krishnachandra drew in a deep breath and said—Give me some poison and then get on with your suit.

Umanath got upset—Why are you so afraid?

Krishnachandra—Have you already decided to bring a lawsuit?

Umanath—Yes, I have. Yesterday, several famous lawyers and barristers were gathered in the city. The lawsuit is an excellent strategy for us. The lawyer's men thought long and hard before giving me their advice. I have even given my testimony to two lawyers.

Krishnachandra responded with disappointment—Fine. Bring the lawsuit.

Umanath—Why are you so unhappy about it?

Krishnachandra—How can I explain it to you when you won't even try to understand? News that has only reached a few small villages will spread all over. Suman will certainly be called to testify and my name will be ruined.

Umanath—How long do you want me to be afraid of the same thing? I still have to marry off two of my daughters. Why should I ruin their lives by taking this slander on myself?

Krishnachandra—Then you want to bring this lawsuit forward to protect your reputation.

Umanath responded gravely—Yes. If that's how you want to interpret it, then yes. The wedding procession turned back from my door. People suspect that Suman is my daughter. People are only talking about me. I am asking for ten thousand rupees in my lawsuit. And if I win even five thousand rupees, Shanta can be married off into a good family. You know that people will devour rotting and half-eaten things because they are drawn to their sweetness. How will Shanta get married if there is no money to attract suitors with? And there remains the fact that my family name has been ruined. People used to think that knowing me worked to their advantage. Now they won't even speak to me with a straight face. That's what has happened.

Krishnachandra said—Fine. Draw up the lawsuit.

After Umanath had left, Krishnachandra looked up towards the heavens and said—Dear God, please call me up to you. I can't bear this awful world any more.

He had never felt dishonoured like this before. He knew that punishing Suman wouldn't wipe out the shame, just like killing a snake wasn't an antidote to the poison. Her death would only bring more derision, nothing else—The police will arrest me; and for months I will wander around aimlessly and then after all this, I will be executed. It would be better to kill myself, to extinguish the candle whose flame makes visible this unspeakable spectacle. Damn! That accursed Suman has dragged Shanta down with her. She has destroyed her life too. Lord! Now you are her protector. You are this helpless child's only hope. Just take me away from this world so that I no longer have to be witness to her ruin.

After a while, Shanta came to call her father to dinner. Krishnachandra hadn't seen her since the wedding day. Now he looked at her with eyes filled with tenderness. In the dim light, he saw a supernatural glow on her face! Her eyes shimmered with the light of her pure soul. There was no hint of sorrow or sin in her. Ever since she had laid her eyes on Sadan, she could feel a divine ecstasy welling up in her heart. To her, it felt as if a spring of pure emotions had erupted there. And with it had also emerged a strange sense of self-sacrifice. Earlier she would talk back to her aunt but these days she spent hours rubbing her feet. She didn't feel the slightest envy towards her cousins either. She would even laugh as she drew water from the well. And working the hand-mill gave her sincere pleasure. Love had taken shape in her life. She didn't have Sadan, but she had got something even better. And that was her love for Sadan.

When Krishnachandra saw Shanta's blossoming figure, he wasn't just shocked, he was downright terrified. It seemed to him that the wicked pain of sorrow had not opened a flood of tears but had actually turned into a horrible insanity. He even deluded himself into thinking that she thought him responsible for her agony. He looked at her with desperate eyes and said—Shanta!

Shanta looked back at him curiously.

Krishnachandra spoke slowly—It has been four years since my life was lost in that whirlpool. That tragedy has taken everything that I had, and now I can no longer bear to see my children suffer. I know that all this is a result of my sins. Had I been careful from the beginning, none of you would have had to suffer today. I won't live much longer. If you ever see poor Suman again, tell her that I forgive her. I am to blame for everything that she has done. Two days ago, I was bent on killing her. But then God saved me from committing yet another sin. Tell her to have pity on her unlucky father and her unlucky mother's soul.

Krishnachandra stopped before he could finish. Shanta stood quietly. She felt terribly sorry for her father. After a moment, Krishnachandra spoke—I have something to ask you as well.

Shanta—Tell me. What would do you want me to do?

Krishnachandra—Nothing, just remember—never be dissatisfied. This little bit of advice will keep you steady even in the worst of times.

Shanta knew that her father had wanted to say something else but hesitated and changed the subject. His thoughts were not hidden from her. She lifted her head and looked up proudly. Her steady gaze spoke more than words. She thought to herself—a woman who has found means in faithful service of her husband needs nothing else to help her. In it, she finds happiness, contentment, and peace.

It was midnight. Krishnachandra went outside. Nature, that beauty, had wrapped herself in a thick blanket of fog like an old woman lost in sleep. And in the sky, the moon was hiding its face and speeding away to some unknown land.

Krishnachandra suddenly felt a sharp longing—will I see my wife again? It was the only memory of a happy life that remained with him. In the thick darkness of frustration, it was the only beacon drawing him onwards. He stood for a long while in the doorway, and then, after taking a deep breath, set off. It seemed to him as if Gangajali was calling him from the heavens.

And for a while, Krishnachandra had no wants, no desires, and no worries. His mind was disinterested in the world around him. He was thinking about getting to the banks of the Ganga as quickly as possible and drowning himself in its deep waters. He was worried about not being able to do it in the end, so he began running in order to strengthen his determination.

But after he had run a short distance, he was unsure of himself and thought—It's not that hard to jump into a river—it's over as soon as my foot slips on the last bit of earth. His heart skipped a beat as he thought about it. For just a second, he thought about running away from it all—If I leave, I won't have to listen to the insults any more. But he wouldn't allow himself to dwell on the idea. His mind could not play tricks on him. After all, he wasn't a religious man by nature and his heart was racing from some fear of the unknown and the invisible, and so in order to stay firm he kept telling himself that God was both generous and compassionate. His soul had forsaken him. He was like a little boy who had broken a friend's toy and was then afraid of going back to his own home.

Slowly, Krishnachandra covered four miles. As he got closer and closer to the bank of the Ganga, he became increasingly flustered. His heart was racing from fear, but he was trying to rid himself of this internal weakness through speed and defiance—ha! I am shameless and soulless. Even after this tragedy I am still afraid of death. Suddenly, he heard someone singing. As he moved closer to the river, the singing got louder. The singer was coming toward him. In the desolate darkness, the song seemed extremely beautiful to Krishnachandra. He listened intently to the lyrics:

> *There is no master such as Hari.*
> *Protecting his devotees in the way each desires,*
> *There is no master such as Hari.*
> *Here feeding the hungry and there quenching the thirsty,*
> *He roams the earth, providing each with his lot*
> *There is no master such as Hari.*

Although the song wasn't poetic or artistic, it was pious, and so Krishnachandra found it to be full of bliss. He knew this teaching well. It calmed his burnt soul.

The song ended and soon, Krishnachandra saw a colossal sadhu with matted hair coming towards him. The sadhu asked him his name and where he was from. From his expression, Krishnachandra gathered that he knew who he was. Krishnachandra wanted to walk on but the sadhu stopped him to ask—Where are you going at this hour?

Krishnachandra—I have some business to take care of.

Sadhu—What business can you possibly have on the riverbank in the middle of the night?

Krishnachandra, angrily—You are mystic. You should already know the answer to that.

Sadhu—I am not a mystic, just a beggar. I can't let you go there at this hour.

Krishnachandra—Go your own way. What right do you have to stop me from doing what I am doing?

Sadhu—If I didn't have the right, I wouldn't have stopped you. You don't know me, but I am your son-in-law. My name is Gajadhar Pande.

Krishnachandra—What? You're Gajadhar Pande? What are you doing looking like this? I have wanted to see you for a long time. I have questions to ask you.

Gajadhar—I live under a tree on the bank of the river. Come, rest there for a while. I will tell you everything.

On the way, the two didn't speak to each other. Soon, they reached the tree, where a huge log was burning. Straw had been spread out on the ground and there was a deerskin, an ascetic's water pot, and a bundle of books.

Krishnachandra warmed himself by the fire. He said—So, you've become an ascetic. Tell me the truth, how did Suman turn into a woman of that sort?

Gajadhar looked compassionately at Krishnachandra's face in the firelight. He could plainly read his heart from the expression on his face. He was no longer Gajadhar. Association with religious people and detachment from the world had allowed his wisdom to grow. Each moment he spent thinking about Suman and her condition brought him an equal amount of remorse. This perpetual reflection had softened his feelings toward Suman. Sometimes he even longed to go to her and fall at her feet.

Gajadhar spoke—It happened because of my cruelty towards her. It is the consequence of my harsh and inhuman behaviour. She possessed every good quality. She was raised to be the mistress in some wealthy family. She should never have married a roguish, wicked, and evil man like me. Then, I was blind to her good qualities. She was forced to endure every sort of difficulty living with me. But still, she never bore me any ill-will. She respected me. But as I watched her behaviour, I began to suspect that she was playing some elaborate trick on me. It was hard for me to see her happiness, her devotion, and her tranquility. I thought that she was certainly deceiving me. And when, for some small trifle, she argued with me, cried, or cursed me and shouted at me, it would only strengthen my suspicion. Her high standards became the cause of my distrust. I began questioning her virtue. In the end, all it took was her staying a little too long at her friend's house for me to throw her out.

Krishnachandra cut him off and said—Where were your senses at a time like that? Didn't you even think for a moment that your cruelty would ruin the fair name of a well-respected family?

Gajadhar—Maharaj, what can I say about what happened? I neglected her. But her intentions were always pure. She loathed sin. Now she lives in a widows' home and everyone likes her. People are astonished by her piety.

Listening to Gajadhar's words, Krishnachandra's heart began to soften towards his daughter. But just as it softened in one place, it became harder in another, like a stream which normally flows in one direction begins to flow very rapidly when it changes it direction. He scowled at Gajadhar, like a hungry lion staring down his prey. He was becoming convinced that this man had ruined his family—but more than that, he has done a great wrong to Suman. He has given her every sort of trouble. Should I forgive him just because he is now ashamed of his crimes? But why did he tell me these things? Perhaps he thinks I will not harm him. That must be it, or why else would he admit his guilt to me so fearlessly? Krishnachandra was unable to understand Gajadhar's emotions. He stared into the fire for a while, and then spoke sharply—Gajadhar, you have ruined my family. You have made it so that I cannot show my face anywhere. You have stolen the life of my daughter, destroyed her, and now you are sitting here like you are some kind of saint. You should have drowned yourself in a fistful of water.

Gajadhar had been scraping the dirt on the ground. He didn't look up.

Krishnachandra continued—You were poor. That's not your fault. You weren't able to provide for your wife properly—that doesn't make you guilty. You weren't able to understand her feelings, to grasp the true meaning of her thoughts, yet, that doesn't make you guilty. You are guilty because you threw her out of your house. Why didn't you just kill her? If you had any doubts about her fidelity, why didn't you slit her throat? And if you didn't have the courage to do that, why didn't you take your own life? Why didn't you swallow poison? If you had only ended her life, it would never have come to this; there wouldn't be this stain on my family's reputation. And you call yourself a man? I have nothing but contempt for your cowardice and shamelessness. A man who is so low that his blood doesn't boil at seeing his wife love another is even worse than a beast.

Gajadhar now knew that by relating how he had kicked Suman out of the house, he was stuck in a moral trap. He regretted having been so open. He was surprised at the way Krishnachandra seemed to reject him and how hurt he felt at this rejection. A troubled heart can only tolerate a rejection that has compassion and gentleness in it, not the kind that smacks of dishonour or cruelty. A blister needs the prick of a lance, not the blunt blow of a rock. Gajadhar regretted his mistake. He was impatient to get back to their earlier argument.

Krishnachandra howled—Why? Why didn't you kill her?

Gajadhar replied soberly—My heart was not hard enough.

Krishnachandra—Then why did you kick her out?

Gajadhar—Because there was no other way out of the situation.

Krishnachandra, annoyed—Why? Couldn't you have taken poison?

Wounded, Gajadhar responded—Kill myself needlessly?

Krishnachandra—Killing yourself needlessly is better than living needlessly.

Gajadhar—You cannot call my life needless. Pandit Umanath may not have told you anything, but I have begged for money and raised fifteen hundred rupees for Shanta's wedding and I was just going to him with another thousand rupees for the expenses of the marriage.

Gajadhar became silent. He felt that he had said too much and revealed his arrogance in the process. He hung his head in embarrassment.

Krishnachandra responded with skepticism in his voice—He didn't tell me anything about it.

Gajadhar—It was not important. I have only told you the beginning of the story. You must forgive me—all I wanted to say was that I wouldn't have been able to help anyone had I killed myself. These mistakes have obliged me to change my life. In waking a sleeping conscience, our mistakes are like a divine tremor, making us careful for the rest of our lives. Even education, good counsel, and relationships don't have as much influence on our lives as observing the consequences of our mistakes. You may call this cowardice, but this cowardice has turned into a regular source of peace and inspiration for me. Having destroyed one life, today I am able to help thousands of desperate young women and it brings me immense pleasure knowing that this has had a positive effect on Suman as well. From my hut, I have seen her bathing in the Ganga several times and have been amazed by her faith and devotion. You can see the perfect radiance of her pure soul on her face. If she was a happy housewife before, then now she is among the most enlightened women, and I am confident that one day she will be a jewel among them.

At first Krishnachandra heard these words like a clever customer listening to the slick talk of a salesman who never forgets to say things only in his own interest. But slowly Krishnachandra began to be affected. He realized that his harsh insults had hurt a man who was ashamed of his mistakes and who was burying him underneath the weight of his favours to others—look how cruel I am! His eyes began to fill up at this realization. A gentle-hearted man hardens as quickly as wax, but melts just as quickly.

Gajadhar looked at him compassionately and said—How would you like to be the guest of an ascetic? Tomorrow, I will set out with you. This blanket will protect you from the cold.

Krishnachandra spoke humbly—The blanket is not necessary. I will be fine as I am.

Gajadhar—You think that by using my blanket you will be associating yourself with my sins, but this isn't my blanket. I have kept it aside for times like this.

Gajadhar didn't protest any more. He was catching a cold. He lay down covering himself with the blanket and immediately fell into a deep sleep. But it wasn't a peaceful sleep, it was a condensed history of his suffering. In his dreams, he saw himself lying on his deathbed in prison with the warden staring at him with hatred and saying—You will not be set free today. In the meanwhile Gangajali and his father came and stood by the bed. Their faces were distorted and blackened. Gangajali cried and said—It is because of you that we are in this awful state. His father looked at him with scorn and said—Will the only thing you accomplish be ruining of the family name? Is that why we brought you into the world? We will never be able to wash the soot off our faces. We will suffer this tragedy till the end of time. You have put us through this torture so that you could live your poor, meagre life, but we will take your life this very moment. As he said this, he picked up an axe to attack him.

Krishnachandra's eyes opened with a start. His heart was racing. When he had fallen sleep, he had forgotten why he had set out from his home. This dream reminded him. He cursed himself. I am an irresponsible oaf. He was certain that it was not a dream, but an omen.

The effects of Gajadhar's narrative on his heart slowly began to evaporate—Suman can become a saint if she wants to, even a nun, but that stain on her character, which has blackened all our faces, will not be wiped out. The Mahatma says that sin has an incredible power to reform. But I don't see its effect anywhere. I have sinned several times and have never felt this power. It's meaningless. It's all a word game—he's hidden his own cowardice in a parade of words. It's a lie. Sin gives rise only to more sin. If there were good things in sin, there would be no sinners in this world.

Thinking thus, he got up. Gajadhar, too, was lying next to the fire. Krishnachandra got up quietly and set out towards the bank of the river. He had decided that he would finally put an end to his torment.

The moon had disappeared and the fog had got thicker. Darkness made it impossible to distinguish between the trees, mountains, and the sky. Krishnachandra walked along the path, but he had to feel his way rather than see it. He was so absorbed in avoiding the rocks and the bushes that he didn't think about his condition.

As he approached the edge of the water he saw a little light. He stepped into the water. The Ganga, wrapped in a thick blanket of mist, lay groaning. The only difference between the surrounding darkness and the Ganga was the flow of water. It was a fluid darkness. It was enveloped in sadness, like a house that has had a death.

Krishnachandra stood at the edge of the river. He thought to himself—hai! My end is so near. Who knows where my soul will be in the next moment, who knows what the future will be? Today, I will break all my relations with the world. Lord, I surrender myself to you, have mercy on me. Save me, Lord.

For a moment, he estimated the strength of his convictions. He found himself to be fearless. He waded into the water. Krishnachandra's entire body began to tremble. He continued wading into the water. When the water reached his neck, he turned around once more to view the overwhelming darkness. It was his last chance to love the world. It was the final test of his courage and his pride. Everything that he had done so far was merely in preparation for this last test. It was his final battle between desire and illusion. Illusion used all its strength to pull him away. Suman stood before him like a wise, educated woman, and Shanta was the embodiment of sorrow itself— What have I to lose now? I, too, can become an ascetic. I am not some famous person whose reputation and honour will concern the world. Who knows how many young women fall into the snares of sin in the same way? And which one of them does the world remember? I am a fool to think that the entire world will laugh at me. His heart wanted more than anything to argue against this logic, but it was useless—it needed only one more dip in the water. Only one step separated life from death. The supporting leg was so steady and calm; the leading leg, dangerously fearful.

Krishnachandra tried to take a step backwards. Illusion had demonstrated the brilliance of its romantic powers. But in truth, it wasn't the love of life but the fear of the unknown that pulled him back.

At that moment, Krishnachandra realized that it was impossible for him to go back. Slowly, he began sliding deeper and deeper into the water. He screamed loudly. He tried to pull his cold, weak legs back, but such was the fate of his action that it drew him farther along.

Suddenly, he heard the voice of Gajadhar calling to him. Krishnachandra shouted back, but the words didn't even have the chance to escape from his lips before they were lost amid the waves—like a candle extinguished in the wind and absorbed into the darkness. The heat of his grieving, shamed, and worried heart grew cooler in the cold waters. Gajadhar heard the words 'I am drowning' and then nothing more save the demonic squeals of the waves.

Mournfully, Gajadhar stood on the banks of the river for a long time. He heard those same words ringing all around him. The nearby mountains, the waves before him, and the impenetrable darkness surrounding him echoed those very words.

39

THE NEXT DAY, this sad news reached Amola. Apart from a few men, no one came to offer condolences to Umanath. Had it been a natural death, even his enemies may have wept a few tears, but suicide was a terrible matter altogether—something for the police to investigate. On an occasion like this, even friends behaved like enemies.

When Gajadhar told Umanath what had happened, he was bathing near the well. He didn't feel an ounce of pain or surprise. Instead, he was angry at Krishnachandra, and the fear of being heckled by the police suppressed all sorrow. It took him longer to bathe and get ready that day. An unsteady mind gets no respite from worry. At that moment, wisdom disappears.

Jahnvi raised an enormous commotion. Seeing her cry, both her daughters began wailing as well. The women from the neighbourhood came over to comfort her. They were not afraid of the police, but still her tears of sorrow dried quickly. A debate about Krishnachandra's shortcomings and merits began. There was a consensus that he had more merits than faults. When Umanath came home in the afternoon for a glass of *sherbet* and mentioned how self-absorbed Krishnachandra had been, Jahnvi looked at him with a sideways glance and said—That's absurd.

Umanath was embarrassed. Jahnvi wanted to keep her heartfelt happiness to herself. She knew that her joy was so vicious and unwarranted that she wanted to keep it a secret even from Umanath. Shanta was the only one to experience genuine sorrow—no one else. Although she had thought her father to be quite helpless, at least she had had someone to support her. Her father's failings had been the cause of her devotion to him, but now she was completely alone. But her frustration did not make her hopeless. Her heart became even more tender. The teachings that Krishnachandra had passed on to her now produced in her a strange compulsion. From this day onwards, Shanta became patience itself. Like the last drops of rain, the last words of a man are not fruitless. Now Shanta would not speak words she thought might disturb her father's memory. While he was alive, she had not always been respectful, but now she would not let even unkind thoughts enter her heart. She was certain that a soul free of its material body did not know the difference between inside and outside. Even though she did everything to please Jahnvi, yet Jahnvi would certainly taunt her a few times through the day. Shanta would be upset, but she would swallow her anger and wouldn't even cry to herself. She was afraid that her father's soul would be distressed by her tears.

For Holi, Umanath bought the best saris for his daughters. Even Jahnvi wore a new sari that day, but Shanta had to wear her old one. Her heart was torn to pieces but her face showed no sign of it. While the two sisters pouted about the fact that their saris hadn't been hemmed, Shanta happily occupied herself with housework—even Jahnvi felt sorry for her. She took out an old silk sari and gave it to Shanta. Shanta didn't mind at all. She put it on and began to prepare dinner.

One day, Shanta forgot to wash Umanath's dhoti. The next day, when Umanath went to bathe, his dhoti was still wet. He didn't say anything, but Jahnvi scolded her so severely that Shanta began to cry. She wept as she washed the dhoti. It hurt Umanath to watch her weep and he thought to himself—we are making this orphan suffer so much for her daily bread. How will we justify ourselves before God? He didn't say anything to Jahnvi, but he decided that there must be a quick end to this torture. Having completed the mourning rituals, Umanath had become absorbed in the proceedings to bring a suit against Madansingh. The lawyers had assured him that he would win. Things will be so much better after I win the five thousand rupees—the thought made Umanath exceedingly happy; it awakened his hopes. He began to make plans for a new house. He had traced out a picture of the house in his imagination. Talk had begun about a proper location for it. He had quite forgotten Shanta amid these blissful dreams. But Jahnvi's scolding reminded him. The thousand rupees that Gajadhar had rustled up and which had been set aside for legal costs were still with him. One day, he talked to Jahnvi about it. There was a chance of finding a suitable groom somewhere. Shanta overheard them talking. Listening to them talk about the lawsuit hurt her, but she thought it inappropriate to intervene. But when she heard them talk about her wedding, she could no longer remain quiet. A strong catalytic force did away with her embarrassment and her hesitation.

As soon as Umanath left, she went to Jahnvi and said—What was uncle saying to you just now?

Jahnvi replied in an annoyed voice—What was he saying? That wretched Suman has brought this calamity upon us, otherwise, why would there be any need for all this hypocrisy? Now, we can't find as good an opportunity or as suitable a groom. There is a small village not too far from here.

Shanta looked down and said—Am I so much trouble for you that you want to just throw me out? You should tell uncle not to trouble himself over me.

Jahnvi—You are his favourite niece. He can't bear to see you unhappy. I have told him to let you be. When we get the money from the lawsuit, we can do something without too much worry, but when does he listen to me?

Shanta—Why doesn't he just send me away?

Surprised, Jahnvi asked—Where?

Shanta replied simply—Maybe Chunar, maybe Benares.

Jahnvi—What kind of childish nonsense is this? If it was that easy, why would there be all these tears? If they had wanted to take you into their home, why would they have made such a commotion?

Shanta—Maybe not as a daughter-in-law, but perhaps as a servant.

Jahnvi spoke coldly—Then go. Your uncle will never take you there just to be insulted, and then have to carry you back. He plans to trample on them and make them pay.

Shanta—Aunt, no matter how proud those people may be, if I go and stand at their doorstep, they are bound to feel sorry for me. I am sure that they won't turn me away. Even when your enemy stands at the door, you hesitate to turn him away. And then I am ...

Jahnvi became impatient. She couldn't bear this shamelessness. She interrupted her and said—Hold your tongue. It's as if you've never heard of shame or modesty. Do you even care what we feel, how insulting it would be? Those who don't brother about you, even if they were the richest Seths in town I wouldn't look up to them. That's my decision. Even if they were to come here now and start showering flattery on us, your uncle would run them out of town.

Shanta was silent. No matter what the world thought, Shanta considered herself married. That a married woman should be married into another home was, for her, most shameful and unbearable. In the month before the wedding procession arrived, she had repeatedly heard good things about Sadan and was already in love with him. During the *dwarpuja*, she saw him at the doorway as if he were her own husband, and as if he were some stranger. Now the thought of another husband was like a blow to her chastity. Having considered Sadan her husband for so long, she couldn't remove him from her heart, whether he asked about her or not, accepted her or not. After the dwarpuja, if she had seen Sadan, she would have met him as if he were her husband, even if there had been no wedding, no circling of the sacred fire, or vermilion in the parting of her hair—even if it was just a feeling.

So far, Shanta had hoped that she would eventually go to her husband's home and find solace at her husband's feet, but now that she heard talk of her marriage—or rather her next marriage—her already betrothed heart began to race. Without hesitation, she entreated Jahnvi to send her to her husband's home. At least as far as she was able. What else could she do? But when she saw Jahnvi's merciless contempt, she felt her courage slipping away. But she couldn't help herself. When everyone had gone to sleep that night, she began writing a plea to Padamsingh. This was her last option. She had already decided what her fate would be if it didn't succeed.

She quickly finished her letter. She had written that letter many times in her mind. The only thing left was for her to put it on paper.

'Revered Father-in-law, please accept the greetings of your humble servant, Shanta. I am in great difficulty. Have mercy on me and take me into your home. My father has drowned in the Ganga. Here, preparations are underway for a lawsuit against your family. There is talk of a second wedding for me. Please reply quickly. I will wait for your reply for a week. After that, you will not hear the cries of this woman.'

In the meantime, Jahnvi awoke. Mosquitoes had bitten her all over. She scratched and said—Shanta! What is that girl doing?

Shanta replied unafraid—I am writing a letter.

Jahnvi—To whom?

Shanta—To my in-laws.

Jahnvi—Why won't you drown yourself in a handful of water?

Shanta—I will, in seven days.

Jahnvi didn't reply and slowly drifted back to sleep. Shanta wrote the address on the envelope, put it in the bundle of her clothes, and went to sleep.

40

PADAMSINGH'S FIRST MARRIAGE took place while he was still studying in college. By the time he received his MA, he was the father of a son. But his child-bride did not know how to care for an infant. The child was healthy when it was born, but soon it turned sick. Six months later, both mother and child were dead. Padamsingh had decided that he wouldn't remarry. But after he got his law degree he was again shackled in the bonds of marriage. Subhadra Rani came into his house as a bride. She had been there for seven years.

For the first two or three years, Padamsingh didn't even think about children. And if Bhama complained, he would brush her off. He would say—I don't want children. I won't be able to bear that burden. Still, he was hopeful that one day he would have children and so was not impatient.

But after four years had passed, he began to feel a little dejected. He began worrying—will I really remain childless? As the days passed, he became increasingly anxious. Now he began to feel an emptiness in his life. He didn't have the same love for Subhadra any more; Subhadra guessed that. She was hurt, but she consoled herself by thinking that it was the consequence of the deeds of her past lives.

Padamsingh would tell himself repeatedly—what are you going to do with a child? From the day he is born until he is twenty-five you will educate him, play with him, and teach him; when he's thirty, you'll worry about whether he has amounted to anything or not. If your son dies, you will weep at the mention of his name. And if you die, his life will be ruined. You don't need this kind of happiness. But these thoughts wouldn't bring him peace. He tried to hide his feelings from Subhadra and, thinking that this was hardly her fault, tried to love her, but when the shadow of despair has fallen over one's heart, how can light shine from one's face? Any person with an average intelligence could tell you that there was something wrong between husband and wife. It was fortunate that Subhadra lacked nothing in love and devotion for her husband. She tried to suppress her longing for children with romance, and in this impossible task she was no more successful than a doctor who tries to cure a patient with music. When it came to even the smallest details of housekeeping, which were unacceptable to her but met with her husband's approval, she was forced to keep quiet. Ever since Sadan had begun living with them, she had been reproached many times on his account. A woman can bear the darts of her husband, but even a sideways glance from someone else is unacceptable to her. Sadan was like a thorn in Subhadra's flesh. In the end, she boiled over. The summer was harsh. For some reason, the cook hadn't reported for work, and Subhadra was forced to make dinner. She made *phulka*s for Padamsingh. But since she was tired out by the heat, she made thick *roti*s for Sadan. When Padamsingh sat down to eat, he saw the rotis in Sadan's plate and, in anger, placed his phulkas in Sadan's plate and took Sadan's rotis for himself. Subhadra got upset and said some harsh things and Padamsingh replied in kind. As the bickering escalated, Padamsingh became so angry that he got up and left the kitchen. Subhadra didn't try to appease him. She put away the food and went and lay down. But even then, neither would give way. The cook made dinner the next day, but neither Padamsingh nor Subhadra ate. Sadan tried to entreat each in turn, but one would say—I am not hungry, and the other—I will eat later, he's not about to leave anyway. If he were going to leave, would I have to bear anyone's anger? The strange thing was that Subhadra would laught and talk to Sadan all the time, and yet he was the root cause of this argument. The stag knows well whether the arrow that flies from under the cover of the bushes is really a symbol of the hunter's hunger for meat or of his love of hunting.

It was morning and Padamsingh, having just woken up, was yawning. His heart was dripping with scorn, hate, and anger towards Subhadra. He was ready to feel sympathy for anyone but Subhadra. At that moment, the postman came and handed him an unstamped letter. He looked at the postman with such displeasure as if the postman had committed some crime in bringing him an unstamped letter. At first, he wanted to send it back—some poor client, perhaps, crying about his misfortune, but after he thought about it, he took the letter and read it. It was Shanta's letter. He read it once and then put it on the table. After a moment, he read it again and then began to pace in the room. If Madansingh had been there, then he would have shown him the letter and said—Here is the fruit of your family pride and your fear of gossip. You have murdered one human being—his death is on your head. After reading about the lawsuit, Padamsingh was somewhat pleased—It is very good that he faces a lawsuit and will see his family pride kicked in the dirt. Umanath will certainly win the case and then my dear brother will understand just how expensive family honour is. What can possibly be going through that poor girl's mind? Padamsingh read the letter again. In it, he found a stream of faith flowing towards him. It awakened the justice-loving part of him. The address, 'Revered Father-in-law', overwhelmed him. It made his heartstrings vibrate. He got dressed and went to Vitthaldas' house, only to find that he had gone to Kumvar Anirudhsingh's place. He immediately turned his bicycle and set out in that direction. He wanted to work out something for Shanta immediately. He was afraid that any delay would cool off his enthusiasm.

A xylophonist from Gwalior had arrived at Kumvar Sahib's house. He had invited his friends today to for a performance by the man. When Padamsingh arrived, Vitthaldas and Professor Ramesh Datt were arguing loudly, and Kumvar Sahib, Prabhakar Rao, and Sayyid Teg Ali sitting around watching the cockfight. As soon as he saw Sharmaji, Kumvar Sahib invited him in. He said—Come, sit. Just look at the fierce battle going on here. Please find some way to separate the two of them, or they will surely kill each other.

Professor Ramesh Datt was saying—It's not an insult to be called a Theosophist. I am a Theosophist and everyone knows it. Because of the efforts of our organization, you can find devotees of Ram and Krishna and lovers of the Gita, the Upanishads, and other ancient books in America, Germany, Russia, and other countries. Our organization has extended the fame of the Hindu race, spread its teachings all over, and has placed it back on the pedestal from which it has been displaced for centuries because of our idleness. We would be extremely ungrateful indeed, if we didn't recognize the importance of those people, who through their own enlightenment have rid us of ignorance and shown us that jewel that we didn't have the ability to see ourselves. It could be the light shown by Blavatsky, or perhaps Olcott or even any of a number of men—it doesn't matter to me. It is our duty to be grateful to anyone who erases our ignorance. If you call this servitude, you are being unfair.

Vitthaldas heard this speech with such indifference it may as well have been meaningless babble. He said—That's exactly what servitude is. At least slaves are free in one respect. Slavery affects the body, not the soul. But you folks have sold your very souls. Your English education has made you so spineless that until some European intellectual demonstrates the merits and demerits of an issue, you have no position on it. You don't praise the

Upanishads because they are praiseworthy in themselves, but because Blavatsky and Max Mueller have praised them. You no longer possess the ability to use your own intellect. Until a few years ago, Tantric wisdom did not mean a thing to you. But now that European intellectuals have started revealing their secret insights, you suddenly see the merits of the Tantras. This mental servitude is far worse than physical slavery. You read the Upanishads in English, and the Gita in German. You betray your mother tongue by calling Arjun 'Arjuna' and Krishna 'Krishnaa'. And because of this mental servitude you have already accepted defeat in that realm in which we could proudly wave the standard of our ancient fame and fortune for all time.

Ramesh Datt was still searching for an answer to this when Kumvar Sahib spoke up—Friends! I can no longer sit here and remain silent. Lala Sahib, you must take back this word 'slavery'.

Vitthaldas—Why must I take it back?

Kumvar Sahib—You have no right to use that word.

Vitthaldas—I don't understand what you mean.

Kumvar Sahib—I mean that none among us has the right to call another a slave. In the alley of the blind, who can call another blind? We may be princes or paupers, but we are all slaves. Those who are illiterate, poor, and rural are only partly slaves. They pray to Ram, raise their cattle, and bathe in the Ganga, and they are wise, tall and handsome. But those who speak foreign languages, raise dogs, and consider their countrymen vulgar, they are the real slaves. The entire race is separated into these two types. That's why no one can call anyone else a slave. It is not proper to separate servitude into mental, spiritual, physical, and other types. Slavery is only spiritual, and all other kinds are included in it. Cars, bungalows, polo, and pianos are fetters. And only those people who have not worn these shackles can experience the bliss of real freedom, and do you know who those people are? They are our humble peasants who eat by the sweat of their labour, who respect their racial dress, language, and custom, and bow before no one.

Prabhakar Rao smiled and said—You should be a peasant.

Kumvar Sahib—Then how would I pay for the sins of my past life? How could I afford the baskets of fruit on important occasions? How could I flatter my superiors like a butler? How could I make trips to Nainital for a promotion? How could I give dinner parties and carry the dogs of English women in my lap? How could I offer my disapproval in matters of national good and keep the gods happy and content? These are the final signs of human downfall. I cannot be free until I have been through these experiences. (To Padamsingh) Well Sharmaji, when will your resolution come up before the board? You seem a little distant these days. Will this resolution face the same fate that so many of our social programmes have suffered?

Actually, for the past several days, Padamsingh's interest had been fading. As it became more likely that his resolution might be accepted, he became less confident. A student constantly prepares for an exam until the appointed day, but once he has successfully passed the exam, his worries about life's future battles begin to discourage him. He understands that the accomplishments that have brought him success thus far will be ineffective in the new, larger and unknown realm. Sharmaji's condition was the same. His resolution seemed useless to him. And not just useless, sometimes he was even afraid that it would do more harm than good. But he didn't have the courage to voice his doubts, and so he looked at Kumvar Sahib confidently and said—No, of course it won't. Yes, it's true that work on that project has fallen behind because I haven't had time.

Kumvar Sahib—There's nothing preventing it from being passed now, is there?

Padamsingh looked at Teg Ali and said—It all depends on the Muslim members.

Teg Ali responded seriously—Trusting them would be like trusting a castle on a sandy foundation. You don't realize the kinds of things that are going on there. It would not be surprising if they betray us when it matters most.

Prabhakar Rao—Isn't Seth Balbhadradas coming? We should find some way to convince him.

Kumvar Sahib—I didn't invite him because I knew that he wouldn't come. He hates debate. Practically all our leaders are the same. This is the only subject in which he has any interest. But if you have even the slightest disagreement with him, he will become an enemy for life, won't speak to you, won't even look at you, and given the opportunity, he will complain about you to other members. Among his circle of friends, he will criticize your ideas and your behavior. If you are a Brahmin he will call you a beggar, and if a Kshatriya, he will call you a peasant. If you are a Vaishya, he will call you a thieving merchant, and if a Shudra, you must be an untouchable in disguise. If you have a love for music, then you are a sinner, and if you are religious, you will immediately receive the title of 'a calf's uncle'. He will even go so far as to falsely slander your wife and mother. In our circles, disagreeing with him is a cardinal sin and there is no repentance. Look, there's Doctor Shyamacharan's motorcar.

Doctor Shyamacharan got out of his car and looked at the assembled men and said in English—I am sorry. I'm late.

Kumvar Sahib greeted him. Everyone else shook hands with him and the doctor took a seat and added again in English—When is the performance going to begin?

Kumvar Sahib—Doctor Sahib, you forget, this is an assembly of blacks.

Doctor Sahib laughed and said—Forgive me. I had forgotten that speaking the barbarian's language was forbidden here.

Kumvar Sahib—And yet you never make that mistake when you are among the gods.

Doctor—Well, sir, then you will have to mete out a punishment.

Kumvar Sahib—The only punishment will be that you conduct your business with your friends in your mother tongue.

Doctor—You are princes. This is a promise that you can keep. But why do you ask such things of me? English is quickly becoming our *lingua franca*.

Kumvar Sahib—People like you have conferred that privilege on it. The fellowship between simple soldiers from Persia and Afghanistan and Hindu businessmen created a language like Urdu. If the intellectuals from the various regions of our country spoke to each other in their own languages, there would have been a national language by now. And if intelligent people like you are devoted to English, a national language will never be born. But this is an onerous task. Who will take it on? Here, people have found a lofty language like English and have sold themselves over to it. I don't understand why people think it honourable to speak and write in English. I, too, have studied English. I spent two years abroad and learned to speak and write from the best English teachers, but I hate it. It feels like I am wearing an Englishman's soiled clothes.

Padamsingh didn't take any sides in this debate. As soon as he got a chance, he called Vitthaldas aside and showed him Shanta's letter.

Vitthaldas said—What are you planning to do now?

Padamsingh—I don't know what to do. Ever since I got this letter, I feel like I am being carried upstream by a river.

Vitthaldas—Something will have to be done.

Padamsingh—What should I do?

Vitthaldas—Send for Shanta.

Padamsingh—No one in my family will have anything to do with me.

Vitthaldas—Fine. Why should you be afraid to do your duty?

Padamsingh—Of course, you are right, but I don't have that kind of strength. I don't have the courage to go against my brother.

Vitthaldas—Don't keep her at your house. Let her stay in the widows' home. That's not a problem.

Padamsingh—Yes, that's a good idea. I didn't even think of that. In moments of crisis, my mind starts wandering.

Vitthaldas—But you will have to go and fetch her.

Padamsingh—But why? Couldn't you go just as well?

Vitthaldas—Look, why would Umanath send her with me?

Padamsingh—What reason could he possibly have not to?

Vitthaldas—Sometimes you are such a child. Shanta might not be his daughter, but for now he is her father. Why would he let her go with a stranger?

Padamsingh—Please don't get angry. I am really not thinking straight. If I go, there will be a huge commotion. If my brother hears of it, he will kill me. He pushed me during the wedding. I have not forgotten that.

Vitthaldas—Fine, don't go. I will go by myself. You don't have a problem in writing a letter to Umanath, do you?

Padamsingh—You may call me a complete coward, but I don't even have the courage to do that. You have to come up with a plan so that I can get away from it if I have to. I don't want to give my brother the opportunity to accuse me at all.

Vitthaldas responde dangrily—I can think of no such plan. And you call yourself a man. Over there, you give these grandiose speeches, filled with such noble sentiments, as if you were a free soul, but here you are a coward.

Embarrassed, Padamsingh replied—You can call me whatever you want, but you must handle this task entirely.

Vitthaldas—Fine. At least send a telegram, or will you not even be able to do that?

Padamsingh (fidgeting)—Yes, I can send a telegram. I knew that you would be able to come up with a way out. Now, if something happens, I can just say that I didn't send the telegram, that someone must have sent it in my name—but the next moment, he changed his mind. He was ashamed of his cowardice. He thought to himself—my brother is not such a fool as to get upset at me for doing my moral duty and even if he is, then I should not worry about it.

Vitthaldas—Then send the telegram today.

Padamsingh—But then it will be a deception.

Vitthaldas—Yes, that it is, as you can see.

Padamsingh—What if I too go with you?

Vitthaldas—That would be best. It will ensure everything goes well.

Padamsingh—Good, then you and I will go together.

Vitthaldas—When?

Padamsingh—I will send the telegram today saying that we are coming to get Shanta, and we will leave by train the day after tomorrow.

Vitthaldas—Are you sure?

Padamsingh—Yes, I'm sure. You can drag me by the ears if you have to.

Vitthaldas looked at his simple-hearted friend proudly and the two returned to listen to the xylophone whose beautiful melody was ringing up to the heavens.

41

When you go to the hills to improve your health, you take great care not to stray from the prescribed regimen. You exercise religiously and the hope of improvement remains constantly in your mind. Suman went to the widows' home to improve her spiritual health and she didn't forget that for one moment. She was always ready to serve her sisters and she read religious books. Her troubled heart found peace in worship and bathing in the river.

Vitthaldas had kept the news from Amola hidden from her, but once the decision to move Shanta into the widows' home had been made, he thought it best to prepare Suman for it. After he left Kumvar Sahib's place, he went straight to the home and told her everything.

A silence had fallen over the ashram. It was late at night, but Suman was unable to sleep no matter how hard she tried. She now saw the real nature of her foolishness. Suman's condition was exactly like that of the patient who wakes from chloroform, sees the deep wounds of his lanced boils and falls unconscious from anguish and fear. It seemed as if her father, mother, and sister were all sitting before her. Her mother hung her head in shame and wept. Her father was standing, staring at her with enraged, bloodshot eyes. And Shanta was the very picture of grief, sorrow, and scorn, sometimes staring at the ground, sometimes at the sky.

Suman was confused. She got up from the cot and began banging her head against the hard ground. In her own mind, she was a demoness. The cuts in her head made her dizzy. After a while she regained balance; blood was flowing from her head. She slowly opened the door. The courtyard was dark. She ran to the gate, but it was locked. She shook the lock but it wouldn't open. The old watchman was sleeping not too far from the gate. Suman slowly crept up to him and tried to get the keys that lay next to his head. The watchman jerked awake and began screaming 'Thief! Thief!' Suman ran back to her room and shut the door.

Like the morning wind, the tumultuous anxiety of the mind also finds peace. Suman wept a great deal—Hai! There is not another witch like me in this world! I have destroyed my family with my longing for pleasures. I am my father's murderer. I have put a knife to Shanta's throat. How can I show her my blackened face? How will I look her in the face? When father heard this news, it must have hurt him deeply. And thinking this, she began to cry again. This pain seemed more unbearable than all her other hardships. If instead of telling her father, Madansingh had crushed her feet, had her trampled by elephants, cast her into a fire, or had her torn to pieces by dogs, she would not have made any noise. Had the desire for luxury and false freedom not loosened the control of shame, she might not have even stepped outside her house. She would have endured her husband's harshest torments and remained locked up at home. When she had left her house, she couldn't have imagined that she might one day be forced to reside in Dalmandi. She had left her home without thinking ahead. Amid her grief and frustration she had forgotten that she had a father, a sister.

Having been separated for so long, she had stopped thinking about them. She thought that she was alone in the world. She thought—I am in another country and nothing that I do will reach them. But now it had come to pass that she felt connected to them by spiritual threads. Those whom she had forgotten now appeared before her and as soon as their souls touched each other, the light of shame exposed her.

Suman spent the rest of the night in psychological turmoil. At four o'clock, she went to bathe in the Ganga. Since she often went by herself, the watchman didn't even stop her.

When Suman reached the bank of the Ganga, she looked in all directions to make sure no one was around. She hadn't come to bathe in the river this day. She had come to drown in it. She had no doubts, fears, or concerns. Tomorrow, Shanta would be in the ashram. It was so much easier to lose herself in the embrace of the Ganga than to have to face her.

Suddenly, she saw that a man was walking towards her. It was still quite dark, but Suman could tell that it was a sadhu. Suman still wore a ring on her finger. She decided to offer it to the sadhu, but as he came closer, Suman hid her face in fear, disgust, and shame. It was Gajadhar.

Gajadhar fell at her feet and, in a strained voice, said—Please forgive my mistakes!

Suman stepped back. The scene of her dishonour was once again before her eyes. The wounds became fresh again. She wanted in her heart to scream at him, and say—you are my father's murderer and the man that destroyed my life, but Gajadhar's compassionate generosity, partly because he looked like a sadhu and partly because of the detachment which becomes manifest after the resolution for self-sacrifice, melted her heart. Her eyes became moist. In a gentle voice she said—You haven't done anything wrong. Everything that has happened is the fruit of my karma.

Gajadhar—No Suman, don't say that. This is all the result of my stupidity and ignorance. I thought that I could do something to repent, but seeing the terrible effect of my crimes, I know that I can never do enough penance. With my own eyes, I saw your father drown in the Ganga.

Eagerly, Suman asked—You saw him drown?

Gajadhar—Yes Suman, I saw him drown. I was going to Amola one night and I met him along the way. He was surprised to see me walking towards the river in the middle of the night. I brought him back to my place and tried to calm him down. And then thinking that my work was done, I went to sleep. When I woke up a little later, I didn't see him. Immediately, I ran towards the river. At that moment, I heard him calling my name, but before I could make out where he was, the merciless waves had seized him. That rare soul departed for heaven before my eyes. Till then, I hadn't realized how terrible and unforgivable my sins really were. Who knows what will happen when I meet God.

Gajadhar's tale had the same effect on Suman's heart that soap has on dirt. It cut through and lifted the grime right up. And those accumulated feelings, which Suman had tried to repress, came to the fore. She said— God has given you wisdom. You can do much with your good reputation, but what about me. I am not worthy of either world! Hai! My desire for comfort has made me a permanent migrant. Why should there be any secrets now? Your poverty, and even more than that your loveless behaviour, infected me with unhappiness, and once I saw, in every direction, the respect and elegance of a life of sin, this germ turned me into a wandering nomad. And then, even a little pressure would have been enough to pop that blister. Your gentleness, your love, your sympathy, your kindness would have been like medicine on that blister, but you crushed it, and I, overwhelmed with anguish, fell unconscious. When I recall your beastly, demonic behaviour, I can feel a fire burning in my heart and curses begin to flow at you from my heart. This is my final hour. In a moment the Ganga will devour this sinful body. I will be with my father again. That's why I am praying to God to forgive you your mistakes.

Gajadhar responded with concern in his voice—Suman, if killing oneself could actually be penance for one's sins, I would have killed myself a long time ago.

Suman—At least it will end the pain.

Gajadhar—Yes, your pain will end, but it won't end the pain of those who are worried about your suffering. Your mother and father are dead, but their bodiless souls are always around you. All of them will be happy in your happiness and hurt by your pain. Just think whether you would rather bring them grief by committing suicide or better yourself and bring them happiness and peace. Remorse is the final warning, offered by God, to motivate us to improve our lives. If we fail to recognize it and end our lives out of grief, then it is as if we have thrown away our last chance for salvation. Also, think about what will happen to that poor girl Shanta, who knows nothing of the good and bad in the world, if you are not here. Who else does she have in this world? You know Umanath's situation. He won't be able to provide for her. He possesses kindness but even more greed. Eventually, he will get rid of her. And then where will she go?

Suman got a glimpse Gajadhar's genuine pain while he spoke. She looked at him with humility and said—It is easier for me to kill myself than to face Shanta. It has been a few days since she sent Padamsingh a letter. Umanath wants to marry her off to someone. She doesn't want that marriage.

Gajadhar—She is a goddess.

Suman—What else could poor Sharmaji do, he decided to send for her and keep her in the ashram. And if his brother finally agrees, then things will be better, otherwise who knows how many days that suffering girl will have to spend at the ashram. She will be arriving tomorrow. The fear of looking her in the face, the shame of looking into her eyes—it's killing me. When she looks at me with longing in her eyes, what will I do, and what if instead she is disgusted with me and hesitates to embrace me. I would rather swallow poison that instant. Suicide is much better than that.

Gajadhar looked at Suman with confidence. He felt as if he would act in the same way that Suman wanted to in that situation. He spoke—Suman, your feelings are real, but no matter what happens in your heart, for Shanta's sake, you will have to bear it all. No one else can do as much good for her as you can. Till now, you have been living for yourself. Now you must live for others.

Saying this, Gajadhar left the way he had come. Suman stood on the bank of the Ganga for a while and deliberated about what he had said. Then she took a bath and returned to the ashram like a man returns home, having been defeated in battle.

42

SHANTA HAD SENT the letter, but she didn't think that there would be a reply. Three days had passed and her despair grew greater by the day. If she didn't get a favourable response, Umanath would certainly marry her off, and every time she thought about it, Shanta's heart would sink. She would go to the temple several times during the day and make various kinds of offerings. Sometimes she would go to the temple of Shiv and pour out her heart. There was never a moment when Sadan was not in her thoughts. She would sit before the idol of him that she had created in her mind's eye and fold her hands and plead—Lord of my life, why won't you accept me? Because you are afraid of being slandered? Hai, is my life so worthless that it can be sold so cheap! You are forsaking me, casting me into the fire, and my only crime is that I am Suman's sister, and this is justice. If ever I meet you, I will hold you, and then I'll see how you run away from me. You are not made of stone that you will not be moved by my tears. Just look at me once with your own eyes and you won't be able to live with yourself. Your large heart cannot be insensitive. What can I do? How can I show you the condition of my heart?

On the morning of the fourth day, Padamsingh's letter arrived. Shanta was mortified. Her hopes of finding love vanished. She became worried about her future.

But Umanath was beside himself with joy. He hired a band. He got the wedding procession together, sent out invitations to the entire village, and set up a tent and laid out carpets for the guests. But the village folk were confused—What kind of wedding reception is this? The wedding never took place, so how can there be a reception? They were sure that Umanath had done something underhanded—he is a first class scoundrel. At the settled time, Umanath went to the station and, with the band playing all the way, brought his guests to his house. They were put up in the tent. There were only three men: Padamsingh, Vitthaldas, and a servant.

The next evening, it was time for Shanta to leave. It was late, yet none of the village women had turned up at Umanath's house. He paced in and out of the house, changing his expression, and cursing at the walls—I will show them all. He got upset with Jahnvi and said—I will show each and every one of them. But such threats, which would once have sent the village headman trembling, had no effect on anyone. The community would not be threatened by a sinner. It lies in wait for such moments when it can make the proud bend their heads.

Dusk fell. The servants brought the palanquin to the door. Jahnvi and Shanta embraced and cried copiously.

Shanta's heart welled up with emotion. She had forgotten all the hardships that she had had to endure while she was here—I won't meet these people again, will never see this house again, and from now on, I am no longer related to these people, she thought as she felt her heart torn asunder. Jahnvi's heart was also filled with compassion—we have truly made this orphan child suffer, she thought and then could not hold back the tears. Waves of true, pure, and delicate emotions began to rise in both hearts.

When Umanath went back inside, Shanta threw herself at his feet and pleaded with him—You are my father. Don't forget your daughter. Give my sisters jewels and clothes, send for them at Holi and Teej, but all I want is a two-line letter from you.

Umanath looked at her and said—Daughter, you are just like my own two girls to me. May God keep you happy always.

He burst into tears.

It was evening. The cow, Munni, came to the house and Shanta hugged her and began crying. She had looked after the cow for three or four years. Who would she run to feed straw to now? For whom would she make necklaces of black string and shells? Munni lowered her head and licked Shanta's palms. The pain of separation moistened her eyes.

Jahnvi took Shanta and seated her in the palanquin. The servants picked it up. Shanta felt as if she were flowing away in an endless ocean.

The women from the village stood at their doors and cried as they saw the palanquin leave.

Umanath went with her to the station. Before he left, he took off his turban and placed it at Padamsingh's feet. Padamsingh embraced him.

When the train had left the station, Padamsingh turned to Vitthaldas and said—Now, it is time for the most difficult part of this tragedy.

Vitthaldas—I don't follow.

Padamsingh—Can we just put Shanta in the ashram without explaining anything to her? We should prepare her.

Vitthaldas—Yes, you are right. Should I go and speak with her?

Padamsingh—Just think for a moment about what you will say. Right now she is probably thinking that she is on her way to her husband's home. This hope is sustaining her in this time of separation. But when she realizes what is really happening, she will be hurt immeasurably. I am beginning to regret not telling her sooner.

Vitthaldas—So what's the problem with telling her now? The train will stop for a while in Mirzapur. I will go and explain it all to her.

Padamsingh—I have made a terrible mistake.

Vitthaldas—Well, if you can make do by regretting your mistakes, then by all means, regret all you want.

Padamsingh—Do you have a pencil I could use? I want to write a letter that explains everything that has happened.

Vitthaldas—No. Send her a telegram. That would be the best thing. You are a strange man. You take a simple matter and make it terribly complicated.

Padamsingh—These are the cards that I have been dealt. What can I do? I have a plan. The train will stop for a while in Mugalsarai. I will go and explain everything to her.

Vitthaldas—You have been chasing wild geese all this time. That's why wise men say that you shouldn't start something without thinking it all the way through. Your mind finally comes to the right conclusion, but in such a roundabout way. You should have thought of this in the first place.

Shanta was sitting in the women's section of the second class compartment. Two Christian ladies also sat with her. They looked at Shanta and began speaking in English.

'She looks like a newlywed.'

'Yes, from a fine family. Going to her in-laws.'

'She's crying as if she's being forced.'

'She probably hasn't seen the groom's face. How can she love him? Her heart is probably trembling with fear.'

'These are their backward traditions. A poor girl is sent into an unfamiliar home, where she has no one to call her own.'

'These are all customs from barbaric times when women were carried away by force.'

'Why, dear (to Shanta). Are you going to your in-laws?'

Shanta slowly nodded her head.

'You are quite lovely. Is your husband a good match?'

Shanta responded meekly—A husband's looks don't matter.

'And what if he's dark and ugly?'

Shanta proudly responded—He's like a God to me, whatever he looks like.

'Okay, suppose that two men are brought before you. One is handsome and the other ugly. Which one would you prefer?'

Shanta responded firmly—The one that my parents choose.

Shanta knew that the two were trying to critique marriage customs. After a while, she asked them—I have heard that you choose your own husbands.

'Yes, we are free to do so.'

'Do you think that you are smarter than your parents?'

'How can our parents know whether we will like the husbands they choose for us?'

'Then you think that love is the most important thing in a marriage?'

'Yes, what else? Marriage is a union of love.'

'We consider marriage a religious union. Our love follows our religion.'

At nine the train reached Mugalsarai. Vitthaldas came and got Shanta; he put down a cushion on the platform for her to sit on. There was still half an hour before the train for Benares departed.

Shanta saw her countrymen carrying huge bundles on their heads, falling all over each other trying to get out through a narrow passage. At another narrow passage, thousands of men were pushing each other trying to get in. But in the opposite direction, Englishmen were twirling their canes and walking their dogs through wide gates. No one stopped them or questioned them.

In the meanwhile, Padamsingh came up to her and said—Shanta, I am your father-in-law, Padamsingh.

Shanta stood up, folded her hands, and head bowed.

Padamsingh said—You must be a little surprised that we didn't get off at Chunar. It is because I haven't spoken to my brother about you yet. When I got your letter, I was scared and I knew that I had to send for you immediately. I didn't get the chance to speak to my brother. That's why you will have to stay in Benares for a few days. I thought it best that you stay in the same ashram where your sister, Sumanbai, is staying. You will have no trouble while you are staying with Suman. Forget the slanderous things you have heard about your sister. Now she is like a goddess. Her life is completely pure and enlightened. I would never send my daughter-in-law to stay with her if that were not the case. In a month or two, I will straighten things out with my brother. If you have any problems with this arrangement, please say so openly so that we can come up with something else.

It was difficult for Padamsingh to end his monologue. He himself didn't believe the praise that he had just showered on Suman. He also said much more about Madansingh to her than he would have liked to. It troubled his conscience to deceive this simple-hearted girl.

Crying, Shanta fell at Padamsingh's feet and forced out words filled with shame, despair, and melancholy—I am in your custody. Please do what you think best.

Shanta's heart felt light. Now it was not necessary for her to worry about her future, and for the next few days she could even forget the direction her life was taking. At that moment she was like a man who doesn't mind having his hut on fire because for a while he is no longer afraid of the darkness.

It was eleven o'clock when the three of them reached the ashram. Vitthaldas got down to tell Sumanbai that they had arrived, but when he went in, he found her lying unconscious with a fever. Some women from the ashram were looking after her. One was fanning her, one massaging her forehead, and one was rubbing her feet. Occasionally, she could be heard moaning. Vitthaldas asked with concern—Have you called a doctor?

He received an answer—Yes. He examined her and left.

Some women helped Shanta down from the carriage. Shanta stood next to her sister's cot and said 'Sister!' Suman didn't open her eyes. Shanta stood still like a statue, looking at her sister with compassion and tenderness— This is my dear sister. Three or four years ago, we used to play together. Where are her long flowing locks? Where is that bright, golden complexion? Where are those playful, always smiling eyes? Where has she lost that delicate, lovely gait, that glowing skin, and those dawn-like cheeks? Is this Suman or her corpse or her lifeless statue? That pale face shone with the pure and peaceful light of serenity, restraint, and self-sacrifice. Shanta's heart filled with forgiveness and love. She gestured to some of the women to leave and then she wrapped her arms around her sister and cried and said—Sister, open your eyes. How are you feeling? It's me, Shanta.

Suman opened her eyes and with a crazed look of surprise she looked at Shanta she said—Who? Shanta? Go away. Don't touch me. I am a sinner, cursed, a whore. You are a goddess, a saint. Don't let yourself be polluted by me. Lust, desire, and sin have sullied this heart. Don't bring your bright and true spirit near me. Run away from here. The fires into the gates of hell are burning before me, and the messenger of death is dragging me into that fire. Run away from here—she said, and then became unconscious again.

Shanta sat next to Suman, fanning her through the night.

43

It HAD BEEN more than a month since Shanta had arrived at the ashram, but Padamsingh still hadn't said anything about her to his family. Sometimes he planned on writing a letter, at other times he wanted to go himself and tell them, and sometimes he wanted to send Vitthaldas. Most of all, he couldn't make up his mind.

In the meanwhile, his allies waited for the presentation of the resolution about courtesans at the municipal board meeting. They had complete confidence in its success. But perhaps another hurdle had presented itself since there had been such a delay. Padamsingh had been putting it off and now it was May. Vitthaldas and Ramesh Datt had been harassing him so much that he was forced to make a formal presentation of his resolution to the board. The date and time had been settled upon.

And as the day approached, Padamsingh became increasingly anxious. He began to believe that merely passing the resolution would not be enough to solve the problem. In order to make it workable, it would require the agreement and assistance of the most important men of the city, and that was why he wanted Haji Hashim, one way or another, on his side. Haji Sahib was so influential in the city that even the courtesans did not dare oppose his wish. In the end, Haji Sahib melted as well. He was convinced of Padamsingh's good intentions.

The resolution was presented before the board today. There was much commotion within the municipal board. The courtesans attacked the board with an army of supporters—let's see what the board does now.

The board meeting was convened. Every member was present. Doctor Shyamacharan had postponed his trip to the mountains. Munshi Abulwafa hadn't slept last night. He had paced in and out of the house all night. Today, there would be no limit to his efforts or energy.

Padamsingh presented his resolution and spoke in favour of it in measured words. It was divided into three parts. (1) The courtesans would be removed from the centre of the city and moved to a place away from the population, (2) they would be prevented from going into the city's main thoroughfares and parks, (3) there would be a high tax on those who hired courtesans to dance, and such performances would under no circumstances be open to the public.

Professor Ramesh Datt offered a summary.

Shafakat Ali (Deputy Collector) said—I am completely in favour of this resolution, but I cannot accept it without one principal amendment. I suggest that the first part of the resolution be amended thus—'Except for those who, within nine months, either get married or learn a skill by which they can properly provide for themselves'.

Kumvar Anirudhsingh said—I completely support this amendment. We have no right to consider these women sinners. It would be extremely arrogant on our part. We, who take bribes at all hours of the day, charge high interest, bleed the poor to death, hang the helpless out to dry, are never worthy of calling any part of society depraved or worthless. The most depraved are we, the biggest sinners, criminals, and perpetrators of injustice, who consider ourselves to be educated, civilized, generous, and truthful! It is because of our educated brethren that Dalmandi is thriving, that there is life in the Chauk, that there is elegance in the markets of sex. We are the ones that have built Minabazaar. We have trapped these songbirds. We have made these marionettes. Why wouldn't Dalmandi thrive in a society where criminal landowners, bribed government officials, greedy merchants, and selfish relatives are the standard of honour and respect? What else does sin generate but more sinfulness? The day that bribes, gifts, and high interest rates are done away with, will be the day that Dalmandi is destroyed. Those songbirds will fly away—but not before then. The resolution without the amendment is like a stab wound that won't heal. I cannot vote in favour of it.

Prabhakar Rao spoke—I don't understand what the amendment has to do with the resolution. You could present it in the form of a separate resolution. Whatever you can do to aid in social improvement is completely commendable, but it is just as easy to do this outside the city limits as inside, and there the benefit is greater.

Abulwafa said—I am completely in favour of this amendment.

Abdullatif said—I will never vote for this resolution without the amendment.

Dinanath Tivari also spoke in favour of the amendment.

Padamsingh said—We do not intend to harm the courtesans through this resolution, but to bring them to the correct path, and so I have no problems with supporting this amendment.

Sayyid Teg Ali advised—I am afraid that the amendment destroys the significance of the original resolution. You are closing the front door of the building while building a back door at the same time. It is impossible that these women, who have been living their lives in pleasure and licentiousness, will agree to lives of hard work and suffering. They will take unfair advantage of this amendment. Some of them will set up sewing machines in the same upper quarters and provide for themselves, some will buy machines to repair socks, some will open paan shops, and some will set up stalls on their balconies to sell apples and pomegranates. The black market for fake engagements and false marriages will come alive and under this cover, there will be even more improprieties than there were before. Approving this amendment is to admit our ignorance of human nature.

Hakeem Shoharat Khan said—I find Sayyid Teg Ali's logic faulty. First we should separate these women from their wicked existences. After that, if they want to live their lives in a proper manner, and when we have confidence in them, we should allow them to enter the city limits and settle down. The door to our city is open, not closed. Anyone who desires can live here. I am certain that the amendment is in line with the intention of the resolution.

Sharifhasan, the lawyer, spoke up—There is no doubt about the fact that Padamsingh is a very good and wise man, but by accepting this amendment he is attempting to pander to populism instead of keeping his sights on the original intent of the resolution. It would have been better if the resolution had never been presented at all. Had Sayyid Sharafat Ali Sahib thought at all about what he was doing, he would never have proposed the amendment.

Shakirbeg said—Compromise may be very praiseworthy in administrative matters, but it is always objectionable in matters of morality. Compromises are only a way of covering over our failures to our duty.

Chairman Seth Balbhadradas took a vote on the first part of the resolution. Nine votes were in favour, eight against. The resolution was passed.

Then a vote was taken on the amendment. Eight were in favour, eight against. The amendment was passed. The chairman had cast the deciding vote in its favour. Doctor Shyamacharan abstained.

Professor Ramesh Datt, Rustam Bhai, and Prabhakar Rao considered it a defeat that the amendment was passed and they looked over at Padamsingh as if he had betrayed them. They had decided that Kumvar Sahib was garrulous, shifty, and unprincipled.

Abulwafa and his circle of friends were pleased; it was as if they had won. Their jubilation was a thorn in the sides of Prabhakar Rao and his allies.

The vote on the second part of the resolution was taken. This time, Prabhakar Rao and his allies voted against it. They wanted to punish Padamsingh's betrayal. This resolution failed. Abulwafa and his allies were overjoyed.

Now it was time for the third part of the resolution. Kumvar Anirudhsingh presented it. Hakeem Shoharat Khan, Sayyid Shafakat Ali, Sharifhasan, and Shakirbeg also approved of it. But Prabhakar Rao and his allies spoke out against it. After the amendment was passed, all further efforts in this matter seemed pointless. There were those who take everything, or else take nothing. The resolution failed.

It was well into the night before business was concluded. Those who were afraid of defeat were seen laughing as they left, and those who were certain of victory had a shadow of silence over their faces.

As they were leaving, Kumvar Sahib said to Rustam Bhai—What have all of you done?

Rustam Bhai answered sarcastically—We did the same thing that you did. You merely made a hole in the water pot; we smashed it. The effect of both is the same.

Everyone left. The watchman and the groundskeeper had also shut the gate and gone home, but Padamsingh was still sitting there on the grass like the very picture of frustration and concern itself.

44

Padamsingh didn't at all believe that he had made a mistake in accepting the amendment. He hadn't thought that his allies would so strongly oppose him on such a minor point. He wasn't upset because he was being blamed for the failure of one part of the resolution, because he was completely certain that it was because of his friends' inflexibility and lack of foresight that it had failed. He considered the amendment a minor point. Padamsingh didn't put any stock in the criticism of its loopholes. He blamed the men for the lack of confidence in the resolution. He was beginning to realize that, in the present social conditions, the hopes that were embodied in his resolution had no chance of being fulfilled. Occasionally, he regretted that he had needlessly brought so much discord on himself. He was amazed that he had fallen into this thorny bush and if the success of the plan rested on this amendment, then he could not be blamed, but that seemed like a false hope to him. Now, the entire blame would rest on his shoulders, the opposing camp would laugh at him, they would mock at his confidence, and he would have to endure all of these insults by himself. He had no friends left, no one to comfort him. He had been sure that Vitthaldas would be fair to him; and he was planning on making up with his friends, but Vitthaldas, instead, had turned them against him. He said—By accepting this amendment, you have turned everything to mud, ruined years of planning. Kumvar Anirudhsingh was the only person who comforted Padamsingh's troubled heart and sympathized with him.

For a full month, Padamsingh couldn't go to court. He would just sit by himself and deliberate over the same issue! His thoughts had turned strangely impartial. Whereas his friends' malice had once troubled him, he now concluded that if educated and intelligent men went against their firm beliefs over trivial issues, then there was no hope for this nation—even if I made a mistake in accepting the amendment, why should my mistake have distracted the others from the right decision?

For the first time, in his mental anguish, Padamsingh realized how much strength a helpless woman possessed. If there was anyone in the world who completely understood his condition, it was Subhadra. She thought, as he did, that the amendment was just as necessary. She knew how to offer sharper criticism of his friends than he did. Padamsingh found relief in listening to her talk. Although he thought that Subhadra didn't have the ability to understand and evaluate such complicated issues, that she was merely echoing his words, yet that knowledge didn't, in any way, diminish his happiness.

But before the month had passed, Prabhakar Rao began publishing a series of editorials about the resolution in his newspaper. It launched such hurtful accusations at Padamsingh that he was caught off guard. In one editorial he dwelt upon the intimate connection between Padamsingh's character and the amendment. In another, he criticized his actions and wrote—Such are the servants of the nation in this modern age, that they can forget their country, but never forget their selves, who use the cover of the country to serve their own self-interest. If the young people of our this country fall into a ditch then so be it, at least the Muslims of Benares will be happy. Padamsingh was just as surprised, as he was angry, about this insulting and misplaced venom. He saw, for the first time, how far the incivility of the 'civilized' could go—that man pretends to be the arbiter of civility and decorum, but his soul is absolutely filthy! And still, no one had the courage to speak out against him.

It was evening. The editorial was lying on his charpoy. Padamsingh was sitting at his table trying to write a response, but he couldn't write a word, Subhadra came up to him and said—Why are you sitting in the heat? Come, sit outside.

Padamsingh—Prabhakar Rao has really slandered me today. I was writing a response to him.

Subhadra—Why is he after your life like this?

As she finished her sentence, she began reading the editorial and had read it thoroughly in five minutes.

Padamsingh—What do you think?

Subhadra—This isn't an editorial. It's a series of insults. I used to think that only women hurled insults at each other, but I now see that men are worse than we are. He is educated, too, no?

Padamsingh—Yes, why wouldn't he be educated? He spends all his time licking a world's worth of books.

Subhadra—And still, this?

Padamsingh—I was writing a response to it. I'll remind him who he's dealing with.

Subhadra—But what can be the right response to an insult?

Padamsingh—More insults.

Subhadra—No. The response to an insult is silence. Even an idiot can answer an insult with an insult. Then what's the difference between the two of you?

Padamsingh looked at Subhadra with gratitude. She had convinced him. Sometimes, the people whom we arrogantly find naïve teach us a lot as well.

Padamsingh—Then I shouldn't say anything?

Subhadra—That's my advice. Let him say whatever he wants to. Eventually, he will feel stupid. That's the only punishment for insults.

Padamsingh—He will never feel stupid. These people don't know how to feel stupid. If I go see him now, he will be very hospitable, he will laugh and smile with me, but as soon at it is dark, he will start insulting me again.

Subhadra—So, does he make it his business to insult other people?

Padamsingh—No, that's not what his business is, but these editors need to pull some kind of stunt to increase their subscriptions. These sharp editorials sell more papers. The public gets much pleasure from these arguments, and the editors profit from this love for scandals. They ignore their principles and begin pandering to the public's love for sensationalism. Some editors go so far as to say that it is their duty to keep their readers happy. They are our bread and butter so we have to think of them.

Subhadra—Then these men are merely slaves to money. You should feel sorry for them, not angry.

Padamsingh got up from the table. He gave up on the idea of writing a response. He had never thought Subhadra was capable of so much thought. He realized that although he had studied much, he could never acquire her generosity—she has nobler ideals than I do even though she is uneducated. Today, he realized that even a childless woman can be a strong source of peace and happiness for her husband. A new love grew in his heart towards Subhadra. A wave arose which washed away years of ill feelings. He looked at her with pure, genuine affection. Subhadra understood the look and her heart brimmed over with happiness.

45

When Sadan returned home after seeing Suman, he was a like a poor man whose life savings had been stolen by thieves.

He thought—why didn't Suman say anything to me, why didn't she even look at me? Does she think that I am that low? No, she is ashamed of her previous conduct and wants to forget about me. It is possible that she heard the news about my wedding and thinks that I am cruel and unjust. He once again felt a deep longing to see Suman. The next day, he set out for the bank of the river near the widows' home, but halfway down he turned back. He was afraid that he would have no answers if the talk turned to Shanta. And at the same time, he recalled the teachings of Sadhu Gajanand.

Occasionally, Sadan thought about his obligations towards Shanta. It was impossible that months of listening to lectures about social problems would have no effect on him. He began to accept that his family had greatly wronged Shanta, and it seemed to him that he had never once listened to his own conscience, which says what it thinks and does not care what the world thinks.

These days, Sadan had become more thoughtful. Having been cheated by Dalmandi and the Chauk, his life set off on a new path. During a lecture sponsored by the Arya Samaj, he heard what character building meant. After he had listened to it, he was no longer deluded by the notion that everything was fated. There, he learnt that just because a man is very intelligent does not mean that he will have self-respect. For this, it was most important to have a good character. Compared to character, education was of little importance. From that day, he began to read books about character and virtue, and day by day he grew fonder of them. He began to believe that despite being uneducated he could do something for the world. Those books offered advice about how to control the senses and steady the mind; he tried not to forgot the teaching of these books.

He was present for the municipal board meeting where the resolution about courtesans was presented. He was very disappointed that the amendment was passed and admitted that his uncle was wrong, but when Prabhakar Rao started to slander Padamsingh openly, then he enthusiastically began defending his uncle's position. He had written three or four articles and sent them to Prabhakar Rao through the post. For several days, he had expected them to be published. He was sure that once they were printed, there would be a huge commotion, a huge transformation of the world. As soon as the postman brought the mail, he would search for his articles, but in their place he found articles filled with spite and venom. As he read them, anger arose in his heart. When he had finished the last one, he lost his patience. He decided that no matter what, he had to do something about this editor—had he been a gentleman, he would have printed my editorials. They might have been written in a simple language, but they were not without merit. By not printing them, he had proved that he was not interested in the truth, but was only conjuring up slander to keep the masses happy. Sadan didn't tell anyone what he was thinking. In the evening, he went to the offices of the *Jagat* carrying a stick. The offices were closed, but Prabhakar Rao was sitting and writing something at the editor's desk. Fearlessly, Sadan stormed in and stood in front of him. Prabhakar looked up with surprise and saw a well-built young man impertinently carrying a stick. Angrily he said—Who are you?

Sadan—I live around here. I only want to ask you why you have been slandering Pandit Padamsingh for the past several days.

Prabhakar—Yes, were you the one who sent me those two or three articles?

Sadan—Yes, I sent them.

Prabhakar—I thank you for them. Come, sit down. I wanted to meet you myself, but I didn't have your address. Your articles are very good and sound and I would have published them long ago, but it is against our policy to publish anonymous articles, and so I was unable to. What is your name?

Sadan told him his name. His anger cooled somewhat.

Prabhakar—You seem to be one of Padamsingh's top disciples.

Sadan—I am his nephew.

Prabhakar—Oh, then you are one of us. Tell me, is Sharmaji well? He hasn't been seen recently.

Sadan—He's doing fine for now, but your editorials have reduced him to a sliver and now only God knows what will become of him. How can you call yourself his friend and hate him this way?

Prabhakar—Hate? Dear God! What are you saying? I don't have even an iota of hatred towards him. You don't understand the duty of us editors. It is our religion to display our hearts openly to the public. To keep our thoughts private is a sin in our books. We have no friends and no enemies. We forsake our childhood friends in an instant and embrace our blood enemies in the next. We forgive no one when it comes to social issues, because our forgiveness makes their influence even more deadly. Padamsingh is my best friend and I respect him from the bottom of my heart. It hurts me deeply to have to criticize him. Until a few days ago, I was merely opposed to his ideas, but yesterday I came across some evidence which proves that he had an ulterior motive in accepting the amendment. I have no problem telling you that for months he has secretly housed a courtesan named Sumanbai in the widows' home and for about a month he has kept her younger sister in the ashram as well. I still want to believe that I have received false information, but soon, for no other reason, I am going to publish this information so that it can be disputed!

Sadan—Where did you get this information?

Prabhakar—I can't tell you that, but you should tell Sharmaji that if this is a false accusation, he should inform me. I also discovered that before this resolution was presented to the board, Sharmaji regularly went to Haji Hashim's place. In this situation, even you can see that it is impossible for me to remain neutral.

Sadan calmed down. Prabhakar Rao's explanations had won him over. Soon, he began to admire Prabhakar Rao and after a few more pleasantries, he returned home. Now his biggest concern was to find out whether Shanta had really been brought to the ashram.

At dinner, he wanted very much to say something to Sharmaji about this matter, but he didn't have the courage. He had seen Suman go into the widows' home himself, and now that he remembered a few things whose significance he hadn't realized earlier, he began to believe that Shanta was there as well.

He tossed and turned all night—why is Shanta in the ashram? Why did uncle call her there? Did Umanath refuse to keep her in his home? These were the questions that arose in his mind. The next day, he set out for the riverbank near the ashram and decided that if he saw Suman, he would ask her about everything. He had only been waiting a little while when he saw Suman approaching. There was a beautiful woman following behind. Her face was hidden behind her veil.

Suman was startled when she saw Sadan. She had been hoping to see Sadan here for a few days now. Although she had earlier decided never to speak to Sadan again, but for Shanta's sake, she felt there was no alternative. Shyly, she spoke to Sadan—Sadansingh, it is our good fortune to see you today. You have stopped coming here all together. I hope all is well?

Sadan trembled as he spoke—Yes, everything is fine.

Suman—You look very thin. Have you been ill?

Sadan—No, my health has been excellent. Who says I am dying?

We often use false feelings to overcome our own fears and win the sympathy of others.

Suman—Don't talk like that. Don't utter inauspicious words. It would have been one thing if I had decided to die, for then none of this would have happened. I am the Kaikeyi of this Ramayan. I was drowning and dragged others down with me. Why are you standing? Do sit down. Today, I have many things to say to you. You will have to forgive me, but today I will call you 'brother'. Now, we are related—I am your sister-in-law, so if I say something very hurtful, please don't think ill of me. You surely know of my condition. Your uncle has saved me and now I live in the widows' home where I weep every day and will continue to weep. For a month, my poor sister has also been living with me. They were unable to take care of her at Umanath's. May god grant Sharmaji a long life, for he went to Amola and brought her here. But he hasn't thought about her since she arrived here. I ask you, is it right that one brother steals and the other is arrested? Now there are no secrets from you. I, unlucky wretch that I am, forsook the path of morality because of my bad fortune, because of the changes in my fate, because of the sins of my past life. I should have received punishment for it and I did. But what did this poor girl do for which you have abandoned her? You will have to give me an answer to that question! Look, don't hide behind your elders. That's how cowards behave. Tell me truthfully, is this injustice or not? And how did you let this grave injustice happen? Did you not have even a shred of mercy while you were destroying this helpless girl's life?

If Shanta had not been present, Sadan might have had the courage to reveal his true thoughts. He would have accepted that it was unjust. But suddenly, in front of Shanta, he was not willing to accept his own defeat. At the same time, he had to think twice before talking about his family honour. He didn't want to say anything which would hurt Shanta, nor anything which would give rise to false hopes. His wandering eyes, which fell on Shanta, had put him in a dilemma. His condition was like that of a child who looks greedily at sweets that a guest has brought, but who cannot eat them for fear of his mother's anger. He said—Baiji, you have already disarmed me, so how can I say that everything that was done was done by my elders. I don't want to absolve myself of guilt by placing all the responsibility on their heads. I, too, was afraid of what the world would think. You must agree that while we live in the world, we must follow the ways of the world. I admit that it was unjust, but I didn't commit this injustice. It was committed by the society in which we live.

Suman—Brother, you are an educated man. I cannot win a debate of words with you. Do whatever you think best. Injustice is injustice, whether it is committed by one man or an entire race. You shouldn't commit an injustice because you are afraid of others. Shanta is standing right here, so I won't reveal her secrets, but I will say this: You may find wealth, respect, beauty, character, and the rest in someone else, but you will never find this kind of love. If her heart had been like yours, she would have married someone else and been happy today. But it is only because of her love for you that she is here.

Sadan saw the tears dripping from Shanta's eyes and falling on her feet! Her simple heart, longing for love, was filled with grief. In a very tender voice, he said—I don't understand what I should do? As god is my witness, my heart is breaking.

Suman—You are a man. God has given you every ability.

Sadan—I am ready to do whatever you want.

Suman—Do you swear it?

Sadan—What can I say? God knows the state of my mind.

Suman—The words of men don't inspire faith.

Suman smiled as she said this. Ashamed, Sadan responded—If it was a question of my willingness, I would tear out my heart and show it to you.

He lowered his head and tried to look at Shanta.

Suman—Fine. Then on the bank of this river, take Shanta's hand and say, 'you are my wife and I am your husband. I will care for you'.

Sadan's resolution began to ebb. He looked under his arms as if he was looking for a place to hide his face. He felt as if the Ganga was rising in order to engulf him. He looked up at the sky like a drowning man and with shame he looked at the ground and choking on his words, he said—Suman, give me a chance to think about this.

Suman responded tenderly—Yes. You should think well before you decide on anything. I don't want to put you in a moral bind.

She then turned to Shanta and said—Look. Your husband is standing before you. I have said everything that I had to say, but he doesn't melt. He is slipping away from you permanently. If your love is true and there is any strength left in it, then stop him, and make him marry you.

As she said this, Suman began to walk in the direction of the Ganga. Shanta slowly followed her. Her love was buried under her pride. The person for whom she had decided to endure lifelong pain, at whose feet she had offered herself with hope—in front of him now, she stood proudly. He didn't consider her situation, didn't think about her difficulties, didn't worry at all about her helplessness. At that moment, had she stood with her hands folded before Sadan, her desires would have been fulfilled, but she thought it better to be proud than be meek.

Sadan stood there for a moment, and then full of regret, returned home.

46

S<small>ADAN FELT GUILTY</small>, as if he had committed some terrible crime. He pondered over his words again and realized that he had been completely insensitive. He was conquered by her love.

He thought—why am I so afraid of the world? What has the world done for me? Will I forsake this jewel, which is the reward of who knows how much sacrifice in my past lives, merely because I am afraid of false slander? So what if my relatives abandon me in order to perform their own duty? The fear of slander exists to save us from sin. It would be cowardice to fear an obstacle in the path of duty. The irony is that if we falsely accuse an innocent, the world doesn't look down on us. Rather, it assists us in performing this crime, provides testimony and counsel. If we were to steal someone's savings, embezzle his wealth, then the world would mete out no punishment, or perhaps a very minor one. But it does punish us for these other crimes, and places an indelible mark of shame on our foreheads. No, the fear of social scorn will not compel me to deny my responsibilities. I won't let her drown like this. The world can say what it wants, but I cannot commit this grave injustice.

I know that it is my duty to obey my mother and father. They gave birth to me and raised me. I played in my father's lap and drank from my mother's breast. A mere gesture from them, and I could take poison, throw myself onto a sword, or jump into a fire. But despite their certain anger, I cannot ignore this poor girl, whom it is my duty to protect. Mother and father will certainly be opposed. Possibly, they may even disown me and say that as far as they are concerned I am as goods as dead to them, but after a few days of pain, they will get over it. They will forget about me. Time will heal their wounds.

Hai! What a cruel and stone-hearted person I am! That girl, who could have been a princess, stood before me that day, like a beggar seeking charity, and I didn't melt at all. That should have been the moment for me to fall at her feet, fold my hands, and say, 'Goddess! Forgive my mistakes!' I should have brought water from the Ganga and offered it to her feet, like a devotee making offerings to his beloved goddess. But I stood there like a stone statue and sang the discordant notes of my family honour. What an idiot! How my words must have hurt her tender heart is clear from her proud response. She must have thought me cold, heartless, proud, and deceitful. She didn't even once look me in the eye. Truth be told, I am not worthy of her.

Sadan felt guilty for days. In the end, he decided that he should build a separate house for himself and learn to stand on his own feet. There was no other way to provide for himself—now the door to my parents' home is closed to me; even knocking on it would not open it. Uncle will help me, but I will only start a feud by staying with him; mother and father will think that he is corrupting their son. So there is no option other than to live on my own.

He thought about going out and extinguishing the blaze that he had started, but when he tried to walk, he couldn't. In his mind, he would hear questions like 'where will I find work?' or 'where can I find a house?'

Sadan was constantly worried about how he would solve these problems. He had searched the entire town for work, sometimes looking near the offices, and sometimes wandering by the large factories, but always returning home after a couple of hours. So far, he had passed his life in happy excess, and had not learned the lessons of simplicity and modesty. Pride still flowed in his veins. When he walked down the street, he strutted. He didn't think much of the people who came across his path. He had no perception of the real world. He didn't realize that in this world, there would be many occasions when he would not only have to bend but also bow. Here, the only kind of petitioner that was heard was one who knew how to beat his head against merciless blocks of stone, who was industrious, who was able, who was modest, who had conquered his own mind like an ascetic, who bent in the face of injustice, who swallowed his dishonour like it was milk, and trampled on self-respect with the soles of his feet. He didn't realize that those virtues, which make gods of men, were looked upon here with scorn. He was virtuous, honest, sincere, and didn't know how to bend the truth, but he couldn't see that irrespective of the spiritual value of these traits, in the eyes of the world, they couldn't compensate for the lack of an education. Sadan now deeply regretted that he had wasted his time—I haven't learnt a trade through which I could have made a living in this world. Sadan spent more than a month wandering around like this and still didn't find any work.

Frustration slowly led to dissatisfaction. He became angry with his mother and father, his uncle, the world, and even himself. Just a few days ago, he would happily to go out for rides in his buggy, but now whenever he saw a buggy approaching, his blood would boil. And if he saw a fashionable man approaching, he would intentionally bump into him, and thinking—if he so much as makes a face, I'll show him. Often, he paid no heed to the driver's cries. He would be irritated by anyone and everyone and pick fights—These people drive around in their cars, put on suits and get all dressed up to go out but there is no place in this world for me.

Having grown up in a zamindar's family, Sadan had never had to worry about finances. That's why he hadn't paid any special attention to his education, but as soon as he had to worry about earning a living, he began to see that he was completely ignorant in these matters. Although he hadn't studied English, he had acquired a good command of Hindi while he had been at school. Because they placed no faith in their mother tongue, Sadan thought that the members of the educated class were traitors to their country and their race. He was arrogant about his virtues. Ever since his articles editorials had been published in *Jagat*, he began to view English-educated men with scorn—every last one of them is self-centered; they have only learnt English to strangle the poor and fill their own bellies. Every last one of them is a slave to fashion, and their education has taught them to mimic the English, who have no mercy, no religion, no respect for our language, no virtue, no self-respect. Are these even men? These were the kind of thoughts that went through his mind. But now that he had to start thinking about his livelihood, he realized that he was being unfair towards them— they are objects of pity. I am not a scholar of languages, but I do know the language better than most. My reputation may not be great, but it is better than most. I don't have the purest thoughts, but they are not base, and still, all doors are closed to me. I can either become a peon somewhere or if I am lucky a constable. That's all I am qualified to do. This is such an injustice. No matter how good someone is, how smart, how thoughtful, it doesn't mean anything without knowledge of the English language. Who else but we would bear such an injustice silently? Or even be proud of it? No, I should give up trying to find a job.

Sadan's condition was like that of a man who sets out to wander into the forest at night but gets upset at the darkness.

And in this condition of frustration and worry, one day, while walking, he arrived at a spot near the river where several boats had been docked. Tiny boats drifted coyly here and there on the river. Melodious strains could be heard from some of the boats. Boatmen were unloading canvas bags from several of the boats. Sadan went and sat on one of the boats. The peaceful evening and the enchanting scene on the riverbank captivated him. He began to think—this is such a peaceful life, may God grant me such a hut, so that I can be happy, stroll along the bank of the river, walk by the waves and sing songs of bliss. Shanta could be standing at the door of the hut, waiting for me. Sometimes, we could sit in a boat and waft down the river. This poetic picture of a simple, joyful existence so enraptured him that he was engulfed by it. Everything about that place seemed bathed in the colours of happiness, peace, and joy. He got up and said to the boatman— Why Chaudhari, are there any boats for sale?

The boatman was smoking a hookah. As soon as he saw Sadan, he got up and showed him a few boats. Sadan chose a new one. The bargaining began. Several boatmen gathered around. In the end, the boat was sold for three hundred rupees. And it was also agreed that the seller would be the rower of the boat.

As Sadan walked home, he was so happy, it was as if he no longer desired anything else in the world, as if he had just been victorious in some long and hard battle. He couldn't sleep through the night. A boat, with its sails put up, coming over the horizon, danced before his eyes, and he saw the scene over and over again. His imagination had erected a lovely hut, decorated with heavy, green vines, and Shanta's lovely image came and sat inside it. The hut had been illuminated. His imagination went on to erect a palace with a garden on the bank of the river with Sadan and Shanta strolling in it. From one direction came the gurgling sounds of the river, and from the other, the sweet songs of birds. The image of the one that we fall in love with becomes etched in our minds in a certain way. And the moment in which we preserve that image, the feelings of that moment, and its scenic details become seared into our hearts. Sadan imagined Shanta wearing a plain sari and standing on the bank of the Ganga with her head bowed. That image would not vanish from his sight.

As he walked home, Sadan felt as though there were nothing but profit in this business. The possibility of loss did not even occur to him. And the strangest part was that he hadn't even thought about how he would get the money.

But as soon as the next day dawned, he began to worry—who can I ask and who will lend it to me? How should I plead? Should I tell uncle? No, he probably doesn't have any these days. He hasn't gone to court in months and asking father would be like trying to squeeze oil out of rocks. What can I do? And if I don't go now, what will Chaudhari think? He began pacing back and forth on the roof. The huge palace of his desires, which had been constructed in his imagination only a short while ago, began to crumble before his eyes. The hopes of youth are like fires in straw paddies—they take little time in blazing and then burning out.

Suddenly, Sadan came up with an idea. He let out a huge guffaw like a person who knocks his opponent to the ground and then laughs mirthlessly—wow! I am such an idiot. I have a gold necklace in my trunk. It has to be worth more than three hundred rupees. Why don't I sell it? I'll come up with something if someone asks for it. No one ever asks about it and even if someone does, I will just tell them straight that I sold it. And then let what happens, happen and if by then I have earned some money, I will take it out and throw it at them. He went and took the necklace out of the trunk and began to think about how he could sell it. To sell jewellery in the marketplace was no less than to sell one's own honour. He was thinking about this very thing when Jeetan, the kahaar, came into the room to sweep. Seeing Sadan look so upset, he said—Brother, you seem sad today. Your eyes are bloodshot. Didn't you sleep last night?

Sadan said—I couldn't sleep. I have been grappling with a problem.

Jeetan—What kind of problem? Tell me.

Sadan—If I tell you, you'll be running around the house, screaming it to everyone.

Jeetan—Brother, I've become old working for you people. If I couldn't keep people's secrets, I wouldn't have lasted here this long. Rest assured.

Just as the word 'no' escapes the mouth of a poor but virtuous man with difficulty, with helplessness and with shame, the following words tumbled out of Sadan's mouth—I have a necklace. Sell it for me. I need the money.

Jeetan—That's not a big deal at all. Why are you so worried? But what will you do with the money? Why don't you ask Mistress for it? She never says no. It's true that if you ask master, you won't get anything. In this house, the master is nothing. The mistress is everything.

Sadan—I don't want to ask anyone in the family.

Jeetan examined the necklace, weighed it in his hand, and left promising to sell it by nightfall. But he didn't go to the marketplace. He went straight to his room, closed both the windows, and began to dig up the ground under his cot. In a little while, he had uncovered an earthen vessel. This was his entire life savings, a lifetime's worth of stinginess, miserliness, cutting corners, dishonesty, and conniving that manifested itself in the form of money inside this vessel. Possibly, because of this, the faces on the notes had been smudged, but still, what a tiny reward for a life's worth of sin. What little price one gets for one's sins!

Jeetan counted his money and made piles of twenty rupees each. There were seventeen piles in all. Then he weighed the necklace against the money in a scale. It weighed considerably more than twenty-five rupees. Even though the price of gold had gone up in the market, he valued it at twenty-five rupees for each rupee in weight. Then he made piles of fifty rupees. There were thirteen piles with fifteen rupees left over. He had two hundred and fifty rupees less than what the necklace was worth. He thought to himself—I can't let this slip through my fingers. I will tell him that it only weighed thirteen! That will save me fifteen more. Well my dear necklace, why don't you rest inside this box?

The vessel was again buried in the ground, and the shape of sin receded into insignificance again.

Jeetan was, for the moment, jumping for joy inside. He had easily cheated someone out of two hundred and fifty rupees. He had never had such a lucrative opportunity before. He thought—I must have seen the face of an auspicious man when I got up in the morning. Like eyes that have gone bad, there is no light in a conscience that has gone rotten.

At ten o'clock, Jeetan went to Sadan and gave him the three hundred and fifty rupees. Sadan acted as if he had simply found the money lying on the ground.

After he had given him the money, Jeetan turned away selflessly. Sadan took five rupees and held it out for him. He said—Here, this is for your paan.

Jeetan made a face like a Brahmin does when offered wine and said—Brother, I survive on what you give me. How can I accept this?

Sadan—No, no. I offer it to you gladly. Take it, there's no harm.

Jeetan—No, brother, I can't. If I had taken handouts, I would have become worthless a long time ago. May God keep you well.

Sadan was sure that this was a very noble man. He decided he would be kind to him in future.

In the evening, Sadan's boat roamed the waves like a cloud roams through the skies. But instead of bliss and enjoyment, his face was distorted with doubts about the future, like a student lost in worry after he has passed his exams. He felt as though the dam which had been protecting him from the flood of the river of life had broken and he was standing in the middle of a huge ocean. Sadan was thinking—I have put the boat on the river, but will it get me to the other side? He now realized that the waters were treacherous, the wind was strong, and the journey of his life was not as easy as he had once thought. If the waves sang in sweet harmony, they could also thunder with terrible roars. If the wind could playfully pat the waves, it could also hurl them around violently.

47

Much of Prabhakar Rao's anger had been quelled by Sadan's articles and when Padamsingh mailed to him, at Sadan's insistence, Suman's entire story, he started paying more attention.

It had been three months since the resolution was passed in the municipal council, and the criticisms that Teg Ali had made about the amendments had proved groundless. Not only had no stores been set up in Dalmandi, the courtesans also demonstrated no abnormal love by getting married. Yes, a few of the brothels were cleaned out. Those courtesans had found other places to live in out of a fear of violent expulsion. To oppose a law requires greater organization than it does to create a law. This was one of the reasons that Prabhakar Rao had become less vicious in his assaults.

Padamsingh had originally taken up the resolution out of his dislike for courtesans. But now, as he thought long and hard about the issue, his hatred began to look increasingly like mercy and compassion, emotions that had compelled him to agree to the amendment. He thought—these poor women are destroying themselves through their desires and their longings. Their longing for luxuries has made them blind. And in this condition, it is necessary to be compassionate and caring towards them. This sin will only weaken their ability to change and those souls whom we can save with advice, love, wisdom, and education will be lost to us forever. We who are lost in the darkness of delusion have no right to mete out punishment. Their own karmas will punish them enough; we need not make their lives even more miserable by wronging them.

Our thoughts lead us to action. Padamsingh let go of his doubts and hesitations and set about acting on his resolutions. That same Padamsingh who had run away from Suman, could now be seen spending his afternoons sitting in the brothels in Dalmandi. He was no longer afraid of social scorn. Nor was he worried about what people would think of him. His soul had grown stronger and the spirit of service had awakened in his heart. An unripe fruit will not fall even if you throw a stone at it, but once it ripens, it falls of its own accord. The desire for service and love had ripened in Padamsingh's soul.

But in this case, Vitthaldas had no love for Padamsingh. He didn't believe that women who were born courtesans could be reformed. Padamsingh also stopped meeting Sayyid Shafakat Ali, who had conceived the amendment, and Kumvar Sahib who had little time left from his literature, songs, and colloquia; so only Sadhu Gajanand remained to help Padamsingh with his work. The desire for service had taken strong hold of this hardworking man.

48

A MONTH HAD passed. Sadan told no one at home about his new business. He left early every morning, claiming that he was going to bathe in the Ganga. He came back home at ten o'clock. After he ate, he would set out again and wouldn't return home until well after dark. Now his boat was better decorated and more spectacular than all the other boats in the river. There were two or three seats in it and a carpet had been laid out. Consequently, several of the town's most refined and rich men used it to tour the river. Sadan wouldn't spend much time talking about fares. His underling, Jhingur, handled that work. He spent most of his time either sitting on the bank of the river or sitting in the boat. He used to tell himself over and over again—why should anyone be ashamed to work? I haven't done anything wrong, and I am no one's slave. No one can look down on me. But whenever he saw a gentleman coming towards his boat, he automatically took a few steps back and hung his head in shame. He was, after all, the son of a zamindar and the nephew of a lawyer. Stepping down from a higher station and working as a boatman often caused him embarrassment, which no amount of reasoning could inoculate him against. This lack of confidence caused him much loss. He would have to content himself with receiving half a rupee when he could have charged one rupee. A high-class store, even with second-rate wares, does well in the marketplace. Even though his product was good, he lacked a clever and good-looking manager. Sadan understood this, but could not bring himself to say anything. Still, every day brought in two-and-a-half or two rupees and soon his hut would be built on the bank of the river and he would move in. He was becoming independent and it brought him great joy. He often spent sleepless nights dreaming about his plans.

At about the same time, the municipal council decided to build houses for the courtesans away from the city. Lala Bhagatram won the contract for the work. No land could be found on this side of the river where they could set up a brick kiln and a furnace. So he bought land on the other side of the river to do so. To get the bricks and the mortar to the other side of the river he needed to hire a boat. While negotiating with the boatmen he met Sadan. Sadan showed him his boat, and Bhagatram approved. He hired Jhingur to work on the boat, and they agreed on fares for two trips across each day. Bhagatram gave him a deposit and then left.

The taste of money is a bad thing. Sadan was no longer an idling and wasteful youth. His mind was now weighed down with worries and obligations. He wanted to be free. He watched every penny closely. He was determined to earn enough money to be able to build his house. Today, while it was still dark, he got up and went to the edge of the water and after waking Jhingur, started work. As day broke, he was already heading out to the other side of the river. On the way back, he took the oars himself and laughed as he rowed a few strokes, but seeing how a little rowing made the boat move faster, he began rowing harder. Now, the boat could go twice as fast. At first Jhingur merely smiled but soon he was amazed.

After the day's work, he began to respect Sadan much more. Sadan no longer seemed to be just some pile of dirt—if the time ever came, he could row the boat across himself, and it is no longer right for me to grumble at him.

That day, they made two trips. The next day, only one, because Sadan was late in reaching the river. On the third day, he made a third trip at nine o'clock at night, but he was exhausted. He was so tired that walking home was like climbing a mountain. He worked like this for two months and made a good profit. He had hired two more boatmen.

Sadan was now the leader of the boatmen. His hut was also ready. There was a *divan* inside, two beds, two lamps, and some cooking utensils. There was a sitting room, a kitchen, and a bedroom. There was a patio made of bricks just outside the door. There were flowerpots all around it. Two of the flowerpots held vines that climbed the walls of the hut. This patio became the meeting place for the boatmen. They often sat there smoking tobacco. Sadan had helped them out greatly. He had written letters to the officers and got them out of their bonded labour. This arduous work had earned him their respect. By now he had also saved a bit of money and he would lend money to the boatmen without interest. Soon, he was making plans for a bicycle and a nice covered boat in which he could take fashionable men for tours, and he had already put up a notice for a harmonium. This was all preparation for the arrival of that goddess whom he had never stopped thinking about.

Sadan was now able to provide for his household, but he did not dare bring Shanta in without his uncle's permission. Whenever he was home, he would sit down to eat with Padamsingh intending to broach the subject so that he could get on with his plan. But he could never act out his intentions. The words wouldn't come forth.

Although Sadan hadn't said anything about his business to Padamsingh, Padamsingh had found everything out through Lala Bhagatram. Padamsingh was proud of Sadan's hard work. He wanted to buy him two more boats and build up his business. But as long as Sadan didn't say anything, he thought it best to remain quiet. He had always respected Sadan, but now he was sincerely proud of him, too, and Subhadra began thinking of him as her own son.

One day, Sadan was sitting in his hut and looking out at the river. For some reason, the boats had been late in returning. A lamp was burning in the distance. There was a newspaper in Sadan's hand, but he couldn't concentrate on it. The lateness of the boats seemed ominous to him. He put down the newspaper and went to the bank of the river. A delicate quilt of moonlight was spread out on the sand and the rays from the moon hit the moving waves like a pure stream of water from a spring, that grew bigger and bigger as it flowed. A few boatmen were sitting and talking on the patio in front of his hut when Sadan suddenly saw two women walking out from the city. One of them asked the boatmen—We want to cross the river. Can you take us?

Sadan recognized the voice. It was Sumanbai. His heart skipped a beat and an intoxication filled his eyes. Stumbling, he went to the patio and said to Suman—Baiji, what are you doing here?

Suman looked at Sadan carefully as if she didn't know him at all. The woman next to her covered her face with her veil and moved away from the lamp into the darkness. Suman spoke with surprise in her voice—Who is it? Sadan?

The boatsmen formed a circle, but Sadan said—You should all leave now. These women are related to me and they will stay here tonight.

After that he said to Suman—Baiji, tell me how you are. What has happened?

Suman—Everything is fine. I am just fulfilling what my fate dictates. You may not have read today's newspaper. Who knows what Prabhakar Rao published which created such a commotion in the ashram. If we had stayed there any longer, the entire ashram would have emptied out. It was best that we left. Now do us this one favour and get us a boat to get to the other side of the river. We will get a buggy to take us to Mugalsarai. From there we can catch a train to Amola. Isn't there a night train that goes there?

Sadan—Now that you have come home, why do you need to go to Amola? You have already been through so much. I can't tell you how happy I am to see you here tonight. I had been planning to come and see you for several days now, but I couldn't get away from my work. I have been working as a boatman for the past several months. This is your house. Come inside.

Suman went inside the hut, but Shanta just stood there in the darkness and wept silently. Ever since she had heard those words from Sadansingh's mouth, she had passed her days crying in pain. She could only regret, over and over again, how arrogant she had been. She thought—if I had just fallen at his feet then, he would certainly have felt sorry for me. Sadan's image was constantly in her mind and his words echoed in her ears. The words were harsh, but to Shanta, they seemed filled with love. She had explained to herself that this was the consequence of the sins of her past life and Sadan was not to blame—He is really helpless. It is his duty to obey his mother and father. It is a reflection of my villainy that I want to turn him away from the path of his duty. Yes! I was arrogant with my husband. I did not honour my venerable husband. I was overpowered by my ruthless selfishness and was disrespectful. As the days passed, Shanta's spirit grew weak. Grief, worry, and anguish dried her up like a river in the months of summer.

After Suman had gone inside the hut, Sadan slowly walked up to Shanta and in a tremulous voice he said—Shanta!

And as he spoke, his throat constricted.

Shanta was brimming over with love. Her love had reached that spiritual plane where it was free from the limitations of the self.

She said to herself—is there any certainty in this life? Who knows how long I will live, whether I will see him again or not, so why should I leave unfulfilled the desire to fall at his feet and cry? What better chance will I have than this? Lord! If you will just once lift me up and wipe my tears with your own hands, my mind will be at peace, and my life will have some meaning. And as long as I live, the memory of my good fortune in this will bring me joy. I had given up hope of seeing you ever again, but when God has granted me this day, why shouldn't I fulfill my heart's desires? I have found a tree in the desert of my life, so why not sit in its shade and soothe my raging heart?

In tears, Shanta, fell at Sadan's feet, but a wilted flower scatters at even the slightest gust of wind. Sadan bent down to pick her up and embrace her, hold her, but on seeing Shanta's condition, he became confused. When he had first seen her by the river, her beauty was blooming like a fresh lotus bud, but now she was a dry, yellow leaf that falls in the autumn months.

Sadan's heart began flickering like moonlight on the water. With trembling hands he lifted her unconscious body. Helpless, he prayed to God. Weeping, he said—God, I have sinned terribly. I have mercilessly trampled a soft, distressed heart, but this punishment is unbearable. Don't steal this priceless jewel from me yet. You are merciful. Have mercy on me.

Holding Shanta close to his body, Sadan took her inside the hut and laid her down on the bed, and in a desperate voice said—Suman, watch over her. I am going to get the doctor.

Suman went to her sister and looked at her. Beads of sweat had formed on her forehead and her eyes were lifeless. She couldn't find her pulse. Suman's face turned pale. She immediately picked up a fan and began fanning her. The anger that had built up in her heart over the past few months caring for Shanta finally burst open. She looked at Sadan with anger—This is the reward of your crimes. This is all your fault. Your cruel hands have crushed this flower. You have trampled this sapling under your own feet. Look, and now suddenly you can speak. Sadan, ever since this troubled girl heard your arrogant words, she hasn't laughed and her tears have not stopped flowing. I had to force her to swallow a few bites of food. And the only reason that you have wronged her is that I am her sister, at whose feet you spent years wallowing, whose heels you spent ages tending, whose love made you drunk for months. Were you still your parents' dutiful son then, or were you something else? Were you still a high-caste Brahmin then, or were you someone else? Wasn't your family honour ruined by your sins then? Now you walk around as if you are the king of the heavens. You are willing to eat someone else's leftovers in the dark, but in daylight you won't even accept an invitation to dinner. This is the worst kind of deception and hypocrisy. God will punish you in the same way that you have hurt this poor girl. Whatever she had to endure, she has endured. She may not die today, but she will die eventually, and then you will cry desperate tears in her memory. If she had been any other woman, she would not have listened to your words and looked up at you. She would have cursed you, but this poor wretch lives by your name. Go bring me some cold water.

Sadan hung his head in guilt and listened to her words. It made his heart feel lighter. If Suman had insulted him, he would have felt even lighter. He felt that he completely deserved her anger.

He handed Suman a cup of cold water and began to fan Shanta. Suman sprinkled some water on Shanta's face. And when Shanta opened her eyes, Sadan said—I should go and get the doctor, right?

Suman—No. Don't worry. As soon as she gets some air, she will regain consciousness. The doctor doesn't have the medicine she needs.

Sadan felt a little more at ease and said—Suman, you might think that I am lying, but I am being completely honest when I say that ever since that moment, my soul has not found a moment's peace. I regretted over and over again how stupid I had been. Several times, I even wanted to beg for forgiveness for my sins, but I kept thinking that I could I never make reparations. I had no hope of getting any help from my relatives, and you know that I am nothing but a lame horse. So I did nothing but worry about how I would earn four pice to build my own house. I spent months looking for work, but I couldn't find any. Now I don't need anyone's help or assistance. I had this hut built and I think as soon as I get a little more money I will have a house in the city. Why, it seems she is doing better, no?

Suman calmed down. She said—Yes. Now there is no need to worry. It was just a fainting spell. Her eyes have closed and the colour is returning to her lips.

Sadan was so happy that if there had been an idol there, he would have prostrated himself at its feet. He said—Suman, you have saved me and I will always remember that. If anything else had happened, you would have found my corpse next to hers.

Suman—Don't say such things. God willing, she will get better without any medicine and the two of you can live happily together for a long time. You are her medicine. Your love is her life. Now that she has you, she will not long for anything. But if you dishonour or hurt her even accidentally, this will happen again and you will be left wringing your hands.

In the meantime, Shanta had begun to stir and was now asking for water. Suman placed a glass of water near her lips. She drank a few sips and then fell back on the charpoy. She looked around with astonishment as if she couldn't believe her own eyes! She sat up with a jolt and stared at Suman and said—Wait. This is my home, isn't it? Yes, yes, this is it. And where is my husband, the pillar of my life? Call him and let me look at him. I am on fire; I need to extinguish this heat. I will ask him a few questions. Why doesn't he come? Well fine, then I will go. Today, we will argue. No, I won't argue with him, I will just say don't ever leave me again. You can turn me into a necklace or into shackles around your feet, but keep me with you. I can't bear being away from you. I know that you love me. Yes, maybe not. You don't want me. But I want you. Yes, maybe not even that. I don't want you either. I have been married to you. No, no, I haven't! Yes, nothing has happened. I won't marry you. But I will live with you and if you even look at another it will not be good. No, it won't be good. I haven't been born to live a life of tears. My love, don't be angry. That's all that will happen, a few men will laugh and taunt you. Bear it for me. What, your mother and father will abandon you? Don't say such things. Parents don't abandon their sons. You will see. I will drag them back, I will wash my mother-in-law's feet and drink the water, and I will massage my father-in-law's feet. Will they not feel sorry for me?

And as she said this, Shanta's eyes closed again.

Suman spoke to Sadan—Now she is asleep. Let her sleep. Once she has slept well, she will calm down. It's past midnight. Now you should go home, too. Sharmaji is probably waiting up for you.

Sadan—I won't go today.

Suman—No, no. They will be worried. Shanta is fine. Look how happily she is sleeping. In all these days, I have never seen her sleep like this.

But Sadan wasn't convinced. He went out into the courtyard, lay down on the floor, and began thinking.

49

Babu Vitthaldas was a simple and just man. He would always follow his sense of justice, without an iota of reluctance. When he saw Padamsingh straying from the path of justice, he abandoned him and didn't go to see him for several months, but when Prabhakar Rao started criticizing the ashram and began revealing the secret of Sumanbai, Vitthaldas became upset with him as well. Now he didn't have a single friend in the city. Now he felt that as the chief of an institution whose future depended on the sympathy and aid of others, it was highly inappropriate for him to take sides. He felt that for the benefit of the ashram, it was best if he met everyone even if he felt indifferent towards them—this is the best path for me. It was evening. He was sitting and thinking about how he would respond to Prabhakar Rao's criticisms—what he says is true. Suman really is a prostitute. And I brought her into the ashram even though I knew that. I didn't tell the board of directors about it. I didn't even propose it. In all honesty, I have been acting as if the ashram were my private property. No matter how praiseworthy my intentions, it was entirely inappropriate of me to keep this a secret.

Vitthaldas had not yet arrived at any decision when the principal of the ashram came to see him and said—Sir, Anandi, Gauri, and Rajkumari are all set to go home. I tried explaining things to them, but they won't listen.

Vitthaldas was annoyed and replied—Tell them to leave then. I am not afraid of that. I won't kick Suman and Shanta out for them.

The principal left and Vitthaldas began thinking again—who do these women think they are? Is Suman so vile that they cannot live with her? They say that the ashram is getting a bad reputation and that they are getting one as well by staying there. Yes, there is definitely disrepute. Go, I won't stop you.

At that moment, the postman came to deliver letters. Five letters had arrived for Vitthaldas.

The writer of one said that he didn't think it appropriate for his daughter (Vidyapati) to stay in the ashram. He was coming to take her away. A second man threatened that if the prostitutes were not removed from the ashram, he would stop donating money to it. A third letter expressed the same opinion. Vitthaldas didn't bother opening the remaining two letters. The threats didn't frighten him, only strengthened his determination—these people think that they can scare me with idle threats! They don't understand that Vitthaldas doesn't care what anyone thinks. The ashram can fall to the ground, but I will never separate Shanta and Suman. Vitthaldas's rage overtook his good sense. The streams of enthusiasm and frustration come from the same source. The difference is only in their effect.

Suman could see that all the commotion was on account of her. She was sorry that she had ever come. She had cared for the widows with such devotion, but this was how she was being repaid! She knew that Vitthaldas would never let her leave, so she decided—why not leave quietly? Three women had already left, two or three were getting ready to, and countless others had written letters home. The only ones that were silent were those with no other place to go to. But even they wouldn't look at Suman. Suman couldn't bear the insult. She talked it over with Shanta. Shanta was uncertain. She didn't think it right to leave without Padamsingh's permission. It wasn't merely a thin thread of hope which tied her to the place, because she considered hers to be a religious obligation. She thought—when I have placed all my hopes in Padamsingh's hands, I have no right to walk on a path of my own choosing. But when Suman said to her in a resolute voice, 'Stay here if you want, but I won't stay here under any circumstances,' Shanta found it impossible to stay on. Like a man wandering in a jungle who follows someone he has seen because that makes two of them, Shanta prepared herself to follow her sister.

Suman asked—And if Padamsingh gets angry?

Shanta—I will tell him what happened, in a letter.

Suman—And what about Sadansingh?

Shanta—I will accept whatever punishment he metes out.

Suman—Think about it. Don't do anything you'll regret later.

Shanta—I should stay here, but I can't stay here without you. Tell me, where are we going?

Suman—I will get you to Amola.

Shanta—And you?

Suman—God will be my saviour. I will go on a pilgrimage.

The two sisters talked for a long time. Then the two wept together. As soon as it was eight o'clock and Vitthaldas went home to eat, the two slipped out quietly and left.

No one discovered anything that night. In the morning, the groundskeeper told Vitthaldas what had happened. Terrified, Vitthaldas raced toward Suman's room. All the things in the room were in their place but the sisters were nowhere to be found. The poor man was very worried. How would he face Padamsingh? At that moment, he became furious with Suman—this is all her doing. She tricked Shanta into going with her. All of a sudden, he spied a letter on Suman's charpoy. He quickly picked it up and began to read. Suman had written the letter just as she was leaving. After he read it, Vitthaldas regained his composure. But at the same time, he was hurt because he had been made to feel small on account of Suman. Earlier, he had been sure that he could make the people that had threatened him feel sorry, but now that opportunity had slipped through his fingers. Now people will think that I got scared. This thought caused him much grief.

Finally, he left the room. He locked the door and went straight to Padamsingh's house.

When Sharmaji heard the news, he was shocked; he said—Now what will happen?

Vitthaldas—They must have reached Amola by now.

Sharmaji—Yes, it's possible.

Vitthaldas—Shanta can easily get herself that far.

Sharmaji—She's not that sheltered.

Vitthaldas—But Suman wouldn't have gone to Amola.

Sharmaji—Who knows. Maybe they are both dead by now.

Vitthaldas—Why not send a telegram and ask.

Sharmaji—How can I do that? When I couldn't even take care of Shanta myself, how can I ask about her whereabouts without humiliation? I had total confidence in you. If I had known that you were going to be so careless, I could have just kept her at home with me.

Vitthaldas—You make it sound like I kicked them out myself.

Sharmaji—Had you comforted them, they would never have left. You had said the same to me, but now the opportunity has slipped through your fingers.

Vitthaldas—You want to place the entire blame on me?

Padamsingh—Who else? Aren't you the guardian of the ashram?

Vitthaldas—Shanta has been there for more than three months. Did you even go to see her once? If you had occasionally gone and asked her how she was doing, she would have felt strong. But when you didn't even ask about her, what crutch did she have to lean on while she was there? I admit to my responsibilities, but you are not free from blame yourself.

These days, Padamsingh was annoyed with Vitthaldas. He had taken up the cause of reforming the courtesans because of him, but when it was time to take on the responsibility, Vitthaldas was nowhere to be found. At the same time, Vitthaldas eyed him with suspicion after seeing his compassion for the courtesans. Now, instead of telling each other what was in their hearts, they were trying to accuse each other. Padamsingh really wanted to make him feel sorry, but he had to be silent when he heard his reply. He said—Yes, I am to blame in part.

Vitthaldas—No, it is not my intention to blame you. I am fully responsible for this. When you had entrusted me with their care, it was only natural for you to stop worrying.

Sharmaji—No, actually my laziness and cowardice are the cause of all this. You couldn't have forced them to stay.

By acknowledging his guilt, Padamsingh turned the game around. We can make someone bend by bending ourselves, but to make someone bend while remaining stiff is difficult.

Vitthaldas—Perhaps Sadansingh knows something. Call him.

Sharmaji—He didn't come home last night. He has built a hut on the bank of the river. He has hired a few boatmen and he owns a boat. He might have spent the night there.

Vitthaldas—Perhaps the two sisters went there. If you want, I will go and see.

Sharmaji—Hold on. Are you mad? He is not that liberal. He has enough shame to stay away from their shadows.

Suddenly, Sadan stepped into the room. Padamsingh asked—Where were you last night? We waited up for you the entire night.

Sadansingh stared at the ground and said—I am sorry. Something came up and I had to stay. I didn't even have time to come here and let you know. Out of embarrassment, I haven't said anything to you for months, but I have been running a boat service. And I have built a hut by the river. I think that I should commit myself to this work, so I have come to ask your permission to live there.

Sharmaji—Lala Bhagatram has told me all about it, but it is unfortunate that you have kept this from me for so long. Otherwise, I could have helped you. Look, I don't think that it's a bad thing. Actually, it makes me very happy to see you work like this. But I can't allow you to live there while you are so close to us. Do you think that there will be more profit in getting another boat?

Sadan—Yes sir, I've been thinking about that myself. But that would make it necessary for me to live by the river.

Sharmaji—Look, this is an unfair condition. I don't like the idea of living in the same city but apart from each other. It might even cause you some discomfort, but I won't take no for an answer.

Sadan—No, uncle. Please hear me out. I am asking you out of desperation.

Sharmaji—Why are you desperate? Why don't you tell us straight out what the problem is?

Sadan—There will be a scandal if I stay in this home. I have now decided to fulfil my obligation, which I have been putting off for a long time out of ignorance and for a while out of cowardice and fear of what people would think. I am your son. Whenever I face hardships, I will ask for your help. And if I ever need anything, I will let you know. But I will live in my own house and I am sure that you will approve of my decision.

Vitthaldas had already guessed the end of the story. He asked—Did you run into Shanta and Suman yesterday?

Sadan's face grew red with shame like a young girl whose veil has flown off her face. Quietly, he said—Yes.

Padamsingh was now faced with a moral dilemma. He couldn't say 'yes' and 'no' at the same time. So far, he had considered himself to be completely blameless regarding Shanta's misfortune. He had placed the entire blame for this injustice on his brother's shoulders and had always believed that Sadan was just a puppet. But now he felt caught in a web, and wanted to escape. He wasn't afraid of the world, but he was afraid that his brother would think that he had had a hand in all of this, that he had been a bad influence on Sadan—if these thoughts ever cross his mind, he will never forgive me.

Padamsingh was deep in thought for a long while. Finally, he said—Sadan, this news is so troubling that I can't come to a decision by myself. How can I say 'yes' or 'no' without consulting my brother? You know what I think about all this. I am proud of you and glad that God has given you wisdom. But I consider my brother's wishes more important than anything else. It might be possible that he wouldn't be troubled if we could make separate arrangements for the two sisters. Well, that's as far as I can go. After that, I have no power to decide. Do whatever your father thinks best.

Sadan—Don't you know what he will say?

Padamsingh—Yes, I know.

Sadan—Then it is useless to ask him. As for my mother and father, I can give the life that they have given to me, but I will not slaughter innocent people for him.

Padamsingh—Why not find a separate place for the two to stay?

Angrily, Sadan said—I will only do that when I have something to hide. I am not committing a sin that I need to hide. This is the biggest responsibility in my life—there is no reason to hide anything. Now, the marriage rituals that weren't completed before will be gone through tomorrow on the bank of the river. If you will do me the honour of being there, I will consider myself lucky. If not, vows can be exchanged in God's court without any witnesses.

When he finished, Sadan got up and went inside. Subhadra said—Well, where have you been hiding. I stayed up all night. Where did you go?

Sadan told his aunt what had happened the night before. He wasn't afraid of talking to his aunt like he was with Sharmaji. Subhadra was proud of his courage and said—No one walks out of a marriage for fear of one's parents. If the world laughs, let it laugh. That's no reason to destroy your family. I am afraid of your mother; otherwise I would have kept Shanta with me.

Sadan said—I am not concerned about mother and father.

Subhadra—Well you were very concerned just a moment ago. All this while, you have almost killed that poor girl in making her suffer so. Any other son would have put them in their place on the very first day. You have already put up with things for far too long.

Subhadra, had you only said these words out of a pure heart, we would have praised you to the skies! But at this moment, you are merely under the spell of jealousy and envy. You want to embarrass your sister-in-law by provoking Sadan. You are taking pleasure from striking a blow at a mother's pure heart.

After Sadan had left, Vitthaldas spoke to Padamsingh—This is what you have always wanted. Why didn't you just come out and say it?

Sharmaji didn't answer.

Vitthaldas spoke again—You should have come up with this plan yourself, instead you are hesitating to let Sadan go ahead with it.

Sharmaji didn't respond to this either.

Vitthaldas—What's wrong with him wanting to live separately with his own wife? You won't let him live either with you or away from you. What kind of logic is that?

Padamsingh responded with sarcasm—Sir, you will only understand it when it happens to you. I have been doling out advice to other people the same way that you are giving it to me. You, too, used to make long convoluted speeches about the reform of courtesans, but when it was time to work, you cut off all ties. You should understand other people are the same. I can do almost anything, but I can't go against my brother. I hold no principle so dear that I would sacrifice his wishes for it.

Vitthaldas—I never told you that I would turn women born into prostitution into saints. Do you think that there is no difference between a woman who is fallen because of her unjust family or the seductions of rogues and a woman that has been a prostitute her entire life? I think that there is as much difference between them as there is between a curable and a fatal disease. You can put out a new fire, but only a fool tries to put out the fire in a volcano. A wise man never does.

Sharmaji—At the very least, you should have tried to help me out. If you come with me to Dalmandi for an hour, you will see that your so-called 'volcanoes' are merely ashes of an extinguished fire. There are good and bad men everywhere. Prostitutes are no different. You will be surprised to see how much religious devotion, how much hatred for a life of sin, how strong a desire to change their lives these women possess. I myself am surprised by it. All they need is one helping hand, which they can hold on to and lift themselves up. At first they wouldn't even speak to me, but when I explained to them that I brought forward the resolution only for their benefit, so that they could remain beyond the reach of sinners, criminals, and rogues, they slowly began to trust me. I won't tell you their names, but some of the wealthy courtesans are ready to help me out with money. Some of them want to get their daughters married. But for now there are more women who don't want to leave their lives of happiness and pleasure. I hope that Sadhu Gajanand's teachings will have some effect. It is unfortunate that there is no one else to help me. Yes, there are several who mock and criticize. Now we need to build an orphanage where courtesans can keep their daughters and we can make the best arrangements for their education. But no one listens to me.

Vitthaldas listened very carefully to him. Padamsingh had said what he believed in, and speaking from the heart always creates trust. Vitthaldas began to see that the work that he thought was counterproductive really wasn't. He said—Haven't you spoken to Anirudhsingh about this?

Sharmaji—He has nothing to offer except pleasantries and literary criticism.

50

Sadansingh got married. The hut was decorated beautifully, the sacrificial fire was lit, but there were no crowds or relatives.

Padamsingh went back to the village that day and told Madansingh all that had happened. As soon as he heard it, he flow into a rage and said—I will cut off that boy's head. Who does he think he is?

Bhama said—I will go there today. I will explain things to him and bring him home with me. He is still a naive boy. He is just under the spell of that whore, Suman. He will never go against me.

But Madansingh shouted at Bhama and threatened her—If you so much as say a word about going there, I will slit both our throats. He wants to jump into a fire, then let him. He is not a suckling child anymore. This is simply his stubbornness. We'll see if I don't leave him begging for money. He thinks after his father dies he will have a good time. This isn't some hereditary property. I have earned it. I can turn it all over to charity if I want. He won't even get a counterfeit penny from me.

The news had spread to all corners of the village. Lala Bhagatram was convinced that there was no morality left on this earth. When people have begun to do such wicked things, how can there be any morality? If it wasn't for the government, that boy would have been torn to pieces by now. Now we'll see what happens if he dares to show his face here again.

Padamsingh sat with his brother for a long time in the night, but as soon as he so much as mentioned Sadan, Madansingh looked at him with such fury that he didn't dare say another word. Finally, when he was about to go to bed, Padamsingh said hopelessly—Bhaiya, even though Sadan lives apart from you, he remains your son. Whatever he does, good or bad, will be a reflection on us. Those who know the full story may even think that we are not to blame, but society doesn't see any difference between Sadan and us. There is little point in killing the snake if the staff also breaks at the same time. On the one hand, there are two disadvantages—we are slandered and we lose our son. On the other hand, there is only one disadvantage, and we get to keep our son. That's why I think it best that we try to explain things to Sadan and if he doesn't comply, then ...

Madansingh cut him off sharply—Then we should let him marry that whore? Why, that is what you wanted to say, isn't it? Well I can't do that. Not once, not a hundred times.

He was silent for a while, then he spoke again, blaming Padamsingh—The amazing thing is that all of this happened around you and you didn't know a thing about it. He bought a boat, built a hut, and lived with those two women illegally while you sat there with your eyes shut. I sent him there because I thought I could count on you. How was I supposed to know that you were just going to sit there with your eyes closed? If you had handled things with even the slightest bit of foresight, it wouldn't have come to this. You didn't ever give me a hint about any of this, or I could have saved him myself. Now that you have lost all your marbles and the entire game is ruined, you have come asking for my advice. I will tell you openly that I am furious with your procrastination. You knowingly let him fall into the fire. I have done many unfair things to you, and so now you have your revenge. Well, write up a deed tomorrow. Aside from the three acres of inherited land, I am giving all of my land to charity. If you can't write it up here, write it up in Benares and mail it to me. I will sign it and get it registered.

With this, Madansingh got up to go to bed. But he had waged such an offensive on Padamsingh's heart that Padamsingh squirmed through the night. The blame, which he sought to avoid by ignoring his principles and for which his friends had slandered him, was set on his shoulders anyway. And not just that, his brother hated him as well. Now he could see where he had gone wrong. Surely, if he had been wise about this matter, it wouldn't have come to this. But despite the pain, he drew some satisfaction from the thought that at least the poor girl had been saved.

Next morning, when he was about to leave, Bhama ran to him in tears and said—Brother, you can see how stubborn he can be. He is bent on taking his son's life, but you be more careful. Even the best can make mistakes, and that poor boy is still an immature lad. Don't think ill of him. He can't even bear it when people look askew at him. I couldn't bear it if it went so far that he thought about leaving for another country. Please keep an eye on him. Don't let him worry about food and water. While he was here, he would drink a buffalo's output in milk each day. He didn't like butter in his daal, but I would sneak in an entire pot of butter into his food. Now who will watch over him so carefully? Who knows how the poor boy is doing? Here, there is no one to feed, and there, he is probably starving. Why brother, does he row the boat himself?

Padamsingh—No, he's hired two boatmen.

Bhama—But he must still have to run around all day in the heat. The workers don't work unless you watch them constantly. Whatever little I have I give it all to you. Look after him like he was an orphan. Every pore in my body will offer you blessings. For this *Kartik-snaan*, I will definitely come to see him. Tell him that his mother misses him dearly and that she cries a lot. It will bring him some comfort. He is a very immature lad. He probably cries everyday thinking about me. Here is a little bit of money. Take it with you. Have it sent to him.

Padamsingh—There is no need for this. I shall look after him. As long as I am watching over him, he won't want for anything.

Bhama—No, brother, take it. Why not? There is a little bit of butter in this pot, too. Have that sent to him as well. Bought butter doesn't compare with homemade butter—it doesn't have the same smell or taste. He really likes mango chutney. We only used the juice of the sweetest mangoes. Explain things to him, and say, 'Son, don't worry about anything. As long as your mother is alive, she won't let anything happen to you.' He is as dear to me as his staff is to a blind man. Good or bad, he is mine. Because of the world's prejudices I may have to keep him far from my sight but he will never be out of my mind.

51

Just as the incorporation of beautiful sentiment gives life to poetry, and beautiful colours to painting, the arrival of the two sisters brought life to that hut. Blind eyes learned to see once again.

Shanta, once a wilted flower, was now blooming with matchless radiance. Dried riverbeds were flooded over with currents. Just as a cow that has suffered from the summer heat is refreshed and begins to roam the pastures in the monsoon, the young woman, after the pangs of separation was now rejuvenated and overcome with love.

Every morning, two stars emerge from that hut and dip themselves in the river. Of the two, one is heavenly and swift, and the other is earthly and slow. One of them dances in the water and the other does not overstep its boundaries. The golden rays of dawn do not outshine these stars but make them even more luminous.

Shanta sings while Suman cooks. Shanta combs her hair while Suman sews. Shanta devours the food on her plate like a starving man while Suman, like an invalid, wonders if she will ever get better.

Sadan's nature, too, has been transformed. He is rapt in the pleasures of love. Now, he gets up late, bathes for hours, combs his hair often, changes his clothes, puts on cologne, is not ready to meet anyone before nine o'clock and when he does, his mind is always somewhere else; he cannot concentrate on work. Every few moments, he returns inside and if it takes too long to talk to someone outside, he becomes bored. Shanta had bewitched him.

Suman does all the work in the house and all the work outside, too. She gets up while it is still dark and after taking a bath and saying her prayers, she makes Sadan's breakfast. Then she goes to the riverbank and unlocks the boats. At nine, she starts cooking lunch. By eleven, when she is done, she finds something else to busy herself with. By nine o'clock at night, when everyone has gone to bed, she sits down to read. She dearly loved Tulsi's *Vinay-Patrika* and the Ramayan. Sometimes she would read *Bhaktmaal*, sometimes lectures by Vivekananda, and sometimes the writings of Ramtirth. She zealously read stories about the lives of educated women.

She was completely devoted to Meera. She generally read only religious books, but compared to knowledge, piety offered her greater peace.

The wives of the boatmen respected her immeasurably. She would settle their arguments, sew clothes for some of their children, and for others, she made kohl for the eyes and other medicines. If any of them fell ill, she would visit them in their homes and arrange for medicines. And so, she repaired the walls of her crumbling life. All the neighbouring men and women praised her. Yet, her own home was the one place that she was not appreciated at all. Suman broke her back doing all the housework, but Sadan didn't utter a single word of gratitude. Shanta didn't seem to care about her efforts either. Neither of them thought about her at all. It was as if she were a slave and it was her duty to remain chained to the grindstone. Sometimes she would get a headache, and at other times she would get ill from running around in the heat, but she would never neglect the housework. Occasionally she would weep by herself at her wretched situation, but there was no one to comfort her or wipe away her tears.

Suman was, by nature, a haughty and proud woman. All her life, she had lived like a queen. In her husband's home, even when she endured hardships, she was still queen. In the brothel, everyone listened to her. In the ashram, her piety and service had made her most respected. Naturally, therefore, living in such demeaning conditions was unbearable to her. Had Sadan thanked her occasionally or asked her advice or considered her the mistress of the house, or if Shanta had sat next to her, listened to her and comforted her, Suman would have worked even harder and would have lived happily. But these two lovers had eyes for no one but each other. While shooting a target, a marksman's sight is fixed on only one point. A lover is no different.

But it wasn't entirely clear that the only reason Shanta and Sadan ignored her was because they were lost in love. Sadan avoided Suman like the plague, and even when he felt sorry for her, he couldn't make himself go near her. Shanta didn't trust Suman and was afraid of her beauty. Thankfully, Sadan never once looked at Suman, otherwise Shanta's rage would have known no limits. And even though both of them wanted to be rid of this resident snake, they were nonetheless afraid to broach the subject, even between themselves.

Slowly, however, these things could not be kept hidden from Suman.

One day, Jeetan brought some gifts from Sharmaji's house for Sadan. On earlier occasions when he had visited, Suman would usually hide when she saw him coming. But this time, Jeetan spied her. And then, of course, he was ready to burst. Here was a man who could digest a stone, but he couldn't digest a secret and keep it down. He went to the Chaudhari on the ruse of wanting to smoke a hookah and managed to tell him the entire story—Arrey! She is a prostitute. Her husband kicked her out of his house, so she was a cook at our house for a while. When she was kicked out of there, she started whoring around the Chauk. And now I see that she is living quite nicely here. The Chaudhari was dumbstruck and the boatmen started making gestures at one another. After that, none of the boatmen would drink the water from Sadan's house, and their wives stopped talking to Suman. Then, once, Lala Bhagatram came by to settle accounts with Sadan. When he grew thirsty, instead of asking Sadan, he asked one of the boatmen to bring him some water. It stabbed Sadan to the heart to have a guest in his house ask for water from outside.

Eventually, after the second year, things got so bad that Sadan would get angry at Suman over the slightest thing and even when he didn't say anything, it was clear how he felt.

Suman began to realize that she couldn't live there any longer. She had hoped that she could pass her life with her sister and brother-in-law—I would care for them, eat their scraps, and sleep in a corner somewhere. She didn't want much from life but a few simple things. But dear God! Even this foundation slipped from beneath her feet and she found herself tossed in the merciless waves again.

But no matter how much her condition grieved her, Suman had no complaints against Sadan or Shanta. Partly because of her religious piety and partly because of an honest account of her own condition, she had become a very humble and gentle woman. She would often fantasize about a place where no one knew her, but she didn't know where it would be. Her tired spirit still longed for some support. Her heart began racing at the thought of going through life without any help. Alone and helpless, she had no hope of surviving on the battlefield of life—how can I survive in a battle where the skilled, virtuous, and the courageous are eaten alive? Who will help me? Who will protect me? Despite being hated here, she couldn't make herself leave—she was afraid of being alone.

One day Sadan came home at ten o'clock and said—How long until dinner? Hurry up, I have to meet Pandit Umanath. He's at Uncle's place right now.

Shanta—Why has he come?

Sadan—How am I supposed to know? Jeetan just came and told me the news that he had come and he is leaving tonight. He wanted to come here, but (and making a gesture towards Suman) didn't for some reason.

Shanta—Then sit down. It will be another hour.

Suman was upset and said—Why the wait? Dinner is ready. Give him some water and I will set his plate.

Shanta—Arrey, what's the harm in waiting? Is a mail train about to leave? Why should he eat half-cooked food?

Sadan—I don't understand what you are up to all day. It takes you so long to make just a bit of food.

After Sadan had left, Suman said to Shanta—Shanta, tell me the truth. You hate my living here, don't you? I know what you are thinking, but I won't even think about leaving until I hear it from your own lips. So say it. I have no place here.

Shanta—Sister, don't say such things. The house is manageable because of you. What would I do without you?

Suman—Don't say things you don't mean. I'm not stupid. It seems to me that the two of you have been distant.

Shanta—Well, then you must have magic eyes that are able to see into my thoughts.

Suman—Look at me. Am I wrong?

Shanta—Why ask when you know the answer?

Suman—Because even after having seen everything, I can't believe my eyes. The world can think what it wants of me. I don't care. It doesn't know what is in my heart. But you have seen it all, and you still think that I am loathsome. I still can't believe it. We have been together for two years. In all that time you must have understood what kind of person I really am.

Shanta—No sister, I swear to God it's not that. Don't accuse me of such a great sin. I can never forget what you have done for me. But the fact is that he is getting a bad reputation. People say all kinds of things. He [Sadansingh] used to say that Subhadra was willing to come here, but she didn't when she heard that you were here. And sister, don't get me wrong, but what can we do when these are the customs of the world?

Suman didn't argue. She had heard what she needed to hear. Now there was only one obstacle. Shanta was pregnant. Suman knew where her duty lay—If I leave now, it will be very difficult for her. I can bear this for a few more days. I've already spent years here, what's another few months. It is my fault that she is in this bad situation anyway. It is not right for me to leave her in this condition.

Each day felt like a year to Suman but she bore it patiently.

A wingless bird considers itself lucky to be living in a cage.

52

FIVE MONTHS OF earnest work by Pandit Padamsingh led to twenty or twenty-five courtesans agreeing to send their girls to the orphanage. Three of the courtesans offered all their wealth for the maintenance of the orphanage, and five courtesans agreed to work in the orphanage itself. Deeply longed for desires always come true. When a community is confident that you are its faithful servant, that you want real reform, that you are selfless, it will readily help you. But this confidence never develops without a true desire for service. If a conscience is not clear and bright, it cannot be a beacon for others. The desire for service had dawned in Padamsingh's heart. There are so many among us who never think of serving their country, and even when they do, they do so out of a desire for fame and fortune. We want to do the kind of work which puts our names in history books, to write the kinds of books and articles which people will praise freely, and often we even get something in return for our selfishness but one cannot make a place for oneself in the community on this basis. A man, no matter how troubled he is, will never show his pain to someone whom he considers his real friend.

Padamsingh now had many chances to go to Dalmandi and the sympathy that he felt for the courtesans brought him an equal amount of pain. Seeing these delicate women waste their lives in the pursuit of pleasure made his heart fill with compassion and his eyes well up with tears. He now recognized that these women were not thoughtless, without virtue, or stupid, but illusion was leading their lives astray. Desire had made their souls weak and helpless. Padamsingh wanted to tear through this web of illusion. He wanted to enlighten these lost souls, to free them from their ignorance. But the illusion was so strong, the ignorance so powerful, and the sleep so deep that he was unable to achieve any more in six months than what has already been mentioned. These courtesans were in the same condition as a man intoxicated with liquor.

And then Prabhakar Rao and his friends presented the remaining parts of the resolution in the municipal council again. Initially, they had opposed Padamsingh's position merely because they were angry with him, but when they saw his devotion to the courtesans, they began attacking him with weapons of his own making. Padamsingh didn't go to the board meeting that day, and Doctor Shyamacharan was in Nainital. As a result, both resolutions were passed without any obstacle.

At the board's request, buildings were being made close to Alaipur for the courtesans. Lala Bhagatram took on the work with full determination. Some structures were of brick and mortar, others of mud, some were two-storeyed, and a small pharmacy and a school were also being constructed. Haji Hashim was building a mosque and Seth Chimmanlal was constructing a temple. Dinanath Tiwari had broken ground for a park. Everyone hoped that Bhagatram would finish his project in the allotted time. Mister Datt, Pandit Prabhakar Rao, and Mister Shakirbeg would not let him rest. But there was a lot of work, and even after rushing through it, it still took a full year to complete. As soon as the new buildings were ready, the courtesans were given notice to leave Dalmandi and take up residence in these buildings.

People were afraid that the courtesans would oppose the move but they were all pleasantly surprised to see them obeying happily. All of Dalmandi was vacated in a day. The place where once a brilliant glow had illuminated days and nights had, by evening, been enveloped by an eerie silence.

Mehboobjaan was a wealthy courtesan. She had given everything she had to the orphanage. By evening, all the courtesans had gathered at her place for a meeting. Shahzadi said—Sisters, today marks the beginning of a new era in our lives. May God fulfil our wishes and guide us on the path to righteousness. We have spent many days living disgracefully and in the company of villains. We have spent many days slowly murdering our souls and our virtue, and lost many days making love and seeking pleasure. The soil of Dalmandi has turned dark with our sins. Today the merciful God has had pity on us and has freed us from a life of sin, and we should be thankful for that. There is no doubt that some of our sisters are anxious at being forced out of our homes, and there is also no doubt that the days to come seem like being in exile. But I have this prayer for those sisters. May God never close the door of opportunity on anyone. May he grant you the wisdom and skill that will always be of use. But even if we face adversity again, we should remain content and calm. The greater the adversity we endure in the future, the lighter will be the weight of our sins. I again pray to God that he illuminate our hearts with his light and give us the strength to be righteous.

Rambholibai said—We should thank Padamsingh Sharma from the bottom of our hearts. He has shown us the righteous path. May God keep him happy always.

Johrajaan said—I only want to say this to my sisters that they should know the difference between the things sanctioned by Islam and those that are forbidden. Music is a sanctioned skill. We should acquire this skill and become experts. But we should stop becoming the playthings of lusty noblemen. We have been slaves to sin for too long. Now we should liberate ourselves. Did God send us into this world so that we could sell our bodies, our youth, our spirit, our virtue, our shame, our honour to sex-crazed men? We are overjoyed when a captivated young noble falls madly in love with one of us. Our madams are beside themselves with joy. The midwives begin to dance and sing and it feels as though we have trapped a golden sparrow. But sisters, this is just our naiveté. We haven't ensnared him in our love, but have become trapped by his love. He has purchased us with gold and silver. We have lost priceless things like our chastity. From now on, we should all conduct ourselves in such a way that if we see one of us doing something wrong, we should immediately exile her from the community.

Sundarbai said—Sister Johra has offered excellent advice. I want the same. If someone starts coming here frequently, we should first find out what kind of man he is. If he loves one of us and she feels for him, then they should get married. But if he doesn't want to marry and has only come seeking sex, we should immediately castigate him. We shouldn't sell our honour for pennies.

On this note, twenty to twenty-five courtesans raised their hands.

Rampyari said—Those who disagree should raise their hands.

No one raised a hand.

Rampyari—No hands were raised. This means that we all agree with Johra. Today is an auspicious day.

Old Mehboobjaan said—I am afraid that you will all think I am like the cat who goes on a pilgrimage after having killed hundred mice, but truly, I am going on a pilgrimage in seven days from now. One way or another, my life is over. But seeing your determination today has made me happier than I can tell. May almighty God grant your wishes.

A few of the courtesans were whispering to each other. From their faces one could tell that they didn't like what they heard, but they didn't have the courage to speak up. Small minds were silenced in the face of righteous sentiment.

After the meeting the courtesans set out for Alaipur on foot, like a caravan going on some holy pilgrimage.

Darkness had fallen over Dalmandi. No beats on the tabla could be heard nor conversations between *sarangi*s, nor songs in melodious voices, nor the comings and goings of gentlemen. Dalmandi was like a field that had been completely harvested.

53

FOR MONTHS, PANDIT Madansingh was so angry that he would slander Sadan to anyone ready to listen—He is undutiful, depraved, licentious, wicked. I won't give him a one-eyed coin. He will have to beg for food, and only then will he realize its worth.

He wrote to Padamsingh on several occasions about the deed. If Bhama ever mentioned Sadan, he would be furious with her, threaten to kick her out of the house, and say—I will become a monk or an ascetic, but I never want to see that boy's face again.

Then there came about a change in his psychological condition. He stopped talking about Sadan altogether. If someone mentioned Sadan, he would become agitated, and say—Sir, why do you curse him now? He will suffer for what he has done. He may be good or bad, but he is far away from me. He earns his wages, eats, sleeps. Let him be.

Lala Bejnath made it a point to talk about Sadan's shortcomings. One day he brought news that Umanath had given Sadan a thousand rupees. Now, he is building a house by the river and planting a garden by it. He has purchased a mortar mill. He spends his money as fast as he makes it.

Madansingh responded angrily—What would you rather he do, beg for money? Eat other people's scraps? What kind of money could Umanath possibly give him? He has just married off two daughters. He is slowly becoming a pauper himself. Whatever Sadan is spending, he has probably earned himself. He may have done a thousand wrong things, but he is not worthless. He is still young, fun-loving. Who does he harm by spending the money he earns? There are so many useless men in this village who don't earn anything, but who steal from their own homes to spend on their low-caste mistresses. Sadan is much better than them.

Munshi Bejnath was embarrassed.

After a while, Madansingh had a reaction. Images of Sadan would float before his eyes, he would think about the things Sadan used to say—Look how cruel he is, he is mad at me, as if I will carry this house, this land, this wealth, and these things with me when I die. He couldn't even come here once. He has applied mehndi on his feet, has he! Sinner, that he is, he is being stubborn with me. But when I die of frustration he will weep at my name, and then he'll come running. He isn't coming now. Fine, we'll see how far he can run away from me. I will go there and see for myself.

When he relaxed after dinner, he would talk to Bhama about Sadan—That loafer was bratty even as a child. And he wouldn't give up until he got what he wanted. Surely you remember what a tantrum he threw over the things in my prayer bag and how he wouldn't be quiet until he got them. He is so stubborn, just look at his cruelty. He hasn't sent a single letter. He is just sitting there minding his own business as if we were dead.

Bhama would cry when she heard him say these things. Madansingh's pride gave way to his love for his son.

And so, a year passed. Madansingh made several plans to go see Sadan, but he could never put the plans into effect. On one occasion, he had all of his property locked up. But then a little later he had everything opened up again. Once he even walked all the way to the railway station and then came back home again. His heart had become the slave of love and pride.

Now his heart wasn't in his work. The fields weren't watered on time and the entire harvest was ruined. He didn't collect rents from his tenant farmers. The poor men would come with their rents, but it was too much for Madansingh to take the money and write the receipts. He would say, 'Brother, go now. Come back later.' The jaggery was rotting in the storeroom because no one had bothered to sell it. If Bhama ever said anything about it, he would become angry and say, 'Let the house burn down for all I care. What use is this house to me when the one for whom I took all the trouble isn't even here?' Soon he began to realize that his entire life, his piety, and his happiness all depended on one person, and that was Sadan.

Even Padamsingh hadn't visited for quite some time. His was the exhaustion that overcomes one's mind after a gargantuan task has been completed. Madansingh hadn't sent him any letters either. Yes, when Madansingh got his brother's letters, he read them with excitement, but when there was no news of Sadan, he would get depressed again.

One night, Madansingh was sitting near the door, reading *Premsagar*. He got a childlike pleasure from reading stories of Krishna's childhood. Evening had fallen. He couldn't read the words clearly any more, but he was so enraptured that he didn't want to get up. Suddenly, a dog's bark warned him that a stranger had entered the village. Madansingh's heart began to race—was it Sadan? He put the book down and got up, only to see Padamsingh approaching. Padamsingh touched his feet and then the two brothers began talking.

Madansingh—Is everything well?

Padamsingh—Yes, by God's grace.

Madansingh—Well, what news of that scoundrel?

Padamsingh—Yes, he's doing fine. He comes to see me every week or so. I ask about him occasionally. There is no reason to worry.

Madansingh—Fine. And does that sinner ever ask about us or has he written us off as dead? Has he sworn never to come here again? Will he only come here after we are dead? If that's what he wants, we can go someplace else. He can take this house and keep it. I heard that he is building a house there. Is he planning on staying there permanently? Who will stay here, then? Who is he leaving this house for?

Padamsingh—No, he's not having a house built. Someone has lied to you. Yes, he has bought a mortar mill and I do know that he is planning to buy some land on the other side of the river.

Madansingh—Then just tell him to come here and burn this house down before he buys any new land.

Padamsingh—Don't say such things. The only reason that he doesn't come here is because he is afraid that you will be upset. If he hears that you have forgiven him today, he will run here as fast as he can. When he comes to see me, he spends hours talking about you two. If you wanted it, he could be here tomorrow.

Madansingh—No, I won't call him. What are we to him that he should come and see us? But if he ever comes here, tell him to make sure he has a strong back. As soon as I see him I will be possessed by demons and I will beat him with a stick. That idiot thinks he can sulk with me. I didn't get angry with him when he drooled on the prayer books or when he pissed near the dinner plate. I couldn't keep any of my clothes clean because of him and wearing white was impossible. Whenever he saw me wearing anything clean, he would take his dirty hands and climb all over me. He didn't cry then. But he wants to cry now? The next time I see him, I will twist his ears so hard that he will cry for his mother's breast.

The two brothers went home. Bhama was laying out straw for the cows and Sadan's sisters were cooking. Bhama stood up as soon as she saw her brother-in-law and said—Well, at least we got to look at you. You live four feet away and still you never bother to come here every month and see if we are alive or not. Tell me, everything is fine, isn't it?

Padamsingh—Yes, by your grace. Tell me, what's for dinner? Right now, feed me some *kheer*, halva, and cream so that I can give you the kind of good news that will make you jump with joy. It's a boy! Congratulations on becoming grandparents.

Bhama's dark face began to glow with happiness and her eyes opened up like new blossoms. She said—Come, and I will let you eat all you can out of the butter and sugar pots.

Madansingh made a face and said—This is the worst news yet. Does God's court deliver its verdicts upside down? I lose my son and he gets one. Now there are two of them. How can I defeat him now? I was bound to lose. This will surely drag me there. My feet are already moving. Truly, God grants rewards to those who do bad things. Is this topsy-turvy or not? But now I am not worried. Sadan can go wherever he wants, because God has heard our prayer. When was he born?

Padamsingh—It's been four days. I couldn't get away from work, otherwise I would have come on the day itself.

Madansingh—So what. We'll be there by the sixth day and have a huge sixth-day celebration. We'll leave tomorrow.

Bhama was beside herself with joy. Her heart was brimming over. She wanted to give out gifts and spend lavishly. She wanted to light up the house, have *shehnai* play at the door, and call over her neighbours. She wanted the whole village to reverberate with song and music. It seemed to her as if something extraordinary had happened in the world, as if the entire world was childless and she was the only grandmother alive.

A servant came up to her and said—Mistress, there is a sadhu at the door.

Bhama immediately gave him enough alms to feed more than four sadhus.

As soon as dinner was over, Bhama sat down with her two daughters and a drum and stayed up singing half the night.

54

LIKE A MAN overcome by greed, who steals jewels but then can't bear to look at his loot once he comes to his senses, Sadan, too, avoided Suman at all costs. But more than that, he looked down on her and tried to avoid her. After a hard day's work, he hated his line of work, in particular the business of making mortar which required him to work extraordinarily hard. He would think to himself—it's Suman's fault that I have been kicked out of my house. She is the reason that I am in exile. Life was so easy for me at home. There were no worries, no problems, I could eat in peace and enjoy myself. It's her fault that these problems plague me now. When his love for her was sprouting, he had loved the food that she had served him, but now he regretted it deeply. It didn't matter how, but he wanted to be rid of her. This, oddly enough, was the same Sadan that had once been madly in love with Suman and was ready to give his life for her smiles, her sweet words, and her merciful glances. But today, Suman meant nothing to him. Despite having been a victim of it himself, he had forgotten how fickle human nature really was!

Sadan hadn't read or written anything for years and ever since he had bought that mortar mill, he didn't have the time to read even the daily newspaper. Now, he felt that the only people who had time to read were those without any work, who spent their entire day loafing around, swatting flies. So perhaps it was a mystery even to him how he found the time to style his own hair and play on the harmonium.

Sometimes, he would remember things from the past and think to himself—I was such an idiot then. I was crazy about this Suman! Now he would brag about his character. He saw women on the bank of the river everyday but he didn't have a single impure thought about any of them. Sadan thought this was a reflection of his strong character.

But as Shanta came closer to delivering her child, she would often be lying down, locked up in her room, drenched in sweat and tired, and Sadan felt like a fool—what I used to think was strength of character was really just a symptom of my decaying desires. When he came home from work, Shanta would no longer greet him with a sweet smile, but would lie around on her charpoy. Sometimes her head would ache, sometimes her body, sometimes she had a fever, sometimes nausea. Her face was lacklustre and it seemed as if there was no longer any blood in her body. It hurt Sadan to see her like this, and he would sit next to her for hours and try to comfort her, but it didn't look like he enjoyed being there. He would get up early on one pretext or another. Desire and longing for pleasure would tempt him, and he had illicit thoughts. He began flirting with the young women nearby and went to the bank of the river to leer at the bathing women. It went so far that one day he was overwhelmed by longing and set out for Dalmandi. He hadn't been there for several months. It was eight o'clock. His lust kept pushing him on. At that moment, his common sense and wisdom were buried beneath his sex-drive. He would take a few steps forward, then stand in silence, think about a few things and turn around, but after taking a few steps, would turn back again. He was like an invalid who goes wild when he sees sweets in front of him and doesn't think how it will set back his treatment.

When he got to Dalmandi, he didn't see the traffic in the streets that he had seen there before. There were a few paan shops, but the breadmaker's and confectioner's stores had been shut down. He did not see any courtesans hanging from the balconies, nor did he hear the sounds of sarangis or tablas. He then remembered that the courtesans had been evicted. He was sad, but the next moment, he felt a strange happiness. He had conquered his lust as though he had escaped from a strict policeman. The real story was more like this: the policeman had been dragging him around and Sadan hadn't have the strength to escape from his clutches, but when the policeman got to town, he saw that the police station was closed, there were no policemen or constables, and no watchmen. Sadan was now embarrassed by his weakness. The pride that he had had in his virtue was now dashed to pieces.

He wanted to go back home, but he thought—as long as I am here, why don't I have a good look around? As he kept walking, he saw the building where Suman used to live. There, he heard the sweet notes of a song. He looked up in surprise at a big signboard. It read 'School of Music'. Sadan went upstairs. This was the very room where he had spent months with Suman. His mind brought up many memories. He sat down on a bench and began listening to the music. Twenty or twenty-five men were sitting there and learning how to play music. Someone played the sitar, someone a sarangi, someone a tabla, and one old man was teaching each of them in turn. He seemed to be very knowledgeable about music. Sadan's mind was so engrossed in listening to the music that he sat there for fifteen minutes. He wished that he could come here to learn to sing, but for one thing his house was far away, and for another, it was dangerous for him to leave the women alone at night. He wanted to get up when the music instructor began playing this song on the sitar—

> *Merciful Mother, accept Bharat as your own.*
> *Console us, O Mother for separated from you, we are full of anxiety.*
> *Call me beloved child and laugh and embrace me.*
> *Merciful Mother, accept Bharat as your own.*
> *Awaken again, dear mother! the pride of the sleeping Aryan race.*
> *Break the chain and throw off the fetters of our slavery.*
> *Merciful Mother accept Bharat as your own.*

This song opened the floodgates of noble sentiment in Sadan's heart. The purest desire to make the country a better place, serve one's people, and national pride began to ring in his heart. This song produced within him an enormous, internal melody. The image of the compassionate goddess-mother stood before his mind's eye. A poor, hurt, starving, and exhausted child was staring at the goddess with humility, and with both arms raised. With tears in his eyes, he said—Accept, Merciful Mother, Bharat as your own. In his mind, he saw himself helping the poor peasants. He was pleading with the official representatives of the zamindars to have mercy on these poor people. The peasants fell at his feet and their wives gave him blessings. Having become the bridegroom in this imaginary wedding, Sadan left the place vowing to serve his people. He became so caught up in his thoughts that he didn't speak to anyone. As he walked a little further, he saw a group of men gathered in front of Sundarbai's house. He asked one of them—What's going on here? He found out that Kumvar Anirudhsingh was starting a 'Peasant Auxiliary Society' today. The society's purpose was to save peasants from exploitation by zamindars. The sympathy that had just taken root in Sadan's heart for the peasants suddenly disappeared. He was a zamindar and wanted to be kind to the peasants, but he didn't like it that people should suppress his rights and try to foment the peasants against the zamindars. He said to himself—these people want to wipe out the zamindars. Since these people have started this society out of jealousy, we should be on our guard and prepare to defend ourselves. Human nature abhors coercion. Sadan found it useless to stay. It was nine o'clock. He headed home.

55

IT WAS EVENING. There was a rosy glow in the sky and a mild breeze was playing with the waves of the Ganga, tickling them. She smiles with her tender eyes and sometimes laughs in ecstasy, and then one can see her pearly teeth. Sadan's beautiful hut was decorated today with flowers and plants. There was a crowd of boatmen at his door. Inside, their wives were singing auspicious songs. An oven had been dug in the courtyard and there were giant pots on the fire. Today, Sadan's newborn baby was six days old, and this was his celebration.

But Sadan seemed very sad. He sat on the patio in front and stared out at the Ganga. The waves of the river mirrored the waves in his own mind. No! They won't come. If they wanted to come, they would have been here by the sixth day, wouldn't they? If I had known that they wouldn't come, I wouldn't havegiven uncle the news. I am dead as far as they are concerned.

They don't want to have anything to do with me. They don't care whether I live or die. At times like these, people even visit their enemies. They didn't have to come out of love for me. They could have come just for a look, or out of habit or custom—at least I would have felt that I had relatives in this world. It's just as well that they haven't come, at least there's one thing less for me to worry about. I will go to the village once and settle all my accounts for good. He's such a beautiful boy, what red lips. He looks just like me. But the eyes are Shanta's. How intently he stares at me. I can't speak for my father, but the first time mother sees him, she will take him in her arms. Suddenly Sadan began to think—what will happen if I die? Who will provide for this child? No one. No, if I die, father will certainly take pity on him. He can't be that cruel. We'll see. I have some money in the savings bank. But it doesn't add up to a thousand yet. Not too much, but if I save even fifty rupees a month, I will have six hundred rupees by the end of the year. And as soon as I have two thousand, I will have a house built. Two rooms in front, five rooms in the back, an arched canopy over the doorway, and if there are two rooms on the second floor then it will be a good house. A high foundation makes the house nicer. It must be at least five feet high.

Sadan found great happiness in these fantasies. Darkness had fallen all around when he saw a buggy coming down the street. Its lanterns shone like a cat's eyes. Who could be coming here? Who could it be other than uncle? Who else is there whom I can call mine? In the meantime, the buggy stopped and Madansingh stepped out. There was another buggy behind. Subhadra and Bhama got out of that buggy. Both Sadan's sisters were with them. Jeetan got down from the coachbox and shone the lantern. Sadan realized that his family had arrived when he saw so many people get down, but he didn't run out to meet them. The time had passed when he was still willing to make peace with them. Now it was time for pride. He left the patio and went inside the hut as if he hadn't seen anyone. He thought to himself—They all probably think that I can't live without them, but I am not worried about them the same way that they are not worried about me.

Sadan went inside and waited to see what they would do. And then he saw Jeetan come up to the door and call out. A few boatmen ran over. Sadan went back out and greeted his mother from afar and stood in the corner.

Madansingh said—You are standing there like you don't even recognize us. Maybe not mine, but at least touch your mother's feet and ask for her blessings.

Sadan—My touch will pollute you.

Madansingh looked over at his brother and said—Do you see what he is saying? I told you that he had forgotten about us, but you dragged me here. Even after seeing his parents standing at the door, he doesn't have any compassion.

Bhama stepped forward and said—Sadan, my son! Touch your father's feet. You are old enough to know better than to say such things.

Sadan couldn't stay stiff any longer. With tears in his eyes, he fell at his father's feet. Madansingh began to cry.

Then he fell at his mother's feet. Bhama picked him up and hugged him to her chest and blessed him.

What a celestial and beautiful scene of love, devotion, and forgiveness it was! The hearts of his parents were overwhelmed with joy and waves of devotion started up in the ocean of the son's heart. The dark chambers of his heart were filled with the pure light of this love and devotion. The germs of false pride, social scorn, and fear had been chased out. Now only justice, love, and decency lived there.

Delirious with delight, Sadan was walking on clouds. Now he was showing off his influence in the community by asking the boatmen to run errands for him. One of them went to bring a charpoy and one of them ran to the bazaar. Madansingh was beside himself with joy and he whispered into his brother's ear, 'Sadan turned out to be very clever. I used to think that he just loafed around all day. He's really living it up here.'

Bhama and Subhadra went inside. Bhama looked all around in amazement—It is so clean. Everything is in its place! Suman's sister seems to have many good qualities.

She went to the bedroom and Shanta touched her mothers-in-law's feet. Bhama took the child in her arms. She felt that he was the incarnation of Krishna. Tears of joy began flowing down her face.

After a while, she went to Madansingh and said—Whatever else she may be, but your daughter-in-law is very beautiful. She is a rose blossom and the child seems to be the incarnation of God.

Madansingh—If he wasn't so attractive, how could he have dragged Madansingh here?

Bhama—Our daughter-in-law seems very gentle.

Madansingh—Why else would Sadan have forsaken his parents for her?

Everyone was lost in his or her happiness, but no one thought even once about where poor Suman had gone.

Suman had gone to the bank of the river for her evening prayers. When she came back, she saw the buggies parked next to the hut. There were a few men sitting near the door. She recognized Padamsingh. She knew that Sadan's parents had arrived. She couldn't go any closer. It was as if there were chains on her feet. She knew this was no longer her home, that she had no relations here. She stood there like a statue and thought—where will I go?

For a month there had been much ill-will between Shanta and Suman. The same Shanta that had been the very image of compassion and peace in the widows' home, was now bent on making Suman miserable and depressed. If we could only be today as devoted to propriety and duty as we were in the days that we were waiting, then we would be like saints today. At that moment, Shanta had needed sympathy. Love had made her generous, gentle, and soft, but now that she possessed her jewel of love, like a man rising above his poor friends, her heart became cold. She was constantly afraid that Sadan would be caught in Suman's wiles. In her eyes, Suman's piety and her faithful devotion had little meaning. It seemed like hypocrisy to her. Shanta only saw the Suman who longed to put oil in her hair and wanted clean clothes to wear. She watched everything Suman did with critical eyes. And Suman said to Shanta the things she should have said to Sadan. It went so far that at dinner time, Shanta would find some excuse or the other to come and sit in the kitchen. She wanted to get rid of Suman before the baby arrived, because after she was confined to bed, she couldn't watch over Suman. She could bear every other hardship, but she couldn't bear this jealousy.

And Suman who saw everything, still didn't see, and who heard everything, still didn't hear. Like a man drowning in the river, she couldn't let go of the piece of wood that was keeping her afloat. She knew that she wouldn't survive on her own, but when she saw Sadan's parents here, she had to let go of her safety line. What she had been unable to do by will power alone, circumstances did for her.

She crept silently and walked to the back of the hut and pressed her ear to the wall to find out if they mentioned her or not. She stood like that for half an hour. Bhama and Subhadra were talking about this and that. Finally, Bhama said—What, doesn't her sister stay here any more?

Subhadra—Why not, where else would she go?

Bhama—I don't see her.

Subhadra—She's probably gone to run an errand. She does all the work in this house.

Bhama—If she comes, tell her to sleep outside. Does Sadan eat food that she makes?

Shanta spoke up from the bedroom—No, I've been cooking his meals till now. These days he cooks for himself.

Bhama—Well then she must have touched the pots and pans. Throw this pot away. Wash the dishes again.

Subhadra—There is no place to sleep outside.

Bhama—So what. I still won't let her sleep in here. Who can trust such women?

Subhadra—No, sister. She isn't like that any more. She has become very religious.

Bhama—Well, well, religious, is she? She has slept with every man in sight and now she thinks that she is religious. An idol of the gods cannot be put back together once it has been broken. Even if she were to turn into a saint, I still wouldn't believe it.

Suman couldn't listen any longer. It felt like someone had pierced her heart with a red-hot iron. She turned around and walked into the darkness.

It was pitch black, and she couldn't make out the road, but Suman stumbled along, who knows where and in which direction she went. She wasn't in her right mind. Like a scared dog that has been beaten with a stick, she limped along in a trance. She wanted to steady herself, but she couldn't. Ultimately, a large thorn wedged itself in her foot. She sat down, holding her foot. She didn't have the strength to go on.

She looked around like an unconscious man suddenly regaining consciousness. A silence had fallen. Only the jackals were howling out their songs. I am all alone, Suman thought, as her hair stood on end. She discovered today what loneliness really meant. But even though she knew that there was no one around and that she was alone, she imagined that she saw small demons hovering around her in the air and was frightened. She was so terrified that she shut her eyes. Her lonely mind became a plaything for her overactive imagination.

Suman began to think—I am so unlucky. How unfortunate I am that my own sister can't stand the sight of me. I wanted so much to love her, but she wouldn't love me back. I have this mark of shame on my forehead and it won't wash off no matter how hard I try. Why should I trouble her or anyone else? This is all the result of my karmas. Oh! My foot hurts so. How will I ever get this thorn out? A piece of it has broken off inside. Oh, how it's throbbing. No, I can't blame anyone else. I was the one who sinned. Who else will bear the consequences? Longing and desire have done this to me. I was so blind. I set out to destroy my soul just for sensual pleasures. Yes, my life was difficult. I wanted clothes and jewels, craved for good food, longed for love. And then, my life seemed painful to me, but even that was the result of karmas from my past life, and besides aren't there women who endure much worse and are still able to protect their souls? Damayanti had to suffer terrible things, Sita was kicked out of her house by Ramchandra and she had to suffer all kinds of hardships in the jungle, Savitri endured all kinds of pain but was still firm in her duty. But why even go that far, there are many women in my own neighbourhood who pass their days in tears. In Amola, that poor milkmaid went through so much. Her husband had abandoned her. The poor woman fasted and waited. Hai! This beauty has ruined my life. It has come to this because I was so proud of my beauty.

Dear God! Why do you make people beautiful and their hearts fickle? Most of the beautiful women I know give in to temptation. Perhaps this is the way that God tests us, or rather how he wants to make our souls stronger by blocking the path of our life with the obstacle of beauty. He wishes to purify our souls in the fire of beauty. But yes! In our ignorance we see nothing, and this fire burns us down, makes us weak.

It's stuck, what kind of a thorn is this? And if someone were to come up and grab me, who would be able to hear my screams? No, this isn't the fault of my desires, nor is it the fault of my beauty. This is all the fault of my ignorance. Lord! Grant me wisdom! You are the only one that can save me now. I made a mistake in going to the widows' home. I was also wrong to stay with Sadan. It is useless to depend on human beings to save you. Sadan was just as stupid as I was. How could he help me? I will go to Him. But how does one go to Him? Which path leads there? I've been reading religious books for two years, but I don't understand a thing. God, how do I find you? Get me out of this darkness! You are heavenly, wise, and in your enlightenment, it is possible that this darkness could dissipate. Why are these leaves rustling? I don't see any animals. No, someone is surely coming.

Suman stood up. Her mind was clear. She became fearless.

Suman had been lost in her thoughts for some time. They didn't bring her any peace. She hadn't, until now, thought about her soul this way. And in this dilemma, her real desires came forward.

The night had passed. The mild breeze of spring began to blow. Suman collected the folds of her sari and put her head down on her knee. She remembered the day when, in this same season and at about the same time, she was sitting at her husband's door and thinking about where she would go. Then, she was being burnt by the flame of her desires. Today, the mild shade of devotion offered her security.

Suddenly her eyes shut. She saw Sadhu Gajanand wearing a deerskin and standing before her, looking at her compassionately. Suman fell at his feet and said with desperation—Swami! Save me!

Suman saw him touch her head softly and say—That's why I have been sent to you. Tell me, what do you need. Money?

Suman—No, Maharaj, I don't want money.

Swami—Luxury?

Suman—Maharaj, don't even mention it. Give me wisdom.

Swami—Fine, then listen. In the golden age, human liberation came from wisdom, in the bronze age, from truth, in the iron age, from devotion, but in these dark ages, there is only way and that is service. You must follow this path and you will find salvation. Go to those people who are worse off than you and their blessings will be your salvation. In these dark times, God resides in this very ocean of misery.

Suman's eyes had been opened. She looked all around and realized that she was now awake. Where had Swamiji vanished so quickly? Suddenly, it seemed to her as if Swamiji was standing under the tree before her, holding a lantern. She got up and limped towards him. She estimated that the tree was less than a hundred yards in front of her, but instead of a hundred, she went two hundred, three hundred, four hundred yards but that group of trees and Swamiji with the lantern in his hand were still the same distance away.

Suman began to think that she was still asleep—this isn't a dream is it? I've covered the distance but he's still that far away. She cried out loudly—Maharaj, please wait.

She heard these words—Come on, I'm waiting.

Suman started walking again, but after she had walked two hundred paces, she sat down from exhaustion. That tree and Swamiji were still one hundred yards in front of her.

Suman's hair stood on end from fear. Her chest began heaving and her feet were trembling. She wanted to scream, but her voice failed her.

Suman steadied herself and tried to understand the mysterious things that were happening—I'm not seeing some kind of ghost, am I? But some unknown force was pulling her against her will.

Suman walked on again. Now she was near the city. She saw Swamiji go into a small hut and the tree before her had vanished. Suman realized that this was his house and felt much better. Now she would certainly meet Swamiji. He would solve this mystery.

She went to the door of the hut and said—Swamiji, it's me, Suman.

It was Gajanand's hut, but he was sleeping. Suman didn't get an answer.

Suman got up the courage to look inside. The hearth was lit and Gajanand was sleeping, wrapped in a blanket. Suman was shocked. Just a second ago he was walking, how did he fall asleep so quickly and where did that lantern go? She called out loudly—Swamiji!

Gajanand got up and looked at Suman in surprise. He looked at her for a full moment carefully. Then he said—Who? Suman!

Suman—Yes, Maharaj. It's me.

Gajanand—I just saw you in my dreams.

Suman was taken aback and said—You just came inside your hut a second ago.

Gajanand—No, I've been asleep for quite some time. I haven't left this hut. You were in my dreams.

Suman—But I have been following you along the bank of the river. You were walking in front of me with a lantern.

Gajanand smiled and said—You have been tricked.

Suman—If it was a trick, then how did I get here without looking or listening at all? I was alone on the bank of the river thinking about how I would find salvation. I was pleading with God to have mercy on me and to take me under His protection. And in the meantime, you arrived and told me about the path of service. I wanted to ask you so many things, but you vanished. But the next moment, I saw you standing a little ahead of me with a lantern in your hand. And then I followed you. I don't understand what's going on. Please explain it to me.

Gajanand—It is possible that things happened just as you say, but they won't make sense yet.

Suman—It wasn't some god, was it, who was dressed like you and who led me to you?

Gajanand—That's possible, too. The things you are describing are the things that I saw in my dream and I was telling you about the path of service. Suman, you know me well. You have had to suffer much because of me, endure many hardships. You know what kind of a vile-natured, horrible person I am, and when I remember my wickedness, my heart goes insane. You deserved respect and I dishonoured you. This is the primary cause of our tragedy and our grief. When will we see the day when the women of our race are respected? Women can live their lives happily even when they have to wear dirty, tattered clothes, eat dry bread to fill their stomachs, live in cramped huts, work like slaves, and endure all kinds of hardships. All they need is respect in their homes, and love. Without love and respect, women cannot survive even in palaces. But I was stupid, lost in the darkness of my ignorance. I didn't know how to save myself. I didn't have wisdom, education or devotion, or even the ability to work. I decided to help those closest to me. That was the easiest thing for me to do. Since then I have been doing as much as I can in this way and now it seems to me that the only difference between all the various paths to salvation is in their names. I have found peace on this path and I think that this is the best path for you as well. I saw you in the ashram, and in Sadan's house. You had lost yourself in serving others. That's what I prayed to God for you. There is compassion and love and sympathy in your heart, and these are the main requirements for the path of service. That door is open for you. It is calling to you. Enter it. God will reward you.

Suman saw a pure light shining in Gajanand's face. Wonderful feelings of faith and devotion dawned in her heart. She thought—his soul possesses so much love and compassion. Hai! I scorned this jewel of a man. Had I continued to serve him, my life would have been better. She said—Maharaj, you are like God to me. My salvation can only take place through you. I offer my mind and body to serve you. I made this promise once before, but foolishly, I didn't keep it. That promise has not left my heart. Today, I make this promise with true intentions. You have given me succour. Now, even though I am fallen, you must forgive me out of generosity and lead me towards the path of righteousness.

Gajanand saw, in that moment, the rays of love and purity on Suman's face. He was confused. Feelings that he had suppressed for years, resurfaced. New hopes of happiness and peace arose within him. His life seemed dry, meaningless, and troubled to him. These hopes scared him. He was afraid that if these feelings took hold in his mind, then his vows of celibacy and service would flow away in their stream like blades of grass. He asked—Do you know that they have opened an orphanage here?

Suman—Yes, I have heard something.

Gajanand—For the most part, the orphanage has girls who have been given up by courtesans. There must be about fifty girls there.

Suman—This is all because of your teachings!

Gajanand—No, it's not that. The full credit must go to Pandit Padamsingh. I am only his servant. This orphanage needs a pure soul and that pure soul is you. I have searched far and wide, but I couldn't find a woman who could do this work with love, who could care for these girls like a mother, and with her love could take their mothers' place. Who will care for them when they get sick, won't turn in horror from their bodily secretions, and by her example, introduce them to feelings of piety so that they can erase their earlier bad habits and live their lives in happiness. This aim cannot be achieved without affection. God has given you wisdom and reasoning, your heart has compassion, tenderness and piety, and you are the only one that can carry the weight of this work. Will you answer my prayers?

Suman's eyes welled up with tears—this is what a wise man thinks of me, she thought as her heart was overcome. She hadn't in her wildest dreams believed that someone would have so much faith in her and she would be given such a great opportunity to serve. She was sure that God had directed Gajanand to do this. A few moments ago, if she had seen a child covered in mud, she would have made a face and turned away, but Gajanand's faith in her conquered her disgust. Love entered her heart. We do not want to disappoint those that have faith in us and we are suddenly ready to undertake tasks that we used to find unbearable. Confidence breeds confidence. Suman said in a very gentle voice—I am extremely fortunate that you think me worthy of this work. It is my deepest desire to be of use to someone, to be able to help someone. I may not be able to reach the standards that you have set, but I will do what you ask to the best of my abilities. And then Suman became silent. Her head bent low and she began to cry. The things that she was unable to say were clearly displayed by the expression on her face. It was as if she was saying—it is because you are so merciful that you have faith in me! On the one hand, there is fallen and wicked me, and on the other hand, there is this important work. But God willing, you will not have to regret this gift of faith.

Gajanand said—That's what I had hoped for you. May God keep you well.

Gajanand got up. Dawn was breaking and the sparrows were beginning to chirp. He picked up his water pot and went to bathe in the river.

Suman went out of the hut and looked around, just like one does when waking up from sleep. It was so beautiful, peaceful, and joyful. Would her future turn out the same way? Would her future life rise anew, too? Would the rays of morning light touch her life as well? Would the sun's light shine? Yes, it would, and this beautiful, peaceful dawn would be the dawn of her coming life.

56

A YEAR HAD passed. Pandit Madansingh had sworn that he wanted to go on a religious pilgrimage. It had seemed as if he would not stay with Sadan for more than a day and wouldn't actually stop until he had arrived at Badrinath. Ever since Sadan had come, however, he hadn't even mentioned the pilgrimage. With his grandson in his lap he would review the accounts of the tenants and survey the fields. Worldly ties took an even stronger hold of him. Yes, Bhama seems a little less worried. The only duty she still performs is conversing with the neighbouring women. The rest of the housework is looked after by Shanta.

Pandit Padamsingh has stopped practising law. Now he is a high-ranking official in the municipal council. It is work that he greatly enjoys. The town improves every day. Within the year, several new streets and parks have been built. Now he is working on laying new streets on the the outskirts of the town for motorcar and buggy drivers. People who were once Padamsingh's friends have become his enemies and so many that were once his enemies have made peace with him, but his faith in Vitthaldas grows day by day. He wanted very much to offer Vitthaldas a position in the municipal council, but Vitthaldas wouldn't accept it. He didn't want to compromise his freedom by doing so. He thought that he could not do as much good as a member of the municipal council as he could independently. His widows' home was improving greatly and these days he got special help from the municipal council. Now he was working on plans to establish a fund for peasants so that they could be lent seeds and money at a nominal interest. And in this work, Sadan was Vitthaldas' right-hand man.

Sadan couldn't occupy himself for long in his village. He left Shanta there and returned to the hut on the bank of the river and built up his business. He now has five boats and makes hundreds of rupees in profit each month. He plans to buy a steamship.

Sadhu Gajanand now mostly lives in the countryside. He has devoted his life to the cause of helping poor girls. When he comes to the city, he doesn't stay for more than a few days.

57

It was the month of Kartik. Padamsingh had taken Subhadra with him to bathe in the Ganga. On their way back, they passed through Alaipur. Subhadra kept looking out of the carriage window and thinking—how do people live in such desolation? How do they manage to feel at home? Just then she caught a glimpse of a beautiful building with a board outside that read 'SEVASADAN' in bold letters.

Subhadra turned to Sharmaji and said—Is this Sumanbai's Sevasadan?

Sharmaji replied disinterestedly—Yes.

He regretted ever having come this way—she will definitely want to stop and look inside. I will have to go as well. What an awful predicament. So far, Sharmaji had not been inside Sevasadan. Gajanand had wanted him to see the place on several occasions, but he would always come up with some excuse or the other. He would do anything for the cause, but meeting Suman face to face would have been too much for him. He could never forget the words that Suman had said that day in the park when she was returning the bracelet. Then he had run away from her out of shame. Since then, he hadn't been able to stop thinking about the incident—That woman, who used to be so chaste and moral, became a sinner because of my own sins—I have pushed her into this hell.

Subhadra said—Stop the buggy. I want to take a look.

Padamsingh—It's getting late. Come back some other time.

Subhadra—It seems as if I have been coming back some other time for a year now. This is the first time I have actually come here. If we leave now, who knows when we will come back?

Padamsingh—I don't have a problem with you visiting. I am just concerned about the time. It must be nine o'clock by now.

Subhadra—Who could stay too long here? It will only take us ten minutes.

Padamsingh—You are very obstinate. Even after I have told you that I will be late, you persist in arguing with me.

Subhadra—You can make the horse gallop faster on the way back. You'll make up for lost time.

Padamsingh—Alright, you go visit but come home before it gets dark. I am going back, but I will leave the buggy for you. I will rent a carriage to take me home.

Subhadra—You don't have to do that. Just sit here. I'll be back shortly.

Padamsingh (getting down from the buggy)—I am leaving. Come back when you like.

Subhadra knew why he was so uncomfortable. She had read about Sevasadan in *Jagat* several times. Pandit Prabhakar Rao had recently been quite favourable towards Sevasadan. As a result, Subhadra had become enamoured of this ashram and she felt pangs of devotion in her heart for Suman. She wanted to see Suman in her new surroundings. She was still astonished at how Suman had become such an enlightened woman, after having fallen so low, that the newspapers were printing stories that praised her. She wanted very much to drag Panditji along with her, but the driver was standing around, so she couldn't say anything.

As soon as she entered the courtyard, one of the women went inside to inform Suman of her arrival, and a few moments later Subhadra saw Suman approaching. She was startled to see Suman with head shorn and simply attired. She no longer had her earlier softness, youthful coyness, smiling eyes, or laughing smile. A lamp of purity shone through her instead of beauty and elegance.

Suman approached Subhadra and fell at her feet. Tenderly she said—Bahuji, I am so blessed to see you here today.

Subhadra's eyes filled with tears. She lifted Suman up and embraced her. Choking on her words, she said—Baiji, I have wanted so very much to come, but I have been unable to bring myself to, until now.

Suman—Is Sharmaji with you or have you come alone?

Subhadra—He was with me, but it was getting late for him, so he rented a carriage and left.

Suman spoke sadly—It's not that he was getting late, he didn't want to come here. It's my misfortune. What hurts is the fact that he is the founder of this ashram and, on my account, he loathes it so. My heart had hoped that both of you would come to visit once. Well, half of my wish has come true today, someday all of it will come true. That will be the day of my salvation.

Suman showed Subhadra around the ashram. There were five big rooms in the building. In the first room, about thirty girls were sitting and studying. They were between the ages of twelve and fifteen. The teacher came up and shook Subhadra's hand. Suman introduced the two to each other. Subhadra was surprised to learn that this woman was the wife of Mr Rustam Bhai, Barrister. She came for two hours every day to teach the girls.

There were as many girls in the second room. They were between the ages of eight and twelve. Some were cutting cloth, some were sewing, and some were pinching the girls next to them. There was no teacher in this room. There was an elderly tailor working in a corner. Suman showed Subhadra the kurtas, jackets, and other clothes that the girls had made.

In the third room, there were fifteen or twenty very young girls, but none older than five years. Some were playing with dolls, others were staring at the pictures hanging on the walls. Suman herself taught this class.

Subhadra walked out into the garden and began admiring the flowers and plants that the girls had planted. A few girls were watering the potato and cabbage patches. They offered Subhadra a bouquet of beautiful flowers.

In the dining hall, a few girls were still finishing their meal. Suman showed Subhadra the pickles and sauces the girls had made.

Subhadra was quite pleased to see the place so peaceful and well maintained as well as to observe how good-natured the girls were. She thought to herself, how does Suman manage this entire place all by herself? I would never be able to do such a thing. None of the girls seems dirty or sad.

Suman said—I have taken all of this on, but I don't have the strength to keep this place going. Whatever advice people give me, I act upon it. If you see any shortcomings, please tell me. It will be of great assistance to me.

Subhadra laughed and replied—Baiji, don't tease me. I am amazed by everything that I have seen here. What advice could I possibly offer? All I can say is that I have never seen an orphanage under such excellent management.

Suman—You are reluctant to tell the truth.

Subhadra—No, I am telling you the truth. This place has turned out to be even better than the reports I had heard about it. At least tell me this—do their mothers come to visit these girls?

Suman—They come, but I discourage their visits.

Subhadra—And how will they get married?

Suman—That will be difficult. It is our duty to ensure that these girls learn to be good housewives. Whether or not society will respect them, I cannot say.

Subhadra—It seems as though the barrister's wife really enjoys this work.

Suman—You might as well consider her the mistress of this place. All I do is follow her orders.

Subhadra—What can I say? I don't really have any skills or else I would work here as well.

Suman—You only came today in passing, and even then, you have irritated Sharmaji. He won't let you come near this place again.

Subhadra—No. This Sunday I will definitely drag him along with me. Then I will teach the girls how to make paan and prepare dinner.

Suman (laughing)—You will find that there are several girls more skilled than you at these things.

In the meanwhile, ten girls wearing beautiful clothes stood in front of Subhadra and began singing in a melodious voice:

Dear Father, Dear Lord, give us your love and affection.
Rid us of desire, our hearts are content in devotion.

Subhadra was overjoyed hearing this song and she offered the girls a five rupee reward.

When she was leaving, Suman said piteously—I will be waiting for you this Sunday.

Subhadra—I will definitely come.

Suman—Shanta is well, isn't she?

Subhadra—I just received a letter from them. Doesn't Sadan come here?

Suman—No, but he sends a few rupees each month in donation.

Subhadra—It's time for me to leave, but you don't need to see me off.

Suman—I am deeply grateful that you came here. Your devotion, your affection, your extraordinary efforts—which shall I praise first? You are truly the jewel of the community of women. (With moist eyes) I shall consider myself your servant. As long as I live, I will be grateful to you. You held my hand and saved me from drowning. May god always grant you good fortune.

Glossary

Aashaadh	fourth month of the Hindu calendar (June–July)
akhada	wrestling or sports ground; arena or ring
badshah	king/ruler
Bhagvad Gita	central religious-philosophical text from beginning of the Common Era
bhaiya	brother
Bhaktmaal	hagiographical text (ca. 1600); lit. 'garland of devotees'
bhang	a narcotic preparation of hemp, often mixed with food or drink
Brahmin	highest of the four main divisions of Hindu society; originally a priestly/scholarly class
Chait	first month of the Hindu calendar (March–April)
Chamaar	formerly untouchable caste; traditionally leather workers
Chandaals	traditionally the lowest sub-caste among Shudras; a derogatory term today
Chandrakanta Santati	or the progeny of Chandrakanta was written by Devakinandan Khatri (1861–1913) as a follow-up to his earlier novel *Chandrakanta* (1888), a modified version of the Urdu *tilasm* or thriller, which proved to be an all time bestseller.
Chauk	town square or market-place
chauth	fourth day of the lunar fortnight in the Hindu calendar
daal	pulse or lentil dish; an Indian staple
dakshina	honorarium to priests or teachers
daroga	subinspector

dhoti	traditional lower garment for men
dwarpuja	a Hindu marriage ceremony performed at the doorstep of the bride's house
ekadashi	eleventh day of either fortnight of a lunar month in the Hindu calendar
ghazals	stylized Urdu or Persian lyrical poetry
ghee	clarified butter
hakim	physician using traditional remedies in India and Muslim countries; a judge or ruler
halva	type of sweet dish
Hari	epithet of Vishnu
holi	Hindu spring festival
jalebis	type of fried sweet
janab	respectful form of addressing
janmotsav	birthday
Kahaar	formerly low caste group; traditionally, water-carriers
Kaikeyi	second wife of King Dashrath in the Ramayan, responsible for exiling Ram to the forest for fourteen years
kajal	collyrium
Kala Pani	infamous colonial prison on the Andaman Islands
Kartik-snaan	a ritual bath taken in the eighth month (October–November) of the Hindu calendar
khas	fragrant root of a grass used for cooling purposes
kheer	sweetened preparation of rice and milk
khichri	preparation of rice and lentils
Krishna	an incarnation of the Hindu god Vishnu
Kuber	Hindu god of wealth
Kurmi	formerly low caste group; traditionally, agriculturalists
kurta	long, loose shirt-like upper garment
Kshatriyas	second of the four main divisions of Hindu society; originally a warrior/ruler class

Lohaar	formerly low caste group; traditionally, blacksmiths
Magh	eleventh month of the Hindu calendar (January–February)
malai	cream
Mangalacharan	benedictory verses recited on auspicious occasions
maulana	title given to a Muslim scholar
maulud	celebration of the birth of the Prophet Mohammed
maulvi	scholar of Islamic law
Meera	devotee of Krishna and author of many works of devotional poetry
mehndi	henna dye
Minabazaar	fancy fair offering jewellery and trinkets for women
navratan	nine gems
paan	betel leaf folded over lime, tobacco and spices; usually taken after a meal
paandaan	box for storing paan
pandit	lit. 'learned'; a term of respect for Brahmins
Phagun	twelfth month of the Hindu calendar (February–March)
phulka	thin, delicate unleavened bread
pipal	tree native to India (*Ficus Religiosa*); sacred to Hindus and Buddhists
Premsagar	pioneering work of Hindi prose authored by Lalluji Lal in 1810
pujari	priest
purdah	term for the separate space reserved for cloistered women
qawali	form of group vocal music
raag	melodic sequence of notes
Radha	consort of the Hindu god, Krishna
Ramayan	classical epic tale of the hero-king Ram; sacred to Hindus

Ramlila	celebration involving the enactment of the story of Ram
ramnami sheets	shawl printed with the name of Ram; sacred to the Ramnami sect
roti	plain, flat bread
sadhu	ascetic
sarangi	stringed instrument
sarkar	respectful form of addressing
Shankar	epithet of the Hindu god Shiva
Shankar's tandav nritya	mythological annihilatory dance performed by the Hindu god Shiva
Shastras	sacred scripture (religious or secular)
shehnai	musical instrument like the clarinet
shirni	creamy milky sweet
Shudras	lowest of the four main divisions of Hindu society; originally a class of artisans and labourers
Shyam-kalyan	a raag traditionally sung or performed in the evening
sindoor	vermillion
Tilak	ornamental or religious mark on the forehead
thumri	form of vocal Indian classical music
tillana	musical expression
Vaitarani	a mythological river in hell
Vinay-Patrika	Tulsidas' devotional composition; lit. 'Petition to Ram', composed in the late sixteenth century.